TASTE ME

Candace —
Rock on! Enjoy.

TAMARA HOGAN

Tamara Hogan

sourcebooks
casablanca

Published by Sourcebooks Casablanca, an imprint of Sourcebooks, Inc.
P.O. Box 4410, Naperville, Illinois 60567-4410
(630) 961-3900
FAX: (630) 961-2168
www.sourcebooks.com

Printed and bound in Canada
WC 10 9 8 7 6 5 4 3 2 1

Prologue

HE WAS DESPERATE FOR A HIT. JUNKYARD DOG DESPERATE.

Stephen eyed the late night sky as he drew closer to the grimy club bordering Block E. Thunder rumbled like timpani, and the chains on his motorcycle boots rattled as he walked. Rubbing at the gnawing behind his breastbone, he unconsciously paced his movement to the beat thumping out of the club called Subterranean.

He stopped dead when he turned the corner. An overflow crowd seethed in the Indian summer heat, and two huge bouncers flanked the door like implacable marble columns. It had been a long time since he'd had to wait on the wrong side of the velvet rope, and he wasn't about to start now. Christ, he needed something, anything. His skin felt ready to burst off his bones.

He took a shaky breath, knowing that he'd have to play the "do you know who I am?" card and hope for the best. How low could you go? But he had to get in. Now. Straightening his shoulders, he walked alongside the line, his eyes flitting over the people who waited. Where were the couples with their hands on each other's asses? With their tongues down each other's throats? Right now, even inhaling some secondhand lust might ease the clawing and scratching on the backside of his ribs.

"Stephen! Is that Stephen?" The woman's high-pitched squeal floated into the humid night air, setting off a chain reaction that sounded like birds chirping in an aviary. Excitement pulsed. He huffed quickly, but it was there and gone. He turned on a carefully calibrated showman's smile, dripping accessibility and "so pleased to meetcha!" to pull more of the crowd toward him.

It worked better than he'd hoped. He was quickly surrounded, then swamped. Energy swirled, momentarily soothing the infernal gnawing behind his sternum, but it didn't last long. He desperately worked the crowd like the pro he'd become, shaking hands, accepting kisses, dodging a few wandering tongues, suckling on a few choice others. Energy surged, and he inhaled greedily. *More, more.* Men wearing baggy jeans and black T-shirts knocked knuckles with him and flashed devil horns while their friends' camera phones clicked. Snippets of conversation eddied around him: "Steve, Stephen? Stefan? I don't care what his name is, I just want to…" "Drummer for Scarlett's Web, idiot." "He's a lot… smaller than he looks on stage."

Two women bookended him and kissed his cheeks as their friend snapped pictures. He felt a hand creep along his hip, then cup his groin. "You're going commando, aren't you?" the chick on the right breathed into his ear.

He grinned but didn't answer, setting off more squeals. No one noticed that the grin didn't meet his eyes; they never did. Dread rose like water in a leaky boat. *Her hand is right on my dick, and I don't feel a thing.*

The pulsing music beckoned, crooked its finger from the door. If touch alone wasn't doing the job, maybe a music chaser would do the trick. He waded toward the door, pulling the crowd along in his wake. An elbow tagged his kidney, and he felt fingers yanking at his shirt. Someone grabbed a handful of his ass. "Leave me some skin, love," he called back, a smile pasted on his face as he tugged his butt out of the man's grasp. *This could get ugly*.

All momentum stopped when a glacial blonde stepped in, pushed a black Sharpie into his hand, and pulled up her halter top to expose her world-class Scandinavian rack. A small space cleared around them, and cell cameras clicked as he grinned, cupped her right breast in his trembling hand, and scrawled his autograph just above her stiff pink nipple. A punch of lust glittered in the air—hers, for him, and the crowd's, for her—but once again, the energy dissipated too quickly. It was there, then gone. His frustration surged.

"Hey!" the blonde said, recoiling from the shock he'd delivered with his hand.

He kissed her cheek in apology, shoving down the panic. *What the fuck was that?* His body was acting like a blown transformer, sparking and crackling. Not normal, not good. "Sorry, love." He had to get inside. Now. He raised his arm and caught the eye of one of the 300-pound badasses at the door. The bouncer dove into the melee and snagged him around the waist, half-carrying him out of the crowd to the door.

"Thanks, man," Stephen said, tucking in his rumpled shirt. "That got a little more out of hand than I thought it would."

The bouncer grinned and straightened his immaculate suit coat. "No problem. Everyone's excited about tomorrow night's show."

"Well, thanks. You really saved my skin." He tried to slip a folded bill into the man's kielbasa-fingered hand.

The bouncer waved it off and unhooked the black velvet rope. "Glad I could help. You enjoy your evening now, sir."

Curses, squeals, and offers of blow jobs rained over him as he shouldered his way into the club. The thing in his chest had nibbled on appetizers, but now it was simply ravenous. Standing in the cave-dark entryway, Stephen wiped at his clammy forehead with his T-shirt sleeve and let the tsunami of sound pound over him.

A small zing, then… nothing.

Sex, then. He'd have to hook up with someone.

Oooh, what a horrible problem to have. He almost laughed. He was living the life, nailing groupies left, right, upside down, and sideways, but the sad truth was he didn't even enjoy it anymore. Nope, shuttling his dick in and out of a warm, willing body had become a means to an end: Just produce the orgasms that would feed the beast. And it had been fun at the beginning of the tour, grand fun. Men, women, anything in between—it didn't matter. Two at a time, three at a time, groups—hell, whole parties. A week ago he'd been so desperate he'd had a three-way in a fetid festival Porta Potty. Their road manager was still scrubbing the pictures off the Internet.

The thing was always hungry, never satisfied. But now that the band was back on home turf, he didn't have to make do with weak humans anymore. He just had to find… some of *them*.

A cloud of the club's energy—gutter-glam techno, grinding dancers, blinking lights, and the scents of spilled beer, stale cigarettes, and hot, clean sweat— drifted over him as he walked from the entryway into the club. Pheromones permeated the place like sweet chloroform, and he huffed greedily as he approached the dark wood bar. *Yeah, this is more like it.*

"Diet cola, no lime, please." While the pierced and tattooed bartender poured his drink, he scoped the place out, mentally sorting energy into groups: light and shadow, sound and silence, smells, people touching each other. They all produced energy which he could use, but tonight he needed… *Ahhh. Jackpot.* A good dozen patrons who had that something extra blipped strongly on his internal radar.

The bartender—a vamp, he thought, but having escaped to the planet only a few years ago, he was still learning these nuances—placed his drink in front of him and waved off his money.

"On the house, man," he said, acknowledging Stephen's identity with a nod. He held out his black-nailed hand for Stephen to shake. Bracelets clanked. "Welcome home. When did you guys get back to town?"

"The tour bus just pulled in," Stephen answered, taking a sip of his drink. Were their comings and goings really the source of so much interest? "I thought I'd re-acquaint myself with the nightlife before Scarlett starts cracking the whip."

The bartender moaned playfully. "Jesus, don't torture me like that." He acknowledged the approaching waitress's hollered order with a nod and gestured back to Stephen's drink. "Let me know when you're ready for another."

Stephen thanked him, dropped a ten-spot onto the bar, and turned toward the dance floor. Bodies blended and writhed to the bass-heavy beat, and his toe automatically tapped like he was behind his kick drum.

Humid colognes drifted through the cramped space, and Stephen scanned the crowd. Who would it be tonight? The leather-clad, Cuervo-sipping redhead eyeballing him from the end of the bar? The Beckham-looking guy drinking beer who sat with his dark-haired friend at the table tucked into the corner? Both of them? All three?

A laugh drew his attention back to the dance floor, where a tall brunette danced with two friends. She was dressed like most of the other women in the club, in low-riding jeans and a knit halter top that clung to excellent breasts and exposed a taut stomach—but in his eyes, she lit up like she was radioactive. Her pleasure and happiness crackled through him like a Fourth of July sparkler. He watched her whirl and grind in time to the blinking lights for a good half hour, saw her cheerfully decline offers to dance from three men and one woman. She finally separated from her friends and peeled off to the restrooms.

She was the one. For tonight, anyway. He levered himself off the bar and followed.

Chapter 1

"Shit. Shit, shit, shit." Lukas Sebastiani pounded down the narrow stairs separating his warehouse living space from the business floors of Sebastiani Security, tucking his black T-shirt into yesterday's jeans on the run and trying not to trip on his boot laces.

He was late.

As he thundered down the hallway, several employees working the night shift craned their heads above cubicle walls then descended, like Whack-A-Mole gophers.

Lukas shouldered into his office, dropped into the battered leather chair, elbowed a pile of case files out of the way, and quickly fired up the secure computer and one of the oversized monitors on his desk. "C'mon, c'mon," he muttered, his large hands twitching over the keyboard. The Council meeting had started over an hour ago—a 3:00 a.m. start time to accommodate the vamps—and Sebastiani Security's proposal to allow their newest employee unlimited access to the archives was first up on the agenda. Lukas looked at his watch. "Damn." Council meetings were run with unwavering efficiency. Thankfully Jack Kirkland, Sebastiani Security's managing partner, had authorization to issue the Security and Technology seat's vote.

He flexed his stiff shoulders, rolled his neck. What a shitty start to the night, and the long day to come. He'd been rocked from sleep by waves of lust, pain, and lightning-hot adrenaline that he'd been forced to gulp like he was being water boarded. The tastes and smells had twisted on his tongue, filled his nasal cavities—pinecones, ashes, ozone—and, just in case he hadn't gotten the message the first time, he'd vomited it right back up.

Lukas closed his eyes and drew in a careful breath through his teeth. Someone had died. One more person he hadn't been able to save.

The sour aftertaste still sat on the back of his tongue, rolled in his stomach like a greasy stew, and he couldn't get the scent of ashes out of his nostrils. Reaching for the ever-present bottle of antacid on his desk, he cursed his hyperactive senses. Why couldn't he be more like his father, his brother and sisters? All incubi absorbed emotional energy for sustenance, could sense and interpret the emotions as they were absorbed, and take vicarious pleasure in them. But through some quirk of genetics, Lukas's interpretation abilities were snarled—he sometimes tasted emotions, sometimes smelled them—and however he experienced them, they were always heightened.

Some fucking gift. He pulled the wastebasket closer to his chair as his stomach lurched.

But his genetic quirk had a practical application. Because he could taste and smell emotions, he could sometimes match an emotional energy signature to the person who'd experienced the emotion—like a glorified police dog. He took calls from their police force at all times of the day or night, visited grisly crime scenes, to gather that one additional piece of the puzzle before the taste or smell dissipated. It was just one more piece of data, like DNA, nothing magical about it. And not admissible in court. It took strong detective work to connect that taste to a specific person.

Lukas sighed and keyed his obscenely long password. What had happened? To whom? He'd learned from experience that he'd just have to wait. But damn, it was frustrating. He wanted to do something physical, hit the street, make some calls. Anything but sit here and attend a fucking meeting.

Be careful what you wish for, you just might receive it. He'd asked for this. In the aftermath of the attacks of September 11, 2001, and the uptick in Homeland Security surveillance, he'd convinced the Council that a Security and Technology division with full voting rights was necessary to manage the risks to their people, to keep their species' existence under humanity's radar. And now attending meetings was part of his job, and took way too much time. What the hell had he been thinking?

He leaned in for the retina scan. His gritty eyes stung. The only reason he was awake now, sitting at his desk with shower-wet hair, burning eyes, and pillow creases on his face, was that Jack had sent a message to his mini-comp from the boardroom. Its vibrations against his bedside table had woken him up, annoying as a buzzing mosquito.

His eyes darted to another monitor, to where the Hot Sheet taunted him with its serene Code Green status indicator. There were a few yellow blips here and there, reflecting their police force responding to calls, but the overall status was green.

Bullshit. He did not have time for this PowerPoint rodeo. He needed to be out on the street, looking for...

He dropped his head into his hands. He had no clue what to look for. But he'd be doing… something, instead of sitting in his office. If he looked long enough, he'd find someone doing something they shouldn't be doing.

The conferencing software finally engaged. It was officially too late to go to the break room and snag some coffee.

His hair was soaked. He considered blocking outgoing video, but then decided not to. It wouldn't be the first time that he'd attended a Council meeting looking less-than-professional, but with a couple days' worth of beard and dripping-wet hair, right now he probably looked like a wild man. His father was going to shit an elegant brick, ask to meet with him afterward to discuss appropriate protocol now that Lukas held his own Council seat.

As water dripped down his neck and saturated the soft cotton of his T-shirt, the conferencing software worked its magic. On his monitor, he watched a holographic version of himself, dripping hair and all, shimmer into his chair next to a suited-up Jack. The boardroom chairs were too damn small for someone their size to sit in all day long, but somehow Jack managed to look like he was ready to walk a fashion runway—and kick a few asses along the way. But him? Even his holograph looked uncomfortable, spilling over the arms of the seat.

He took a minute to blink away the cognitive dissonance this technology produced in him. But it was worth it, because another benefit of attending the meeting holographically was that the distance buffered the buffet of tastes which inescapably leached from the group. While most of the women on the Council had fruity essences that combined very pleasantly, he didn't think his stomach was up to Krispin Woolf's mothballs tonight.

"Good morning, thank you for joining us, Mr. Sebastiani," Willem Lund, the Chairman's executive assistant, greeted him, his fingers tapping as he efficiently took notes at his keyboard.

"Sorry I'm late, Willem," Lukas said, zooming his camera to the boardroom's windows to ensure the security screens were engaged. Even though it was still dark, and the Sebastiani Labs corporate campus was located way out in the boonies southwest of the Minneapolis metro, you could never be too careful.

He then pulled back so he could see the whole room. The Sebastiani Labs boardroom looked like any large conference room found in corporate America—if that corporation had lifetimes of experience, proprietary technology, and obscene financial assets at its disposal. Against a side wall, a tableclothed credenza groaned with a selection of juices, water—fresh and saline—and synthetic blood. And coffee, damn it. A huge silver urn of coffee.

A pale maple table dominated the room, large enough to seat the Council members, their Seconds, and Willem. His father, Elliott Sebastiani, sat at the head of the table wearing an exquisitely tailored steel gray suit, his lighter gray hair brushing his shoulders. Willem Lund managed the meeting from his seat at the Chairman's right. At his father's left, chic and intelligent, was Claudette Fontaine, representing the sirens, and probably holding his father's hand under the table. Next to her sat Valerian, the elderly vampire historian and sage, who was leaning across the table to gently scold the Valkyrie

Second, Lorin Schlessinger, about her wardrobe. Lorin was an archeologist, and in her cargo pants and denim shirt, she looked like she'd just come from the field. Next to Valerian, his chosen successor, Wyland, silently watched. Facing off with his father from the other end of the table was Krispin Woolf, the WerePack Alpha. Jack sat jammed into the chair next to Lorin, but unlike Lukas, he was far too urbane to allow any discomfort to show. There were several empty chairs. Annika Fontaine, the Siren Second, was not present. Neither was Lorin's mother Alka, the formidable Valkyrie Chair, nor was Krispin's son Jacoby.

"So nice of you to roll out of bed and join us." Krispin Woolf looked Lukas's holograph up and down with distaste.

"Mr. Woolf. Let's get back to the agenda, please," Willem said firmly. "Mr. Sebastiani, we were discussing a candidate to replace Dr. Sagan."

Krispin Woolf pounded his fist on the table. "Let the Humanity chair stay empty! It was a mistake to invite a human to join the Council in the first place, and it's a blessing he died. For a millennia, each of the species has had Council representation. Species," he repeated, looking directly at Lukas and Jack. "Not humanity, not Security and Technology. Species."

"Mr. Woolf…" Willem tried again.

"Until Sagan and Kirkland joined the Council, humans had no idea we existed," Woolf said. "We should never have confirmed our existence to even one human, much less two. And this morning we authorized a third."

Lukas could almost feel the other members of the board mentally push back from the table as Krispin

Woolf derailed the meeting. He did the same, clicking the meeting's "Step Out" option, flicking Krispin Woolf a virtual middle finger. With outgoing video deactivated, his holographic doppelganger sitting flash-frozen with eyes firmly rolled—oops—he could move freely about his office. He looked at the Hot Sheet again, still mocking him with its Code Green status. Nothing yet. When would something break?

He sighed as he examined what remained of the Council's agenda. Another petition from the Genetic Purity League urging them to require registration of bond relationships. A sentencing decision to be made for an incubus tailgater who'd huffed emotions off gang members robbing a gas station. Lorin had a status update on the Isabella dig, and would talk about actions under way to prepare for her mother's upcoming sabbatical. Lorin hadn't been interested in assuming temporary leadership of Sebastiani Labs' Physical Sciences division during her mother's absence—she practically lived up at the northern Minnesota archaeological dig which each season exposed more about their ancestors—but she wasn't at all happy about reporting to her peer, by-the-book geologist and metallurgist Gabe Lupinsky.

ping

[JKirkland]: Woolf's on a roll today. Earlier he asked Willem to cite the exact bylaw allowing a human to lodge a Council vote.

From his vantage point, Lukas could see Jack surreptitiously typing on the mini-comp resting on his thigh. No one attending the meeting in person would know Jack's entire attention wasn't on Krispin Woolf's bombastic performance.

[LSebastiani]: <sigh>. I have zero patience for Woolf's shit today.

Lukas drew himself up to his full height, leaned in to his webcam, and toggled himself back into the meeting. Watched his virtual self loom over the boardroom table, as if he was about to reach across the table and...

A second box opened with a soft *ping.*

[ESebastiani]: STOP.

Lukas speared Woolf with his eyes, and then sat back in his chair.

[LSebastiani]: Dad, this guy's a waste of oxygen.

Elliott Sebastiani sighed from his seat at the head of the boardroom table. "Krispin, we can't keep revisiting this. We established the Humanity chair to pave the way for our eventual discovery, and the Security and Technology chair to manage the risk to our people in the meantime." His voice got louder and firmer. "These decisions were made years ago and will not be revisited today. As for Dr. Brown, we need someone with her skills to secure our archives. Yes, her background is... unusual. But she's the best person for the job. And she's paid her debt to society."

Woolf shot up from his seat and pointed at Jack. "She's his friend! How objective can their risk assessment be?"

Elliott Sebastiani stood slowly. "Krispin. The vote to open our archives to Dr. Brown was taken and passed half an hour ago. The decision has been made. Please take your seat. Your opposition has been noted for the record." Elliott looked to Willem, who nodded. "Let's move on." He sat down.

Willem opened a new window in the meeting

software, displaying a resume. "Back to our discussion about the candidate, theoretical physicist Dr. Michio Kaku. The floor is open for comments."

[JKirkland]: you OK?

Lukas paused.

[LSebastiani]: rough night

[JKirkland]: ??

[LSebastiani]: Waiting it out. What was the final vote for Bailey?

[JKirkland:] 5/1, Weres against. Easy pass.

Easy pass, my ass. It had taken a lot of legwork. But the vote had gone as he'd expected. He wouldn't have brought this issue to the Council in the first place if he hadn't secured the votes first.

A luscious smell wafted from his doorway. Coffee. Dr. Bailey Brown, Sebastiani Security's newest hire, computing wunderkind, convicted felon, and the catalyst of a multi-species dust-up she was at this moment blissfully unaware of, lounged against the doorjamb, sipping coffee from a gigantic insulated mug. The spicy roasted red pepper flavor Lukas had come to associate with Bailey—always thinking, always curious—hit his tongue. His stomach rolled as her essence mixed with the ash that wouldn't go away, but he swallowed it down. Lukas hit the conference software's PRIVACY key to block the meeting. "Hi, Bailey. You're up late."

"Or early, as the case may be." Bailey nodded in approval at his actions to secure his desktop—even from her. "You look…" She paused, then shrugged. "Well, anyway, good evening, good morning, whatever." She took a noisy slug off the mug.

Damn it. Right now, he would sacrifice his left nut for even one sip of that coffee.

Lukas was glad the Council had authorized them to share their people's history with Bailey, because after three months on the job, she was getting twitchy, looking for the next challenge. Jack had warned him that when Bailey got bored, she got curious. And so Lukas had put his fledgling political capital on the line with the Council, recommending that a human hacker work hip to hip with Valerian to digitize and secure their people's most precious documents.

If humanity had to learn that they shared their planet with other species, the Council was going to damn well control the timeline.

Bailey walked up to his desk and extended the mug to him, and revealed her own, which she'd been hiding behind her back. Lukas raised the mug to his lips and sipped as if from a holy chalice. It was all he could do not to whimper as the viciously strong blend finally washed away the ashy residue of some sick fuck's depraved midnight adventure.

[ESebastiani:] Anything break yet?

Lukas sighed. He should have known his father had felt something too.

"I'll let you get back to work." Bailey turned away. "Catch you later."

"Thank you," he called to her back. Lukas flipped audio and holo back on, and watched his body shimmer into his chair once again. Several of the Council members were typing, getting other work done, while Krispin Woolf busily worked Willem Lund's last nerve.

[LSebastiani:] Nothing yet
[ESebastiani:] Tailgater?

It hadn't felt vicarious to Lukas. Whoever had force-fed him that noxious midnight snack had been wallowing in a swirl of pain and pleasure.

[LSebastiani:] Don't think so.

"Mr. Sebastiani?" Willem said. "Lukas?"

Oops. Busted multitasking. And Woolf's cheekbones were rippling with anger. "I'm sorry, Willem. Could you repeat the question?"

"Mr. Woolf has asked about the timeline on the archiving project."

"The archives will be opened to Dr. Brown today," Lukas responded. "The timeline is hers to establish. We'll report status at next quarter's meeting. Willem, my apologies once again for pulling us off the agenda."

Lukas watched as Willem tapped at his keyboard and lodged an action for Sebastiani Security. Jack made a notation on his mini-comp, thank gawd. He did not have the patience to close action items—

Saliva spurted, and the taste of wet ashes flooded Lukas's mouth. At the meeting, his father's eyes narrowed slightly.

Lukas hunched over the wastebasket and vomited.

Krispin Woolf spoke from the boardroom. "Well, at least there's no messy cleanup on this end."

A red-rimmed dialog box exploded onto Lukas's monitor as the Hot Sheet registered a Code Red. His mini-comp vibrated furiously. *Finally*. Lukas took a swig of coffee, swirled it around his mouth, and spit into the wastebasket. He clicked "Step Out" once again, and quickly read. Homicide. Werewolf club called

Subterranean, two responders on scene. He saw Jack excuse himself and exit the boardroom.

An icon pinged as Jack came online, and they both watched the split-screen live feed streaming from the headsets being worn by the Commander In Charge and his partner.

"Don't you dare yack at my crime scene," Commander Gideon Lupinsky snapped to his trainee, who was identified at the bottom left of the video stream as "J. Williams." Lukas blocked the rookie's audio as his stomach lurched in sympathy. He opened up an audio channel to Lupinsky instead. "I'm here, Gideon."

Lupinsky stopped just outside the entrance to a public bathroom, creating an establishing shot for the record. "Call came in about fifteen minutes ago," Gideon said, looking around the room slowly. "Cleaning staff found her after closing."

Lukas mentally sniffed. Ammonia. Incense, potpourri. Ozone? Something... electric. And yes, the slightest hint of ashes on the air. "Go ahead," he said to Lupinsky.

Williams, pale and clammy, re-entered the room, looking anywhere but at the body sprawled in the handicapped stall. He reactivated her audio.

While Williams collected shards of broken light bulbs and placed them in evidence bags, Lukas watched Gideon snap on some gloves and approach the body. Unmistakably female. Brunette, looked to be about his sister Sasha's age. Lukas quickly pushed the thought aside and focused on the details: jeans, a pair of those high-heeled boots he was amazed women could actually walk in, much less wear dancing. Her shirt was pushed down, exposing her breasts. It felt like a violation to film her condition for the record, but he told himself she was long past caring. Her face, neck, and shoulders were covered by waves of dark brown hair.

Gideon looked around. "I don't see a purse," he said. He knelt next to her, sniffed. "Were." He carefully swept her hair away from her face. And recoiled. "Holy shit."

Her identity kicked Lukas in the gut. Andine Woolf. Andi, Krispin Woolf's daughter. He looked at the other open window on his desktop. Krispin Woolf's day—hell, his life—was about to take a nasty 180.

"What the..." he heard Gideon say. Lukas looked back to the crime scene.

Andi Woolf's ankle had twitched.

"Jenny, call the EMTs," Gideon rapped out to his partner. "She's not dead. Move it!"

Lukas absorbed the Commander's shock and adrenaline as he moved with speed, preserving the scene now forgotten as Andi, sprawled in the handicapped stall, seized uncontrollably.

Gideon leaned over her, examining her face, her crushed throat, the flecks of blood on her lips. Lukas could see the damage as well as Gideon could. Andi tried to drag breath through her ruined airway. No go.

"Lick her," Lukas said softly.

Gideon's head whipped up. "What? Jesus."

Lukas closed his eyes against the vertigo Gideon's sudden motion had caused. "You'll have to help her shift. She has a better chance of surviving in werewolf form."

"Jesus, I don't know if she has the energy reserves to..."

"She'll die if you don't," Lukas snapped. "Just do it."

A sweet clover essence swirled onto his tongue. This girl wasn't ready to die yet.

Andi seized again, her head rhythmically bumping into the cold tile wall. Lukas saw Gideon reach to her, hesitate, then lay his hands on her torso, avoiding her exposed breasts, her damaged throat. And as Lukas had hoped, Andi instinctively responded to the scent of Pack pumping off the werewolf male kneeling next to her.

Gideon pulled her out of the stall by her stiletto-booted feet, her head bumping over the rough floor tiles, her arms dragging overhead. As he dropped onto the floor and ranged his upper body over her bare torso, Lukas got a better look at Andi's crushed throat, using the bathroom's unforgiving fluorescent light to note the placement of the blooming bruises. Gideon finally lowered his head, dragged his tongue along her jaw line, over her open lips, over her cheekbones, eyelids, eyebrows. Gideon's physical reaction pulsed through the room as he used his scent, his sexuality, to catalyze Andi's shift.

"C'mon, c'mon," Gideon breathed as Andi's nostrils twitched, her eyelids fluttered. "Good girl, good. Keep going." He snuffled his nose into her ear, and a moan escaped along with her precious air.

The bathroom door opened as the EMTs arrived. "Stay back," Gideon ordered from his position atop her body. "Lupine, shifting. Get ready to intubate, her airway's gone."

The EMTs goggled at the sight of the straight-laced Commander stretched prone over their patient.

Time dragged as Gideon worked. He finally backed

off as nostril became snout, as sleek brown fur sprouted over Andi's ruined neck. Her torso pulsed. Whiskers sprouted. Her hands turned to paws, her fingernails to claws. And all the time she instinctively lurched toward Gideon. To Pack. It was wrenching to watch, and seemed endless, her bones shifting, popping, with yelps of pain coming from her mouth.

"Shit, she's losing it." Gideon quickly shrugged off his jacket, unbuttoned his cotton oxford shirt, and pressed their torsos together, skin to skin. He grasped her head, brought their faces together, and locked his lips to hers.

His desperation flooded the room.

Several minutes passed. Finally, through Gideon's vid feed, Lukas saw the color of Andi's eyes as they fluttered open, then closed—a mossy green, like her father's.

"Gideon, let the EMTs at her now," Lukas said softly.

Through Jenny's eyes, Lukas watched Gideon shakily lever himself off her body and lean wearily against the bathroom wall. "Okay," he growled to the EMTs through a bloody, half-lupine mouth.

The EMTs scooped Andi up, quickly found a vein, and inserted an IV. At the board meeting, Krispin Woolf listened while the siren, Claudette Fontaine, spoke, unaware that his daughter was fighting for her life.

"Jack and I were attending a meeting with her father when you called," Lukas said. "We can notify him and meet you at the hospital."

"Okay. Give us a few minutes here," Gideon said as the gurney rolled briskly out of the bathroom, wheels clattering against the uneven tile.

Through Williams' video feed, Lukas watched

Gideon raise his hand to his mouth, pause, put it back down again. Gideon looked to his trainee. "Can you bring the kit over here, Jenny? We're going to have to process me for evidence."

Williams gulped audibly as she brought her commander the kit. Through her vid, Lukas watched Gideon extract a tarp and spread it on the floor, then step onto it. He removed a large evidence bag from the kit, set it on the tarp, and opened it. *Snap.* His gloves dropped into the bag. His shirt quickly followed. "Get a swab," he said grimly. "I tasted semen."

Lukas's stomach dropped.

ping

[JKirkland:] *I'll bring Krispin to the hospital.*

[LSebastiani:] *k*

While Lukas opened a chat with his father and gave him a quick update, he saw Jack approach Krispin Woolf, put a hand on the man's shoulder, talk quietly. The other man's flint-tinged fear, his father's horror, spilled onto Lukas's tongue.

Lukas sat for a moment, his bleary eyes staring sightlessly at the glowing monitors. Rancid tastes and toxic smells converged: the rookie's diesel-tasting horror, Gideon's soil-scented helplessness. Andi Woolf's sweet, grassy musk. Cooling coffee. Krispin's mothballs. His own vomit.

As he took a healthy swig of antacid from the bottle on the desk, Lukas watched Claudette Fontaine rise and put her arms around Krispin Woolf.

From this angle, Claudette looked more like Scarlett's sister than her mother.

Shit, where had that come from? Lukas wearily

speared his hands through his still-damp hair. He'd managed to put the Scarlett's Web show out of his mind, for a while, anyway. Thankfully, Scarlett Fontaine was Jack's client, not his. Jack's problem, not his. And if Lukas knew that her tour bus had already pulled into Underbelly's underground parking ramp, right on schedule?

It was only because it was his name on the door, not Jack's.

Chapter 2

SCARLETT FONTAINE TRIED NOT TO WINCE AS LAUGHTER exploded around the table like shrapnel. The band's traditional "welcome home" celebration was just getting warmed up, and she could barely keep her eyes open. She rolled her shoulders and tried to get comfortable in the padded chair. Her apartment—her bed—was ten floors overhead, so close, yet so far away.

Just hold it together a little bit longer. What's a half hour more after a year on the road? She sighed and took a sip of the excellent Chianti that Flynn, Underbelly's night manager, had just poured. "Mmm, just what I needed," she said to Flynn, burrowing into his hug.

"The wine?"

"The hug," she replied with a smile. "It's good to be home."

"Glad to have you back. And don't think I don't notice how bony you are under that floppy sweatshirt. Are you okay?"

No. I'm not. "Just tired," she responded instead. And other than a raised eyebrow, he didn't call her on it, thank the universe—not that he'd hold off for long. But she couldn't explain how she felt to herself yet, much less to someone else.

"Hey, Flynn!" a disembodied voice hollered from the club's back office. "Are you going to close out the tills here or what?"

Flynn hesitated.

"Go count some money," she said, shooing him with one hand and picking up the bottle he'd set beside her with the other. "You'll have all the time in the world to browbeat me."

As Flynn departed, Michael, the band's incubus lead guitarist, said something that made the group guffaw once again. Clangs and curses echoed from the industrial kitchen as the last pots and pans were washed. Plastic cups and bottles clacked as one of the closers pushed a huge broom across the darkened dance floor. Behind the bar, backlit liquor bottles gleamed like rough-cut jewels, and glasses clinked as everyone's drink orders were filled. Sound bounced off every surface, hitting the back of her skull with the subtlety of a nail gun. She wanted to plug her ears. Put on her headset. Scream for silence.

But if she let herself scream, she wouldn't stop. So she breathed deeply, tried to push the noise, the panic, into the background. *Focus on something else, anything else.* Her eyes cruised over the plum-colored walls, nearly black in the shadowy light, and locked on to the most dominant thing in the room: the sculpture that surrounded the stage and formed most of the club's west wall. Steel, aluminum, and pewter undulated three stories to the ceiling, in a functional piece of art that cleverly directed sound from the stage out into the performance area. It was gorgeous, and both *Architectural Digest* and *Audiophile* had featured it in their magazines.

"Toasts!" Tansy, their valkyrie bassist, called from the far end of the table with a glance at her watch. "Let's get this show on the road, people!"

Scarlett smirked. Tansy's bondmates, gorgeous twin vampires, were probably waiting up for her. Naked, in bed.

"Stephen, here's your—where's Stephen?" Flynn asked as he strode from the back carrying the bottle of absinthe the drummer preferred.

"He didn't feel well and went home awhile ago. He'll meet us at Crackhouse for brunch before sound check," Scarlett said, referring to the other business housed in the Sebastiani Building. Her best friend Sasha Sebastiani managed both Underbelly and Crackhouse Coffee, and they also shared one of the building's penthouse apartments with Scarlett's sister Annika. "But he left me his toast." She waited for the table to quiet down, for Flynn to fill a delicate glass with the glowing green liqueur. Scarlett raised it. "To groupies."

The toast was so like Stephen, and so not like Scarlett, that laughter rolled.

"He's the reason the tour bus smelled like sex all the time," Tansy grumbled. "On the next tour we need to have a 'no sex on the bus' rule."

"You can't be serious," one of their roadies said. "Good luck with that."

"You and your rules," Michael said with a roll of his eyes. "You'd have to wallpaper it from stem to stern to cover all the places Stephen's had sex on that bus. And then he'd just find places no one had thought about yet."

"Those damn socks of his. Jesus, he's got some foot funk," Joe, the vampire who played rhythm guitar and keyboards, chimed in. He raised his creamy Guinness. "Here's to clean socks."

"To 3:00 a.m. greasy spoon breakfasts!"

"To room service!"

"To Nessie, who got us here safely!" "Nessie" was the band's nickname for their workhorse tour bus, which had covered over 50,000 miles on this last tour, with only one stop for repairs outside Calgary.

A cheer went up. "Hear, hear!"

"To the next tour!" someone called. Everyone groaned again. Scarlett laughed as she was expected to, but her gut bubbled in warning. "Let's finish this one first, okay?" she said. "We *do* have one more show to go." And she was dreading it.

Flynn appeared at her elbow again and lifted the bottle of wine, but she put her hand over the top of her glass before he could pour. "Nope, I'm cutting myself off."

He peered at her. Too closely. "Good call. Ready to call it a night?"

"Yes, yes, yes." A yawn escaped, and she shivered through her layers. "Brrr. It was freezing when we left the hotel in Chicago this morning, and when we pulled in tonight, it was hot enough to steam rice. Now I'm cold again."

Flynn nodded in agreement. "Fall in Minnesota. Why do we live here again?"

"So we have something to bitch about, of course." Scarlett snagged her purse off the floor and stood.

Accusations of "party pooper" rained over her as the others noticed she was leaving. "I'm following Stephen's lead and getting some sleep. We have one more show, boys and girls, and I, for one, need my beauty sleep."

"Scarlett, what's your toast?" Tansy called.

Shit, the last toast was hers. She paused and closed her eyes. "To…" *To silence, to solitude. To hibernating until the snow melts next spring*. When she opened them, everyone was looking at her expectantly. No way could she say what she really felt. She picked up Stephen's absinthe and raised the glass. "To our homecoming. To sleeping in our own beds tonight—whether alone or with company—and to a great show tomorrow night," she finally said. A cheer went up as she drained the shot of glowing green liquor.

She responded to the calls of "Good night" and "See you tomorrow!" with a wave and almost sagged against Flynn as he walked her through the unmarked door leading to the back of the house.

"Want to raid the refrigerator, have a bedtime snack?" Flynn said as they passed the noisy kitchen.

"No thanks, I'm not hungry."

Flynn eyed her. "You look like you haven't been hungry for a while. You sure? How 'bout a Milky Way milkshake?"

Scarlett's stomach lurched. "No thanks, I just want to go to bed."

They stopped at the private elevator leading to the penthouse apartments. Scarlett stood there blankly, blinking when Flynn pulled a card out of his pocket and swiped it. The elevator doors opened with a swish. Flynn bundled her in and smacked a kiss on her temple. "Welcome home, darlin'. Get to bed. Sleep well."

"Good night," she called as the elevator doors closed. "Thank you, Flynn."

The butter-smooth ride to the tenth floor started, and she turned her back to the elevator's smirking mirrored walls. She didn't need an up-close-and-personal view of the damage the road had wreaked, thank you very much. Her weight loss and the condition of her skin had had

Jesse, her bodyguard-cum-stylist, tsk-tsking for the last month or so. With no makeup on, her green eyes were the only shot of color on her face, and her red hair was wilted and limp. While Tansy had recently started complaining that her favorite leather pants were getting too tight— "too many damn Hot Pockets"—Jesse had had to alter some of Scarlett's performance clothing. But on the plus side, shopping had been required. What woman didn't get a zing out of buying her jeans a size—okay, two sizes—smaller than usual?

The elevator drew to a stop, and the doors opened onto the dimly lit foyer for the two penthouse units on the top floor of the Sebastiani Building. Scarlett forced herself to move before the elevator doors closed on her and took her back downstairs.

The foyer was blissfully silent. On the table directly across from the elevator, a Tiffany lamp burned in welcome. A trio of pictures of the aurora borealis still hung on the wall above the table, greenish blue magnetic sheets coating the night sky. A single, exquisite orchid stood in a crystal vase, its petals a pink so pale they seemed white. She picked up the small lavender note card leaning against the vase, and read. "Welcome home, darling. Love you, Mom." Smiling, she touched the flower's delicate petals with her forefinger, and then tucked the card in her back pocket.

Elliott Sebastiani's stately apartment was off to the right. She veered left, to the four-bedroom unit.

Key, key... where was her key?

It was a sign of everything that was wrong with her life that she didn't know where her own damn house key was. When was the last time she'd unlocked anything other than a hotel room door for herself? She wearily opened her landfill of a purse, pawed through candy wrappers, pens, matchbooks from the clubs they'd played, enough tubes of lip gloss to stock a cosmetics counter, a stray tampon. Her wallet. She found the right card, slid it into the slot underneath the doorknob, waited for the light to turn green, and opened the heavy door. Closed it softly behind her.

Home. She was home at last. Away from the incessant attention that made her feel like a wild animal pacing behind bars at the zoo. Alone. At least for a few hours. No autograph seekers, no star fuckers, no paparazzi. And, love 'em dearly, no band mates, no roadies, no crew. They were all overdue for some time to themselves. It had been months since she'd slept in her own bed, and it was just fifteen strides away. She just… had to convince her feet to move.

She took a step in the dim light and promptly stumbled over a suitcase. "Damn." Had she wakened Sasha and Annika? It had been so long since she'd been home that her roommates would be more apt to think a robber was opening the door than her.

Nah. No robber would ever reach this door, because with his sister living here, and his father living across the foyer, Lukas Sebastiani had used every bit of his legendary skill to ensure the place was locked down tight.

Her own safety? Just a happy coincidence. Lukas avoided her like the plague. She sighed. Yeah, okay, the avoiding was reciprocal, but occurred for completely different reasons. Lukas didn't care about her, and she… cared too much. Hurt too much. But that was going to change. Once she felt better rested, she would deal with Lukas, once and for all.

Scarlett made her way to her bedroom without turning on the lights or waking her roommates. She shut the door behind her, flipped the switch, and flooded the room with light. Though the turquoise walls glowed and there was no dust, the room felt a little sterile after such a long period of disuse. For a few minutes, she simply puttered, reacquainting herself with her things. A faint scent of rain permeated the room from a candle that someone—Sasha, most likely—had left burning in welcome on her bedside table. Passing the sound system, she unclipped her iPod—facetiously named Sigmund in honor of the psychiatrist Sigmund Freud—from the hip pocket of her jeans, docked it, and pressed Play. She barely blinked when the shuffle feature queued up Michael Jackson's "Scream."

It just figured.

As the music throbbed softly into the room, she trailed her hand over the intricate contemporary quilt covering her maple four-poster bed. Priceless, too precious to take with her on the road. The faerie quilt swirled with all the colors of the ocean: teal, turquoise, tanzanite. Indigo and midnight blue tipping to nearly black, the occasional flash of lime green. She'd commissioned it the day she'd turned eighteen, the youngest age the faeries would consider such a request—her illustrious lineage be damned—because in addition to providing warmth and beauty for a lifetime, faerie quilts catalyzed dreams, and such things could not be trusted to youth. During her hypnotic blur of an interview, Scarlett had apparently described her favorite childhood fantasy: She

was a mermaid, swimming through the bath-warm trop-
ics, caring for the creatures feeding near the towering
kelp forest.

Not a siren singing men to their deaths, thank you
very much.

Her eyes were drawn to the plum-framed Annie
Leibovitz prints lining the walls, pictures of the musi-
cians she respected, some of whom she'd been lucky
enough to collaborate with and now counted as friends.
Her own photograph by the famed rock photographer
hung around the corner, tucked in the alcove which
held her desk and computer—part of the collection, yet
not. Hers was a matted pair of prints: first, the staged
shot which had appeared in *Vanity Fair* about a year
ago as part of a story on emerging female songwriters,
Scarlett presented as a majestic siren luring ships into
the cliffs with her voice, standing strong and sinuous on
a bluff overlooking the pounding Irish Sea near dusk,
barefooted on the rocks, arms stretched to the elements.
Power pulsed off the picture, and Scarlett stared at it in
amazement. Who was *that?* Was even a fraction of it
real, or was it all smoke and mirrors?

She looked at the second print and smiled. She and
Annie were hugging after the shoot, Annie seemingly
impervious to the weather, but Scarlett bundled into
an ugly, ankle-length, down jacket, UGGs on her feet,
knit cap on her wet hair, her hands wrapped around a
steaming mug of tea. Bedraggled, runny nose, blue lips
and fingernails.

This Scarlett she had no problem recognizing.

The bed called to her, but she checked for messages
first, and then quickly flipped through the piles of mail

someone had deemed important enough for her to see, but not urgent enough to deliver to her on the road. How did Garrett receive her mail? How had he delivered her latest house key when he was on the road with them most of the time? She'd never thought about it before. She'd gotten used to being hustled and bundled from location to location, conserving her flagging energy for the next performance. The road was a bubble in which real life fell by the wayside. An escape. Just like she'd wanted, had asked for.

But now it was time for real life again. She wanted to sort through her own mail. She yearned to sort laundry into colors, choose which temperature to wash them in, turn the knobs. To go to the grocery store and choose her own fresh oranges, shop for her own damn tampons—not just have them magically appear when she needed them.

Her face blazed with heat. Garrett even managed her period.

She looked up to the picture of The Pretenders' Chrissie Hynde, met her wise, kohl-rimmed eyes. Would Chrissie let some man manage her menstrual cycle? Hell no.

She had to make some changes—starting with confronting her pitiful feelings for Sasha's lunk of a brother.

She made herself think back to Annika's Succession Ceremony late last summer, the day her sister had officially become the Siren Second, a member of the Underworld Council. The weather that day had been hot and gorgeous, drenched in history, laughter, and sunlight. Held at Annika's choice of venue, The Calhoun Beach Club in Minneapolis, the Succession Ceremony

itself had taken place in one of the smaller private ball-
rooms, its French doors thrown open to the lake and
the adjoining private beach which was theirs for the
day. Though "succession casual" had ruled the day,
the simple and moving rite had played out as it had for
hundreds of years, with Wyland carrying the Council
Tome to the front of the room where a candle-laden,
white-clothed table had been set up on a riser. Valerian,
resplendent in his black, grey, and white tapestry robes,
had stood behind the table facing them, with Annika and
her mother positioned on each side. Scarlett herself had
been seated in the front row, hyper-aware of Lukas's big
body shifting uncomfortably in his chair at the end of the
row. Even after Valerian had intoned the final emotional
words of the ceremony—"All that was. All that is. All
that shall be"—as he'd scribed Annika's name underneath her mother's with his flashy Mont Blanc pen,
she'd been fine. But when each Council member had
approached Annika, ceremonially kissing her forehead,
heart, left cheek, right cheek, lips... Scarlett gulped.

Admit it. Watching Lukas place his lips on her sister's mouth, even platonically, had fractured something
inside of her. And she'd ducked out of the after party,
dialing up Garrett and setting tour plans in motion before she'd even left the Calhoun Beach Club parking lot.

What had ever made her think that touring for over
a year would be a viable solution, would anesthetize
her useless, pitiful feelings? All she'd accomplished
was burning herself out. The year swirled through her
brain: sold out shows. Music and merch sales through
the roof. Hundreds of thousands of hits to the band's
website, spiking when Scarlett herself posted in their

online road journal. Yes, the tour had been successful beyond Garrett's wildest dreams, but she'd been going through the motions for months. She couldn't write for shit, and looked even worse. About halfway through the tour, she'd started singing other artist's songs more frequently than her own because… it was easier. It hurt less to interpret the emotions in songs other people had written, and she did it very, very well. Wildly popular, Scarlett's Web cover shows had become epic events, guaranteeing an emotional roller coaster ride one would never forget.

But no one knew the sense of failure she felt every single night the band performed. It was bad enough she wasn't writing her own music, but she was also too much of a chickenshit to sing her own backlist.

She couldn't think anymore, couldn't focus. She lost her temper more easily than she used to. Her life felt like it was happening to someone else. And that was going to change, she affirmed as she undressed. She needed to feel her own feelings again, not run from them, no matter how painful they were. And she couldn't move on until she confronted her feelings for Lukas Sebastiani.

The bastard.

Yes, it was time to get her life back on track. Scarlett climbed into bed naked, pulling the puffy quilt over her bare shoulders. *Please, no dreams tonight.* Because in her dreams, she tumbled in the sheets with a rock of a man, with the incubus who'd kissed her, devoured her, initiating her into womanhood so deliciously that she'd… screamed.

Ruining her for anyone else.

Chapter 3

THE NIGHT SKY WAS BRIGHTENING, ABOUT TO TIP OVER to dawn, and the lobby of Memorial Hospital was filled with people who never expected they'd be making a pit stop at the emergency room. The sharp taste of iron spurted under Lukas's tongue as yet another ambulance screamed to a stop at the entrance. Adrenaline pumped as the medical staff jumped into action like football players, choreography he'd become familiar with during the hours he, Jack, and Krispin Woolf had been waiting for Andi Woolf to come out of surgery. First, a medical response team trotted out the door and onto the field. They opened the ambulance door, listened to the EMT squatting like a coach in the back of the vehicle beside the patient. The sleepy resident quarterbacking the play then rapped out a jargon-filled stream of orders that Lukas sure as shit hoped made sense to someone. Snap goes the gurney. Gurney and passenger were quickly wheeled to the end zone.

And sometimes screams fill the stadium.

The place was bedlam. He was in the way everywhere he stood, and he'd seen *way* too much of the lower torso of a valkyrie straining to bring new life into the world, but he wasn't going to leave until he talked to Gideon Lupinsky. Jack was in the cafeteria, getting them an umpteenth cup of awful coffee, and Krispin Woolf waited, tight-lipped, in a family room just down the hall.

He'd declined Jack's offer of coffee with icy politeness. "All I'd like is privacy, please." Despite the closed door between them, Krispin's misery leached into the lobby.

Lukas's mini-comp pinged. He edged into the doorway of an empty family room directly across from the nurse's station, his stomach sinking as he skimmed the preliminary findings that the lab had routed to both him and Gideon.

The skin they'd scraped from underneath Andi's fingernails was incubus. Lukas sighed. Like they didn't already have enough of a problem with bigots thinking incubi were uncontrollable sex fiends.

Lukas stepped into the family room and sat on the institutional couch. Though the thing looked like a torture rack from The Inquisition, he was so damn tired that any horizontal surface looked pretty attractive right now.

He'd been the first to arrive, beating even Andi's ambulance, because Sebastiani Security headquarters was located a mere two blocks away from the hospital. Gideon and his rookie had been delayed at the scene, and Jack and Krispin had hit the morning rush hour exactly wrong, turning the drive from the Chanhassen boardroom from forty minutes into an hour and a half.

And thank the aurora that Krispin had been delayed, because no father, no matter how much of an asshole, deserved to witness what Lukas had seen as the gurney carrying Andi had emerged from the ambulance. She'd looked positively feral, spontaneously shifting between human and werewolf and back again, growls and moans and groans mixing and pushing from her damaged throat like gritty asphalt. She'd clutched at her neck repeatedly, as if she'd tear it open herself if she could. The sour aftertaste of her terror still lingered on the back of his tongue.

If someone did this to a member of his family, there'd be nothing left of the guy except a gut pile by the side of the road.

The doctor who'd run alongside Andi's gurney hours ago emerged from behind a closed door. Lukas watched as he rested his weight against the nurse's station, swung a monitor his way, and started to type. When he finished, the nurse behind the desk pointed to Lukas, who stood as the doctor joined him.

The doctor covered a jaw-cracking yawn with his hand and blearily eyed the couch before shaking Lukas's hand. One of the laminated cards clipped to his coat pocket identified him as Dr. Adnan Penn, MultiSpecies Trauma. The picture on the card was as bad as anything the Department of Motor Vehicles had ever slapped on a driver's license.

"How is she?" Lukas asked.

Dr. Penn dragged a hand through his short, coal-black hair. "We repaired the damage to her throat. She's critical, in Intensive Care, but… holding. Werewolves are so damn strong," he said with a shake of his head. "There's a chance that the trach might be permanent, but…"

The rest of his thought didn't have to be said: better that than dead.

"When can Mr. Woolf see his daughter?"

"I'm off to see him next," Dr. Penn said. "Commander Lupinsky is with Ms. Woolf, but he said he'd only be a few more minutes. Mr. Woolf will be able to visit his daughter after the Commander finishes."

Exhaustion pulsed off of Penn in waves, and Lukas

had to stiffen his knees to stay standing as the other man spoke. "Mr. Woolf has authorized us to update you and the Commander if there are any changes in her status."

If Andi Woolf died.

Penn reached for his waist as his PDA beeped. "Here comes the next one." He eyed Lukas grimly. "Good hunting, Sir."

Across the hall, Gideon Lupinsky emerged from Andi's room, an evidence bag in his hand and a phone clapped to his ear. He was still wearing the thin, half-translucent jumpsuit he'd put on in Subterranean's women's restroom after placing his own clothing into evidence. More waterproofing than anything else, cops usually pulled the jumpsuit on to protect their clothing at messy crime scenes. Gideon's bright red boxer shorts were clearly visible, but from the rigid expression on his face, people being able to see his underwear was the least of his concerns.

Down the hall, Dr. Penn escorted Krispin Woolf into his daughter's treatment room. Suddenly the voices in the waiting room quieted to a hush, then excitement buzzed like a hive of bees.

His father had arrived.

He, Jack, and Krispin Woolf hadn't been recognized by too many people in the waiting room, and those who had recognized them had clearly seen that they were occupied. But Council President Elliott Sebastiani, accompanied by Siren Leader Claudette Fontaine? It was too juicy to ignore, even in the land of Minnesota Nice.

Where the fuck was his father's bodyguard? Lukas stepped in front of their bodies with his own, quickly herding them to the family room he'd just come from.

Lukas closed the door behind them and moved them away from the window. "Damn it, Dad…"

Elliott sighed and hugged him. "He cleared the elevator, watched the doors close."

"If he's not next to you, he's not guarding your body."

"If you're here, why should I bother him?"

Lukas opened his mouth, then shut it. Now was not the time, and his father was right—he *was* here. He hugged his father back, then leaned down and kissed Claudette on both cheeks. He sensed his father's concern—for Andi, and for Lukas himself—but a much more complex set of emotions swirled around Claudette: a woman's fear that he recognized intellectually but couldn't fully appreciate, a helpless, gut-burning anger, and… maternal concern.

He tensed.

Claudette had passed her aristocratic bone structure and coloring down to her younger daughter Scarlett in spades. What was it about the Fontaine gene pool that pulled at the Sebastiani men so strongly? Did his father feel yanked around by his gonads too?

If he did, he seemed pretty damn happy about it. Elliott's wife, Lukas's mother Dasha, had been dead a long time, and Claudette, this woman who'd stepped in out of friendship and practically raised him and his siblings alongside her own little girls, had twined herself around their hearts. After years of guilt and denial, his father had finally reached out and taken what he wanted.

Unfortunately, he couldn't do the same.

"How is Andi?" Claudette asked, her siren's voice soft, empathetic. Lukas felt it comfort him, as she had no doubt intended. Yes, there was no doubt about it. Scarlett's skill came down through the blood.

"She's critical but stable. They've repaired her throat, established an airway, and they're keeping her sedated for the time being." He stretched the stiffness from his shoulders. "She's fighting."

Elliott took Claudette's hand. "And Krispin?"

Lukas shrugged. "He's angry. Upset. Not talking too much." Not talking aloud, anyway. But vengeance pulsed off the man as Lukas had easily interpreted the request Krispin couldn't let himself speak: "Find who did this to my baby."

"His anger is understandable." Claudette pulled Elliott to sit beside her on the couch.

"Yeah." Lukas plopped down in an adjacent chair, and they simply sat for several minutes, the bubbling of the saltwater aquarium on the table punctuating the silence. People walked by the closed door, some undoubtedly curious about what event had brought members of the Underworld Council to the hospital. They'd find out soon enough.

Lukas relayed the information about the skin found under Andi's nails. "Lupinsky is running like crimes, but nothing's popped yet."

"Did you find anything at the scene?" his father asked.

Lukas hesitated, his hand unconsciously rubbing his stomach. How to describe it? "Pleasure. Pain. Violence. All swirled together," he said slowly. "And... ashes." He shrugged. "But maybe someone was sneaking a smoke in the bathroom."

"Or not." Elliott looked at Claudette, then back at Lukas.

Claudette's concern fluttered into the room like a hummingbird, tripping his internal security perimeter. Lukas sat up straight on the couch. *Shit. This was about*

Scarlett. He opened his mouth to speak, but Claudette beat him to it.

"Aah, Lukas. You read me too well." She pushed her silver and red hair behind her ear, and it swept right back onto her cheekbone again. "With what happened to Andi tonight, I'm nervous about the girls. Annika is pretty good at taking care of herself, always has been, but Scarlett..." Claudette ticked off reasons on her slender fingers. "She's a wide-open target when she's performing. She's not street-smart. And just coming off the road? She's absolutely exhausted."

Lukas snorted. "Yeah, a life filled with sex, drugs, and rock and roll might do that to you."

Claudette nailed him with a stare he usually didn't see outside the boardroom.

"Sorry." Tipping his head back, he tried to work the kinks out of his stiffened shoulders, neck, and upper back. "It's been a long day. I'm not usually so subtlety-impaired."

"Yes, you are," she replied. "And you're not being fair to Scarlett. But that's an issue for another day." Lukas sensed her finger hovering over the spring of a trap, and took a careful breath. She took Elliott's hand again. "If there's the slightest possibility someone is attacking the Council through their family members, Scarlett might just as well have a bull's-eye painted on her back tonight."

To Lukas, a political motive for the attack on Andi Woolf seemed tenuous at best, but until he and Gideon could hit the street, he couldn't rule it out, either. Couldn't reassure her with empty platitudes.

"We can't rule out a political motive, but we haven't

found anything to support one either," he responded. "Gideon and I have been at the hospital all night. Give us a chance to investigate, Claudette, to rule it out. As for the show tonight, you know that Underbelly is the safest place Scarlett could possibly perform. I've reviewed Jack's security plan. It's rock-solid. Jack will be there, right at her side."

"And you, Lukas? Where will you be?"

Damn it. Lukas slouched back against the back of the couch and swiped his hands through his hair. He should have been better prepared for this. He knew the trap was about to snap shut; he felt the tension in the fucking hinges.

"Lukas," she pressed. "I want you there."

"No." The instinctive response slipped out before he could stop it. He did not have time to babysit a spoiled rock star, especially this one—and not with Andi Woolf lying in a hospital bed, fighting for her life. "Claudette, I—"

"I know you're busy, and that you and Scarlett rub each other the wrong way. Nothing against Jack, but"—steel entered her voice—"I want you to keep watch over my daughter personally."

It was all Lukas could do to clamp down on manic laughter. If Claudette knew just *how* wrong he and Scarlett had rubbed each other, with which body parts, and how bloody long ago, he'd be strung up. There was no parental statute of limitations for what he'd done. He reached for his only argument. "Scarlett won't agree."

"If you and Jack have problems with Scarlett, we can set Claudette on her," Elliott advised. "She can be very persuasive."

Lukas remembered how Scarlett's barely legal hands had felt on his younger body. *Your daughter is no slouch in the persuasion department, either.*

Ah, shit. He stood and paced the small room, considering the ramifications of Claudette's demand. Physical pain he could manage. Did, nearly every day. But standing in such close proximity to a siren who interpreted and amplified emotions with her voice? This particular siren, who he wanted with every cell of his body, but couldn't let himself have again? She'd lead him around by the dick all night long.

Clenching his jaw, he fought his mind back to Andi Woolf lying in her hospital bed. Was it a random attack, or politically motivated? Andi's injuries went well beyond some guy—some incubus, Lukas made himself acknowledge—losing control, or not being able to handle his liquor. The taste of ashes gave them somewhere to start, but Claudette's request would keep him off the street for nearly twenty-four hours.

He couldn't refuse.

Like you wouldn't have ended up at the show anyway, his mind whispered.

He took a deep breath. He could damn well control himself around her. It would be tough, but he could do it. Even if it killed him. "Okay," he replied curtly.

Claudette stood and hugged him. Her relief smelled like fresh dandelions. "Thank you so much, Lukas."

His father joined them, wrapping his arms around them both. "Thank you," Elliott whispered.

His father had a pretty good idea what the request would cost him.

"Well, then," Elliott said. "We all have work to

do, Lukas more than we do, I think. We should get going." He turned to Lukas. "Will you be heading to Underbelly soon?"

"A couple of hours more, I think. I have to touch base with Gideon first, then we're going back to the scene. I'll catch a shower and a change of clothes somewhere along the way." Lukas looked at his watch and mentally rearranged his day. Any hope he had of catching a catnap had just been shot to hell. Where was Jack with the coffee?

He dialed his father's bodyguard, telling him the president was ready to leave and that he and Madame Fontaine required an escort to the car.

"Is that really necessary?" Elliott groused. "So annoying."

"Good." Lukas stepped out of the room before his father and Claudette, assessing it for threats before they walked down the hall. "Would you rather have a female bodyguard? Have her pose as your girlfriend?"

"There's no need to get nasty." Elliott grasped Claudette's hand. As they rode the elevator down to the parking garage, Elliott turned to him. "Thank you," he said again. "For everything."

"No problem. Just get in the car." Lukas watched closely while his father's stony-faced bodyguard ushered Elliott and Claudette into the backseat of the armored Town Car, and closed the door behind them. As the car pulled away from the curb, Lukas mentally penciled in a serious career chat with the guard. Elliott was increasingly in the public eye due to his "day job" as CEO of Sebastiani Inc., the technology research conglomerate whose activities and subsidiaries uncomfortably straddled the Underworld/humanity boundary. Despite the guard's formidable qualifications, he wasn't going to last long if he couldn't push back against his father.

Thankfully, Lukas could drop himself into the concert's physical protection plan with barely a ripple; all he had to do was change clothes and plant himself backstage. The fact that Underbelly was a Sebastiani property meant that its physical layout was secure, but Sasha's demand that Underbelly be buttoned up tight, but not visibly enough to impact the atmosphere of barely controlled hedonism that made it one of Minneapolis's hottest clubs, had given Jack fits. Just last week Jack had supervised the installation of additional metal detectors, doorjamb prototypes supplied by Sebastiani Labs. Sasha and her team had ticket technology under control; no one would be able to counterfeit the tickets for this event.

Lukas wondered yet again whether he and Jack should have worked harder to convince at least some of the Council members to watch the show remotely, from the boardroom. If anyone or anything got past them tonight, they could take out most of the leadership of the non-human citizens of the planet in one fell swoop.

Why did his father have to choose now to get a love life? Lukas made a mental note to assess the security at his father's penthouse apartment again, and to assign him—them—a larger protection detail. If Underworld Council leadership continuity wasn't a big enough stick for Lukas to swing at his father, he would use Claudette's safety. Ruthlessly.

Extremely dirty pool, given how his wife—Lukas's mother—had died.

He walked back to the emptying waiting room, and saw Jack making his way down the hall. Bright yellow bananas peeked out of each of his suit pockets, and he juggled two gigantic cups of coffee. A good portion of a third appeared to be splashed down the leg of his Hugo Boss suit.

"Hold on a sec," Jack said into his headset as he approached. He handed Lukas one of the huge cups. "I had to fight a gurney for this. You owe me, big-time."

"I'm going to owe you even more before the day is through," Lukas said with a sigh. "Slight change of plans for Scarlett's show tonight." He explained Claudette's request.

"I would have brought it up myself if she hadn't," Jack said. "I'm talking with Bailey now. I'll ask her to meet us at Underbelly instead of the office this afternoon."

Lukas stared at him.

"The meeting about the archiving project?"

He'd forgotten all about it. The Council meeting and its contentious vote seemed like it had happened weeks ago. Lukas dragged his free hand through his hair, and took a slug of the coffee. It tasted like crankcase sludge, but it was caffeinated, and that was all that mattered right now. Jack was right; this meeting with Bailey couldn't be postponed. Luckily one of them still had functioning brain cells.

"Sure. Tell her to bring some party clothes." They might as well drop her in feet first tonight and see how well she coped.

Hell, what was he worried about? Bailey would cope better than he would.

Jack handed Lukas two bananas, and then sat down on the couch to give Bailey instructions. Suddenly he pointed to the waiting room, to where Gideon Lupinsky had emerged from Andi's room carrying more evidence bags.

Adrenaline hit hard. *Finally*. Mouthing "later" to Jack, Lukas cut through the waiting room, taking a bite off a banana, fueling up on the run. Doing something, anything, would be better than all this sitting around.

Sitting around gave him too much time to think—to think about Scarlett, the woman he couldn't let himself have again.

Chapter 4

"SCARLETT! WAKE UP, YOU LAZY BITCH!"

Ugh. Scarlett rolled over and buried her head in her pillow. If Annika's banshee wail hadn't been enough to wake her up, her sturdy body flopping full-length onto the bed beside her certainly was. She stole a quick look at the mermaid clock on the bedside table before rolling into her sister's exuberant hug. She'd hoped to sleep until noon, but seven hours was better than nothing.

"Damn it, Annika." Sasha scowled from the doorway. "I told you to wait. She needs to sleep."

Annika yanked Scarlett's quilt down to her waist, exposing her bare torso to the chilled air. "Wake up! You've been gone for months, and sleeping for hours. I waited as long as I could." She gestured to the panther-black cat twining itself around Sasha's ankles. "And Calamity has missed you, haven't you, you evil beast?"

Scarlett yanked the quilt back up and scraped a riot of hair out of her face. "Come here, sweetie," she crooned. "I couldn't find you last night. Where were you?"

The "sweetie" in question was twenty pounds of muscular bad attitude who adored the taste of flesh. Scarlett tapped her fingers against the quilt to tempt him. From across the room, Calamity's bright green eyes met hers, held, and with a hunch of his back and a flick of his tail, the cat about-faced and skulked out of the room.

"You aren't hurting my feelings one bit," Scarlett called after him. The expression on her face belied her words.

"Oh, he'll be back to gnaw on you before you know it." Annika pulled one of the bed pillows off the mound on the floor and propped herself up against the slatted headboard.

"He doesn't bite," Scarlett muttered. "Much."

"Yeah, right." Sasha pointed to her right ankle, which sported a fresh red weal. "He harpooned me this morning when my alarm went off. Damn cat is a fifth of my body weight, hell of a way to wake up."

"He nipped Jack last week," Annika said.

Sasha smiled innocently. "So I forgot to tell him it might not be a good idea to jiggle his foot like that. Oopsie." She looped her fingers on her belt. "But thank the aurora you're home. The cat—and Jack—are all yours again."

The guilt trickled through her. "Thanks so much for watching Calamity. I know he's a pain in the ass."

"I think it was the other way around—he watched out for us. Lukas should hire that cat for guard duty."

Scarlett yawned and hauled herself up beside her sister, mentally penciling in a nap for later in the afternoon. She'd never get through the show without it. Then she smelled something glorious. Her eyes searched the room. Where was it? "Give it to me now, and no one gets hurt."

Sasha ducked out for a moment, picked up the tray she'd left on a hallway table just outside Scarlett's bedroom door, and breezed back into the room. "Given what time you got to bed last night, I thought a bribe might come in handy."

One of the biggest benefits of living in the Sebastiani Building was the convenience of having a twenty-four-hour coffee shop right on the ground floor.

"A pot of Crackhouse Blend, just for you," Sasha said as she placed the cheerful orange serving tray holding a Holstein-spotted thermal carafe and three oversized purple mugs on the foot of the bed. "I brewed it myself."

It was all Scarlett could do to stop herself from lunging at it. The stuff was addictively good, so much so that Sasha had jokingly named the coffee shop and its signature blend after a place where people scored drugs. Though Scarlett carried a healthy supply of the coffee on the tour bus, it tasted better when Sasha brewed it. Girl had the touch.

Sasha poured a cup of the coffee, added a dollop of cream, and handed it to Scarlett. It was unstirred, as she preferred.

Home was the place where people remembered how you took your coffee.

She paused at the lip of the mug, sipped quietly. The flavor exploded on her tongue, and she finally swallowed. "I think I just came," she breathed, leaning back against her headboard and smiling at her roommates. "I'm so glad to be home."

"It's been awhile since we were all home at the same time. Gonna stick around for awhile?" Annika asked.

She sipped again. "Yeah. I need a break. I'm absolutely wiped."

"I hear ya," Sasha said as she rubbed at her temple.

Scarlett studied Sasha. She looked a little thin, but she was a fine one to talk. Sasha still sported the same black and fuchsia hair she'd had at Annika's Succession

Ceremony almost a year ago. Always darn near aerodynamic, this morning it sprouted up from her pixie face like she'd already been tugging on it for hours. "Headache?" she asked.

Sasha dropped her hand from her head. "No. I don't have time for a headache today."

How much stress had this damned show put on her friend?

Annika elbowed her to get her attention. "First things first," she said, waving a month-old tabloid in her face.

That damn picture. "Where did you get that trash?" Scarlett made a grab for it.

Annika held it aloft. "Please tell me he rocked in the sack."

Scarlett rolled her eyes. "Sorry, he rocked at the sound board and nowhere else," she said. "He's producing a couple of songs for the next record. And if you look at that picture closely, you can see Duncan's practically holding me up, my knees were knocking together so hard. The paparazzi hijacked us coming out of a restaurant, and…" She shrugged.

When Sasha touched her hand in commiseration, Scarlett consciously ratchetted her reaction down. Sasha already had a headache, and she didn't need to absorb her crap too.

"You okay?" Annika asked.

"They gave me a few rough moments," she admitted. Political kidnappings weren't unheard of in their world, and given her profession, she drew plenty of whack jobs all by herself.

"If Lukas had been there, he'd have pounded them into the pavement," Annika said with relish.

Scarlett raised a brow. "I can take care of myself. And Jack drills me every time I'm home. If I need a bodyguard, he's it."

Annika nudged her with her elbow. "Jack can guard my body. As closely as he wants to."

Scarlett eyebrows climbed higher. Her sister and Jack? "Are you two…?"

"No, but not for the lack of trying. He's not biting." Annika squirmed on the bed, a beatific expression on her face. "Mmm, there's a thought."

Sasha wrinkled her nose. "Eww."

"Eww? Eww?" Annika sat up. "I call bullshit. The man is smokin' hot."

"He's impossible to work with, doesn't know the meaning of the word compromise, and he's way too bossy."

Annika looked at Scarlett, and they both burst out laughing. "Pot, meet kettle. And c'mon, a little bit of bossy can be absolutely delicious." Annika collapsed back against the pillows again. "He's always so… buttoned up. Wouldn't you just love to see what he looks like rolling out of bed first thing in the morning? All mussed up?"

Scarlett mentally shrugged. Intellectually she knew that Jack was very attractive, but for some reason he just didn't melt her panties. Not like—she shut down the thought with an emphatic slam. "Would you stop talking about Jack like he's a Happy Meal?"

"I think I just threw up in my mouth a little," Sasha muttered.

Annika laughed at her. "You're just pissed that he's right more often than not."

"Gawd, the last thing I need to deal with is another

oversized know-it-all. The moment I get Lukas out of my hair, Jack steps in to fill the void. Both of them are major pains in my ass. Though Lukas has been less of a problem lately," Sasha mused. "It seems like every time I swing by Sebastiani Security to deliver coffee, he's closeted in a conference room with Bailey."

Every cell in Scarlett's body stuttered. "Who's Bailey?" she asked mildly.

"Bailey Brown, SebSec's newest employee," Sasha answered. "Little blonde, computer savant, great hair, drinks like a sailor. Human. She's been with them for— what?" She looked to Annika for verification. "Three months now?"

Annika nodded and lowered her voice. "Last night, the Council granted her unlimited access to the archives. Some hush-hush computer project with Valerian and Wyland."

"Wow." Scarlett pulled the quilt up over her shoulders. This was huge. This woman must be very special. Would Lukas date an employee? A *human* employee? She didn't care. Not one whit.

"Are she and Lukas...?" Scarlett waved her hand toward the bed vaguely. Hey, not caring didn't mean not asking.

Sasha pursed her lips. "I don't think so. Not that she's not adorable, but I get zero vibe. I heard she hacked NSA or the CIA or something when she was a teenager, just to prove she could. The only reason she got caught was because her bargain-basement equipment couldn't keep up with her." Her voice turned admiring. "That takes some gonads."

Scarlett's jaw dropped. Though she stayed well away

from Council activities, even she knew that keeping their people's very existence a secret was critically important. What was Lukas thinking, hiring someone who'd likely be under Homeland Security surveillance for the rest of her natural life? Her shoulders dropped. Lukas had to be thinking with the little head, not the big one.

Though, if she could trust her memory, the little head was pretty damn big.

"Well, luckily she did this before 9/11," Sasha continued, "or she'd still be festering in some forgotten prison cell. And to her credit, it was a white hat hack. No damage done, except to some old guys' egos." Sasha paused to sip at her coffee. "I've gotten to know her a little, talked to her when I deliver coffee to SebSec, and she's come to the club a few times. Grabs a drink, dances, but doesn't go home with anyone. Sometimes the bouncers get a workout when some dude doesn't want to take no for an answer."

Hmm. Scarlett concentrated on her own cooling coffee. She would not think about Lukas being closeted up in a conference room with a smart, nice, cute—no, make that adorable—human woman who men got into fights over. And who had great hair, one of Sasha's highest accolades. Time for a change of subject. "Annika, aren't you supposed to be at a Council meeting?" Annika worked as a voice actor, supplying dialogue for animated characters in movies and cartoons, and was slowly learning to balance the demands of her profession with her responsibilities as the Siren Second.

"Just as I was about to dial in, I got a text message from Willem that the meeting had been unexpectedly adjourned." She shrugged. "So I stayed at work. I'm not sure anyone will ever see the movie, but the character was interesting, and the dialogue was fabulous." She grinned and stretched languorously. "As was the writer."

No long-term relationships for Annika—not yet, anyway. Her sister was an erotic adventuress, always on the hunt.

"Speaking of fabulous…" Annika readjusted the pillows behind her. "I saw someone down at the Crack a half an hour ago that I thought might be yours. How do you keep your hands to yourself? Or do you?"

"Huh?"

Sasha pawed through a bunch of silver bracelets to look at her watch. "Most of your band is downstairs catching a bite to eat while the roadies finish loading in. Sound check starts in about an hour."

Sound check. Exhaustion washed over her in a wave. *One more show. Just one more show.* "I'd never sleep with a band mate or a member of the crew. That's just… incestuous."

"The one who caught my eye was the new guy— small, dark, wicked tattoos. Looks like the Lucky Charms leprechaun, only hot."

"Stephen," Scarlett and Sasha answered together.

"I think Stephen looks more like a faun than a leprechaun," Sasha mused.

"Whatever." Annika waved her hand. "Love the eyeliner. And those arms! Where did you find him?"

"L.A.," Scarlett said. "You really haven't met Stephen?" It seemed like Stephen had been with them forever. When their former drummer overdosed, Stephen had… been there. She pointed her finger at her sister. "Just leave me something to work with, hmm? A drummer needs all his strength. He's no good to me all worn out." Actually, now that she thought about it, her sister and the hyper-hormonal drummer might be pretty darn compatible.

Metallica's "For Whom the Bell Tolls" chimed from the PDA hanging off of Sasha's hand-tooled leather belt. She looked at the caller's number, muttered "damn it" under her breath, and answered.

"Jack." Silence as she listened. "What?" Her brows jerked up in exasperation. "No, I don't have time to meet with you. Do you have any earthly idea how many logistical nightmares I have to deal with today?" She fell silent, and her expression shifted to worry as she listened. Her body stiffened, and she covered her mouth with her hand. "Is she going to be okay?" She listened again, and put her hand over the mouthpiece. "Andi Woolf was attacked last night," she said to Scarlett and Annika. She listened some more, then looked steadily at Scarlett. "She's right here. Let me put you on speaker."

"What?" Scarlett said to Sasha, who pushed a button on her PDA and placed it on the quilt. Her stomach fell. She was pretty sure she wasn't going to like this.

"Scarlett, it's Jack." His voice was Scotch-smooth, even through the tinny speaker.

Annika fanned her face. "I think *I* just came."

"Shut up," Scarlett hissed, swatting at her. "Is Andi okay, Jack?"

A pause. "She came out of surgery about an hour ago. She's hanging in there, getting the best possible care."

Surgery? How badly had she been hurt? She didn't know Andi Woolf very well, but they ran into each other occasionally at Council family functions.

"I'd like to do a quick review of tonight's security plan," Jack said. "Just as a precaution."

Not smooth enough, my friend. "A precaution for what? Underbelly is the safest possible venue for me to perform in, and we both know it. What's going on?"

Stress finally entered his voice. "We'll tell you more when we see you, Scarlett."

Hmm, the "I" had turned to "we." Suddenly Scarlett had a pretty good idea who really wanted to review security procedures.

"Scarlett?"

Maybe she should blow Lukas off. Tell Jack to tell him to go to hell. Actually, Jack should be telling him to go to hell on his own behalf, because after completely washing his hands of Scarlett's security needs, Lukas was sticking his big, honking nose right back in. She clenched her hands into fists under the quilt. No. No, she had to do this in person.

"Scarlett?" Jack repeated. "Are you okay?"

"I'm really getting tired of people asking if I'm okay," she snapped.

Sasha snatched up the phone, took it off speaker, and quickly finished the conversation with Jack, eyeing Scarlett all the while. "Underbelly's conference room in an hour," she said as she hung up. "The band will have to start sound check without us." Her tiny nostrils flared. "But you'll still have time to catch a nap afterward, easy."

Suddenly Sasha's careful regard was too much. Scarlett's throat clogged with tears, but she tightened her jaw and swallowed them down, watering the seed of anger sprouting inside her. Anger felt more productive than exhaustion. "I'm going to take a bath," she choked out. She dragged herself out of the warm bed and shivered, nude, to the bathroom, closing the door on her sister's gasp at the condition of her body.

I know. Not a pretty sight, is it?

She turned the knob, filling her pond-sized bathtub with hot, steamy water. She climbed in and prepared herself for the battle to come.

Was she okay? Probably not. But that was about to change.

Chapter 5

Bailey Brown looked to the corners of the conference room for hidden cameras. *I'm being punked.* "Could you… repeat that?" She swallowed noisily. "Just the part about the…"

"Crashed spaceship?" Lukas said, watching her closely.

"Um, yeah."

And then he repeated it. The same damn thing. Her boss was an incubus, an incubus whose ancestors' spaceship—yes, spaceship—had crashed on Earth. And the incubi hadn't been alone. Oh, no. Vampires, werewolves, valkyrie, faeries, sirens, God knew what else had been along for the cosmic road trip.

And humanity had shared the planet with them for nearly a thousand years.

She sat back in the large conference room chair, hearing air shushing in and out of her lungs. Intellectually, she knew she was going into shock, but thankfully her brain kept working, the hard drive kept spinning. Because… ho-ly shit. Her employer, her co-workers, most of her new friends were…

Holy shit.

"Sorry I'm late." Sasha Sebastiani breezed into the windowless conference room and dropped into the huge leather chair next to Bailey. "Problem with the delivery from the blood bank. You know how crabby the vamps get when they can't drink an authentic Bloody Mar—"

Her nostrils flared. "Jeez." Sasha grabbed her hands and rubbed them. "Time out, guys. She's freezing. Give her a minute."

For some reason, Sasha's touch, and her blithe reference to Underbelly's vampire clientele's drinking preferences, injected a note of normalcy into the conversation. Just a delivery problem at the bar, because vampires, who drank blood, got really annoyed when they couldn't get their favorite drink. Bailey laughed, a laugh even she could hear veer toward hysteria.

The friction felt good. Why wasn't she pulling away from Sasha, instead of clutching at her hand like a lifeline? She was being touched by a succubus whose ancestors had come from another planet, who'd been cruising through the neighborhood when—oops!—a cosmic fender-bender had altered Earth's history forever.

This succubus was her friend, and the incubus jamming his hands into his streaky, shoulder-length hair across the table was her boss.

She should have known that something was just a little... off. Both Lukas and Sasha were preternaturally attractive—physical ideals, really—even if Lukas dressed more like hired muscle than the owner of the company. And Sasha was gorgeous, with fine bone structure and a delicately muscled body. Wiry and tough, she was built like the dancer she'd been before a blown ACL had halted a promising professional career in its tracks.

She stole a glance across the table at Jack. Her longtime friend watched her closely. Appearance-wise, Jack fit right in, though he'd assured her just a few minutes ago that he was as human as the next guy.

As long as the next guy wasn't an incubus. Or a vamp. Or a werewolf.

Earth still spun on its axis, molecules combined, and gravity still pulled objects to the ground, but Bailey's reality had taken a quick hairpin turn. Just about every-thing she remembered reading about incubi and succubi had negative religious overtones, with the God-fearing women of the Middle Ages swearing to the heavens— and to their judgmental neighbors and clergy—that while their husbands had been away at war, demons had come to them in the night, impregnating them. Considering the beauty and charisma of both Sebastianis—hell, the whole damn family—Bailey could see how night visi-tors this gorgeous just might make you do something you wished you could take back the next morning.

She now had a better understanding of why Jack rarely met Sasha Sebastiani's eyes if he could possibly avoid it.

She took a deep breath and sat up straight in the slouchy leather conference room chair. Jack, Lukas, and Sasha were waiting for her to suck it up and deal. "Okay, I'm fine," she told the three of them. "Curious, yes, and Jesus, do I have a lot of research to do," she muttered. "But there has to be a reason you told me this now. What's up?"

"I knew this wouldn't knock you for a loop for very long." Sasha shot a fake smile at Jack. "It took some people a lot longer."

Jack simply resumed his typing.

"I'll be honest, I have so many questions, and I don't know where to start. But what do I need to know right now?" Bailey said. *And why does Lukas look so wiped out?*

The conference room's integrated projection screen lit up the wall behind Lukas, illuminating his face with its phosphorescent glow. He levered himself out of the chair, dimmed the lights, and stayed standing, leaning against the wall, in the shadows, behind Jack. For someone so large, the man moved like smoke.

Bailey looked to the screen where the familiar-looking Sebastiani Inc. website was displayed. Now they were talking. She'd regain her footing more quickly if she could analyze some data. Jack scrolled down to the bottom center of the page, to where a very small globe twirled and sparkled. He clicked on it, and then drew his index finger across a pad on his laptop. Then he lifted his head and winked.

So, she was finally going to find out what was behind the damn firewall. She'd bumped up against it a couple of times, had circled around it like a wolf cornering prey, but she'd backed off. It had almost killed her, but she'd backed away, not just punched through the damn thing. Because it would have been so damn easy. Her fingers practically twitched as she watched Jack at his keyboard.

"We need you to tighten this up," Lukas said matter-of-factly.

She nodded like this was a request she received every day, but her curiosity spiked like a pegged CPU. What was out here that needed more than strong passwords and fingerprint recognition?

When the screen came back up, it displayed a website that looked very much like the site they'd just come from, except there were now several additional navigational controls presented at the left side of the screen. Jack cruised his mouse over an "Archives" link that hadn't been there before, and then clicked on a link which now read "Council Members" instead of "Board Members." She had to chuckle when Jack clicked again, displaying an org chart. Apparently even extraterrestrial beings couldn't escape PowerPoint.

"The Underworld Council is our governing body," Lukas said. "Each species is represented by one representative, and that representative chooses a backup—a second, if you will."

"A term from the days of dueling," Sasha added, extending her arm like she carried an épée. "'Name your second.' 'En garde!'" She tilted her head. "We like to think that things are much more civilized these days."

"Bullshit," Lukas grumbled.

UNDERWORLD COUNCIL

INCUBUS—Elliott Sebastiani*	Second: Lukas Sebastiani (acting)
SIREN—Claudette Fontaine	Second: Annika Fontaine
WERE—Krispin Woolf	Second: Jacoby Woolf
VAMPIRE—Valerian	Second: Wyland
VALKYRIE—Alka Schlessinger	Second: Lorin Schlessinger
HUMANITY—(Vacant)	Emeritus: Carl Sagan (1934-1996)
SEC/TECH—Lukas Sebastiani	Second: Jack Kirkland
*President	

Bailey could almost feel her synapses snap as she skimmed the information. Carl Sagan? Jack? She blinked, and then swallowed audibly. Yes, that was Jack's name next to Lukas's in its neat little box. Humans were members of the Underworld Council?

"The Underworld Council governs Earth's non-human

species. These are the current representatives," Lukas said. He pointed to the bottom of the list. "As you can see, there have been some recent changes. After long deliberation, a human was asked to join the Council about twenty years ago. Unfortunately, Carl wasn't with the Council very long. But we have to take the long view and prepare for the day when we either decide to, or are forced to, reveal our existence to humanity. We need to find someone to fill that chair."

Bailey remembered the many hours of pleasure she'd gotten from Dr. Sagan's work during the time she'd been incarcerated. She'd have to watch *Contact* again through the lens of a completely changed reality.

"I see you chose a scientist, not a politician." Bailey nodded in approval. "Good call."

"We needed someone less likely to have preconceived notions about our existence." Lukas sat down, the projector casting shadows on his face. "Carl's seat has been empty since his death, but several promising candidates are being evaluated as replacements."

Lukas pointed to his own name. "After the attacks of 9/11 in New York City, I abdicated my seat as the Incubus Second to focus on security and technology risks. Homeland Security is a significant risk to our anonymity."

"Will you become the Incubus Second?" Bailey asked Sasha.

"Hell, no." Sasha raised crossed index fingers in a warding off motion. "As if."

"Sasha's dislike for Council matters is well established," Lukas responded. "Rafe's got his own thing going on. It's Dad's decision, and he's still making it, but Antonia's the obvious choice."

Sasha nodded her agreement. "Clearly. She's a brainiac, scary-smart."

"She's so young," Bailey said quietly. A sixteen-year-old with a seat on their ruling council?

"You, better than anyone here, should understand that sometimes age isn't the most important indicator of someone's competence," Jack said.

The chair creaked as Lukas leaned back and speared his hands wearily into his hair. "I'm serving double-duty until Dad makes a final decision. I hope he hurries up," he muttered. "Okay. To cut to the chase, Jack was the second human to receive the Council's sanction to learn of our existence. As of this morning, the Council authorized a third. You."

What? Bailey's heart pounded like a tom-tom.

"The Archives are a mess. The older materials are barely catalogued. They aren't digitized, aren't searchable. And what is isn't adequately protected." When Lukas kicked back to stare at the ceiling, the chair squeaked alarmingly. "But screw our unsecured archives; screw all of our other work. Today, we're pulling every employee so we can babysit a prima donna rock star."

"This isn't Scarlett's fault," Jack said.

Lukas leaned into the table with an audible growl. "Nearly getting killed wasn't Andi Woolf's fault either. We should be out there finding this asshole."

"So we find a way to do both," Jack replied in a reasonable tone of voice that just seemed to piss off Lukas more.

As Jack discussed staffing with Lukas, Bailey looked at the org chart displayed on the wall behind Lukas's head. The prima donna in question was obviously Scarlett Fontaine. Her mother, Claudette Fontaine, was the Siren Council rep, and her sister Annika, Sasha's other roommate—who could drink six Kamikazes and dance all night—was the Siren Second.

Mythology was full of stories about seagoing men crashing their ships into the cliffs, lulled by a siren's song. Suddenly Scarlett's vocal talent made a whole different kind of sense. But why was Lukas so pissed off? "Who's Andi Woolf?" Bailey asked aloud.

"Krispin Woolf's youngest child," Jack said, quickly explaining the details of Andi's assault. "We don't have any reason to believe that Andi's assault was politically motivated, but unfortunately we can't rule it out yet either. Claudette is worried, and asked us to put additional security measures in place at Scarlett's show tonight." Lukas tossed his pen to the table, and Jack cleared his throat. "Of course we're going to fulfill Ms. Fontaine's request. So here's the plan." He tapped some keys on his laptop and displayed a three-dimensional schematic of Underbelly's performance space. Plucking the stylus off his mini-comp, he activated it and pointed a red laser beam to an area backstage. "Lukas will be positioned in the wings over here, where I was going to be. Jesse will still be standing stage right. I'll be down in the pit," he said, "which frankly, I'm a little happier about."

"Why is that?" Lukas asked.

"In case she stage-dives."

Lukas sat up in his seat, massive, booted feet dropping from the adjacent chair to the floor like blocks of cement. "Damn it, I thought you'd nipped that in the bud, Jack. It's not safe."

Jack shrugged. "You know Scarlett."

Lukas swore, and a flush crawled up his neck. Sasha's nostrils were twitching up a storm. Hmm. Just how well *did* her tight-lipped boss know Scarlett Fontaine? She opened her mouth to tease Lukas about his crush, but then stopped. Sasha looked deadly serious. Something was going on here that she didn't understand.

"So, Lukas and Jesse are backstage. You're in the pit," she said to Jack, not looking at the Sebastiani siblings as some sort of unspoken message bounced between them. "What do you need me to do? Not that I'm complaining, you understand—I couldn't get a ticket to this show to save my life. But how can I help?"

"Just keep your eyes open. Lukas wasn't kidding about reassigning nearly every Sebastiani Security employee to Scarlett's show tonight. We need all hands on deck, all available eyes and ears," Jack replied. "This concert's a high profile event on a couple of fronts. For one thing, it's the last show of Scarlett's tour. She hasn't performed locally for over a year. It's going to get rowdy. Scarlett's manager and I have been working with Sasha on these plans for months. And if Scarlett's security needs weren't a big enough challenge, most of the people on that org chart will be here tonight too."

"A command performance."

"What?" Sasha tugged at her hair, already standing straight up in the air.

"The people on that org chart may be family, but they're also the rulers of your people. Royalty," she added with a shrug. "The pressure on Scarlett must be enormous."

Sasha pursed her lips. "I hadn't thought of it that way. They're just... the Council. Hmm, that might explain why she seemed so..." Sasha trailed off, shook her head slightly, and focused again. "There was a reason you couldn't get a ticket. Due to the security considerations, and the pheromone issue, there's a private guest list." At Bailey's blank look, she glared at the men. "What were you guys doing before I got here, playing grab-ass?"

Lukas ground his teeth together so hard that Bailey thought his jaw would shatter. "We haven't gotten to physiological considerations yet."

Jack picked up the explanation of procedures. "The floor is General Availability, so anyone with a ticket has access. Second floor is reserved seating, a little pricier. Council members and their immediate families will be congregated up here." Jack indicated the third floor VIP boxes at the rear of the venue, facing the stage. "The younger ones will probably creep down to the floor before the night is over, so we'll have to keep our eyes open." He reached into his briefcase, pulled out a small hinged black box, and pushed it across the table. "Here. You'll need this."

Bailey opened the box and looked at the tiny earpiece and matchbook-sized receiver with an integrated clip. "I don't recognize this technology."

"Now that the Council has cleared you, you'll have access to technology you've only dreamed about," Jack said with a smile. "That," he said, indicating the small box, "will patch you in to Sebastiani Security restricted communications tonight. You'll be able to read up on it later," he said, recognizing the interested gleam in her eye. "We don't have time right now. We have"—he looked at his watch—"less than two hours to give you a cultural crash course. Species strengths, weaknesses, susceptibilities…"

"How about protocol?"

Sasha looked at her with an odd expression on her face. "What?"

"Hey, this Council stuff might be old hat to you, but tonight I'm meeting royalty. And everything I know about protocol comes from networking books. Or the Goldie Hawn movie."

"You held Annika's hair out of the toilet when she puked the other night. You're sitting with two Council members right now, people you work with every day. One of them is your best friend. It's way too late for protocol, sweetie."

Bailey froze.

"C'mon, don't freak out on us now," Sasha said, grasping both of her hands again. "You know us. At least, you're starting to know us. You already know that Lukas is an annoying grouch, you've known Jack forever, and you ogle men's asses with The First Daughter."

"True."

"Back to the matter at hand, ladies," Jack said. "Time's tight. Claudette asked for a personal favor, council leader to council leader. We don't have a choice here."

"Our families go way back," Sasha added, examining a chip in her purple nail polish. "I live with Scarlett and Annika. Claudette practically moved in after Mom died and helped raise us." She turned her head to her brother. "Did you know that Dad and Claudette are finally doing the deed?"

Lukas winced.

"What?" Sasha shrugged with a grin. "I'm happy about it. I don't know why they waited so long. And it's so cute to see her doing the Walk of Shame out of Dad's place in the morning." She giggled and singsonged, "Dad's getting la-id."

"So saying 'no thanks' really wasn't an option, no matter how much you might have wanted to," Bailey said to Lukas.

Lukas stiffened. Sasha looked at Jack, and then Lukas.

Bailey sat back in her chair and spread her hands. "Okay, guys. What's up?"

"Sorry. You have to cut us a little slack here," Lukas said. "This is only the third time in history this information has been shared—"

"And Captain Sphincter here is just a little uncomfortable discussing our species' susceptibilities," Sasha said, indicating her brother. "*His* susceptibilities."

If possible, Lukas's jaw clenched even tighter. Bailey feared for his teeth.

"Okay, Incubi Physiology 101," Jack broke in smoothly. "You might notice that both Lukas's and Sasha's nostrils are twitching right now."

They both immediately stopped.

"It's not a twitch," Sasha said, crossing her arms over her chest. "You make it sound like I'm Samantha on *Bewitched* or something."

"It's a definite twitch," Jack informed Sasha, then turned back to Bailey. "Incubi and succubi absorb emotional energy for sustenance. They do this unthinkingly, autonomically. If it's there, they absorb it, like humans breathe air." He kept his eyes on Bailey, his voice clinical. "Absorbing positive emotions is pleasurable, absorbing negative emotions is not. When they're feeling pleasure themselves, they emit pheromones which others around them find pleasurable."

"Creating a feedback loop?" Bailey asked.

"Yes. That incubus sex myth?" Sasha flicked a challenging glance at Jack. "Fact."

Bailey's brain was clicking, processing. "How…?"

"Your guess is as good as ours," Lukas said. "The best we can tell, our species can process and utilize a type of energy that humans can't."

"Like a sixth sense."

"Yup," Sasha responded with a smile. "It's not magic by any means. Just because I can discern"—Sasha gazed at Jack, let her eyes travel over his face and upper body—"lust in the air doesn't necessarily mean I can tell who's feeling it. But sometimes, just by process of elimination, it's pretty easy to guess." She curled her legs in her chair while Jack's face went tight. "I just know if it's there, I absorb it. And it feels really, really good."

Oh my God. They could tell what she was feeling? When she was pissed off? Aroused? By sniffing? Sniffing the air? Bailey put her hands to her own burning cheeks.

"We try not to be invasive about it," Sasha said with a shrug. "It just… is."

Jack rubbed his neck. Bailey was pretty sure he was counting to ten. "So, tonight's show," he finally gritted out. "The club holds nearly a thousand people. No humans tonight, other than you and me. Weres, vamps, hundreds of incubi and succubi in an enclosed space, drinking, dancing, having fun. And where there's fun, there's pleasure, and where there's pleasure, there are pheromones. Now, factor a siren into the equation—a siren who interprets and amplifies emotion with her song."

If Bailey understood Jack correctly, Scarlett's voice would ratchet the pheromone level sky-high.

"Yes," Sasha said, her voice dripping with anticipation as she confirmed Bailey's suspicion. "It'll be bacchanalia."

Lukas abruptly stood. "Can you take it from here, Jack? I have some work to do." He stalked to the door without waiting for an answer.

"Um, good-bye!" Sasha called to her brother's back. She stood up to follow him. "He can be such an asshole."

"So can you," Jack snapped. "You know how hard this is for him. Andi's assailant shoved some nasty shit down his throat not twelve hours ago, he's had no sleep, and Scarlett's show is the last place he wants or needs to be. But he's doing it. He's sucking it up and doing it. So back the hell off."

The silence hummed.

"Bite me," Sasha finally muttered. But it was said without heat.

"You wish."

Sasha's eyes wandered over Jack—all over Jack. Bailey felt a tug between her thighs as their eyes locked in battle. She barely stopped herself from writhing against the leather seat, and she was just sitting on the sidelines.

Sasha smirked. "Don't forget to take your meds," she reminded him airily as she followed her brother. "Catch you later, Bailey." The door slammed behind her.

"Meds?" Bailey finally said.

"There's a drug that humans can take to make them less susceptible to the pheromones."

"Hmm, handy. Something that Sebastiani Labs conjured up?" At his affirmative nod, she sat silently for a moment. "Is Lukas okay?"

Jack reached across the table and turned off the overhead projector. "He's under a lot of stress right now, but he'll deal with it." He looked to the door, and sighed in relief. "It'll be easier to explain this now that they're gone. I swear, she picks on him for entertainment. I hope Lukas can catch a nap."

She could use one herself. In the last hour, she'd found out humans weren't alone in the universe—hell, weren't even alone on Earth. She'd learned her boss was an incubus, and his sister a succubus. She'd learned her best friend was a member of a Council governing Earth's non-human species. "So, this is what all the secrecy is about."

Jack raised his eyebrows in question.

"The rooms at SebSec that I can't badge into. The servers and files I can't access." She looked away from him for a moment. "I thought you didn't trust me."

"I trust you implicitly. But Lukas and the Council were a little more challenging to convince, and it wasn't my secret to share." Jack rose and sat in the chair Sasha had just vacated. He looked her in the eye. "I'm so glad you backed away from that firewall when you did."

"Yeah, well, it was close," she muttered, "and we both know that at one time I probably wouldn't have." They both sat in silence, let it wrap them comfortably. "Wow," Bailey finally said.

"Yeah, it's a lot to think about," Jack agreed. "There are aspects of their world that I'm still trying to learn about, to absorb. But tonight, all that has to be put aside. Scarlett's safety is the priority."

"What is Lukas so uptight about?"

"Lukas has a genetic anomaly which forces him to taste and smell emotions as he absorbs them. He's battered by stimuli 24/7, and a lot of it isn't pretty."

"Kind of like emotional synesthesia?" she asked, referring to the sensory integration disorder which enabled some humans to see numbers in color, smell music, and taste scents.

"Yeah. He doesn't talk about it, but the bottles of antacids scattered around the office speak for themselves. And yes, before you ask, he and Scarlett have a history. He'll be struggling tonight."

Bailey pursed her lips. "So, let me get this straight. Basically, the Underworld Council is coming to an orgy." She started giggling as she tried to imagine some of humanity's historic rulers doing the same, but stopped as a horrible thought struck. "Is Dick Cheney a vampire?"

Jack blinked. "Not that I know of."

Bailey took the mouse from Jack and clicked on the "Species" link. "What do I need to be on the lookout for? Cliffs Notes version, please."

"The werewolves tend to be vocal, physical, and exuberant, and will probably shed clothes as the night goes on. The vamps might flash some fang, but most of them aren't about to strip off in public. The valkyries have been officially reminded that they can't fight in the building. The sirens shouldn't be a problem, unless they band together and start singing along with Scarlett. Jesus, I hadn't thought about that one," he muttered, grabbing his mini-comp and tapping a note. "But in terms of crowd control, the incubi and succubi will pose the biggest challenge. They're the most vulnerable due to their susceptibility to siren song, but they emit pheromones which loosen everybody's inhibitions."

"No meds?"

"So far, the pheromone meds only work for humans."

And only three humans in history knew of their existence in the first place. Damn it, Jack had allowed himself to be used as a lab rat.

Jack clicked deeper into the website, explaining what he knew about the species. Bailey took mental notes on the areas where she needed to spend more time, do more research. And as the facts and factoids scrolled by, she learned Earth's unvarnished history: how the Underworld Council's guiding hand had been poised behind countless thrones, influencing events to their benefit, and about how many of *humanity's* accomplishments weren't actually humanity's at all.

But it was the small facts that mesmerized her: that vampires' mythological aversion to the sun was simply because they were allergic to the sun's UV rays; that incubi drew energy from the aurora borealis, and that pictures of the aurora were prominently displayed in most incubi homes—rather, Bailey thought, like some Christian homes featured pictures of Jesus or Mary, or of that old guy praying over a loaf of bread; that sirens had an affinity for water and waves, and a lot of them kept tabs on America's big surf breaks, dropping everything when word of epic waves went out over the surfer's grapevine; that werewolves were the only species capable of shifting physical form; that all of the species could breed with each other, and could breed with humans.

And had, for generations.

Incubus clubs. The Underworld Council. Siren song. Sexual feedback loops. Jack continued on, and the web pages kept scrolling by.

Finally, the information all started to swirl together. Bailey held up her hand in the universal gesture for enough. Buffer overflow. Her mind needed to rest.

She tucked her small hand into Jack's big one. Humanity wasn't alone. And neither was she.

Chapter 6

As Lukas left the conference room, he ran into Scarlett—literally bumping into her, full body contact. She ricocheted against the wall.

"Jesus." He instinctively yanked her to his body as she rebounded, and every inch of her, from her knees on up to her torso, imprinted itself on his body.

The seconds hung. She finally shoved back—hard, like she'd been defibrillated—but he didn't let go of her arms.

"Are you hurt?" The taste of flat orange soda swam onto his taste buds. *What the hell?* What happened to the mandarin champagne that tingled on his tongue whenever Scarlett was in the vicinity? She was barely registering, her energy pulsing so low he literally had not sensed her coming.

His fingers nearly met his thumb as he grasped her upper arms. When she continued to struggle, he loosened his grip slightly but didn't let go, half-convinced her knees would crumple if he did.

Lukas tried to assess her appearance objectively: the dark circles under her eyes. The freckles sprinkled across her nose, stark against her chalky, pale complexion. The sagging neckline of the sweatshirt exposed collarbones pushing up against the backside of her skin. The black sweatpants she wore bagged at the ass. Even her blazing red hair seemed dim and dull.

What was wrong with her? What the hell had she been doing to wreak such damage?

"Watch where you're going," he growled, giving her a soft shake. "Did I hurt you?"

It seemed to take forever for her to lift her head and meet his eyes. And... yes, there she was. He surreptitiously swirled his tongue as mandarin oranges crept onto his taste buds, as her green eyes sparked to life. Even if her annoyance and anger were targeted at him, he'd take it.

But she hadn't answered his question. "Did I hurt you?"

"No."

"Liar."

"Why ask if you're not going to listen to my answer? Stop manhandling me and move out of my way," Scarlett snapped, twisting her arms out of his hands and rubbing at them. "I'm late for a meeting."

He gestured to her damp hair, pulled back in a messy ponytail. "Yeah, I can see what a priority it was for you. Lounging in the tub, making everyone wait. Jack and Sasha have a lot more patience with your crap than I do."

Her delicious fury spiked. She stepped up to him and poked him in the chest with a finger whose nail was bitten to the quick. "Fuck you."

His most fervent wish, put into words. Lukas grinned nastily. "Again? Hey, I'm game if you are."

He felt his words hit, saw her lips wobble before she firmed them back up. What the hell was he doing? By unspoken accord, neither of them ever referred to the single, incendiary night they'd spent together so many years ago. Nope, it was the elephant in the living room that only they could see, and they ignored it with impunity. But with his unthinking, dick-addled words, he'd swung a fucking sledgehammer at the foundation of their carefully constructed détente.

Instead of turning her back on him, or flipping him off and stalking down the hall, she tipped her head to the side and just gazed at him. Like she actually might be… considering it.

Sweet zombie Jesus, what had he done?

She must be at the end of her rope, absolutely exhausted, because her eyes were taking the long route over his body instead of focusing on some far point over his shoulder, like she typically did when they couldn't avoid talking to each other. Her gaze stroked him like a fingertip.

"So, you're game?" she breathed. She sidled closer, stopping when her stomach was a mere molecule away from his violently aroused flesh. Her hands lifted, poised tantalizingly over his abs.

Lukas held his breath. Was she going to do this? Was he going to let her?

Yes and yes. He bit back a groan as she leaned her slight weight against him. His dick cuddled into the layers of clothing covering her flat stomach, her hipbones digging into his upper thighs like tiny fingers. As he lost the battle and reached for her ass, to drag her more firmly against him, she slithered around him instead.

"As the great philosopher Mick Jagger once said, 'You can't always get what you want.'"

Before he was aware of doing it, he snaked his arm around her waist and pinned her against the wall with a forearm wedged right under her breasts. And time slowed to a crawl. They both stood there, breathing heavily, each of them waiting to see what the other would do. Her eyes snapped with annoyance, but her mandarin arousal effervesced on his tongue, filled his head. Scarlett might deny it with her eyes, with her words, but her body couldn't lie about her desire. Reluctant desire, to be sure, he admitted to himself, but it was there, regardless.

She squirmed under his arm. *Shit, he was pressing too hard.* He eased back, her movements brushing the underside of her fleece-covered breasts against the sensitive hair on his forearm. *No bra.* He was actually touching her again—something he'd consigned to his memories, to fevered dreams which made him sweat through his bed sheets, and awaken with his hand moving on his hard, aching flesh.

Despite being pinned up against a wall, she wasn't pulling away from him, wasn't saying no. If anything, her taste was darkening, deepening, and her hips tipped toward his body as if pulled by a magnet. She watched his mouth with dilated pupils that practically dared him to do something, anything. When her soft pink tongue licked her chapped lips, Lukas could practically see his common sense shake its head, reach for the popcorn, and settle back to enjoy the show.

He leaned in with his body, lightly and carefully fusing them together from torso to knee. *So thin,* Lukas thought. Christ, he could feel her very bones. Stroking her delicate cheekbones with his thumbs, he clasped her head in his hands. Scarlett latched onto his wrists—to stop him? To pull him closer? A whisper-soft moan escaped from her lips, giving him his answer.

It had been so long. He lowered his head slowly, centimeter by centimeter, waiting for her to call a halt to this mutual psychosis. It would kill him to stop, but if she asked him to, he'd find a way to do it. Instead, she wrapped her arms around his waist and stood on tiptoe to bring her lips closer to his. Her hot breath puffed against his chin, and he leaned down to—

The conference room door opened not three feet from where Lukas plastered Scarlett to the wall with his body. Sasha eyed them both, raising a brow. "Scarlett, you're finally out of the tub." Her nostrils twitched, then she smiled mischievously. "Are you... coming?"

What the hell was he doing? He peeled himself away. Watching Scarlett sag, then support herself against the wall sent every predatory cell in his body to howling. *Get away. Now.* "I've got work to do." Lukas mentally swore at his sister's knowing grin, her damn twitching nose, her horrible/fabulous timing, at his hypersensitive dick. He quickly turned away from them and stalked down the hall toward Sasha's office.

It was too much to hope that his sister hadn't noticed the erection tenting his jeans.

Reaching Sasha's office, he barged in and closed the door behind him. Striding to the beat-up mini-fridge, he grabbed a Coke and gulped it, trying to wash Scarlett's taste off his lips, out of his mouth. He shook his head to clear it, and acknowledged that—yes, even half-wrecked and wiped out—all Scarlett Fontaine had to do was breathe in his general vicinity, and he was as intoxicated, as addicted, as ever.

Nothing had changed.

He slumped into Sasha's doll-sized desk chair,

ignoring its squeaking protest. He'd probably bruised Scarlett's upper arms with his grasp.

Again, nothing had changed.

———w———

As Lukas finished his phone call with Gideon, he heard the conference room door slam down the hall. Footsteps pounded, becoming less audible as Scarlett beat feet away from the meeting. He could taste her fury from here.

"Thanks for the update, Gideon. Keep in touch."

Lukas ended the call and looked at his watch. Fewer than twenty minutes had passed since his sister had stopped him from doing something monumentally stupid, something he wouldn't be able to take back. He didn't quite have his equilibrium back, and he was kicking his own ass for leaving it to Jack to break the news of his involvement in tonight's show to Scarlett and her business manager, Garrett Wilder.

Thankfully Gideon had called with an update, giving him something else to focus on, because he'd flooded Sasha's office with pheromones she'd be able to read as easily as the children's book *Go Dog. Go!*

Damn it.

Okay, what had happened—had almost happened—with Scarlett really wasn't that big a deal. Nothing had changed, really. He and Scarlett did not talk, didn't interact in anything other than the most desultory fashion, and then only if forced to by the presence of others. They certainly didn't touch. Touch lips, especially. Or grope each other. Like they just had.

He dropped his head into his hands.

Sasha's high-heeled boots tap-tap-tapped down the hallway, and he quickly sat up and adjusted the front of his pants as the door opened. Sasha theatrically sniffed, then made a wafting motion with her hand that only Lukas could see while she finished her conversation with Scarlett's business manager.

It sounded like Scarlett had left no one in the conference room with any doubt about how she felt about Lukas's involvement in the night's plans. The corners of his mouth kicked up as he envisioned the scene. At least he'd catalyzed some reaction in her. Even rage was better than that scary void he'd sensed earlier.

"We're late for sound check," Garrett was saying. "We'd better count Scarlett out. She was, um, quite agitated when she left the meeting, wasn't she?"

"Let her work off her mad. We really don't need her," Sasha said. "All we really need to do is reacquaint the band with the sound system. Shouldn't take long."

Garrett finally noticed Lukas sitting at Sasha's desk and came into the office to shake his hand. "Lukas," he said. "I heard about Andi. How is she? Are you any closer to finding who did this to her?"

No, because I'm stuck here babysitting your client. "She's holding her own," he answered.

"She's too damn stubborn to do anything else," Sasha added.

"Yes, that she is." Garrett put a hand in the front pocket of his tailored Italian pants. "Well, despite Scarlett's feelings on the matter"—he exchanged a rueful glance with Sasha—"I'm glad you'll be on board tonight."

"She knows that it would be flat-out stupid to not have every hand on deck." Sasha glanced at Lukas.

"And when Jack told her it was Claudette who'd re-quested additional security coverage…" She shrugged. "There wasn't much she could say. Which pissed her off even more."

Lukas felt a muscle tick in his jaw. While he ap-preciated Sasha's oblique message, he wasn't about to hide behind Claudette's designer skirts. And first things first. He nailed Wilder with his gaze. "What's wrong with Scarlett?"

The werewolf hesitated, clearly about to say "nothing," but changing his mind. "I think she's just… exhausted."

"You think? Isn't it your job to know?" Lukas leaned forward, and the chair squeaked in protest. "And what the hell are you doing about it? Jesus, anyone can see she's about to drop, that she's nothing but skin and bones." He voiced one of his concerns. "Is she using?"

"Using? What, drugs?" Garrett's laughter was spon-taneous and genuine. "Hell, no. She was ready to fire her last drummer because he wouldn't go to rehab and get help. He died before she could do it."

"Eating disorder?" Lukas suggested. "Has she seen a doctor?"

"Her appetite's been off a little, and yeah, she's lost some weight. But bulimia? No. There's no way you can live on a tour bus and keep something like that a secret. She's been getting plenty of sleep, staying hy-drated, not partying." Garrett sighed. "She says she's fine. Being she's a competent adult, I have to take her word for it."

"Why the hell would you do that? Her judgment's obviously not worth shit right now." Lukas pushed the vase of mums sitting on the corner of Sasha's desk out of his way. Their cheerful color annoyed him. "Why didn't you cancel some dates, make her take a break?"

"You seem to be under some mistaken impression here," Garrett replied dryly. "I work for her, not the other way around. She wanted to stay on the road, so..." he gestured with his hand, "we stayed on the road."

"And you couldn't influence a weakened, shaky woman to change her mind?" Lukas said as he stood up, not even attempting to hide the derision in his voice.

"Lukas." Sasha stepped between them.

Garrett budged Sasha out of the way. "No, he's right, Sasha. Scarlett insisted we stay on the road, finish out the bookings. I don't know why, but there it is. The good thing is that the tour is over after tonight's performance. She's home, and she can rest. If you have questions about Scarlett's health, you need to ask her yourself."

Garrett's PDA chirped. He extracted it from the breast pocket of his suit jacket, glancing at the small display. "Tansy," he said to Sasha. "She's asking if sound check is being pushed back." He quickly text-messaged a response. "If we don't go now, Tansy will drag those boys of hers off for some afternoon delight. Then the rest of them will scatter and I won't be able to find anyone for hours. We have to go. Now."

"Start walking. I'll be right behind you," Sasha said.

"If you happen to see Scarlett before I do, please let her know I need the set list as soon as she can swing it. God knows where her head will be at tonight," he muttered as he left the office. "We could be listening to anything from Gregorian chants to Marilyn Manson."

Sasha pursed her lips as she watched him walk away.

"That is one excellent ass." She shut the door behind her and rolled her shoulders.

"He's lucky I didn't carve it into rump roast."

"He's just doing his job, Lukas. Cut him some slack. You know how stubborn Scarlett can get." Sasha made a beeline for the lime green crushed velvet love seat. "I need to sit down for a few minutes."

His high-energy sister needed nothing of the sort. The inquisition was about to begin. Lukas watched her flop onto the couch, stretch her body out full-length, and pull her right leg up so her shinbone touched her nose. She repeated the movement with her left leg, her leather boots creaking as she flexed and pointed her toes.

"Show-off."

"I've been called worse. By you. It's your fault I have such fragile self-esteem."

"Yes, you're obviously permanently damaged."

She pulled herself into a sitting position, crossed her legs. And then she looked at him, waiting silently.

Lukas met her blue eyes, stared her down with a glare she wouldn't find the least bit intimidating, damn her. Just to be an asshole, he made a show of looking at his watch. "Aren't you late?"

She held his gaze for about ten seconds, and then threw up her arms. "Screw this. I don't have time for a game of chicken. And I always win anyway."

Unfortunately, this was true.

"Damn it, Lukas, when are you and Scarlett going to stop this masochistic dance? It used to be entertaining to watch and all, but now it's just getting sad and old."

BAM. Jab to the ribs. He leaned back in her tiny

chair as Sasha's frustration, her concern, crept onto his tongue, a sting of tin.

Sasha glared at him. "If you blast out the sides of that chair, I'm going to shave you bald."

As usual, she'd served up her verbal sucker punch, and then gave him a chance to step back and recover his equilibrium. Only to set him up for the uppercut he knew would be coming. He was being danced around the ring by an expert, a fuchsia and black-haired flyweight less than half his size. Lukas glanced down at the tiny desk chair he was wedged into. And, meeting her eyes, shifted his hips side to side so it creaked and groaned even louder.

"If you had something other than doll furniture in here, it wouldn't be a problem."

Sasha watched him, nostrils twitching. He stopped punishing the chair and looked at her with a scowl. "Do you know how annoying it is to have your sister know everything you're feeling?"

"Duh. There's no such thing as a secret in this damn family." She stretched her arms overhead with a sigh. "Now you know how I felt when you and Rafe kept cock-blocking me and Jacoby back when we were dating."

He leveled a steely glance at his sister. "Sasha. You were fourteen. The cock needed blocking."

"It's a wonder I ever had sex with anybody, with you two on the job."

"Well, it sure as hell backfired," Lukas grumbled. "You just learned to be sneakier."

She grinned, but then became serious again. "When did you last sleep?"

He shrugged and didn't answer. It felt like years ago.

"You're tired, frustrated. Horny. Worried. And trying to hide it." She looked up at him and sighed again. "Me too. She's not registering much of anything, is she?"

He hesitated before answering, considered brazening it out. But it was worthless to front when the other person could pretty much tell exactly what you were feeling. It was almost a relief to ask. "Do you know what's wrong with her?"

"I think she's just plumb worn out. Their road schedule was outrageous. Sustaining a pace of four shows a week is challenge enough, but five? For over a year? Obscene."

"It's Garrett's job to keep her healthy, damn it, to overrule her when she's pushing too hard."

"Your hypocrisy is staggering."

"Sasha, this isn't about me."

"It just as well could be. I swear, you and Scarlett are like two peas in a workaholic pod," she shot back. "I bet you can't tell me the last time Scarlett was home."

Four months, three weeks, and two days ago. He'd made sure they avoided each other, but no one had said a damn thing about Scarlett looking like she'd just been sprung from Bergen-Belsen. He mentally added Jack to his shit list. "Okay, you might have a point. But do you know what's up? Has she talked to you?" It drove a stake in his heart to ask. "Relationship trouble?"

Sasha got up off the couch, stood behind him, and rubbed at the slabs of muscle in his rigid shoulders. "Annika barged in and woke her up this morning, and we chatted a bit about that picture in *The Tattler*— they're not dating, by the way. Then Jack called, asking for a meeting, and then we were off and running." She karate-chopped her hands up and down his right bicep. "She's... thin, but not anorexic. If you didn't know her, weren't familiar with what she looked like before, you wouldn't think anything of it. But she's lost those edible curves." She nudged him with her sharp elbow. "Though you seem to find the ones she still has tasty enough."

Lukas didn't respond; the spike of lust he pumped into the room as he remembered her slim wand of a body pressed against him said it all. But he was relieved to hear that Scarlett wasn't involved with the musician who'd been with her when that paparazzi shot had been taken. Seeing the man's hand on Scarlett's shoulder, reading the suggestive caption, had given him a jolt. He'd almost started a background check on the guy—deep background. Proctology-level background. But once he settled down and looked at the picture objectively, he noticed things he'd missed the first time around: the fear in Scarlett's eyes, the tension in her body. The man's defensive position. Musician or not, the guy had been ready to fight.

"The tour's been a huge success, the reviews are great," Sasha was saying. "But thank the aurora it's over. Like Garrett said, she'll get the break she needs now." Her voice firmed. "I'll make sure of it."

"No more sex, drugs, and rock and roll. How sad. Might be too quiet for her here at home."

Sasha's head snapped up. "The rock and roll part is certainly true. Scarlett doesn't do drugs. As for the sex..." She shrugged.

Lukas's temper surged.

His sister sensed it, and went in for the kill. "Hey, why shouldn't she fuck a dozen fanboys a week? You won't go near her." She examined her nails. "A girl's gotta do what a girl's gotta do."

Lukas opened his mouth to speak, but before he could, Sasha barreled on. "And you're a fine one to talk. You treat sex like a workout, like it's mere body maintenance. Safety in numbers, no emotional involvement. As soon as someone wants more from you than your admittedly spectacular body, you move on." Her voice gentled. "How much longer are you going to punish yourself?"

BAM. Solar plexus shot.

"You big dolt." Sasha clenched a tiny fist and slugged him. "Pull your head out of your ass. She wants you, and you want her. Finish what I interrupted in the hall."

He swallowed before answering, trying to lubricate his suddenly dry throat. "Sasha, you said it yourself. She's tired, exhausted. She didn't realize what she was doing." The universe help him if she did. He wasn't certain he could fight himself and her at the same time. "It wouldn't work anyway."

Sasha burst out laughing, a laughter so knowing it made the blood rush to his face. "Looked like it was working just fine to me." She stepped around the chair and put her hands on his shoulders. With him sitting down, they were almost the same height, and he couldn't avoid her eyes, damn it. "You're scared to let your guard down, to meet her halfway."

Lukas didn't deny it.

"You're scared it could work too damn well."

When Sasha's cell phone rang, Lukas welcomed the interruption.

She pointed at him. "Don't move." She huffed a breath, chanting "there are no tickets left. There are no more tickets. No, I don't have any tickets put aside or tucked away" like a mantra.

"Did I mention that there are no more tickets?" she said to Lukas, her frustration palpable. "My phone has been ringing off the hook for weeks. I should make a damned recording." But despite her annoyance, she picked up. His sister was too much of a businesswoman to let a phone call go unanswered during business hours.

Distorted bass pulsed in the background, making the phone's tiny speaker buzz in protest. "Tomas! Turn that damn music down, I can't hear you."

The caller was probably Tomas Diego, the drummer for Ten Inch Screw. Lukas had seen his name on the VIP list. He'd slapped cuffs on the man himself nearly a decade ago, after that notorious sex tape featuring Tomas and his pneumatically blessed wife had been beamed to all of humanity. The investigation had cleared him, determining that the tape had been stolen from Diego's home and hadn't been purposely leaked, but Lukas still thought the man took too many chances, drew too much attention to himself—to them all—with his hedonistic lifestyle.

Sasha's job certainly brought her into contact with some real characters.

"Yes, I have your ticket right here," she said, "and I swear if you're late I'll give it to the first mutt sniffing on the sidewalk." Her eyes narrowed. "It's not my fault you haven't been to bed yet." She looked at her watch. "Check into the hotel, take a nap. No, I will not give you a wake-up call. You're not that adorable, you degenerate."

Lukas worked hard to keep his eyebrows stationary. What kind of relationship did his little sister have with

Tomas Diego that the man felt comfortable asking such a thing?

Some things a brother didn't want to think about.

As she hung up, she silenced the ringer on the phone. "Did you see that Jacoby called to cancel the Woolf family's RSVP for the show tonight? With everything going on with Andi right now, it was completely un-necessary—but so like him."

They both sat silently for a moment. It didn't take long for Lukas to fume once again that he wasn't out on the street, helping Gideon to find the maggot who'd assaulted Jacoby's sister Andi.

"Hey."

Shit, she'd snuck up on him. Looping her arms around his shoulders from behind, she scrubbed her product-stiff hair into the nape of his neck. "Damn it, stop that," he said.

"Lukas."

Her voice was too soft.

"What are you going to do when Scarlett gives up on you? Bonds with another man?" She rested her chin on his shoulder. "Has children with him?"

BAM. BAM. BAM. Knockout blow. He took a shaky breath. "Damn, you fight dirty."

She stroked the hair at his temple, and then gave it a yank. "I'm just tired of watching you punish yourself for nothing. 'I should have known better.' 'She was too young.'" Sasha threw up her hands. "Bullshit. You're just scared."

Lukas stared at her. How did she—this was one se-cret he thought was tucked way, waaaaay back in the dark corner of the safe, never to see the light of day. He drove his hands into his hair, swore when his fingers got caught in snarls. "I... lost control."

"You're supposed to lose control."

"Yeah, right." His self-disgust filled the room. "Enough to leave bruises? Her first time? Jesus."

"Hey, some bruises a woman enjoys earning," she said with a knowing smile which made him really uncomfortable. "Knowing you caused your man to lose control like that is very empowering. Perform a root cause analysis, Mr. Risk Management. The problem isn't that you think you hurt her—it's that she made you lose control in the first place."

Lukas didn't respond. She was wrong.

"And I don't suppose you've discussed this with her?" She held up her hand, an expression of disgust on her face. "Why did I even ask? Of course not." Sasha broke off in frustration, popping him with her fist once again. It felt like a pebble against his bicep, but he wasn't about to tell her that. "You know, Lukas, some people actually like to make decisions for themselves."

Lukas finally spoke. "Look at the condition she's in. Do you really think she's making good decisions right now?"

"You're a fine one to talk. Don't think your family hasn't noticed that you're well along the way to burnout yourself. If you stay busy enough, there's no time to feel, no bandwidth to spare for those pesky emotions." Wrapping her arms around him from behind, she whispered, "But it doesn't work for very long, does it?"

No. He allowed himself to lean into her hug for a moment.

"Will you think about it? Think about what could be.

And talk to her, Lukas. Talk *to* her, don't decide *for* her." With a smacking kiss to the back of his head, she removed her arms and walked to the door. "I'm going to sound check. Since you've already reeked the place up, you might as well stay awhile. Take a nap, clear your head." Before he could say a word, she left, closing the door with a snick.

His head was already plenty damn clear, thank you. And if his emotions were buried so damn deep, why was his throat tightening up? Sasha didn't know shit.

"What could be?" Lukas scoffed aloud. Nothing could be. He'd evaluated all the data, analyzed all the angles and risks, both then and now. Nothing was possible.

Nothing had changed.

But as he sat there in Sasha's quiet office, the minutes ticking by, he twirled the combination lock on that mental safe and pulled out his most precious memory: he and Scarlett in her bedroom, their youthful bodies writhing together in the moonlit darkness, her siren's moans luring him closer to the cliffs with every minute that passed. Languorous hours spent stroking her with his body, his hands, his mouth and tongue, learning what she liked, teaching her what her body wanted, her gasp of pain quickly becoming pleasure as she exchanged innocence for knowledge with a single, inevitable stroke of his body. And afterward, Scarlett looking up at him with her luminous eyes, saying simply, "More."

He'd obliged, until they were both exhausted.

When he'd awakened the next morning, his body was curled around hers, and a place inside him that he hadn't realized was so parched and thirsty had started to fill. Holding her exhausted body, stroking his fingers through her glorious hair, he'd let himself start thinking about a future—until the moment the rising sun illuminated the bruises he'd left on her delicate wrists and pillow-soft breasts. Bruises his massive hands had inflicted as he'd mindlessly lost himself in her untried body.

She'd given him the gift of her innocence, and he'd... hurt her.

His hands clenched into fists against his thighs. Sasha didn't know the whole story, because if she did, she'd agree that he'd done the right thing by backing off. And if anything, Scarlett was more delicate now than she had been then, a fragile, crystal stem that would snap the minute he wrapped his fingers around her.

No, she was safer without him.

And yeah—he was safer too.

Chapter 7

STEPHEN SHUFFLED OUT OF THE BATHROOM STALL AT Crackhouse like an old man, ignoring the PDA vibrating in his pocket, and extended his arm to turn on the faucet. His elbow cracked, and pain shot up to his shoulder. He could practically hear his muscle filaments groan with each movement. If something as simple as washing his hands was this difficult, how the hell would he get through sound check?

Moving cautiously, he sluiced hot water over his face, stole a quick glance at his watch, and swore. There was no time to contact his favorite masseuse to work the kinks from his carcass before sound check.

When he'd woken up, his body had been stiff and tight, like he had rigor mortis, but his first thought had been about his Candy Girl. She'd been responsible for the most sublime sex of his life, and how had he thanked her? By leaving her dead on a cold bathroom floor.

What was he going to do to recapture that feeling again? He'd killed the source of his pleasure.

Standing in the buzzing, fluorescent light of the restroom, Stephen started his warm-up sequence, a series of motions usually as mindless and automatic as walking. Pain zinged down his spine as he shifted his shoulders and scapula. He made himself continue, instinctively disassociating the way he used to when he'd worked on the pleasure cruiser. Small moans escaped as he stretched and flexed, working his pecs, delts, biceps, triceps. Each movement felt like one of those pinching, skin-twisting "snakebites" his older brother used to torment him with when they were young. When Stephen bent his arms at the elbows, they snapped audibly, but he made himself repeat the motion, over and over, and, sure enough, each movement hurt a little less than the previous one. Minutes ticked by as he worked his forearms, wrists, and the small twitch muscles in his hands, palms, and fingers. They felt positively arthritic.

The door swung open, and one of the employees came in. He set a takeout cup on the counter, and the loamy scent of coffee filled the air. Stephen peered at the man's name tag, written in the same faux-seedy font as the sign over the door. Padrick.

"Hey, Stephen," Padrick said. "Tansy asked me to bring this in, said they'd meet you next door." He untied the black apron he wore over an equally black T-shirt and hung it on a hook on the wall. The T-shirt set off the red, orange, and yellow flame tattoos licking up his muscular forearms.

Padrick was… really hot. And here he was, looking like he'd just rolled out of bed.

The other man stepped into a stall and closed the door behind him.

"Thanks," he called over the sound of Padrick's belt clanking. A zipper whooshed. Denim rustled.

"Did you hear about what happened to Andi Woolf?" Padrick called from the stall.

"Hmm?" Stephen pried the top off the coffee and sipped. *Bless you, Tansy*.

"Andi Woolf. You know Krispin Woolf, the

Underworld Council? His daughter." The sound of liquid hitting the water stopped. After a pause, Padrick zipped up. "Someone attacked her at Subterranean last night."

As the toilet flushed, fragments of the previous evening started snapping together like puzzle pieces: the howling wolf tattoo riding low on her back. The nips on his lips as she kissed him. Andi Woolf. His Candy Girl was the daughter of the WerePack Alpha.

Damn, he sure could pick 'em.

The stall door opened. "Yeah, she was in surgery for hours," Padrick said. "Someone really did a number on her."

The ground dropped out from beneath Stephen's feet. "She's still alive?"

"Yeah," Padrick said as he turned on the faucet and washed his hands. "I guess she's in a coma, and her throat's a mess, but Andi is one tough bitch."

Stephen was so stunned that he didn't register how Padrick subtly brushed against him as he crossed to the bathroom hand dryer. What the hell was he going to do? Part of him was relieved that he hadn't snuffed out the glorious energy which had lit him up like... He shook his head, hard. What the hell was he going to do if she survived? Recovered? Came out of her coma and identified him as her attacker? Had anyone seen them together? He wasn't exactly anonymous anymore. Next to Scarlett herself, he was the band member with the most notoriety. The bad boy, up for anything.

Damn it. It would only take a couple of questions for law enforcement to place him at the scene, for his band mates to learn that he'd blown off their welcome home celebration to get laid.

In his pocket, his PDA vibrated again. Garrett. But Stephen met Padrick's Irish blue eyes, read their invitation. In case there was any mistake, Padrick raised a brow and tilted his head toward the stall.

The scratching in his chest started anew. Garrett— and worry—could wait.

Ten minutes later, Stephen stepped into Underbelly's cavernous performance space carrying his cooling coffee in one hand and rubbing at his sternum with the other. While his muscles were still uncomfortably tight, an excellent blow job had taken the edge off. Thanks to Padrick, he just might make it through sound check without his arms breaking off.

Despite the scrupulously mopped floor, the slightest whiff of stale beer permeated the place. Right now, hours before a show, Underbelly was brightly lit, and bustled with pre-show industry. Up on the stage, an army of blue-jeaned, black-shirted instrument techs went about their work, tuning guitars and placing them in stands where Michael, Joe, Tansy, and Scarlett could easily grab them. Their custom rolling storage crates still littered the stage. Roadies crawled on the floor, employing their ever-present duct tape. His own drum tech, a taciturn man with an aggressive gray brush cut, was still setting up his high hat.

He wasn't officially late.

A loud crash echoed through the space as a light tech dropped a bulb from three stories up. "Everyone okay?" Sasha Sebastiani called from behind the sound board at the back of the dance floor. Randy, their magician of a sound guy, huddled beside her, his tongue practically hanging out of his mouth. Knowing Randy, it was because of the sound system, not the woman.

Still unnoticed back in the shadows, he eyeballed Sasha Sebastiani. Even if he hadn't known who she was by name or lineage, her aura would have tipped him off immediately. Succubus. Sexual power rolled off her, and he really liked her look, especially her punk-pixie hair, black with hot pink streaks. Her chopped up T-shirt showed off collarbones that would snap at a touch, and her viciously expensive jeans looked like they'd been pulled out of a Dumpster.

"Hey, move those tables further apart," she hollered to the workers setting tables up along the rails bracketing three sides of the second floor, where patrons who wanted a chair, bottle service, and a little elbow room could obtain it—for a price. The workers quickly followed her orders. A vacuum moaned from one of the coveted VIP boxes ringing the third floor, each with sliding glass doors and heavy plum curtains that could be pulled shut for privacy.

Standing at the lip of the stage wearing walking shorts, a sweater, and flip-flops, Michael noodled the opening guitar riff of Guns N' Roses' "Sweet Child O' Mine." Stephen winced as the high notes shrieked through him, raising gooseflesh on his arms and back. His PDA buzzed again. "I'm here, I'm here," he muttered, shutting the unit off. He slowly emerged from the shadowy back corner into the full light of the performance space, the jingling of his boot chains giving him away.

"There he is. Hey, Stephen." Joe stepped down from the L-shaped, multi-level riser where he was setting up keyboards, synthesizer, and the computers used to run them. Wires and cables slithered across the stage. As

Stephen approached, Joe leaned over the edge of the stage and extended his arm to give him a boost up.

Stephen looked at the short stairway leading up to the stage, then back to Joe's arm.

"You fuckin' pussy."

Tansy stopped tightening the strings on her bass. "What did you say?"

"I said, 'Allow me assist you onto the stage, fine young gentleman,'" Joe called back.

"Yeah, I thought so." She slung her bass over her torso, settling it against her muscular upper thighs.

Joe crouched down closer to Stephen. "Ears like a bat."

Stephen took a deep breath. He *would* look like a pussy if he took the stairs. His tendons audibly snapped as he accepted Joe's boost up the six-foot stage. It was all he could do not to whimper.

"Jesus, you're tight. I thought you went home to get some sleep last night," Joe said under his breath. "What did you really do? Orgy with the American Gladiators? Bar fight? Something I couldn't imagine, even if I tried?"

Those final, euphoric moments in Subterranean's bathroom—Andi Woolf's throat crunching under his thumbs like potato chips, the light bulbs shattering over-head like hot stinging rain—probably qualified.

Joe scanned him for injuries, but the other man wouldn't find anything, thanks to the wide wristbands he wore. At the very end, Andi's fingernails had dug in to his wrists—hard. Under the wristbands, gauze-wrapped wounds still oozed blood.

Joe glanced at his watch. "You don't have time to loosen up with a hot shower—which, might I add, you could use anyway. Whew." Reaching for the tight muscles in Stephen's neck, he muttered, "If you can't move, Garrett's going to skin you alive."

Joe's strong hands hurt like a mother, but Stephen gutted it out. Joe was right about Garrett. While sound check ran a bit more loosely than an actual performance, there was no such thing as "just" rehearsal. Every member of the band took sound check as seriously as a heart attack. If they didn't get the sound balanced correctly now, the show would suck later.

"Ouch," Stephen hissed when Joe hit a particularly touchy spot.

"Why the hell are you so tight?" Joe lessened the pressure and lowered his voice. "Must have been some night."

Stephen thought about Andi's hips, moving and swaying as the music pounded. Her candy-sweet taste. Her near feral expression as she shoved him up against the bathroom stall wall. The suction of her soft, wet mouth on his dick, pulling him up onto his toes. Her life force, slamming into him like a speedball.

Michael's amp shrieked feedback.

"Jesus." Joe jerked his hands away.

Randy trotted the length of the wooden floor up to the stage, tool belt clanking. "What the hell was that?" He looked accusingly at one of the roadies. "Do I have to do everything myself?"

"Hey, don't ask me," the guy said, eyeing the amp like it was a baby who'd suddenly filled its diaper.

Snap. The amp crackled again. Randy looked at it, nonplussed.

Stephen's forearm muscles jumped and twitched like they were attached to a car battery. He hid the arm behind his back.

"Time to saddle up, boys and girls." Garrett's amplified, disembodied voice filled the venue, Wizard of Oz style. Heads swiveled as the members of the band looked for their manager. They finally found him seated at one of the tables on the second floor rail, near the back.

Randy finished his careful examination of the cords and wires around Michael's amp, ripping off a long piece of duct tape from his own roll and slapping it over cords that were already securely fastened. "Looks okay here." He jumped the six feet from the stage back down to the floor, and trotted back to the soundboard.

"Ready when you are, Randy."

Randy put on a headset, pressed a button, and the crisp opening percussion of Bauhaus's "Bela Lugosi's Dead" snicked out of the massive, three-floor amplification system, bouncing off the floor and the acoustic panels on the side walls and ceiling. Stephen couldn't help but smile—Jesus, you could practically hear the air vibrating around the notes. Thankfully, Randy could test some of the balances and levels using recorded music, and he wouldn't have to play every damn song himself, but he only had a few more minutes to work the kinks out, and to ensure his kit was set up well enough to get him through sound check. Climbing the riser which elevated his drum kit for greater stage visibility, he dropped gratefully onto the padded stool, carefully stretching his arms out to verify the spacing of the snare, the cymbals, his high hat. He grabbed a set of 5B sticks from the bin at his feet, and made sure 5As were available. Three bottles of room temperature water, caps off, were already lined up at attention at the side of his kick drum.

From her position at his left, he watched Tansy's fingers twitch as she unconsciously played along to the recording. At his smile, she cursed and put on her "ears," the custom-made, in-ear monitors that allowed each band member to hear their own voices and instruments in the amplified mix. Stephen grabbed his own headset and slung it around his neck.

The next song queued up, segueing from new wave crispness to lush, dissonant harmonies. Michael strolled back to the drums. "Look at Randy. I think he's about to come in his pants."

Randy was almost bouncing with glee as he stood next to Sasha Sebastiani.

"Hell, so am I." Stephen paused. "What do you think the chances are of us actually playing some originals tonight? I'm so tired of this cover song shit."

Michael shrugged. "It's up to Scarlett—your guess is as good as mine. But the crowd loves it." He walked back to his position, putting in his own ears.

Stephen's shoulders screamed as he slipped on his headset. Christ, the next half hour was going to be brutal. As Randy cued up "Slide" by Dido to work out the sound system's higher range, the stage lights came on unexpectedly, bright as a supernova. Stephen winced and reached for his sunglasses as the heat washed over him. "Give us some warning, will you?"

"Hard night, Stephen?" Garrett said laconically.

He answered Garrett's question with a raised middle finger, but he could feel their manager's gaze linger on him as the song continued. Damn it. He definitely looked like he'd been on an all-night bender instead of resting at home. His hair's bedhead style was 100 percent authentic this morning, and it showed. Putting the sunglasses on over his bleary eyes had probably tipped his unkempt look over into degeneracy.

His abdominal muscles clenched. It would be just like the son of a bitch to choose songs with the most difficult drum parts in creation for sound check, just to teach him a lesson.

The song ended. Michael stripped off his Argyle sweater and stretched from side to side. Joe simply stood, waiting for the abbreviated set list Garrett would call on the fly. Tansy made eyes with her bondmates standing in the wings. Devotion and lust drifted over to him, and the beast in his chest stirred.

Shit. Not now.

"Okay, showtime," Garrett said, eyeing each member of the band.

"Did Scarlett give you a set list yet?" Michael called. "Are we playing any originals tonight?"

"Not yet, and I don't know. So let's be ready for anything."

Stephen watched Garrett's thumb twirl over the iPod in his hand, a duplicate of the one they all carried. Every band member had to be ready to play any song stored on the damn thing, and there were thousands upon thousands of them, spanning folk to death metal. While Scarlett had a marked preference for '80s New Wave, Garrett, being a sadist, would as likely call out a Broadway show tune as something that Scarlett might actually choose for them to play, just to keep them sharp. Stephen wasn't about to admit that this practice had saved their asses any number of times during the last few months, as Scarlett deviated from the set list more often than not, or took requests from the crowd.

Stephen listened as Garrett rattled off the five songs he'd chosen: "Barely Breathing" by Duncan Sheik, a medium-paced rocker to get them warmed up. "Ice" by Sarah McLachlan. Restraint and delicacy, and hardly any drums, thank gawd, but Stephen saw Tansy grimace at the thought of the vocals. Next was Duran Duran's "Save a Prayer," Joe's preferred song to test-drive his synthesizers and computers. Tansy's grimace turned to a grin as Garrett called Duran Duran's "Rio," with its raucous bass lines, and damn it, a drum workout too.

There was a pregnant pause as Garrett looked directly at him, his thumb twirling slowly, a fucking Catherine Wheel.

"Call it," he called from his riser, stretching his arms overhead.

The slightest smile stole over Garrett's face. "Foo Fighters' 'Come Alive.'"

The man was trying to kill him. Really, he was. The song Garrett had chosen, about how a man's life changed forever with the birth of his child, was deceptively difficult. The drummer didn't have much at all to do for the first two minutes of the song, but the second half was a fucking drummer's showcase, and would tax his abilities even at full strength.

"You suck," he called up to Garrett, who now leaned urbanely against the rail.

Garrett raised an eyebrow. "So I've been told. Ready, Randy?" he called down to the sound booth. "Nice and easy to start. Michael, Tansy, nothing fancy, just mark the vocals."

"Thank you," Tansy muttered with a look to the heavens. Michael and Tansy sang harmony with Scarlett when they performed, but someone needed to handle lead vocals during sound check so Randy could verify the microphone levels and set the balance where he wanted.

Michael counted them down. "Five, six. Five, six, seven..."

And Stephen missed the opening cymbal riff on the second half of eight. "Sorry," he called.

"Again," Garrett replied with a steely look in his eye.

Stephen flexed his hands and wrists. His forearms and thumbs were so sore he wondered if he'd be able to hold on to his sticks. An amp crackled again, and he took a deep breath, wrestling his thoughts back to the task at hand. He met eyes with Michael and nodded.

And they were off.

He held it together as the band plowed through the abbreviated set list, but thankfully there were no paying customers, because he was flailing away like an eighth grader in his first garage band. "Rio" was galloping to a close, and his stomach was already rolling, thinking about the song to come. He almost wished he didn't have to wait out the first portion of the song, because now that he was moving a little, he felt better. It was when they stopped between songs that everything tightened up again, when everything snapped and sparked like a live wire.

He jerked as he heard Michael's light touch on his guitar, starting "Come Alive." Having several minutes to wait, he moved and stretched, chose sticks, adjusted his headset and wrist bands. Took a deep breath as he joined in at about the two minute mark with a soft kick drum, then subtle snares. The song layered and built as it went on, as he supposed labor pains did. His body struggled and strained as the volume picked up, and he gritted his teeth as he crashed cymbals on every one-beat. More pounding, more fills. In the original, Foo Fighters' front man Dave Grohl practically shreds his vocal cords screaming his daughter into the world, but Michael was not about to do that, especially just before the show.

When they reached the last minute of the song, Stephen played like his life depended upon it. His arm and back muscles burned as he drove, flew, pounded. Sweat dripped down his neck. *Okay, almost there. Just twenty seconds more.* He just had to find enough strength for the final push, for that last monstrous set of rolls, riffs, and crashes.

They arrived before he was ready, but he had no choice but to push through it. *This was it.* "Aah!" he groaned aloud, his body moving instinctively.

And then… it was over. His groan hung in the air along with the last soft guitar chord, and his arms dropped heavily, uselessly, to his sides. His sticks dropped from his hands to the floor, clattering onto the wooden stage below.

They waited.

"All right, then," Garrett said after a pause, still eyeing Stephen but otherwise not making comment. "See you backstage in two hours. When I get the set list, I'll zap it to you. And Randy, fix that damn amp, will you?"

Tansy approached and handed him a bottle of water, which he swigged gratefully. "Are you okay?"

He reached for one of the towels stacked in a pile behind his stool and wiped his sweaty face. "Nothing a shower won't fix. I'll pull it together by showtime."

Yeah, right. This wasn't something he could shower off. Was he going to be wrecked every time he...

Snap.

Every time you almost kill someone?

No, he assured himself. What had happened with Andi Woolf had been a horrible, horrible accident. It wouldn't happen again. Couldn't happen again. Now that he knew what to expect, he'd find a way to control himself.

He had to, because he couldn't fathom not feeling that narcotic, orgasmic blast again.

High-heeled boots tapped against wood. A hot brunette joined Sasha Sebastiani at the soundboard, wrapping an arm around her waist and kissing her cheek. Stephen narrowed his eyes. *Yowza.* She looked vaguely familiar, but he just couldn't place her. As the woman shook Randy's hand, Stephen jerked his head toward them. "Who's that?"

"Hmm?" Tansy looked up from where she wiped down the neck of her bass.

"Who's that woman with Sasha and Randy at the soundboard?" *The woman tossing her dark hair over her shoulder, looking at me like I'm catnip?* His nostrils flared as lust bloomed across the empty dance floor.

"That's Scarlett's sister Annika, and don't you even think about it." Tansy put her hands on his shoulders and squeezed.

"Ouch." Wow, that was Scarlett's sister? While he'd never found Scarlett all that physically appealing—unlike most of the known world—her sister's alluring smile tugged at him from across the room. He could feel her lips on him already.

"Stephen." Tansy shook him. Hard. Snapped her fingers in front of his face until she was sure she had his attention. "We have a show in less than three hours, and you're a mess."

"Yeah," he said to Tansy, the muscles in his midsection clenching as Annika Fontaine met his eyes across the expanse of the performance space.

Tansy just shook her head. "You're not even listening to me, are you?"

"Yeah, I am."

But the beast gnawing on his rib cage was drowning her out.

Chapter 8

AN HOUR BEFORE THE SHOW, LUKAS SHIFTED HIS arms over his head as he walked the hallway leading to Underbelly's third floor VIP rooms, punishing the fibers in the V-necked black cashmere sweater he'd swiped from his father's closet. Though noticeably small, it would have to do; there was no way in hell Sasha would let him through the doors in the T-shirt he'd been wearing for over a day. There was no help for the jeans and boots.

Sasha should be thankful they weren't spattered with blood.

Though the short nap he'd caught on Sasha's lime green love seat—and the obscenely long shower he'd taken up in his father's place—had refreshed him somewhat, the cost had been high. Sasha had painted his nails with shiny black polish while he slept in her office. Despite his picking and chipping, he hadn't managed to remove the color worth a damn, though he should probably be thankful for small favors. At least she'd chosen black, not pastel pink. He'd considered stalking across the foyer, pounding on her apartment door, and demanding some remover, but enough of Scarlett's residual fury saturated the floor that he'd thought better of it. No sense tempting fate.

Yet, anyway.

Feet hammered behind him. Lukas whipped around.

"Calamity!" Antonia hollered. "You come here, right now."

Scarlett's huge black cat streaked around the corner, ears pinned against his head, big belly swinging from side to side as he galloped down the hall. Lukas's body relaxed, but his mind flashed to scratches. Bites. Lawsuits.

His younger sister barreled around the corner, her butt-grazing hair flying out behind her, tottering a bit on her high-heeled boots. Lukas blinked as he registered the changes in the tiny sprite's appearance. Since he'd seen her last, Antonia had made that inexplicable tip from girl to woman. Who had given her permission to grow up?

And when was the last time he'd seen Antonia? Really talked to her? Antonia's whirlwind teenage social life kept her busy, and away from home on the weekend evenings when Lukas typically stopped by his father's place to cadge a meal that wasn't takeout.

What a shitty brother he was. Catching the cat could wait.

"Hey, hold on a sec," he said, snagging her arm before she could pass.

Antonia looked at Lukas with a withering glance which teenaged girls the world over were masters of. "Damn it, I almost had him. What do you want?"

He picked his sister up under her arms, lifted so her face was level with his, and kissed her hello. "Do I need a reason to hug my favorite sister?" Her lips were slathered with aromatic pink bubble gum lip gloss, but her eyes were elaborately and expertly made up. "You have way too much shit on your eyes."

She halfheartedly kicked her legs so he would put her down, and batted her mascara-blackened eyelashes.

"Jesse did it," she said, referring to Scarlett's stylist-cum-bodyguard. "In matters of makeup, I trust his judgment, not yours."

Yeah, well, she still had way too much shit on her eyes. His gaze narrowed on the black-edged Celtic knot tattoos bracketing her wrists.

She rolled her eyes at him and snapped her gum. "Don't get your jock in a twist—they're temps."

The door to the VIP room suddenly opened, and laughter and chatter spilled into the hall. Calamity streaked into the room. Seconds later he heard someone say, "Hey, there's a cat on the buffet table." There were no shrieks of carnage. Yet.

Reluctantly, he put Antonia down, holding her shoulders until she was steady on her feet. When had his little sister sprouted curves? He could see a lacy black bra strap nestled in with the layers of camisole T-shirts she wore. How could so many shirts leave so much skin uncovered? Her jeans were a crime against circulation. "Are you wearing underwear?"

Antonia shrugged away from his grasp and said loudly, with theatrical projection, "Lukas Sebastiani, you are such a perv."

Sound in the VIP room momentarily stopped. Lukas closed his eyes, and took a deep breath. She hadn't answered his question—which answered it, damn it.

"Kayla," Gideon Lupinsky's younger brother Gabe said as he was tugged from the VIP room by his fiancée and backed against the wall. "Let's wait until we get home."

"Don't want to." Her voice was barely audible; she was busy nibbling Gabe's neck, trying to change his mind. She leached reckless abandon, but it was clear to

Lukas that Gabe wasn't quite on the same page. Gabe worked for Alka Schlessinger at Sebastiani Labs, and Alka had invited Gabe and a guest to watch the concert from the VIP box, much to Lorin's disgust. When he noticed Lukas and Antonia, Gabe pushed Kayla away with a muttered curse.

Definitely annoyed.

Gabe made the introductions. "Nice to meet you, Ms. Andersen," Lukas said, extending his hand to the small werewolf female.

"Mr. Sebastiani," she responded, shaking it with a respectful bow of her head.

"Please, it's Lukas."

Antonia also shook the woman's hand. Her nostrils twitched. "If you want to have sex, the bathroom's right down the hall."

Lorin exited the VIP room. "Mind if I use it first?" she asked, shooting Gabe a withering glance as she walked past everyone.

Lukas lifted a weary hand to his forehead. Why was everyone so pissed off tonight? "Antonia…"

"What? They want to have sex," Antonia said with a shrug. She glanced at Gabe. "Well, one of you does, at any rate."

Jesus. "Enjoy the show," he said to Gabe and Kayla, tugging Antonia down the hall by her arm. She inhaled deeply, her eyes drifting closed as she tailgated off the secondhand desire blooming in the hallway. Puberty turned incubi and succubi into walking, talking hormones.

"Lukas, you're about ten years too old to pull off that nail polish."

"Forget the nail polish. You can't just say stuff like that."

"Why not?" she retorted. "I was right. Even though they're fighting now, they wanted to have sex—she did, anyway."

"Yeah, you're right. But that doesn't mean you say anything about it." Lukas paused, looking for the words to explain to his sister. "It's important to give people at least the illusion of privacy, especially about sexual matters. And it's especially important with people we don't know well, or just met."

"Gabriel isn't a stranger."

It shook him to hear that twist, that sexual liquor, in her voice. Had she and Gabe—nah. Lukas discounted the idea almost as soon as it winked into his brain. Gabe was engaged, and a devoted Sebastiani Labs employee. He wouldn't touch his boss's daughter, no matter how hard she worked her fledgling wiles. But if not Gabe, someone else. And if not already? Soon. At sixteen, Antonia had reached the age of consent, and for all he knew, she'd already had a lover. Lovers, plural. He certainly had at sixteen.

Okay, fourteen.

No wonder his father's hair was gray.

"Hey." Their brother Rafael stepped through the open door with Calamity in his arms, using some serious muscle to control the big animal. Calamity yowled his displeasure and clamped his teeth into Rafe's shoulder. "Jesus. This isn't a cat, it's an anaconda."

Antonia jabbed her elbow into Lukas's rib so he'd release her. "Calamity! Bad cat. Let's get you back upstairs where you belong."

Rafe looked at his sister's bare arms and held on. "Let me take him; he'll scratch you to hell."

"You won't scratch me, will you, sweetheart?" she crooned to the cat, who leaped away from Rafe into Antonia's arms. She grunted like she'd been tackled—not surprising, since the cat was about a fifth of her body weight—but once the cat settled in her arms, he purred like a motorboat. Antonia rubbed her cheek against the cat's massive head.

Looking at his watch, Lukas considered escorting her to the penthouse, but throttled back on the protectiveness. She'd be walking from one secured area of the facility to another, and back again. Five minutes, tops. "Time to get him back upstairs, kiddo. The show's about to start."

"Be right back."

They both watched as their little sister walked down the hall with a sway of her hips exaggerated by her high-heeled boots. Rafe turned to Lukas with a puzzled look on his face. "When did she…?"

"Damned if I know."

"Looks, brains, and mean as a pit viper. Jupiter help us." Rubbing at his shoulder, Rafe said, "Claudette wants to talk to you."

"Did it look to you like she was wearing any underwear?"

"Claudette? Antonia is right—you *are* a perv."

"Not Claudette," Lukas replied between clenched teeth. "Our little sister."

"If you've added Underwear Police to your long list of duties, you're going to have a really busy night."

"Just… shut up. I need to talk to Claudette."

He and Rafe entered the dimly lit VIP room, where

the party was low key but in full swing. Lorin, back from the bathroom, chatted quietly with Wyland back by the bar. Valerian and Alka stood in the back corner nibbling appetizers. His father and Claudette stood hand in hand by the waist-high rail overlooking the dance floor, talking with Annika. It gave Lukas a jolt to see them there, so exposed, but earlier this evening, Sebastiani Security staff had swept the place up, down, and sideways. He knew the metal detector was working, because they'd already snagged several knives and one gun at the front entrance. Bailey was wiring a few last-minute cameras backstage. Jack was down on the floor, coordinating the activities of the Sebastiani Security employees working the event who would mingle with the crowd. Sasha was backstage somewhere. He'd received a report that Scarlett was in her dressing room with her manager and her stylist. Once Antonia came back to the VIP suite, everyone on his mental checklist would be accounted for.

He sighed. The place was as safe as he knew how to make it. He approached his father and Claudette.

"Do you have Calamity in custody?" Annika laughed and kissed him hello on both cheeks, following it up with one of her exuberant hugs.

He hugged her back, allowing her uncomplicated happiness to give him a boost. She was easy to read—so different from her sister. "Calamity's on his way back upstairs where he belongs. Antonia's got him." Looking around the room, he was relieved to notice that no one was bleeding out or cradling a mangled limb. "Did he bite anyone?"

"No, Rafe saved the day. And the spinach dip."

Despite his father's lighthearted words, Lukas watched his father's fingers tangle with Claudette's tense ones, trying to comfort.

"I'm going to go get some of that dip," Annika said. "Excuse me for a moment, will you?"

Lukas, Elliott, and Claudette silently watched the activity on the floor for a few minutes. Music, voices, and pheromones drifted, jumping noticeably when the house lights darkened slightly and the DJ turned up the music. People started to dance. In his earpiece, Lukas heard Jack giving their crew last-minute instructions about consensual touch, urging them to keep an eye out for anyone in the pit who might need help if things got rowdy.

He needed to get backstage. He turned his attention back to his father and Claudette.

"I understand Scarlett wasn't very happy with you this afternoon," Claudette said. "I apologize for my daughter."

"Not necessary, Claudette," Lukas responded evenly. Of course Claudette knew about the scene Scarlett had caused earlier in the day. Her information network was as solid as his own.

"How did she look? What did you sense?" A look of annoyance crept over Claudette's face, there then gone. "She's avoiding my calls and my mother-sense is shrieking." She looked up at Lukas. "I know my daughter. If she doesn't want me to hear her voice, something's wrong."

His stomach bumped. It wasn't just him, then. But how did he answer Claudette's question? The limited time he'd spent with Scarlett that afternoon hadn't exactly yielded observations and impressions he was comfortable sharing with her mother. "She seemed tired.

And it looked like she'd lost some weight." He smiled ruefully. "But she was feisty enough to give me hell."

"Please keep an eye on her, Lukas. I know what I'm asking you to do," she said, gesturing to the music, the dance floor. The energy and pheromones leached off the crowd, swirling upward with their body heat. "But... something's wrong."

"I won't take my eyes off her, Claudette."

Truer words never spoken. You're weak, Sebastiani. Weak.

The VIP room door opened, and Gabe and Kayla Andersen returned, tense and annoyed instead of satiated. Antonia was right behind them, with no new scratches or bites on her bare arms. She immediately butted in to the conversation Wyland and Lorin were having, certain of her welcome. Annika, PDA in hand and mischievous expression on her face, caught the door before it closed, calling back to her mother that she had something she had to take care of.

Lukas turned his attention back to his father. "Dad, I know that now's not the right time, but we really need to talk about Antonia."

"What about her?"

"She's..." He watched Antonia talk with Lorin and Wyland. She was years younger than the two Council members, yet certain of her place. Lukas could only imagine the topic under discussion. Knowing Antonia, it could be anything from *Project Runway* to the G20. How could he put his complex concerns into words? "Would you make her go upstairs and put on some underwear?"

Elliott blinked, and Claudette's laughter tinkled

merrily. "Lukas Sebastiani, I'm certain you've seen a thong or two in your day."

A thong? That seemed worse than her wearing no underwear at all.

"Lukas?" he heard Jack say in his earpiece.

After excusing himself from his father and Claudette's conversation, he responded. "Yeah, go."

"Is Stephen up there by any chance? Scarlett's drummer?"

"No."

He heard Jack relay his answer to Sasha, who swore ripely.

"Get down here. We have a problem."

"Be there in a sec. I have to go," Lukas said to Elliott and Claudette.

Claudette brushed a kiss on his cheek. "Thank you, Lukas. Thanks for giving Scarlett your personal attention. I know my daughter is safe in your hands."

Lukas barely held back a bark of hysterical laughter. *Don't be so sure of that, Claudette.*

"It doesn't fit." Jesse clutched a handful of black leather at Scarlett's hip. "We just had this fitted two weeks ago."

"Can we pin it?" Scarlett said with a full-body shiver.

Jesse noticed, and flipped on the heat lamps recessed into the dressing room bathroom's ceiling. "Nope, the fabric won't take it. With another hour before curtain, I might have been able to take it in, but we don't have an hour. Step out."

"I'm sorry." Scarlett let the ball gown slither to the floor.

"Don't apologize, sweetheart," Jesse said as he

picked it up. "I'm the one who's sorry. I should have asked you to try it on earlier today."

Scarlett's eyes stung as he carefully put it back on its padded hanger. She loved the dress, and had counted on it to give her a boost of confidence. The skirt was a black leather mini no wider than a place mat, but yards and yards of black-violet tulle exploded from its hem to flutter down to her calves. It had a matching leather corset that laced up the back. When she'd tried it on last, Garrett had declared that she looked like a Goth ballerina.

Everything that could go wrong today had, and the damn dress not fitting just added insult to injury. It didn't help that her traitorous mind wouldn't stop replaying that hallway encounter with Lukas Sebastiani on continuous loop: her, melting over his oversized body like chocolate. Him? As cold and unaffected as ever. Walking away.

Lukas was really good at walking away.

"Sweetie, you really have to do something about this," Jesse said softly, snatching the purple calf-length fleece bathrobe hanging on the back of the door and bundling her into it.

She blinked quickly at the weak, reactive tears. "I'm working on it, Jesse." At his "yeah, right" look, she nodded and amended, "Okay, I *will* work on it. Now that we're off the road, I'll let you all fatten me up. I'll stay in bed for a week and eat nothing but your truffles. You'll need a forklift to move me."

While Jesse snorted and zipped the dress into a protective wardrobe bag, she tried to calm her queasy stomach. The pre-show jitters were especially bad tonight, and hadn't let up even though she'd thrown up over an hour ago—in her own toilet, which was a bit of a luxury; she didn't have to wonder how many strange asses had used the facilities before she had. Her stomach lurched again as she thought of the set list she'd just delivered to Garrett, explicitly crafted to make Lukas Sebastiani writhe. What the hell had she been thinking? What had possessed her? That gorgeous hunk of rock would be standing mere feet away from her, all night long. She'd be wading through his luscious pheromones for hours.

She dragged breath through her suddenly tight throat. This idea was sure to boomerang back on her, big-time.

"Scarlett? Let me see the dress," Garrett called from the dressing room's large common area, a tranquil, Zen-like space decorated with overstuffed couches, plenty of lamps for indirect lighting, and grass-scented candles.

Jesse carried the wardrobe bag over his arm as he left the bathroom. "Time for Plan B. The dress doesn't fit. We need to find something else for her to wear." On the way to the closet stretched across one full wall, he detoured momentarily to brush a smooch against Garrett's cheek. "Thank Jupiter we unpacked her trunk, or else she'd be wearing that bathrobe onstage."

"The bathrobe is an improvement over those ratty-assed yoga pants," Garrett said with a shudder. "Scarlett, promise you'll let me put them out of their misery. I want to do the honors."

Garrett and Jesse had very firm opinions about her "look," which was good, because she sure didn't. She dressed for comfort—and more importantly, for warmth. If Garrett wanted her favorite lounging pants, he was going to have to pry them off of her cold, dead body.

While the men stood at the closet muttering about knits versus leather, and debated the merits of this belt or that one, Scarlett sipped her cooling Throat Coat tea, brushed her teeth, and practically danced around the bathroom trying not to scratch at her head. The hot rollers Jesse had set her hair with had cooled off, and tiny teeth bit into her scalp something fierce.

Exclamations of success emanated from the living room. Jesse hurried into the heated bathroom carrying a handful of black cotton knit, and Garrett was on his heels with a long leather wrap belt.

As she slipped off her bathrobe, Scarlett caught a glimpse of the three of them in the vanity mirror and burst out laughing. Garrett was all suited elegance. Jesse was rough and ready in black leather pants and a white wife beater. And standing between them was her—shivering, pale, and nude, except for a miniscule black thong and the rollers in her hair.

"Blackmail shots, anyone?"

"Where are the paparazzi when you need them?" Jesse said, leering at Scarlett playfully. "I can see the headlines now: 'Scarlett Fontaine's Pre-Show Manwich.'"

Scarlett rolled her eyes. "I wish." If anybody knew how long it had been since she'd had sex, it was these two. "Get these damn things out of my hair, will you?"

Jesse quickly pulled the cooled rollers out of her hair, and she scratched her skull with a blissful sigh. "Time?"

Garrett looked at his watch. "Twenty minutes to curtain."

Jesse handed her the wad of fabric, and Scarlett pulled it over her head without question. Fine-gauge cotton knit slid down her body, stopping at mid-thigh. Hmm, a T-shirt dress. The belt would wrap twice around her hips. Casual, fun, though a little… um, *breezy* with her choice of undergarment. It didn't have quite the oomph of the ball gown, but it would absorb sweat like a sponge. "Good call," she told Jesse.

"It fits," he responded dourly. "Go pick out some boots."

Scarlett went to the closet, where her performance footwear marched across the floor like soldiers on parade. Her eyes flitted over the options, mentally bypassing any boot that had a high heel. Her feet just weren't up to it tonight. Where were those… *Aha*. "You cannot hide," she intoned, kneeling so she could reach back into the corner of the closet.

"Whoa, full moon alert," Jesse called from the open door of the bathroom. "Want some different underwear?"

"They're all upstairs. We don't have time," Scarlett said, emerging with a pair of thigh-high pirate boots with wraparound studs at the ankles. The top of the boot folded over a couple of inches south of the hem of the dress, and best of all, they were nearly flat. Her feet wouldn't be screaming ten minutes into the show.

"Perfect," Garrett said.

"Duh." Scarlett quickly put on the boots, then scurried back to the bathroom, where Jesse opened his makeup kit and selected the magic wands he'd wave to turn wan, pasty Scarlett Fontaine into Scarlett!! Fontaine!! "Are you sure twenty minutes will be enough time?"

"They'll wait for you, honey."

"I guess that answers that."

She focused on the face emerging under Jesse's

skillful hand. Who was this woman? Her familiar, flaky face became exotic and dewy. Her eyes, now smoky and emphasized, blazed with mystery. Separating her lips, Jesse applied her favorite matte lipstick, the one that didn't come off on her microphone. Cheekbones? No problem, she had cheekbones to spare—except now they looked sophisticated rather than emaciated.

Jesse put down the lipstick and picked up a can of hair spray. "Assume the position, please."

Scarlett stood and bent over from the waist, closing her eyes and holding her breath while Jesse sprayed her hair. Once she stood up and sat again, he busily brushed and back-combed near the roots to create some volume. Sprayed again.

"You know this is a losing battle," Scarlett said. "I'll sweat through this in a half hour, tops."

"But you'll look great until then."

Scarlett snagged a black elastic band off the vanity table, snapping it onto her wrist so she could pull her hair into a hasty ponytail if she wanted to.

A knock came from the dressing room's outer door. "Scarlett? Garrett? We need you out here. Now."

"Thank you," Garrett called back. "Breathe," he told Scarlett.

She felt flop sweat bloom on her forehead and upper lip. "I'm going to throw up," she muttered to Garrett as Jesse bundled her back into the purple fleece robe.

"No, you're not," Garrett replied, though she noticed he patted his suit pocket to make sure he had the airline sickness bag he carried for just such an event. "You know how this goes. Once you get through the first song, you're home free."

Scarlett breathed through her teeth, trying to ignore the sour sting at the back of her throat. "Ready as I'll ever be."

Garrett and Jesse each took an arm and hustled her out of the dressing room door. Everywhere she looked, faces stared back. Scarlett shrank into Jesse's body, letting it shield her from at least some of the inquisitive eyes. Four men she didn't recognize joined them, walked with them. "Just some extra security, remember?" Garrett said comfortingly. "Ignore them, sweetie. Remember to breathe."

One foot in front of the other. Scarlett counted off the steps in her head until they reached the common area adjacent to the stage, where the band gathered before the performance. In contrast to the Zen calm of Scarlett's personal dressing room, this area snapped with motion and energy. Burgundy, purple, and turquoise couches popped against the charcoal gray walls, and over on the food table, the destroyed tray of sandwich fixings and nearly empty candy bowls indicated to Scarlett that, as usual, her band mates hadn't had any trouble with pre-show nerves. Three insulated coolers labeled Beer, Pop, and Water had been placed on the floor next to the table, and a recycling bin stood nearby.

Though she was vaguely aware of Michael waving to her as he nibbled on a very rare roast beef sandwich, of Joe talking on his cell, and of Tansy lying across the laps of her bondmates over on the burgundy couch, what she noticed most was Lukas, standing like a monolith in the middle of the room, sucking away all of the oxygen. He was talking with Sasha, who was clearly upset about something. Whether Lukas was doing the upsetting or was trying to alleviate it wasn't quite clear.

"Excuse me a moment," Garrett said, joining them. Scarlett watched him listen to Sasha, who punctuated her words with slashing hand gestures. He shook his head "no," his face locking into an expression she privately called "Battle Stations."

No matter how much she didn't want to get close to Lukas, something was obviously wrong. "What's up?" she asked when she reached the small group.

He smelled so good.

"Have you seen Stephen recently?" he asked.

It was all she could do not to let her eyes drop to half-mast as his voice shivered into her nervous system. The air around them practically pulsed. Lukas's eyes narrowed and his nostrils flared as he absorbed her helpless reaction to him. *Damn it. Damn it.* She stiffened her buckling knees. "No. I haven't seen Stephen since we all got off the bus last night. What's up?"

"Little shit's MIA," Sasha said tightly.

"He's got to be here somewhere." Scarlett turned to Garrett. "You gave him a set list about an hour ago, right?"

Garrett nodded.

"But then he disappeared. His drum tech checked the bathrooms. We've checked all the dressing rooms except yours. We've searched the dance floor; we've looked behind the damn curtains. Nothing." Sasha balled her fists. "That hormonal little shit."

"He's usually not so unprofessional," Scarlett murmured. When Garrett cleared his throat, she amended her comment. "Okay, his personal behavior is flagrantly unprofessional, but anything having to do with the job?

With the music? He's usually the first person at practice, and he's never missed a gig."

When Jack Kirkland arrived and pulled Lukas away for a quick confab, Scarlett, Sasha, and Garrett had one of their own. Sasha nibbled at a nail. "He might very well show up in a couple of minutes tucking in his shirt and wiping pussy off his mouth, but what will we do if he doesn't?"

"That's the easiest problem to solve," Scarlett responded. She gestured to the dance floor. "You can't throw a stick out there tonight without hitting a great drummer."

A crafty smile lit Garrett's face. "Who do you want?"

"Give me a set list," she asked Garrett. "And something to write with." Her efficient manager produced both from his breast pocket.

Scarlett tapped the pen against her lip as she considered how to adapt the set list. "Tomas will do it, for sure," she muttered. "Dave, how about Dave?" she said, referring to Dave Grohl, current Foo Fighters' front man and past Nirvana drummer.

Garrett's smile grew. Scarlett knew he was already envisioning how he could spin the situation, and the substitute drummers, to publicize and market the concert DVD they'd be filming tonight. Well, that's what she paid him to do. Let him earn his paycheck; she had other problems to solve. Sigmund was still in her dressing room, so Scarlett mentally shuffled through the songs in the Ten Inch Screw, Foo Fighters, and Nirvana back catalogs, and then considered the flow of the show and the vibe she wanted to create. Stealing a covert look at Lukas, she crossed a few of the most egregiously sexual songs off the set list, and scribbled in several songs to replace them.

She showed the adapted list to Garrett and Sasha.

Garrett scanned the changes, and then smacked a kiss on the top of Scarlett's head. "You're a genius."

"I'm on it," Sasha said, already walking away to find the men and propose the idea. "It's early yet. They're probably both still sober. Maybe." She spoke into her headset. "Tell the DJ to keep the music coming. We have a half-hour delay."

Scarlett listened as Lukas described Stephen to his staff. "Fan out," he ordered tersely. Lukas sounded as annoyed as she felt.

Stephen, where the hell are you? When he emerged from whichever little hidey-hole he was undoubtedly fucking someone in, she was going to kick his ass.

Chapter 9

"DIM HOUSE LIGHTS TO 50 PERCENT, PLEASE," SASHA hollered into her headset, having no idea if the light tech could actually hear her instructions with the music pounding to every corner of the dance floor. From her position backstage, Sasha saw Scarlett shrug her purple robe into her manager's arms and take a careful sip of water from one of the dozen or so bottles standing ready.

Scarlett was still shaking off pre-show nausea, and Lukas watching her like a hawk didn't help. On the other hand, watching her doff that robe had pretty much made her big brother swallow his tongue. She didn't have anywhere near Lukas's sensory strength and skill, but even she could feel the reciprocal jolts of lust.

As the house lights dimmed, a flash of blond caught her eye, on the floor just beyond the lip of the stage. Bailey was already in position, laughing, twirling, and finally staggering into the hard-bodied guy standing next to her. He caught her with a laugh, and clamped his hand firmly to her butt.

"Shit." Which Einstein had forgotten to give Bailey her meds? Um, that Einstein would be her. With everything else going on, with Stephen disappearing, she'd clean forgotten to give Bailey a dose of the medication that would render her immune to the effects of pheromone intoxication. Sidestepping a roadie, Sasha trotted down the backstage stairs, emerged from an unmarked door tucked in the shadows of the dance floor, and hurried over to the other woman. "Bailey?"

"Sasha!" Bailey slurred, her eyes glassy. "Hi, Sasha! This is my friend Sasha. This is... what's your name again?" Bailey breathed into his muscular chest, her mouth grazing the nipple ring clearly visible under his sheer excuse for a shirt.

"Chadden," he replied slowly, amusement in his eyes.

"Sorry, Chad. She's buzzed."

"No problem, Sasha," the vamp holding Bailey said, his interest reflected clearly on his face. Chadden was an Underbelly regular. Sasha knew that he knew the rules, but Bailey sure didn't. Glamour pulsed off of him; he was way too gorgeous for his own good. His long black hair was loose and already damp at the temples, but in the way of vamps, the sweat simply made him more attractive rather than less. "Who is my adorable new pal here?" He grinned down at Bailey. "You'd fit right in my pocket, wouldn't you, tidbit?"

"No she wouldn't," Sasha muttered. "Your pants are too tight." Frustration boiled. The show was about to start, but she couldn't just leave Bailey out here on the dance floor to fend for herself. She heard Jack's deep, smooth voice on the Sebastiani Security communication band. Maybe he had some extra meds he could spare. "Lukas? Jack? Problem," she said into her headset.

"Go," Lukas's tight voice responded.

"Bailey's intoxicated, didn't get her meds."

"Hi, Lukas!" Bailey said giddily, hearing the conversation in her own earpiece.

Even above the noisy crowd, Sasha could sense her brother's tension crackling over the line.

"Damn it," she heard Jack say as he joined in.

"Jack? Is that Jack?" Bailey slurred. "Do you know what the women at work call Lukas and Jack? 'Beef' and 'Cake.'" She leaned into Sasha conspiratorially. "'Beef' because Lukas is so big, and 'Cake' because Jack's so pretty. Beefcake. Get it? Get it?"

"Yup, I get it," Sasha said, trying to avoid Bailey's jabbing elbow.

Bailey tipped her head toward Sasha's. "Don't tell them, but a lot of women at work stare at their butts as they walk down the hall."

"Jesus," Lukas muttered under his breath.

"Okay, Bailey," she said loudly. "Your secret is safe with me."

"And Jack helped me get this job. Isn't he the nicest? Sasha?" Bailey repeated when Sasha didn't respond.

Nuh-uh, not touching that one.

"Sasha?" Lukas barked.

"Sorry, guys." She swiped away her other headset so she no longer had dueling soundtracks in her head. "I've got a missing drummer and two substitutes who, while very talented, haven't rehearsed dick. The first floor men's room is already out of condoms. We just had a small grease fire in the kitchen. Three cars are being towed from Reserved Parking at this very minute. Scarlett's about to barf up all that water she just drank, and I don't know when the curtain is going up." She took a deep breath, cursing as Chadden eyed Bailey like she was a tasty amuse-bouche. "Bailey's out of commission until we get her some meds, and I'm fresh out."

"Hey, Sasha." Rafe's voice joined the conversation. "Meet me back at the soundboard. I'll take Bailey up to your office, get her some meds, babysit her until they hit. She'll be back on the floor in a half hour, tops."

"Do it," Lukas said curtly.

Putting her other headset back on, she tugged Bailey away from Chadden and his friends to the perimeter of the room where it was less crowded, and started the long trek back to the soundboard. Bailey latched on with both arms, rubbing her cheek against the cups of the leather bikini top Sasha wore as a shirt. Inhaling as they walked, Sasha let the throbbing music, the pulsing lights, and the club's emotional energy seep into her. The buzz was heightening as people laughed, hugged, danced, drank. Everywhere she looked, people stroked and touched. As soon as Scarlett took the stage, the energy would spike and surge, building through the night, like some invisible giant hand had shaken the club like a bottle of soda and then gleefully unscrewed the top.

Sasha spared a moment's pity for her brother, standing in such close proximity to Scarlett backstage. Had he seen the set list? Did he know what he was in for? She didn't know what Scarlett was thinking, but she heartily approved.

A werewolf howl split the air, louder than the music banging through the club. Things were getting raucous, and the show hadn't even started yet. But so far, a fine tension was keeping everyone behaving in an evolutionary game of Rock, Paper, Scissors: the werewolves had immense physical strength for their size, second only to the valkyries, but both species were more susceptible to incubi and succubi pheromones than the vamps were. Vamps tended toward slender frames but possessed massive personal glamour—and having fangs didn't hurt.

Humans, physically the weakest—chum in the water, really—would actually have the clearest heads in the house, if they took their meds. She looked at Bailey, currently planting a string of tiny kisses along her jaw line.

Some friend she was.

For the next few hours, it would be the gentle sirens sitting at the top of the food chain. Scarlett, with her incomparable voice, was about to take them all on a journey of her choosing.

Why couldn't Lukas just strap in and enjoy the ride?

———

A helpless shiver wracked Scarlett as Lukas's body heat bled into hers from where he stood, not two feet behind her. Did he have to stand so close? Her sex clenched at his scent, a wild night forest.

Whoa. Head rush. She stumbled backwards, and his massive hands steadied her.

"Are you okay?"

She shivered again as his humid breath puffed into the crook of her neck. His fingers momentarily flexed, gently biting into her hips as he steadied her. For a moment, just for a moment, she allowed herself to lean into his body. Into his heat. His… size.

Her eyes widened slightly as she felt the unmistakable erection pressing against her back. If the only thing she had to go on was the expression on his face, she would think that he was contemplating cutting his toenails, or maybe having his taxes done, but his body told a different story completely.

She stepped away. "Thank you."

"Have you eaten at all today?"

"What?"

"Won't be much of a show if you drop from hypoglycemia."

"My blood sugar's just fine," she said crossly. "And if I drop, isn't it your job to catch me?" She stared blindly at the set list duct-taped to the backstage wall. What the hell had she been thinking? Anticipation and dread swam in her stomach. Damn it, she hadn't factored in her own reaction to the man when she'd crafted the set list. She wasn't even singing yet, and it was all she could do not to lean toward him like a compass needle seeking true north.

She jumped when a hand touched her shoulder. "Hey, sorry," Dave Grohl said. He eyed Lukas, who didn't show any sign of stepping back to give them a little room. Shrugging, Dave asked, "Has Stephen showed up yet?"

"No," Scarlett said. She pushed Dave's long scraggly bangs out of his face so she could see his eyes. "But even if Stephen were to show up right now, you're my guy for tonight. Are you okay with the set list?"

He grinned around his ever-present gum. "I'll muddle through. This place is gonna pop its fuckin' cork."

"Excuse me," Lukas said tightly. He moved a couple of body lengths away, though his eyes didn't leave her. Scarlett watched his lips move as he talked. Anyone who hadn't noticed the miniscule, flesh-toned earpiece he wore would probably think he was talking to himself.

"Scarlett?"

She turned back to Dave, whose grin had turned knowing. Her face flaming, she punched him on the shoulder. "What?"

Dave backed away, hands jokingly raised. "Hey, I

didn't say anything but your name. Did I?" he said to Tansy, who'd joined them.

"I have no clue what you're talking about," the bassist replied, taking Dave's arm and leading him to where Michael stood near the curtain. When she heard them talking Dave through the timing of the band's entry onto the stage, her stomach clutched. At least someone was thinking. Their opening number, "Desire (Come and Get It)" by Gene Loves Jezebel, had a precision unison start for the drummer and the lead guitar. There was no room for slop, no opportunity to drift in or catch up.

As Tansy explained the countdown to Dave, Scarlett examined the set list once again, shoving down a growing panic. Her body was throbbing already; she was halfway to an orgasm and he'd barely touched her. Where was Sigmund? Who had a pen?

It was too late for second thoughts. For better or for worse, she'd do her best to bring things to a head tonight, using the most ruthless tool she had at her disposal.

It would help if she could tear her eyes away from the bulge at his crotch.

Then again, why be coy? She was done walking on eggshells. The goose bumps surged once again, each hair standing straight away from her body. This time she let the shiver wrack through her, watched him watch it happen.

His golden brown eyes missed nothing.

She remembered just how much painstaking attention he paid to the details of a woman's body, how he'd known just how much pressure it took to bring her to that perfect knife edge of pain and pleasure that she now recognized she craved, and had not been able to recapture since. She'd never had a lover to match him, and it was entirely his fault.

When a girl's first lover's a sex demon, it's all down-hill from there.

His eyes locked onto hers, his nostrils flaring. She acknowledged it with a quirk of her lips that said, "So? What are you going to do about it?" She mapped his body with her eyes, taking in his big, Frankenstein work boots, the jeans he'd had on earlier in the day, with the same brass button that had pressed into her stomach when he'd backed her against the wall in the hallway, with the same faithful cupping of the bulge at his crotch. The sweater he wore looked expensive, soft, but slightly too small for his linebacker shoulders. It clearly wasn't his. She moved up to his face—to the firm jaw line, the crooked nose, the fine lines that time and responsibility had creased into the corners of his eyes and mouth. The sharp planes were stubbled by a beard, and his heavy eyebrows were furrowed with annoyance. Other than the borrowed sweater, the only soft thing on the man was his tabby cat hair.

He may have thought the wardrobe helped him blend into the background, but if he did, he was delusional. He was too big, too much a force of nature, and as usual, she couldn't manage to drag her eyes away from the son of a bitch when she should be getting ready for what suddenly felt like the most important show of her life.

She interpreted emotions with her voice, so… she'd interpret. She would throw down the gauntlet in a way he couldn't possibly ignore.

Red, orange, and yellow lights exploded against the huge digital screens covering the back and side walls of the stage as the band opened the show, hitting the first note crisply. The cheering crescendoed as recognition of who was sitting at the drum kit rippled through the crowd. When Scarlett sauntered onto the stage, they positively roared, nearly drowning out the sound of the band. Over his headset, Lukas heard Sasha order, "Levels!"

Before she could finish the sentence, Randy rapped out, "I'm on it."

The sound ratchetted up, a match held to a powder keg. The metal sculpture surrounding the stage seemed to undulate as Scarlett waved to the crowd, called out a quick "hello!" and made her way to the spotlight at center stage. There was no posing, no rock star preening. Instead, she quickly got to business, planting her feet with one foot slightly in front of the other like she was bracing herself against the firestorm that swirled around her. The music thrummed and pulsed, and the crowd swayed and reached for her before she even opened her mouth.

And the first words she crooned wrapped around his dick like a prehensile tongue. Fifteen seconds into the show and he was already locking his knees.

Lukas gritted his teeth as the yearning wave of energy pulsed through him, muting outgoing communications on his headset so everyone on the security channel wasn't treated to his increasingly loud and labored breathing. Blood rushed to his face and he could feel each individual heartbeat pound into his groin. Even the tug of his hand through his own hair felt hypercharged against the nerve endings in his scalp. His stomach sank as he skimmed the set list taped to the wall: "Do Ya Wanna Touch Me." "Maneater." "I Touch Myself." "Too Drunk to Fuck." "Stripped." "Erotic City."

Scarlett had sex on the brain.

Concentrate. The minute he allowed himself to enjoy the forbidden feelings raging through him, the second he actually entertained following up on them, he wasn't doing his job. Thankfully, Jack was doing his. His partner's bright blonde head was in position in the pit at Scarlett's feet. Sasha stood immediately to Jack's right. Nearly a dozen undercover Sebastiani Security workers stood near them in the jostling crowd.

He stared at the proximity of Scarlett's open lips to the microphone she clasped with such authority. The feeble, phallic symbolism was inescapable. *Look away*. But damn, there was no safe place to rest his eyes. How could a man be expected to do his job when everywhere he looked was terrain straight out of his Top 10 fantasies list? Those leather boots climbing her taut thighs. The vulnerable slice of moon-pale skin above the boots. The soft T-shirt fabric clinging to her ass. The leather belt, slung twice around her hips, hanging on for dear life. The scissor-slashed neck of the T-shirt dress, exposing her collarbone and shoulder, threatening to drift south. Her nipples, crested proudly against the fine fabric.

Her champagne mandarin arousal, blooming on his tongue.

Stalking the stage like a huntress, she already had the people in the crowd bouncing in unison, reaching blindly toward her. As she leaned over the lip of the stage, she extended her free arm above the writhing crowd. She was used to the love and adulation of thousands. How could one man ever be enough for her? How could—

Shit, someone had her hand.

"Jack?" he snapped. But before he could clear the curtain, she'd already released herself—which was good, because his freakin' audio was off. Screw Claudette's request; he should have assigned someone else to this job—he wasn't objective enough. It was never a good idea to guard someone you were invol—

They weren't involved except in his imagination. He looked down to his unruly dick, which didn't care about such foolish distinctions. He'd always thought he was a practical man, but in his imagination—in his dreams and fantasies—he and Scarlett were involved all right, involved for hours on end, cycling through every position in the *Kama Sutra*, and some that simply hadn't been documented yet.

"Hey," Garrett said, joining him. "She's whipping 'em up fast tonight. I'm glad you're here. Any sign of Stephen?"

"Negative." Where was the guy? Despite Scarlett's blithe response earlier, he knew just how worried she was. "We're keeping our eyes peeled."

His staff was executing cleanly, doing the job, and despite the volume of blood flowing south, he'd better find a way to do his.

And his responsibility was to watch Scarlett, all night long. As if he could help it.

—∿∿—

Standing under the blazing lights a half hour later, sweat dripping down her backbone, dampening her dress, Scarlett leaned over the lip of the stage again,

barely out of range of the bouncing heads and waving arms, and yowled the angry, sex-charged words of
Orgy's "Blue Monday."

Things were going well. Other than some initial
problems with the levels, quickly resolved, the band was
performing like a well-oiled machine, despite Stephen's
absence. They were tight, everyone at the top of their
game. Indeed, having Dave sitting at the kit had introduced a spark of spontaneity which had been lacking as
they slogged wearily toward the end of the tour.

A hand grasped her ankle through the fine leather of
her boots. Her toes curled and shrank in reaction, but she
stood her ground and kept singing. She'd give Jack and
the security staff about ten seconds to get the guy back,
get him off of her, before stomping on his fingers.

In her peripheral vision, she saw Lukas's eyes narrow. He shifted his weight to the balls of his feet, relaxing slightly as the guy let her go. She was far too attuned
to him. When she performed, she wanted each person
in the audience to feel like she was singing to each of
them individually, but tonight they were being cheated.
Reality was that her words were challenges, being flung
with force at the feet of a single person: the massive
lump of testosterone who hadn't moved out of her line
of sight all night long.

Not that it was working, she thought grumpily as
the band tore into the end of the song. No, he simply
stood there, his expression carved in stone. Every now
and again she caught a whiff of his wild, dark pheromones, and yes, he had a hard-on that wouldn't quit,
but so did every other man in the place. No, he simply
stood sentinel, her plan to make him miserable clearly

a stellar failure. If anything, her plan had boomeranged back on her times three, as the childhood faerie tales had portended. Watching the minute movements of his tongue shifting and swirling in his mouth distracted her to no end. Just looking at him made goose bumps ripple, her nipples tighten, and her sex pulse and clench on... emptiness.

She was empty. She wanted to be filled, and Dave's heavy hand at the drums didn't help. The vibrations pushed at her from the back, and buzzed up her legs from the wooden stage floor. Her body pulsing with each note, she surfed the wave of anger and frustration, nearly head-banging as the band finished out the song. When it ended, she stood in the blinding hot light and acknowledged the cheering and clapping. "Thank you!" she called.

While the applause eddied around her, she looked down at the set list taped to the floor at her feet. If the next three songs didn't chip away at Lukas Sebastiani's marble façade, nothing would.

"Are we having any fun yet?" she asked the crowd, giving the band a chance to swig from bottles and towel off some sweat. "Stephen couldn't be with us tonight, but what a treat to have Dave sit in. Dave Grohl, everybody!" Scarlett indicated Dave with a wave of her hand, and started the clapping herself. Dave acknowledged the applause by lifting his bottle of beer with a toasting gesture and slinging his sweaty hair out of his face.

"Are you ready?" she called out to the crowd, her eyes shooting a challenge at Lukas as Dave tore into the opening tom-toms of Joan Jett's "Do You Wanna Touch Me?" She extended her arms over her head, clapping on the two and four beats. Before long, most of the crowd had joined her. The song banged and throbbed, the band crisp and steady as a metronome behind her, Tansy and Dave laying down the beat like they'd been playing together for years rather than minutes.

Holding Lukas's gaze, she spread her legs, planted them, and swayed her hips back and forth in time to the music. The crowd pulsed in time with her, swaying back and forth like a single organism. She saw Lukas swallow, his nostrils flare, but his eyes didn't leave hers. No. They blazed with heat, with intent. Of what, she didn't know, but a shudder tore through her body nonetheless. She was a hair's breadth away from coming, and he hadn't touched her with anything other than his eyes.

She tore her gaze away from his and strutted back to center stage, focusing on what she could see of the people in the crowd. After the first couple of rows closest to the stage, individual faces blurred. The pheromone level had noticeably spiked, and the crowd surged toward the stage, trying to get closer. Almost before she saw Jack's lips move, a perimeter formed to hold back the crowd. Lukas was ready to step out from behind the curtain. To do… what? Snatch her out from beneath the ravening horde? Rescue her like a damsel in distress?

And then what?

His hands clenched, then released. *Ahhh, finally. The first crack.* She felt his eyes travel her body from head to toe and back again. His tongue moved subtly in his closed mouth.

What did she taste like to him?

Time to raise the stakes. She found a familiar face in the second row. Crooking a grin at Chadden, she reached her hand into the crowd to pull him onstage. She wrapped her arm around his waist and held the microphone up to their mouths. He easily picked up her rhythm, singing the "yeahs" in the call-and-response section of the song.

She knew if she gave Chad an inch he'd take a mile, so... she gave it to him. It wasn't long before his cheerful, talented hand drifted from her waist to her hip, then slipped along her ass. The crowd laughed as she moved his hand, and finally the song ended. Chad being Chad, the vamp turned her "thank you" peck into a silky French kiss. Scarlett sank into his touch—very smooth, very nice—but it wasn't the rough, scrappy kiss she knew would satisfy her.

She backed away from Chadden just as Lukas stepped out from behind the curtain. Chad didn't deserve to get the shit kicked out of him because she wanted to make Lukas react.

As Chad jumped off the stage, Lukas stepped back, but not without glowering at her first. She raised a brow in response. He replied by crossing his arms and widening his stance.

Her gaze drifted south. She'd gotten a reaction, all right.

———⌇⌇⌇———

This was absolute torture. Frank sexual energy crackled in the air, and the place was saturated with pheromones. If he had been alone, there was no doubt in his mind that his dick would be in his hand. It was all he could do to keep his arms crossed at his chest.

To stop himself from throttling her.

Scarlett had been building the vibe all night, stoking

it like a bonfire. He estimated that they were about three-fourths of the way through the show. The crowd no longer even pretended to dance, instead swaying and grinding against each other, a frank group frottage.

Thank the aurora that Jack had taken his meds, because things were getting a little dicey at the front of the stage. Scarlett was standing too close to the edge again. Each time she reached out to grasp the supplicating hands that reached up to her, the crowd surged. Stuffed animals, flowers, thongs, and jocks littered the stage. Hands groped wildly at Scarlett, who was posed at the lip of the stage, one foot planted atop an amp as she blithely sang a song about touching herself.

Jesus.

A couple of meatsticks in the front whipped out their cell phones, hoping to snap an upskirt shot. Anger surged at the thought of some asshole having a picture of whatever Scarlett was—or wasn't—wearing under that skimpy excuse for a dress. How could her band mates focus, watching her luscious ass twitch and shift all night long, night after night?

Scarlett was in her own little world, completely unaware that a good portion of the pit was just waiting for a glimpse of her panties.

The crowd was going wild, and understandably so. Since the start of the show, they'd been lyrically invited to line up for a blow job, asked for a one-night stand because they were perfect strangers, begged to be her pleasure victim, informed that all day long she dreamed about sex. And now, after calling out a hasty apology to the mother she couldn't see, watching from the VIP box, she crooned, "I Touch Myself."

The taste of her humid arousal had deepened to mango. She was turned on, horny, and didn't seem to care who knew it. She'd pulled a strange vamp onstage with her and let him bury his tongue in her mouth.

No, Scarlett had left no doubt whatsoever about what was on her mind. Sasha's statement about Scarlett's right to sleep with a different fan every night haunted him. Would she take that slinky vamp home tonight, use his body to take the edge off? Let him use hers?

A collective groan went through the crowd as Scarlett placed her hand on her inner thigh, stroking the cuff of her boot with a delicate forefinger. Every molecule in Lukas's body went on Red Alert, and his dick was raging against his zipper. He wouldn't be surprised if its teeth were permanently carved into his flesh.

But he couldn't look away.

Chapter 10

FROM HIS POSITION BACK IN THE WINGS, LUKAS watched the sweaty guitarist, Michael, throw his head to the ceiling and make his guitar squeal as he and Scarlett traded verses on "Erotic City." When Scarlett stroked the neck of Michael's guitar with her hand, Lukas knew he wasn't alone imagining that small, soft hand wrapped around his dick.

She swayed with the music, power blazing in her eyes, and her suggestive voice swooped and looped around the room before burrowing into each and every person in the audience.

Scarlett was hiding it well, but she looked ready to drop. The band had been performing for over two hours, and standing backstage he'd gotten a brand new perspective on how hard the band worked. Michael's chest and arms were pumped like he'd spent the night quarrying rocks. The drummer's hair was lank and wet, his teeth gritted, his arms pounding the skins like a jack-hammer. Joe was wilting at his rhythm guitar. Tansy alone seemed unaffected, her feet planted, banging out the bass line with methodical steadiness.

When the final notes faded, howls and shrieks of delight split the air. From the back of the room, the crowd surged toward Scarlett en masse. Jack hollered "Perimeter!" to the Sebastiani Security and Underbelly event staff working the front of the stage. Lukas lunged out from behind the curtain, snatching Scarlett back from her precarious position with an arm around her waist. "I've got you."

Scarlett sagged, wrapping her arm around his waist.

"Scarlett?" he repeated, his voice strangling out of his suddenly tight throat. She didn't mean anything by the embrace, but it didn't stop him nuzzling his cheek against her hair.

Her eyes flew open. Locked with his. "I'm... okay. Thank you."

He released her, going back to his position next to Garrett in the wings. Scarlett walked to the front of the stage and spoke softly into her hand mike. "Hey folks, stop pushing, please."

Something in her voice was like an anesthetic. The crowd settled down.

"Thank you."

A sole voice in the audience called out, "We love you, Scarlett!"

Scarlett smiled and responded, "We love you too." Catcalls and applause followed, and when it finally died down, Scarlett simply stood there, staring into the bright, hot lights. The crowd quieted. Waited.

She stepped back, put her hand mike on its stand, and walked back toward the drums, to where a shiny black guitar stood. Garrett, standing next to him, whipped his head to the set list hanging on the wall. "She's off the grid."

Lukas suspected the phrase meant something entirely different to Garrett than it did to him, because Scarlett was standing right there, swiping her damp hair back into a hasty ponytail using an elastic band on her wrist.

"She doesn't need a guitar for the next song they're supposed to play," Garrett was saying. "I have no idea what's coming next. The band doesn't either. Buckle in."

In the silence, Scarlett picked up a towel from the stack on the drum riser and swiped it across her face, over her neck and exposed shoulders, then had a quick huddle with a roadie. A stool was set center stage, and the mike stand repositioned.

She stepped back into the spotlight carrying her guitar and sat, exhaustion pulsing off her in waves as the crowd hooted and called out requests. Silence. Finally, she strummed out several keening chords that had him swallowing before she sang a word.

Beside him, Garrett relaxed slightly. "'Such Reveries.' Duncan Sheik. We've rehearsed this. But I don't know if Dave—"

Tansy stepped over and mouthed the song title to the drummer just in time for him to join in with a soft tap. Swaying on her stool, Scarlett softly sang a tale of two soul mates on vacation, watching the ocean, riding horses on the beach. A fantasy romantic interlude. But her voice shifted from wistful to tear-stained as the song took a surprise twist: the whole thing was just a reverie, a fantasy. It never happened.

Her regret tasted like dirt on his tongue.

The last notes drifted away. There was a moment of hushed silence before the audience responded with cheers and deafening applause. While they clapped, Scarlett momentarily turned away from the crowd and covered her face with her hand.

"Damn." Tomas Diego reached around him to snag one of Scarlett's water bottles.

Garrett looked at his watch, raised an eyebrow. "Good of you to show up. I was taking bets that Dave would play the encore."

Tomas laughed and twisted the cap off the bottle, tipped his head back, and guzzled. He'd lost his shirt somewhere along the line, and Lukas had a clear view of the tattoos layering most of the man's torso and arms. His cobbled abdomen exclaimed CARNAGE in elaborate gothic letters, but his children's names were etched into his wrists in their own childish handwriting. Nothing seemed to be holding up his baggy, wallet-chained jeans except his porn star dick.

Tomas breathed heavily as he finished drinking. "She's in love."

"What?" Lukas whipped his head to the other man as Garrett passed Tomas a snowy white towel from the stack on the table.

"Thanks." Tomas wiped down his chest and hitched up his sagging pants. "Dude, can't you feel it? Homesick, horny, pissed—and in love." He flashed a grin. "Who's the lucky guy?"

Lukas stood ramrod straight, broadening his upper body in response to the sexual energy pulsing off the other man—energy that somehow managed to be both cheerful and lascivious.

BACK. OFF. The words were on the tip of Lukas's tongue when the taste of ashes barreled down his throat.

He snatched one of Scarlett's airsickness bags off the stack and heaved.

―∾∾―

A blue-tinged spotlight picked up a delicate touch at an

electric piano. Applause surged as the people standing closest to the stage realized a drummer change had occurred in the dim light. The moment was magic, and Tomas milked it for all he was worth.

Dispassionately, Scarlett knew it would film beautifully. But... what was wrong with Lukas?

The silence hung. Raucous applause pulled her attention back to the matter at hand. She met Tomas's eyes and nodded.

She was... home.

Her eyes stung as she lost herself in someone else's lyrics, someone else's song. One more show where she couldn't bring herself to sing even one of the songs that had made the band famous—songs she'd written, emotions she'd purged, in the aftermath of the shattering night she'd spent with Lukas Sebastiani.

When she'd awakened the following morning to find him gone.

Lukas reappeared in the wings at the guitar bridge, a little pinched and pale around the lips but still standing strong. Her stomach fluttered, but she aimed the final sustained high note at him like a sharpshooter's bullet.

Want me. Love me.

She watched it hit, saw his abdomen clench under the clingy sweater. Felt his pheromones bloom in response, felt them shiver into her. Their eyes locked across the distance. The final piano notes faded. The moment hung.

And as the crowd broke its silence and roared, with a blink she raised the microphone to her lips, calling over the applause, "Thank you so much. Thanks for welcoming us home." She gestured to Tomas, who stood and blew her a kiss, stoking the applause higher. The band put down their instruments and joined her at the front of the stage, Dave walking from backstage with a fresh beer in his hand. They all took bow after bow. Michael, Tansy, and Joe finally waved and walked off the stage, leaving Scarlett, Tomas, and Dave. The guys stepped back, and the crowd went wild as Scarlett stepped to the front of the stage to take a final bow. She waved to the crowd to acknowledge the applause, and choked out a "thank you" that no one could hear.

After a quick, final wave, she joined arms with Dave and Tomas, and let them escort her off the stage.

"You okay?" Dave murmured as she sagged between them.

She automatically nodded yes as they reached the backstage area, but her knees positively wobbled as Garrett bundled her into her robe, slinging a towel around her neck like a muffler. Lukas handed her an open bottle of water. "Thank you." Was that her hand? It tingled, and she couldn't really make the fingers work. Her vision blackened around the edges, contracted to a tunnel. Lukas spoke into his headset, directing the security staff to clear the hallway to the dressing rooms.

The bottle dropped to the floor. His arm was around her waist, a manacle supporting her weight, before the water splashed his pants.

"Okay, we're moving," Lukas said, practically carrying her down the hall, Garrett and Jesse trailing in their wake.

Scarlett leaned into Lukas's strong body. Pheromones steamed off of him, dark and luscious.

"Holding on?" he asked.

Her eyes were nearly closed, but she nodded in response to his soft question, stroking her cheek against his cashmere sweater.

A low groan rumbled in his chest.

When they reached Scarlett's dressing room, Lukas didn't let go. "Clear it," he ordered the tough-looking guard standing at the door. The man disappeared into the room. Lukas lowered his head to her ear. "We need to talk."

She nearly shuddered at his tone, half-promise, half-threat. *Finally.* "When?" Neither of them was anywhere near done working.

"After the party tonight?"

She nodded. She'd be absolutely exhausted, but she might never get this chance again.

The guard returned. "Clear."

Lukas squeezed her hand before passing her to Jesse. "We've got your door." With one glance back, he left the room, closing the door with a snap.

"I don't have time for a bath, do I," Scarlett confirmed with Garrett.

"Take all the time you need."

"Let's make it a shower tonight, Jesse," she said. She didn't want to keep people waiting any longer than necessary. There were always people waiting.

But the sooner she finished with work, the sooner she could talk with Lukas.

Chapter 11

WHERE THE HELL HAD ALL THESE PEOPLE COME FROM? "Chico?" Lukas snapped into his headset. The scrappy werewolf who'd just cleared Scarlett's dressing room had vanished into thin air, and Lukas needed him at Scarlett's dressing room door. Someone had died, Scarlett was about to drop, and he was stuck playing traffic cop to tipsy hipsters. "Passes. Now," Lukas demanded from each member of the giggling, rowdy group who swarmed the hallway.

"Right behind you," Chico said. The Sebastiani Security lieutenant's shaved head gleamed like an eight ball, and pea-sized diamonds blazed in both ears. The ornamentation made him more menacing rather than less, because Chico only broke out the bling when he didn't care if you saw him coming.

Lukas jerked his head at the crowd. "Get these people out of here."

Chico stepped toward the tipsy group and growled deep in his throat. They hurriedly dispersed, leaving behind a copper-tinged cloud of fear.

"Theatrical, but effective. Why is this hallway such a sieve?"

"Fight broke out at the entrance. Jack needed backup. Do you plan to stay at the door?" Chico indicated Scarlett's dressing room door with a jerk of his head. "If so, I'll take the T in the hallway to keep this area clear."

His silent mini-comp mocked him. The comm channel was quiet. Whatever had caused the ashes to barrel down his throat like a pyroclastic floe hadn't popped yet. "Sure, I've got it," he replied. There was nothing he could do until he got some actionable information.

As Chico disappeared around the corner, Lukas reached to his right front pocket for the small container of breath mints, popping one in his mouth as he paced in front of the closed dressing room door. Humidity leaked from the crack under the door. Scarlett must be taking a shower.

Ah, shit. The woman scrambled his brain. He should already have initiated a check-in of principals. "Jack."

Jack turned on his outgoing audio, but Lukas could barely hear him with all the crowd noise at the entrance. A high-pitched voice screeched, "Is that your hand on my ass?"

"Hold on a sec," Jack shouted. The noise lessened as he walked to a quieter area. "Ah, silence. What's up?"

"Everything okay down there?"

"Fight's over, crowd's clearing. We're pouring people into taxis. What do you have?"

"We need an immediate visual verification on all principals. Can you—"

"Got it," Jack replied. His voice tensed, but he didn't waste time asking questions. "You've got Scarlett?"

"Confirmed."

"Sasha's right here. I'll start at the VIP box and check in shortly."

Lukas swallowed heavily, the essence of ashes still stinging the back of his throat. It had felt—tasted—close.

Turning off his outgoing audio—his crew didn't need

to hear him mutter and swear while he paced—he pulled his mini-comp and checked the Hot Sheet. He wanted to call Gideon Lupinsky, but he had absolutely nothing to tell him yet. All he could do was wait for Jack to check in, damn it—and imagine Scarlett, naked and wet, behind that locked door.

"Hey, dude, feeling any better?" Tomas Diego asked Lukas as he approached from the band's dressing room next door. He dragged a half-dozen people in his wake.

Lukas shoved his mini-comp into his pants pocket. "Passes." He quickly but carefully examined the laminated passes hanging off people's necks, sending everyone except Diego and Tia Quinn on their way.

"Well, look who's here. Lukas Sebastiani," drawled the curvy vampire who possessed a coveted All Access pass. Tia Quinn, an award-winning investigative journalist who'd gotten her start writing reviews for *Rolling Stone*, was here to interview Scarlett. Her pass authorized her to roam anywhere in the venue except Scarlett's dressing room and the VIP box.

Earlier, Lukas had overheard Garrett canceling their interview. Why was she still here? "Ma'am, why don't you go upstairs to the after party, enjoy a drink? Garrett will reschedule your interview before you leave tonight."

She raised her eyebrow slightly, a tiny fang peeking over her purple-glossed lips. "Do I look like a ma'am to you?"

Lukas took in the precision-cut blond hair, the knockout body, the clinging black pants topped by a tiny T-shirt and a battered leather jacket. "No, ma—no, Ms. Quinn," he finished carefully. "But we need to clear this area."

"Okay," she responded agreeably. But instead of walking away, she planted herself on the eggplant-colored leather couch in the alcove directly across from Scarlett's dressing room, her expression saying "not specific enough, doofus." "I'll just wait until she gets out of the shower and say a quick 'hi' before going upstairs."

"Ms. Quinn—"

Tia hitched a thumb at the closed dressing room door, her purple nails filed to lethal points. "That set list was a huge 'fuck you'—or was it a 'fuck me?'—to someone. Whoo-ee." She fanned her face with her hand. "My panties are still steaming. Did she and Duncan break up? Is he here?"

Lukas stood silently in front of Scarlett's door, not saying a word.

"All I know is, if I were incubus, I would have been down for the count—or least had my tongue jammed down somebody's throat half the night. But here you are, standing strong and tall. How is that?" Her eyes narrowed. "*Why* is that? Why is Lukas Sebastiani, of all people, guarding Scarlett Fontaine's dressing room door?"

Why couldn't she be a random entertainment stringer instead of an investigative journalist? "Ms. Quinn—"

"Tia! Dude! What's it been, five years? Seven?" Tomas chose that moment to drag the journalist into a bear hug, whether she wanted to be dragged there or not. Tia looked momentarily annoyed before returning the embrace.

Lukas almost missed Tomas's conspiratorial wink.

"Let me buy you a drink, catch up," he suggested to Tia.

"On the house," Lukas added. Hell, they could drink the place dry if it kept Tia Quinn from asking questions he couldn't answer.

"Thank you," she replied, shooting Lukas a look that clearly said, "Don't think for a minute that I'm dropping this." "I didn't expect to see you playing tonight," she said to Tomas. "Where the hell is Stephen?"

Your guess is as good as mine, lady, Lukas thought grimly. The man had been missing for over four hours. Even for an incubus, it was a marathon session worthy of a Viagra endorsement.

"Ms. Quinn? Tomas? I think the after party is getting started upstairs," Lukas said. "Why don't you go on up? We really need to clear this area."

"And you haven't told me why yet."

His only response was a bland stare.

"Okay, okay. No need to break out the cuffs." She looked his big body up and down, and raised a brow. "Unless you want to? No? Too bad." With a final look at Scarlett's dressing room door, she allowed Tomas to lead her down the hall.

Leaving him free to check in on Scarlett. Dripping wet, singing in the shower not twenty feet away.

It took two groaning tries for Stephen to lift his head off the floor. Around him, speakers popped. He smelled hot wires and melted plastic, and his own semen. The computer monitor nearest him displayed white letters and numbers across a cheerful blue background, and the other monitor had winked out completely.

What the hell happened?

He couldn't hear music pulsing from the floors below any longer; the show must be over. Damn, how long had he been out? They really had to get downstairs. Or upstairs, to the after party. Where he would probably be fired. "Annika. Babe." He nudged Annika's leg, setting it swinging. Her French-manicured toenails glowed in the dim light. "The show's over. We're going to have some serious explaining to do. I'll be lucky if I…"

No response. Had she actually fallen asleep with those knobs digging into her back? "Annika." Again, no answer. His heart beat faster.

Please be sleeping. Please be sleeping.

He pushed himself up, staggering to a stand between her limp legs. She lay slack and unmoving on the soundboard, her mouth stretched open in a soundless "O," staring at him with dry green eyes—expressionless, but accusing him nonetheless.

His heart beat a fast tattoo.

Shards of broken light bulbs glittered like rhinestones on her face and body, and he gently brushed them away from her cheekbones with his thumbs. There was no recoil, no tinkling giggle. Whatever universal energy had made her uniquely Annika was unmistakably gone.

The enormity of the situation, of what he'd done, hit him like a freight train. Pulling up his pants with a yank, he sank onto the couch to think. The speakers snapped, crackled, and popped accusingly.

I need one hell of an alibi. He was very stupidly—and very publicly—not at work tonight. His text message asking her to meet him in the recording studio was on her PDA. His fingerprints were all over the studio, and his DNA all over her body.

He'd killed the Siren Second. He'd killed Scarlett's sister.

His mind raced, erasing a few lines and re-sketching reality to align with the aspects of the story he couldn't change: he'd texted Annika. They'd hooked up. While they were in the act, someone... knocked on the door. Thinking it was Garrett, coming to drag him back downstairs for work, he'd opened it. A man—two men? Yeah, two men—had pushed into the room, attacked him. Knocked him out. He had no idea how long he'd lain there, unconscious—or what had happened while he was out.

But when he woke up? Oh my god. Look at what they'd done to poor Annika.

He nodded slowly, refining the picture, building and layering the story with increasing confidence. Annika had told him earlier that there were no security cameras on this floor. It wasn't perfect, not at all, but... scary how easily it could work. He looked at the room through the eyes of what he and Annika had consensually done, and what had happened to her after—while—he'd fugued out. The large strokes of the scenario were there.

Those damned light bulbs worried him. The same thing had happened when he was with Andi Woolf at Subterranean, and he couldn't afford to have the investigators draw any more parallels between the two crimes than absolutely necessary. Even if he swept up all the glass shards—even if he discovered a way to get rid of them—there was nothing he could do to replace them in the light fixtures themselves. The men must have smashed them after he blacked out. No—after they *knocked* him out. Yeah. They'd gone nuts, smashed the place up. Why? He had no idea.

He was a victim here too.

Yeah, he could sell it.

Stephen's gaze flitted around the studio. Ah. There. Now they were talking. A golf club leaned in the corner by the coffee station. Stephen wrapped the tail of his shirt around the handle. Grasping the club solidly in his hands, he bashed at the computers. Brought the club down hard against the soundboard, on both sides of Annika's body. Her weight shifted a little with the second blow, but her lashed hands kept her from slipping off the soundboard's tilted surface. He smashed the club against the popping speakers, and at the framed art on the walls for good measure. Glass shattered. The head of the putter dug a dozen divots into the drywall. He turned in circles, knocking over mike stands, drums, chairs, music stands, and guitars. He kicked a few amps over, and for the finale, swept the club through the chunky mugs and carafes near the coffee pot, knocking it all to the floor. Dragging a straight-backed chair underneath the one surviving light bulb, he smashed it.

Breath whooshed in and out of his burning lungs as he admired his handiwork. He stared at Annika for long, long seconds, until he heard muffled footsteps and laughter from the nearby stairwell. The after party hosted by Elliott Sebastiani and Claudette Fontaine at the president's penthouse apartment had probably started. Guests using the stairs would pass within ten feet of the studio door. Frankly, he was surprised some incubus or succubus hadn't already been drawn to the floor and discovered them.

He couldn't put it off any longer.

After one final bittersweet glance at Annika, he walked over to the maple coffee table. Eyed the sharp corners.

He threw himself down. There was a flash of white-hot pain, and then… nothing.

———ᴡᴡ———

"Are you sure you don't mind?"

"Go ahead, I'll be right here," Lukas assured Jesse. Apparently Scarlett's favorite body lotion was nestled away in one of the unpacked suitcases upstairs, and Jesse wanted her to have it when she was done bathing. "She's in the shower." *With water coursing over her naked body.* "She won't even know you're gone."

"Okay. Be right back."

After Jesse left, Lukas turned off his outgoing audio and slipped into Scarlett's dressing room. The shower was running full blast, and Scarlett's whipsaw emotions misted the air. Lukas inhaled deeply, her essence washing away the ashy aftertaste lingering in his mouth.

He moved like a sleepwalker toward the brightly lit bathroom. When he reached the door, he didn't bother to hide. He just stood there and watched as she sat in an exhausted huddle on the floor of the shower, her head tipped backward to loll against the wall. The stall's chest-high, glass block wall turned her silhouette into wavy undulations, but he could see her hand move gently between her thighs. Her pleasure shivered into him and back out again, and a breathy groan escaped.

Her hand stopped as she sensed his presence. She slowly rose from the floor to face him, meeting his gaze through the billowing steam, her body hidden by the glass block from the chest down. Her luscious mandarin essence bathed his taste buds. He swirled his tongue to gather as much as he possibly could.

A vicarious taste wasn't nearly enough.

He moved closer—one step, two, three—until his face was so close to hers, he could feel her every breath. A fine spray of water splashed his face, hair, and sweater, but he didn't care.

They stared at each other. Finally, she whispered, "Kiss me. Please."

He didn't have the strength to deny them both. He'd be gentle if it killed him.

He'd barely dipped his head when she grabbed his hair and yanked, crashing their lips together. Gentleness? Scarlett clearly had other plans. Her soft, wet tongue delved hungrily into the cavern of his mouth.

Her taste. He'd never forgotten it, and god knew he'd tried. Not trusting himself to touch her with his hands, he clenched his fists against his thighs, drinking her like ambrosia, glorying in the gasps and moans he produced using only his mouth. If only he could—

"Lukas, come in." Jack's voice crackled through his earpiece.

It nearly killed him to back away from her clinging lips. "It's Jack," he murmured, finally stepping back. "I'm sorry, I have to take this."

He turned his outgoing audio back on. "Yeah, Jack. I'm here." He gulped as Scarlett turned off the water, squeezed her hair, and casually stepped out of the shower. Rivulets of water flowed over her pale body, over her champagne goblet breasts—

"Is Scarlett secure?"

"Yeah."

Tense silence. "Are you absolutely certain? Please verify."

"Confirmed, I have a current visual." And what a visual it was. Scarlett didn't seem to be in any hurry to grab a towel. "What's up?"

"Code Red, fourth floor recording studio. It's… Annika's…" Jack's voice faded out, but Lukas tasted aching grief.

"What? Repeat last message."

"Annika's dead, and we found Stephen. He's seriously injured."

Scarlett was supposed to be the target, not her sister. He took a shaky breath before responding. "Okay. Um, okay. I'll secure Scarlett and get up there as fast as I can. Call Gideon."

"Already have. He's on his way. Get… up here. Hurry."

Scarlett wrapped her arms over her towel-covered breasts. "What is it? What's wrong?"

Failure clawed. *I can't tell her. I… can't.* "I have to go." He saw Scarlett's purple bathrobe hanging on a hook on the back of the bathroom door and bundled her into it before speaking into his headset again. "Garrett, Jesse, Chico. Scarlett's dressing room, please."

When she put her hand on his forearm, it was all he could do not to flinch away. "Lukas. What's wrong?"

He opened his mouth to respond, to say something. Anything. But words were beyond useless.

Garrett and Jesse hurried in.

"Someone, tell me what's wrong," Scarlett repeated. Lukas nearly choked on her rising hysteria.

Garrett and Jesse each took an arm, sitting down

with Scarlett on the couch. As they spoke softly and intently, Lukas headed for the door. Before he could make his escape, Scarlett's polyharmonic wail slammed into his back.

He broke into a run.

Chapter 12

HOURS LATER, LUKAS SAT ALONE IN SASHA'S CHEERFUL kitchen. Gideon had just left for the hospital, and Sasha and Jack had gone downstairs to verify that Underbelly was locked up tight, leaving him with only the kitschy black cat clock for company. Its black tail twitched off the seconds with annoying consistency.

"Damn." Shoving to his feet, he washed the mugs and coffee pot, and put away the snacks. After wiping the table and counter tops with a Holstein-spotted dishrag, he walked like a zombie to Scarlett's room.

Even asleep, her grief sliced him like a thousand tiny razor blades.

He opened the bedroom door. Antonia slept sprawled across the foot of Scarlett's decadent bed, and Calamity sat sentinel, curled into the crook of Scarlett's bent knees, his head up and alert. Scooping up his gangly sister, Lukas carried her into the hallway, past Annika's police-sealed bedroom door to Sasha's room at the end of the hall. In her smudged makeup and Hello Kitty socks, Antonia looked more like his little sister again—but if tonight had taught him anything, it was that his little sister wasn't so little anymore. Nope, she'd been steady as a rock.

Maybe she was ready to take her place in the so-called family business after all.

Scarlett whimpered, the chasm of her grief yawning endless and dark. He quickly bundled Antonia under

Sasha's blankets fully clothed, kissed her forehead, and went back to Scarlett.

To do what? What the hell am I doing?

Scarlett whimpered again, reaching out with her hand. When he clasped it in his own, she settled nearly immediately.

The unoccupied side of the king-sized bed, with its soft mound of pillows, beckoned. *Ten minutes. Just long enough to make sure she stays asleep.*

It was the least he could do.

———

As Scarlett emerged from sleep, her first sensation was of heat radiating into her from behind. She snuggled back, against a man who had his big arm wrapped securely around her, his hand draped over her heart.

She descended back into the twilight world of textures: the delicate scrape of chest hair, the delicious weight of his arm, the scratch of denim against her ass. If Lukas Sebastiani was back in her bed, why on earth was he still wearing pants?

She tensed as her butt shifted against an impressive morning erection. This was no memory, no fevered dream. Why was Lukas in her bed?

Her breath caught. *Annika.* It hadn't been a nightmare after all.

Behind her, Lukas took a deep, shuddering breath, and then drew her against him, so gently that her chest hurt.

And she let the tears come.

She had no idea how long she cried, or why she stopped. Why her grief shifted to urgency, why her lips blindly sought his, or why his latched on to hers. But the sun was streaming into the room, bright and clean. His bed-rumpled body pumped pheromones, and his tongue delved into the dark corners of her mouth like she was a decadent dessert and he was licking the bowl.

He felt so solid, so warm and alive.

His taste. Dark, damp, elemental as the sea. She shifted on top of him, prompting a groan from them both. She separated their lips momentarily and dragged the T-shirt Sasha had bundled her into over her head, throwing it… somewhere, anywhere, as long as it was off. She brought her torso back down to his, stroking her breasts lightly against his chest hair.

The sight of his bare chest was no mystery to her. Their families had spent a lot of time together over the years, particularly at the Sebastiani lake cabin, where everyone lived in swimsuits in the summer. In the fall, the appearance of a football would result in a game of Shirts and Skins, where she could covertly ogle Sasha's unattainable older brother. But to touch him? To run her hands over him, slowly, and in broad daylight? Luxury. The one time they'd slept together, she'd had her hands all over his body, to be sure—but not for long, and because the room had been so dark, she hadn't seen much.

She pushed herself up to a sitting position and swiped her hair out of her face, his abs lurching momentarily as her weight shifted over his crotch. The daylight streaming into the room lit up his masculine terrain. His musculature seemed hewn of granite, a mountain range for her to explore. She dragged her hands over his shoulders, the slabs of his pecs, his cobbled abs. *No wonder no one else had ever measured up*. This was the body of a man in his prime, an incubus of immense power. Top of the food chain.

And she'd had him—once—before he'd simply walked away.

She wanted to have him again. Now. From her position atop the ridge at his crotch, he certainly seemed up for it. His body was, anyway. Who knew about his mind?

As he watched, waited, she threaded her fingers into the hair that draped across her girly lilac pillowcase, all tawny and wild, and lowered her head to his. He nibbled at the vulnerable curve where her neck met her shoulder, his devastating tongue tracing the tendons in her neck, up to where they connected into a bundle of sensitive nerves behind her ear. He painted her with damp lips, his hot breath puffing gently against the shell of her ear.

Not enough.

He finally cupped her breasts in his big hands, worried their tips with his rough fingers. Pushing her mound against whatever piece of his body she could connect with, she dragged one of his hands down her body, until it rested between her legs. His fingers threaded through her soft pubic hair, streaked over her inner lips, separating her petals. The slight tug and pull of her delicate skin between his diabolical fingers, the way he teased her opening but didn't quite breach it, was absolutely maddening. He touched her everywhere except where she ached to be touched.

"Lukas."

At her shaky plea, he finally moved—lifting her and setting her down right over his mouth.

She shattered at the first touch of his tongue. He inhaled madly, filling his lungs with her energy, feeding from her

while he incinerated her with pleasure. Scarlett didn't
know how much time had passed when he finally shifted
her away from his glistening mouth so she sat poised on
top of his upper chest, her legs were spread wide, her quivering flesh open to his gaze. She couldn't bring herself to
care—especially when she caught him licking her wetness
from his lips like a cat at a bowl of cream.

His breath was slowing, returning to normal.

Can't have that.

His eyes flew open as she dragged her wet mound
down his torso, marking him with her essence. Slipping
off of his body, she traced each lump and bump of his
muscled abdomen with her tongue. The flushed head of
his penis poked up from under the gaping waistband of
his jeans. As she gave it a tiny lick, his midnight flavor
burst through her head, a dark, wicked memory.

Lukas groaned.

She finished unzipping his pants slowly, tooth by
tooth, dragging her mouth down each inch of him as it
was revealed, and finally he was exposed to her view.
To her touch, her taste.

"Oh," she breathed. He was beautiful. She'd felt him
inside her once before, but their joining had been fast
and frantic—and she'd been so inexperienced that she
hadn't properly appreciated the bounty before her.

Pleasure buzzed in her head. How in the world had
she survived without this? Without him? His skin was
so soft, silk over steel. Cradling his heavy weight in
both hands, she felt him tense and hold his breath as
she traced the underside of his cock with her tongue.
When she reached the plum-like head, his hips shifted
minutely—but toward her mouth, not away from it.

Got ya.

She lapped at him, over and over again, for endless minutes, learning his textures and tastes with long strokes of her hands and tongue, noting which touches made him writhe, and which made him relax. When she added the slightest purring vibration from her vocal cords, his hips jerked, pheromones blooming ever more dark and damp.

Lifting her head away from the drugging scent, she shook it to clear away the woozy buzzing. The movement swept her hair over his violently engorged cock. He moaned and grabbed her head.

Bzzzzzz. Bzzzzzzzzzzzzzzz.

Lukas glared at the ceiling in exasperation before reaching for the mini-comp pulsing and chattering on her bedside table. "It's Gideon," he said softly.

Gideon Lupinsky. *Annika.*

It all came crashing back.

She shrank away from his hand and stumbled off the bed. His cock was wet from her mouth.

"Scarlett?"

Whirling away, she ran to her bathroom, closing the door and locking it behind her.

Chapter 13

FINALLY.

After days of unnatural silence, of a poise so flash-frozen that it seemed she would shatter if anyone so much as touched her, Scarlett was finally crying again.

Annika's funeral service at Fontaine House, the family's ancestral home located on the rugged cliffs of northwestern Ireland near Donegal Bay, was finally drawing to a close, and when Lukas rose from his front row seat, he felt like he'd popped up his head while under sniper fire. All eyes on them, he nudged Scarlett up out of her chair, escorting her to where his father and Claudette stood in the aisle waiting for them.

He knew speculation was running rampant: Was he at her side as a family friend? A lover? Her bodyguard?

All three theories contained at least a grain of truth.

Seated in the row behind him, Rafe, Sasha, and Antonia would host the after-funeral reception until he, his father, Scarlett, and Claudette returned from performing the ceremony's final steps: casting Annika's ashes into the ocean. In the front row on the other side of the aisle, Wyland discreetly supported Valerian, visibly sagging under the weight of his resplendent ceremonial robes. Underworld Council members and their families filled the next rows of reserved seats. Behind them sat Scarlett's band mates and their families, except for Stephen, who remained hospitalized back in

Minneapolis. After that, rows and rows of friends, both
Annika's and Scarlett's, filled the ballroom. Most of
them had also attended Scarlett's homecoming show,
which had simplified the funeral's security arrangements somewhat; most of their background checks had
already been performed.

Lukas refused to think about the long hours he
and Jack had spent on pre-funeral logistics. While he
couldn't begrudge Annika the service, the arrangements
had taken even more time away from the hunt for her
killer, who was still at large. As he escorted Scarlett, he
felt every accusing eye.

When the small group reached the back of Fontaine
House's ballroom, the massive terrace doors were
thrown open to the elements. The Atlantic Ocean
crashed and pounded into the nearby cliffs, and yes, the
sky was the color of clay. In choosing Sting's "The Wild
Wild Sea" as the final song to be played at her funeral,
it seemed as if Annika had somehow choreographed the
weather to the lyrics.

Annika had planned her funeral in as much exacting
detail as many young women planned their weddings,
and listening to Wyland read her will at the Underworld
Council meeting called within twenty-four hours of
her death had been brutal. Though Annika had taken
a maddening number of liberties with the document's
required contents, her funeral preferences had been documented to the last explicit detail, requiring Claudette
and Scarlett to make very few decisions—certainly her
intention. She'd designated the location of the service,
the decorating scheme, the music to be played at both
the ceremony and the reception... layers and layers of

details, right down to the brand of tequila she wanted poured into shot glasses for the final toast.

Who could have predicted that the Council's newest and youngest member would be the first one to die? Lukas swallowed around the lump in his throat. With his lack of attention, he'd not only cost Scarlett her sister, but probably her career. Now that Annika was dead, Scarlett was the new Siren Second—a job she had no interest in performing.

Footsteps tapped against wood, a dozen tiny hammers, as the siren choir and the kind-faced, white-robed woman who'd performed Annika's service with Valerian filed past them and started walking down the dozens of twisting, weathered stairs leading from Fontaine House's second floor ballroom terrace to ground level. Lukas grabbed Scarlett's arm as she tottered toward the steps in a pair of fuchsia high-heeled boots which were completely unsuited for the weather or the rough terrain.

"You're going to break your neck," he muttered softly.

Her only response was a small pulse of pain-laced annoyance—not much, but it was more emotion than she'd directed toward him in a week. She allowed him to support her as she walked down the slippery steps, and didn't pull away as they made their way across the damp wildflower lawn to the winding dirt path, worn smooth by centuries of footsteps, which led from Fontaine House to the oceanside cliffs where the last part of the ceremony would be performed.

The back of Lukas's neck itched. Seconds later, when they reached the cliffs, he saw light glinting off long-range camera lenses nestled in the rocks just beyond the Fontaine estate's property line. *Fucking paparazzi*. Did

Scarlett even notice them? Or was she so used to being watched that they simply weren't on her radar? Lukas took Scarlett's chilly hand and shifted them so their backs were to the photographers. They might be on the legal side of the property line, but damned if he'd make their job any easier.

And where were Scarlett's gloves? Christ, it wasn't fifty degrees out, and the blowing wind, saturated with moisture, cut to the bone. He didn't remove his hand, hoping some of his body heat would transfer to her— and because, he admitted to himself, he wanted to hold it. To feel some sort of connection, because if the time they'd spent together in Scarlett's bedroom had burned into her psyche the way it had into his, it certainly wasn't showing. Nope, since Annika's death, Scarlett had shut down, had gone through the motions like an automaton, even as she'd signed the document formalizing her as her sister's successor.

If he'd been concerned about her health at their first meeting back from tour, he was even more concerned now. To his discerning eye, she looked even thinner, if that was possible, and she moved slowly, like a sleep-walking wraith. According to Sasha, Scarlett had spent the days between the Council meeting where Annika's will had been read and the flight to Ireland closeted in her bedroom, uninterested in food, in the cards and flowers that streamed to the penthouse, or even in her beloved Crackhouse Blend. Sasha bullied her into eating a few bites here and there, but she accepted comfort only from that feral black cat, who hissed and bared his fangs at anyone who made the mistake of knocking on her bedroom door.

Her silence had continued during the excruciating transatlantic flight that brought them to Ireland, her energy ebbing at such a low level that she barely registered.

A burst of wind buffeted the small group as they assembled on the edge of the rugged cliff. Lukas instinctively leaned in to shelter Scarlett with his larger body. Out of the corner of his eye, he noticed his father doing the same thing for Claudette as she stood in her family's ancestral worship area like a poised ivory statue, her face locked in a rictus of control. In this thin, milky light, her hair looked more gray than red, and her white mourning trench coat whipped around her legs. She cradled a fuchsia suede bag about the size and weight of a sack of sugar in both arms.

Her daughter's ashes.

Compared to her mother, Scarlett blazed with defiant color. She'd made no attempt to harness her hair, and it billowed behind her like a red sheet on a clothesline. Her calf-length wool coat was bright turquoise, her pink boots glowed, and her face was blotchy with tears.

Grief and sadness poured out of her like blood from a wound. Lukas clenched his jaw and held on to her hand as the siren choir gathered around them in a loose semicircle.

"Let us sing our sister home," the Celebrant intoned. She turned her substantial body to the pounding sea and extended her arms to the sky and waves, singing the first haunting notes.

He thought he was prepared. He really did. But when the other women joined in... *Jesus*. Dissonant harmonies shrilled up and down his backbone, and he grasped Scarlett's waist more tightly—whether to support her or to be supported, he didn't really know. Scarlett was as much moaning as singing, her incomparable voice rising above the others as she extended her arms to the sea and tipped her head up to the sky. The collective mourning energy swirled above them like a whirlwind as the sirens sang the Fontaine family lineage, imploring the wind and the waves to accompany the brave siren Annika to her final resting place. Annika, daughter of Claudette, daughter of Signe, daughter of Siobhan, daughter of Siann, of Sorcha, of Catraoine. Of Sinead, Maire, Ceile, and Fiona. On and on, back through the generations, the sirens recited the names the unbroken Fontaine matrilineal line back to Canola, Goddess of the Harp.

It was up to Scarlett to ensure continuity of the Fontaine line.

On and on the singing went, the sirens acknowledging sisters lost to history, sisters who'd protected their families and ensured their species' survival by luring marauders' ships into the cliffs with no weapon but their voices. Lukas surreptitiously popped an antacid and tried to focus on the waves pounding against the cliffs, the swooping gulls—the fall sumac blazing between the rocks, where the paparazzi crouched like fucking jackals. Something, anything, to distract himself from the taste of Scarlett's saltwater mourning mixing with her mandarin essence.

Or how his seed boiled at the thought of fathering Scarlett's child.

Finally, the plaintive song came to a close, and the Celebrant stepped back, gesturing to the churning water.

"I… can't do this," Scarlett whispered brokenly, the first words she'd spoken to him in nearly a week.

Lukas bracketed her chilly face in his warm hands, trying to pour whatever strength he could into her. "You can."

She clutched his wrists with her hands for a long moment, her eyes locked on to his. Finally, she stepped away from the shelter of his body and joined her mother at the edge of the cliff. And as the other sirens chanted, "All that was… all that is… all that shall be," they reached into the bag with their bare hands, casting Annika's ashes to the wild, wild sea.

——∿∿——

Stephen's head throbbed. The scent of alcohol wipes, dinner trays, and overcooked coffee stung his nose as he slowly walked past the patients' solarium and the empty nurses' desk on his way back to his hospital room. Televisions murmured out of almost every room—talk about a captive audience—and far too many were tuned to a so-called journalist with Miss America hair who breathlessly reported the Latest! Breaking! News! on the tragedies which had befallen singer Scarlett Fontaine: the death of her sister, and the senseless attack on her drummer, who "at this moment was lying near death" in an unspecified hospital. "We mourn with you, Scarlett," the anchorwoman emoted like the lead in a bad community theatre production. When she queued up footage of a small group standing on the cliffs—clearly filmed from a helicopter buzzing the site—to the tune of "Wind Beneath My Wings"—Stephen just about puked.

Yeah, he felt like shit, but at no point had he been "lying near death." And there was absolutely no news, breaking or otherwise. If there was one thing he'd learned in the week he'd been hospitalized, it was that when Lukas Sebastiani established a communications blackout, he created a black fucking hole.

He was being well-protected, perhaps too much so. His fan mail was screened, all deliveries to the hospital were searched, and Garrett had told him that packages were piling up at the office. He didn't have computer access, and every visitor on his approved visitor list was scanned head to toe by bodyguards posted at his door.

Keep walking. He did laps around the hospital several times a day, skulking around the ER, the NICU, the morgue, tailgating enough secondhand energy to keep the beast from snapping its teeth. Between the blast of mojo that Annika had hit him with as she died, and the pain and death energy that saturated the hospital itself, his tank was still half-full.

His sleep cycle was all screwed up. Anyone who thought people could actually get some rest in a hospital was nuts, and needless to say, after a year on the road, the hospital routine didn't exactly coincide with his body clock. He really should have asked for a bed on the vamp floor. But he hadn't, so it was blood pressure and temperature checks at six in the morning and breakfast an hour later, whether he was hungry or not. Shower, shave, and then up and at 'em with both physical and occupational therapy, which he'd tried to charm his way out of with absolutely no luck. Surprisingly, he enjoyed the time he spent making woven plastic key chains with three chattering kids. The children didn't know who he was, and they didn't ask questions he didn't want to answer. Instead, they seemed fascinated by his hair.

Maybe Garrett could raffle the key chains off for charity, or give them to fans.

He weaved on his feet. "Whoa," he muttered, slapping a hand against a doorjamb for support. "Sorry, ma'am," he called to the elderly woman lying in her hospital bed.

She lifted her nut-brown head up from her creased pillow, peering at him with rheumy eyes behind thick, thick glasses. Her TV was tuned to the same channel as everyone else, except now the vapid journalist yammered about the supposed Brad-Angie-Jen love triangle.

"You look like that drummer," she said, fingers plucking at her colorful quilt.

"Nah. Do I look like I'm lying near death?" Phlegmy coughs rattled her chest as she laughed. "Are you okay?" he asked, stepping into her room to push the nurse call button. *Damn your flippant tongue.* She was the one lying near death. It wouldn't happen this minute, and probably not today, but the process was well under way.

When he reached her bed, her hand latched on to his with unexpected strength. "Don't bother, son," she rasped. She accepted the water he handed her from the table by her bedside, sipping from the straw. When she finished, she laid her Brillo-haired head back against the pillow. Her voice was weak, but her dark brown eyes snapped with annoyance. "Thank you. Dying's a tiresome business, boy—don't let anyone tell you any different." She patted an empty space on the quilt. "Sit down before you fall down."

He sat before he was conscious of doing so. There was more than enough room on the bed. The old woman's gnarled body was so wasted away that it barely created a bump under the covers, but her wrinkled lips were painted a bright, defiant red. Despite her failing body, a formidable brain clicked behind her eyes. Somehow he felt stripped naked before her, but instead of wanting to leave, he leaned closer.

"Yeah, you look a little shaky to me, but you're nowhere near ready to journey beyond The Pale." She nodded firmly, confident of her diagnosis. "What happened to your head, dear heart?"

His throat slammed shut at the endearment. "I…" Stephen swallowed heavily. How was he supposed to answer this majestic woman's question? "I threw myself against a table"? "I killed a woman while we were having sex, and I'm afraid I'll do it again"? Instead of answering, he simply dropped his head, rubbing his aching sternum with his knuckles.

"It's okay," she said softly.

"No. It's not," he replied before he could stop himself.

She extended her wasted hand. He took it, clasped it in both of his. Somehow, he knew he could tell her anything, and she wouldn't be shocked.

He was actually opening his mouth to do so when a curvy blond nurse wearing bright purple scrubs poked her head in the room. "There you are, Stephen," she chirped as she came into the room. "I see you've met Madame Bouchet. She's one of our star patients."

Madame Bouchet eyed her balefully. "That statement makes absolutely no sense. I'm dying, girl, and we all know it." To Stephen, she added, "Don't get old. People talk to you like you don't have a brain in your head."

"Sorry, Madame," the nurse said cheerfully as she straightened the riotously colored quilt. "Stephen's been on his feet a long time today, and he really needs to get back to bed."

Stephen looked down at their still-joined hands. He didn't want to let go. When he finally released her, the oddest sense of loss fluttered through him.

"You come back and see me anytime, boy, you hear?" Madame Bouchet said softly.

Stephen nodded, smiled, then allowed the nurse to steady him as they left Madame's room. Together they walked the short distance down the hall to his own.

"You're really shaky," Peggy said as they entered his room. "I'm not sure you should be pushing yourself so hard this soon after…"

The attack? After the assault? Funny how even here in the hospital, people were reluctant to state out loud what had happened to him—or what they thought had happened to him. Did other crime victims feel so invisible?

Peggy was a spring bouquet of scents. Her scrubs smelled like those fabric softener sheets people used in the dryer, and he caught a whiff of apple shampoo and baby powder as she helped him climb onto the freshly made bed. She murmured a soft apology as she peeled back the gauze dressing covering his wound. He'd done a bang-up job of gouging the corner of a fricking table into his skull—too good a job, really. Though the pain was getting better by the day, most days his head throbbed like a bitch.

Even though the nurse busied herself tearing strips of adhesive tape off a roll, she couldn't disguise the bump of lust she felt. Regardless, he had to give this one top points for professionalism. She didn't brush her breasts against him, touch him inappropriately, or even let her expression change, which was more than he could say for the nurse he'd caught threading her fingers through his hair as he'd awakened one night.

"I see the guards are giving you a little more space," Peggy said as she smoothed the tape onto the fresh gauze. "If you'd been here any other time, you'd have the VIP suite upstairs, but someone's already using it." The nurse shook her head slowly and bit her lower lip as she took his pulse. "First Andi Woolf is attacked and nearly killed. Then, the attack on you and Annika Fontaine. I don't feel safe walking outside my own house right now, much less going to a club."

Was Andi Woolf upstairs? The beast clattered to its haunches.

Peggy tut-tutted. "Okay, first you were cold, and now you're flushed again. Your pulse is fast. No more walks today. Into bed with you." The nurse was all business as she bundled him under his covers and looked at her practical, white-banded watch. "You're overdue for pain meds. Hang tight. I'll be right back."

Please. Hurry.

Overhead, Andi Woolf's room burned in his imagination, like a glow stick at a rave.

Chapter 14

SASHA STUBBED HER TOE ON JACK'S BOAT-SIZED SHOE, nearly dropping the flower arrangement she carried from the foyer to the apartment. Though the cordovan loafers sat in a perfectly reasonable place—on the rug beside the door, right beside her own Doc Marten boots—she kicked them anyway.

Stalking to Scarlett's bedroom door, Sasha took several deep breaths to get her temper under control. Scarlett had to give her some help here, because she'd had it

Time for some tough love.

Scarlett had disappeared into the cocoon of her room as soon as they'd gotten home from Ireland, leaving her to deal with Lukas and Jack, who'd all but moved in with them. Five days of cardboard boxes, hardware, wires, and duct tape. Of duffel bags no doubt filled with jocks and stinky socks. Of big bodies and big-ass shoes that took up way too much room.

Testosterone bloomed like a roadkilled skunk.

Jack's voice murmured from behind Annika's closed bedroom door, and a moment of dissonance reached out and grabbed her by the throat. It wasn't Jack's fault that Lukas had arrived first and taken the guest room, leaving Jack to choose either Annika's room or the couch. But each day he stayed, more of Annika disappeared.

Annika, Jack's finally in your bed. What do you think?

Sasha shook off the thought. Jack had pulled daytime bodyguard duty, grumbling that he had hours of con-calls to attend today. It was a perfect time to make a break for it—and come hell or high water, Scarlett was coming with her.

Setting the freesia down on the hallway table, Sasha opened Scarlett's bedroom door and closed it behind her. The bed was empty, littered with pages of newspaper, and Scarlett's sad voice wafted from the bathroom. The breakfast tray she'd delivered earlier still sat on the bedside table. The cold cereal hadn't been touched, but the lid was off the thermal coffee carafe.

If Scarlett was drinking coffee again, things were looking up.

Sasha wasn't going to make this easy anymore. After today, if Scarlett wanted coffee, she'd have to get it herself.

The newspaper was open to that intrusive, gorgeous picture snapped at Annika's funeral and zapped around the world in seconds. The paparazzo who'd taken it had hit the jackpot, capturing Claudette Fontaine, blowing a good-bye kiss to the daughter she'd just returned to the sea, secretive titan of industry Elliott Sebastiani holding her other hand, standing stoic at her side—and Scarlett, her mouth open in a cry as she'd thrown herself into Lukas's arms. Sasha ran her finger over her brother's tight jaw line. He cradled Scarlett gently, but his expression was as hard as the very cliffs they stood upon. If it was possible to kill with a look, the helicopter buzzing the site would have crashed into the water.

When Scarlett looked at the picture, what did she see? With a sigh, Sasha went into the bathroom, where she found Scarlett reclined in a tub of bubbles, eyes closed, iPod perched on the tub's ledge, her ever-present headphones clamped to her head.

So much for my dramatic entrance. She can't hear a damn thing.

Sasha snapped the connection between Sigmund and the headphones. Scarlett's eyes flew open. She lurched up, creating a mini-tsunami in the tub.

Sasha held Sigmund over the water with outstretched arms.

Tipping the headphones off, Scarlett half-stood. "What are you doing?"

Sasha danced away from the bathtub, shoving Sigmund in her back pocket. "The question is, what are you doing? Nothing," she continued before Scarlett could respond. "Nothing. Enough is enough. I need some help here."

As Scarlett sat back down in the tub, submerging herself in jasmine bubbles, Sasha inhaled a wisp of remorse. *Gotcha.* She ruthlessly pressed her advantage. "The phone is ringing off the hook. We're swimming in sympathy cards. The foyer is so overrun with flowers that you can barely climb out of the elevator. Your band's server crashed yesterday after Stephen posted a message thanking people for their concern. Why, yes! Stephen *did* get out of the hospital yesterday." Her voice steadily rose. "The whole damn building is swarming with extra security, and two very large bodyguards are eating us out of house and home, because they are living... with... us!" Sasha snatched a violet bath sheet off the closed toilet seat and extended it to Scarlett, who lay wide-eyed in the tub. "You've been perfectly comfortable allowing me to manage your life for the last week, but I quit. You're going to get out of this tub. You're getting dressed, brushing your teeth—"

"I've been brushing my teeth," Scarlett interrupted with a mutter.

"—brushing your hair," Sasha continued through gritted teeth. "You are leaving this bedroom. Then, if we can manage a jailbreak—"

"What?"

"Our bodyguards don't want us to leave the building until Annika's killer is behind bars."

Scarlett's eyes filled.

Damn. "Oh, baby, I miss her. I miss her so damn much. But..." Sasha swallowed as the tears stung. "I need my roommate back."

Scarlett's lips wobbled as she stood and got out of the tub, taking the towel from Sasha. "I still can't believe she's gone. Sometimes I wake up in the middle of the might, thinking I hear her stumbling in late, just like she used to."

"That's Jack. He and Lukas haven't gotten a lot of sleep since we got back from Ireland."

Sasha wrapped her arms around Scarlett, ignoring the water dripping on her feet. "You need to call your mother."

Scarlett drew in a quick breath. "Mom."

"Dad's been taking good care of her—and she understands you need some decompression time—but she's worried." Sasha stepped back, grasping Scarlett's hand and tugging her back into the bedroom.

Scarlett sighed. "I've been a selfish bitch."

"No, honey, you haven't been. But Annika would want you to live your life, not stay in this limbo. So don't even think about sitting down. Let's find you some clothes." Sasha delved into Scarlett's lingerie drawer, throwing pink bikini underwear at Scarlett's torso. A bra and a pair of white sweat socks quickly followed. "Come on, get dressed. Lukas is gone, and Jack just dialed into another meeting. We might be able to make a break for it."

—⁓—

Lukas had moved in? Where was he sleeping? Scarlett's face heated. His scent had permeated her sleep and saturated her dreams, but she thought it was just her imagination.

Sasha handed her a pair of faded boyfriend jeans, a soft white T-shirt, and a gray hoodie embroidered with pale pink and green skulls. "When you open the bedroom door, get ready for a new world order."

The newspaper on the bed caught her eye. Despite the quicksand state of their relationship, at the moment the picture had been taken, some primal instinct had arisen. She'd thrown herself in Lukas's arms, certain she'd find shelter there. And he'd delivered.

Certain events were indelibly burned into her memory: that horrible, tear-soaked Council meeting. The endless flight to Ireland. Annika's funeral. Lukas pushing a snack and a cup of coffee into her hand as she'd zoned out on the couch in the den at Fontaine House, after all the guests left and only family remained. Lukas helping her navigate the rough, starlit path leading to the Fontaine family's primitive henge the night that massive sheets of magnetic energy had lit up the sky. The aurora borealis itself had been beautiful, but the sight of the Sebastianis lifting their heads to the heavens, to something bigger than all of them, had given her inexplicable comfort.

It hadn't taken long for her to pick Lukas's pheromones out of the mix—and then comfort had been the last thing on her mind.

She joined Sasha in the bathroom, picked up her brush, and tried to do something with her hair. Sasha was bent over the bathtub, pulling the drain. Sigmund bulged in her back pocket. "Hey, Sash."

"Hmm?"

"Thanks for the kick in the ass."

"Any time."

Despite the joking tone, Scarlett knew Sasha spoke nothing less than the truth. "Can I have Sigmund back now?"

"No. I'm holding him hostage. We have an important mission to perform. Ready?"

She put the hairbrush down on the vanity. "As I'll ever be."

Sasha slowly opened Scarlett's bedroom door, quickly ducking her head out and back again. At Sasha's "come on" gesture, they tiptoed out of Scarlett's room and past Annika's, where Jack's voice murmured behind the closed door.

"He's going to be so pissed," Sasha whispered.

"You're enjoying this way too much."

They reached the front door without alerting Jack. Sasha grabbed an oversized pair of black sunglasses from the credenza and popped them on Scarlett's face. "Disguise complete."

"Wait!" Scarlett hissed. "I don't have my purse."

"Never mind your purse. I'm buying." Snagging her by the arm of her sweatshirt, Sasha pulled her into the foyer and quietly shut the door behind them.

Scarlett goggled at the condition of the foyer while Sasha pushed the elevator call button. It looked like a flower shop, and smelled like a rainforest. Envelopes overflowed the mail pan atop the table, and more cards were piled in a series of USPS boxes beneath the table and along the wall.

She hesitated. The last thing she should be doing today was—

"They'll be here later. Today, tomorrow, and for weeks to come."

Scarlett sighed. Sasha was right—again.

The elevator door whooshed open, and they stepped inside. "Where are we going?"

"What would Annika do?" Sasha replied, pressing the button that would bring them to the parking garage.

Their eyes met. They both knew perfectly well what Annika would do. "Shoe therapy," they replied together, giggling as the elevator descended and they made their getaway.

———

From her seat on the cracked leather couch in front of Crackhouse Coffee's picture window, Scarlett watched Sasha slither behind the counter and pour their coffee herself, bypassing a long line composed almost entirely of chattering women and their children. Scarlett didn't recognize any of the workers behind the counter, but she'd spent enough time here at the coffee shop that the rhythms of the business came back quickly. With all the mothers and toddlers here, there must be an afternoon family event at the Target Center—"Count with Elmo" or "Ariel Skates In Endless Circles" or some such thing. Most of the kids sported chocolate milk moustaches.

She winced as a toddler's squeal assaulted her eardrums. What had possessed them to come here, after the absolute disaster their trip to the Mall of America had turned into? Lukas had picked them up from the mall's security office himself. The tightly controlled lecture he'd delivered as he'd driven them home had made her feel like a child in the principal's office.

As the espresso machine hissed, Sasha wended her way back toward the couch, slowing to return people's greetings but not quite stopping. She studiously ignored her brother, who glared at them from his own table near the door.

"Here." Sasha handed over one of the two steaming mugs before joining Scarlett on the couch. They both took a fortifying sip of Crackhouse Blend. "Okay, okay. In retrospect, I can see how my idea might have been the teensiest bit shortsighted."

"Yeah."

At a beat-up table across the room, a very annoyed Lukas jabbed at the keys on his mini-comp. Scarlett had to admit that he had a right to be pissed. Their shopping trip had turned into a debacle. A stringer from the local newspaper had picked them up almost as soon as their car had left the parking ramp, and he'd followed them to the mall. After a pleasant hour shoe shopping— Sasha had scored a fabulous pair of riding boots on sale at Nordstrom, but they hadn't had the same pair in Scarlett's size—they'd been minding their own business when the guy had hollered "Scarlett!" so he could get a better shot.

A crowd swarmed, and the jig was up.

"That bank of gumball machines would never have tipped over if the autograph seekers hadn't gotten so pushy-shovey," Scarlett said as she sipped her coffee. The cleaning staff at MOA would be cleaning the damn things up for days.

Sasha nodded. "It's all that idiot reporter's fault."

But her voice was laced with the slightest bit of guilt. As Lukas had so succinctly informed them when he'd showed up at the mall security office, luckily no one had fallen, slipped, or had otherwise gotten injured. Despite his chilly, controlled tone, Lukas's words had been blistering. "Selfish." "Shortsighted." "Ill-advised." Apparently their "childish antics" had pulled Lukas away from a meeting with Gideon, and Jack had interrupted his own meeting once he realized they'd left the apartment.

"Well, despite how it all ended, thank you for busting me out. You were right; a change of scenery was just what I needed."

The scent of a freshly filled diaper wafted from the nearest table.

Scarlett and Sasha both dissolved in giggles. Lukas shot them a disgusted look, and then focused on his mini-comp again like it contained the secret of who killed Kennedy.

"When did the leaves change color?" Scarlett asked as she pulled a fleece blanket off the back of the couch and covered her legs with it. The trees embedded in the Nicollet Avenue promenade blazed yellow, orange, and fiery red. Despite the bright sunlight, the air was crisp as an apple. Minnesotans could no longer deny that fall had arrived, and winter would inevitably follow.

They sat quietly, sipping on their coffee. "There's Jack," Sasha complained. "I can barely turn around without crashing into that man." She shot a dirty look at the guys' table, where Jack had just taken a seat next to Lukas. "What are we going to do about this? We can't get away from them. Even Flynn is in on this. He practically patted me on the head this morning when he told me that he'd check in the deliveries."

"That cad."

"You know what I mean. They don't want us to leave? I feel like sending Jack to Target to buy a year's supply of tampons, just on principle."

Scarlett burst out laughing. "Let's hold that idea in reserve." Her gaze met Lukas's, held for a moment, then he broke contact, focusing on his conversation with Jack.

"So, what's going on between you and my brother?"

"Are you asking me as my friend, or his sister?"

"Both, you nut. But please keep my sensitive constitution in mind. Some things a sister just doesn't need to know."

Scarlett took a sip of coffee as she considered where to start. "Did you know that Lukas was my first lover?"

"Shut. *Up,*" Sasha said sarcastically, sidling closer so their heads nearly touched. "Of course I knew, you idiot."

"Quiet down!" Scarlett hissed. Now Lukas was watching them. Hell, half of the coffee shop was watching them. "Does everybody know?" she asked under her breath.

"No. I suspected, but I just found out for sure a couple of weeks ago. Lukas didn't tell me the particulars. When was this? And where was I?"

"The summer after our senior year. You were in New York dancing half the summer. Lukas had just finished grad school, was getting his business off the ground, immersing himself in the Council's day-to-day activities." Scarlett snuggled more deeply under the blanket. "I'd just come home after a great gig—you know the feeling, high on life, jacked into the universe. And there he was, looking all…" She simply gestured toward him to finish her thought.

Sasha wrinkled her nose.

"Come on. I know you're his sister, but even you can't be that oblivious."

They both sneaked a look at the table near the entrance, where Lukas and Jack worked. Even now, the two men attracted more than their share of attention, Lukas wearing beat-up cargo pants of a nearly indeterminate color, broken-in leather boots, and a snug black T-shirt, his facial structure brought into relief by the hair lashed tight to the nape of his neck. Jack was wearing a pair of khakis and a snowy-white, cotton button-down shirt, open at the neck with sleeves rolled up. His close-cut blond hair glowed in the sun. Two sets of long legs fought for space under the table for four.

"Beef and Cake," Sasha murmured.

"What?"

"Bailey said that's what the women at Sebastiani Security call them. Lukas is 'Beef' and Jack is 'Cake.'"

Scarlett laughed out loud. "I hadn't heard that one."

"I guess I can maybe see the physical appeal," Sasha

said, considering her brother, "but damn, he's annoying. He and Jack are two peas in a pod."

"You know what else is annoying? Having an incubus for your first lover." Under the blanket, her nipples drew tight. "It's all downhill from there."

"Very, very true." Sasha's nose wrinkled mischievously. "So, Mr. Perfect corrupted you."

"I wish. He didn't stay long enough for any real corruption to take place. The next morning he couldn't get away fast enough." She rolled her eyes. "I'm sure he'd had quite enough of amateur hour."

"He thinks he hurt you."

"Well, just for a second. It was my first time, and, well, he's a big guy."

"Geez, TMI." Sasha winced. "Again, he didn't get too specific, he just said that he was too rough, that he lost control. I got the feeling that he backed off for your own good."

"What? Are you kidding me?" The anger rose dangerously, a flash flood spreading over the land.

"I wish I was." Sasha sliced a dire look at her brother. "I'd be pissed too. I told you, they think they know all the answers."

"Damn him," Scarlett whispered. She'd beat herself up for years, certain she hadn't been enough for him—and he'd bailed because of some misplaced sense of guilt?

How dare he make such a decision for both of them? Across the room, Lukas sat upright, his nostrils flaring.

"Damn you." She spoke directly to him, let him read her lips. "Damn you. How dare you—"

The plate glass window exploded into thousands

of tiny shards, and something hot stung her ear. Sasha yanked her off the couch, pulling them to the hard tile floor. They'd barely landed when Lukas's heavy weight crushed them both.

———

His pleasure quickly turned to a curse as Stephen recognized the face framed in the hole where the coffee shop window used to be. Lukas Sebastiani—and he was looking right at the parking ramp across the street, where Stephen had fired the shot.

"Just my luck," he muttered, slumping to a heap at the base of the concrete pillar. Cries and shrieks still echoed from the coffee shop across the street, carrying plenty of fear-laced adrenaline, but he couldn't stay here to enjoy it.

Sebastiani was probably calling in backup, right now.

Stephen tucked the handgun into his sweatshirt's kangaroo pouch pocket, gritting his teeth as energy zipped up and down his spinal column. The mothers' hysteria was particularly strong in the top notes, but... Lukas's alpha male response crashed into him in violent waves, making his balls tingle and pull up tight.

Why the extreme reaction? What the hell was going on over there?

He chanced a quick peek around the edge of the pillar and saw Jack Kirkland herd women and shrieking children away from the window. Sasha Sebastiani had a cell phone clamped to her ear, her anger palpable even from across the street. And Lukas was helping a shaking, flame-haired woman off the floor, protecting her body with his.

Scarlett's pale face dripped blood from dozens of small cuts.

Ah, damn. He couldn't do anything right.

Chapter 15

"LET GO." SCARLETT PUSHED WEAKLY AT LUKAS AS HE tried to scoop her from the passenger seat of his car. "I can do it myself."

"Fine." Lukas stepped back, but not so far that he couldn't catch her at the first hint of a wobble. Despite her feisty words, her voice was thready. Combined with the aftershocks of what had happened at Crackhouse was a seething feminine anger. He didn't understand the reason for it, but her body didn't have the energy reserves to sustain it for long. She was going to crash, and when she did, Lukas preferred that it be inside rather than out in Sebastiani Security's parking lot.

The four-story brick building housing his business and living space sat on the corner of Washington and First Avenue, one of those Minneapolis intersections where the city turned from spit-shined to seedy on a dime. During the short drive from Underbelly and Crackhouse, he hadn't let himself forget the cuts on her face, or the glowing white bandage he'd placed on her right ear himself.

The bullet that shattered Crackhouse's window had taken a nice divot out of her ear before burying itself in the coffee shop's far wall.

He'd nearly lost her.

The adrenaline that had coursed through him at the coffee shop in the aftermath of the shooting had long since burned off. They were both running on fumes.

He'd nearly lost her.

By the time he'd covered Scarlett and Sasha with his body, the damage had already been done. Sasha had had her back to the window and only had a few grazes on her neck, but Scarlett's face had taken a direct hit. Disregarding every procedure he knew he should follow, he'd picked Scarlett up off the coffee shop floor. Quickly telling Jack to check out the parking ramp across the street, he'd carried her upstairs to her apartment to render first aid. Despite knowing that even minor head wounds bled like a bitch, his stomach had positively roiled as he'd held a gauze pad to the nip the bullet had taken from the tip of her ear, applying pressure to stop the bleeding. She'd winced as he cleaned and applied antibacterial ointment to each tiny cut on her face. By the time he'd finished that task, Gideon, thoroughly annoyed that Scarlett and Lukas had left his crime scene, had made his way upstairs.

The taste of ashes had been mild, yet unmistakable.

Claudette was right. Scarlett wasn't safe. And Scarlett had barely changed out of her glass-glittered clothing before he'd grasped her by the elbow, hustled her out the apartment door, down the elevator to his car, and buckled her into the passenger seat.

The fading afternoon sunlight lit the puffy cuts on her face. She closed her eyes momentarily, as if mustering up the effort to get out of the car was simply beyond her means at the moment. And it probably was. How stupid was it to just stand here, an open fucking target? *Get your head in the game.*

"Come on, we need to get inside." He scoped out the parking lot and the shoreline of the Mississippi River, and then stood in front of her to cut off as many angles as he could with his body.

She eyed the space between them. "Can you give me a little room, please?"

"No."

She sighed. "What's up with this car?" she said, indicating his sedate-looking black V8 Impala SS. "It looks like something Valerian would drive."

While the car was nearly twenty feet long and had Barcalounger seats, under the hood, where it counted, it was a completely different story. "Hey, it gets me where I need to go. And I fit in it."

Scarlett humphed disapprovingly. "Where's the 'Screw Global Warming' bumper sticker?"

"Rather than buying something new, small, and politically correct which doesn't meet my needs, I'm using a car that already exists for its complete, useful lifetime." He lightly grasped her upper arm as she stepped away from the car, and this time she didn't pull away from him. Either she was becoming less mad or more exhausted, and frankly either was okay in his book. He needed to get her inside, settle her in.

He'd wait until later to hit the gym and work off some of this killing rage.

Grabbing her duffle bag from the backseat, they finally walked toward the building. Was Claudette right after all? Was someone targeting Council members and their families? First Andi Woolf, then Annika Fontaine, and now Scarlett had been shot at.

No, not shot at—*shot*. The white bandage on her ear was a painful reminder.

"Lukas."

"What?"

"Is that a strip club across the street?"

The color was creeping back into her cheeks, and there was definitely a bite to her voice. Some perverse instinct made him say, "Yes. The dancers are very nice women." Let her make of his response what she would. Sebastiani Security was always happy to provide some neighborly assistance to the bouncers on particularly rowdy weekend nights.

Yes, Scarlett was definitely annoyed. And was that... the tiniest bit of jealousy creeping into the mix? He liked how it tasted.

As he guided her through Sebastiani Security's heavy doors, Bailey's head popped up from under the Reception desk, a screwdriver in one hand and a snarl of colored wires in the other. "Hey there," she called, eyeing them with open curiosity. "Good to see you."

"Jack filled you in?" Lukas said.

"Yeah." Bailey smiled at Scarlett. "I'm glad we'll have one more woman in the building. We need some more estrogen in the mix." Her smile dimmed a bit when she looked at Lukas. "Jack said that the bullet barely missed your head when it slammed into the wall."

"What?" Scarlett tensed in his arms, and he tasted flint-edged fear.

"Hey, the *missed* part is the part that counts." Lukas dropped his hand to the small of Scarlett's back as they said good-bye and crossed to the elevator. After what Scarlett had been through today, he wasn't about to take the four narrow flights of stairs up to his living space.

The elevator ride was short, but her essence filled every corner of the standard-sized conveyance. As

Lukas escorted her to the heavy oak door and unlocked it, he wondered how he'd survive the days to come.

His new roommate would sleep in his bed until they caught this asshole.

———————

Sasha had been full of stories about the long-running effort to rehab and restore the Sebastiani Security building, including Lukas's top floor living space. Scarlett half-expected to see jock straps and sweat socks hanging from the rafters, and pizza boxes used for tables.

Whatever she'd been expecting, it hadn't been… this.

Her initial impressions were of mellow beige brick, glass, and wood, and the faintest scent of fresh paint. And light. Oh, the light. Windows soared along the south and west walls. The living area of the two-story warehouse space was basically one large room, with the ceiling held up by blackened wooden beams so large that she didn't think she could get her arms around them. Different areas of the living space had been cleverly demarcated with area rugs exploding with colors—red, orange, yellow, rust—and natural wood panels with wheels on the bottom served as movable partial walls. Bisecting the room was an unusual floor-to-ceiling wooden wall unit. Scarlett supposed it provided storage space as well as a solid wall of sorts for the bedroom and kitchen on either side of it. The floor's wide wooden planks were slightly uneven and discolored in a way that shouted their age and authenticity. She saw one door in the whole place, which she heartily hoped was the bathroom.

She refused to look at the bedroom area over by the windows, glowing like kryptonite behind hanging curtains.

Lukas kicked off his boots at the door. "Shoes off, please. This place is a bitch to sweep. Then I'll give you the grand tour, though you can pretty much see the whole place from here."

Scarlett sat down on the sturdy bench near the door and unzipped her own boots, reaching into the duffel bag Sasha had hastily packed and extracting her black cat slippers, complete with head, ears, whiskers, and tail trailing off the back. She ignored Lukas's raised eyebrow.

As Lukas hung up her coat, Scarlett wandered through the living area, admiring the huge fireplace, made of rough slabs of river rock, and large enough to roast a boar. Poised at its side was a waist-height bronze sculpture, unquestionably Rafe's work. Chopped wood filled an alcove to the fireplace's right, and small chips and ashes littered the hearth. Lukas had already had his first fall fire.

If she wasn't a prisoner here, she could totally see herself curling up on that oversized and overstuffed leather couch, reading a book or taking an afternoon nap. The only thing missing would be a cat on her lap. Or nibbling on her ankle, as the case may be.

"What's wrong?"

He was right behind her. For such a large man, he moved very quietly. "I'm worried about Calamity," she said. "I just got home, and now I'm gone again. He's going to be so confused. I didn't get a chance to clip his nails before I left."

"I hear he likes the taste of flesh."

"Yeah." She glanced at him, and then hugged her arms around her torso. "So, what do we do now?" As soon as the words escaped her mouth, she regretted them.

Lukas cleared his throat. "Why don't we get you settled, then find something to eat?" He opened two doors on the long shelving unit, exposing a built-in set of drawers topped by empty shelves. "You can put your stuff here." Swishing back the curtains on the bedroom area, he placed her duffle on his bed. "Here's where you'll sleep. I'll, um, have to change the sheets."

Scarlett stopped at the heavy velvet panel, trying not to stare at the king-sized bed. Rumpled, with its pillows askew, it looked large enough to host a party. She felt guilty for kicking him out of his bed, but she wasn't stupid enough to open her mouth and suggest that they share it.

"I'll move another slider across the front here, block it off so you have some privacy."

As if. She had no privacy from this man, who could sense, smell, and taste her body's need. She looked wildly around the apartment. She would have no privacy until Annika's killer was caught.

She looked guiltily at Lukas. *No privacy for him, either.* No matter how much he annoyed her, or how angry she was, Lukas was putting himself out for her—and with her mother's full support. There was little-to-no chance she'd talk her way out of here anytime soon.

She moved closer to the bed, trailing her hand across his faerie quilt. Though the quilt was slightly faded, pyrotechnic shades of red, orange, and yellow exploded across the fabric. "What a beautiful quilt. I'm surprised that you have one."

"Why?" He joined her near the bed. Despite the size and openness of the room, she suddenly felt a little suffocated.

"I can't imagine you ever lowering your boundaries enough for the interview."

He didn't respond to her comment, but a telling tinge of color crept onto his cheekbones.

Her own face heated in response. What in the world had the faeries pulled out of him? What dreams did Lukas have as he lay under his fire-colored quilt?

What dreams would *she* have?

Flashing lights drew her attention. She giggled as she looked out the window.

"What?" Lukas asked as he joined her.

She pointed to the "Sex World" sign, blinking hot pink across the street.

Lukas pulled the window curtains matching the bedroom's faux wall closed with a muttered curse. "Sasha insisted I put the bed over in this corner, and it was months before I noticed why."

With the curtains drawn, the bedroom seemed even more intimate. Lukas must have felt the same way because he quickly maneuvered them away from the bed and out of the bedroom to show her the rest of the living space. Everything was oversized, nothing really matched, yet somehow it all merged into a pleasant and comfortable whole—a real feat, given that the space was large enough to host a half-court basketball game.

And an army of cooks could comfortably work in the kitchen at the same time, Scarlett mused as Lukas showed her the room. It was huge, with sparkling restaurant-quality stainless steel appliances and copper-clad pans hanging over a long center island, but nothing but the coffee maker sitting on the granite counter top looked like it had been used. Pulling open the refrigerator, her stereotypical bachelor expectations were finally fulfilled. The fridge was filled with take-out cartons, bottles of beer, and nearly every condiment known to man. Was that a shriveled garlic clove down in the otherwise empty crisper? She couldn't tell, and didn't want to know. But there were gallons of milk, and a quart of half and half. She picked it up, sniffed. Yup, it was fresh.

She'd have coffee.

And she could cook. She'd missed cooking while she and the band had been out on the road. Even though she wasn't as talented in the kitchen as Annika was, she would certainly pitch in and—

Annika.

"Whoa." Lukas grasped her as she swayed.

She recoiled as his palm pressed on a bruise, blooming to painful life on her hip. "Ouch."

"I'm sorry," he said, immediately removing his hand.

She frowned and rubbed her hip. "I must have hit the ground harder than I thought."

"Let me see."

"No. It's fine."

His voice firmed. "Let me see."

So did hers, and she sidled away from his grasp. "I said it's fine. It's just a bruise." Years of hurt and fury made her voice snap like a whip. "Sometimes a bruise is just a bruise, Lukas."

His big body stilled. She saw him put the pieces together, and the expression on his face was as easy to read as a large-print book: *Let's not go there*. Despite her exhaustion, she suddenly felt like supplemental steel had been welded to her backbone. "This conversation is years overdue. Let's clear the air, shall we?"

Lukas took a deep breath, and one careful step toward her. "Scarlett, within the last few hours, you've been shot, cut by breaking class, and body-slammed to the floor by someone well over twice your body weight. You're sore and tired, and about to drop. I think—"

"I don't give a damn what you think. I understand that, from a security standpoint, you have some expertise that might help keep me safe. But you don't have all the answers." Her voice dropped to a whisper. "When you walked away that morning without saying a word, you hurt me worse than any shooter ever could."

Lukas opened his mouth to speak, but she held up her hand. "Did you really think so little of me? Of what we experienced together?"

He didn't defend himself. He didn't say a thing. A muscle ticked at his cheekbone as the automatic ice maker clattered cubes into the dispenser. Her anger tipped to a clutching, violent need, and a sadness she didn't know what to do with.

"Lukas," she whispered. She didn't know what she wanted to say; she just knew that she had to say something. The pressure building inside her chest demanded it.

"Damn it." Lukas dragged her into his arms, plastering them together from chest to knee. As his head dropped, she opened her mouth like a ravenous baby bird. But instead of the passionate kiss that she'd expected—that she yearned for—he cradled her in a rough hug, pressing her cheek against the soft fabric of his T-shirt.

When his lips nuzzled her hair, the sobs finally erupted, welling like magma. She couldn't stop them, and burrowed into his size, his strength, his heat.

"Let it go, Scarlett. Just let go."

And she did. Endless minutes passed as she cried out the fear, the adrenaline, the pain and grief, the knife-sharp desire, and the endless exhaustion. Finally, she gave a shaky, watery laugh. "Damn you, even when you're providing comfort, you're giving me orders." She wiped her eyes, and met his gaze directly. "That has to change."

He looked steadily back. "That can't change, Scarlett. Not if I'm going to keep you safe. A situation could arise where the only thing that saves your life is you following my orders."

She tried to wrench herself away, but he wouldn't let go. "How do you even know I was this guy's target? Sasha was sitting right beside me. For that matter, so were you and Jack. Maybe you were the target." She smirked. "You pissing someone off isn't outside the realm of possibility."

He acknowledged her point with a single nod of his head. "Okay, at this point we can't know for sure who the target was. But this asshole won't get another clean shot at you." Lukas's gaze flicked to the bandage on her ear. "What happened today is inexcusable. I... we almost lost you." He hesitated before dropping a gentle kiss onto the bandage, touching its edges with his big, rough fingertips. His hot breath heated her cheekbone as he slowly, unerringly—finally—lowered his head to her mouth.

"Lukas." No doubt about it; that was pleading. For his mouth, for his touch. For everything he could give her.

His lips cruised over hers, a wisp of sensation. A soft flick of his tongue over the center of her lower lip teased her unbearably. The softness of his lips contradicted the coiled strength of his body, barely leashed. *Too soft. Not enough.* Grabbing at his hair, she tugged his head toward hers. She wasn't going to let him treat her like a fairy tale princess cocooned in glass.

She almost heard his control snap. Holding her head in place, he crushed his lips down on hers, and plundered. His dark taste swam through her like heady wine. When his teeth joined his tongue in a game of nip and smooth, she wove her fingers into his tabby cat hair—and bit back.

Cupping her butt in his hands, he lifted her off her feet, rubbing her dewy core against his groin with frank hunger. She wound around him, clinging like a monkey on a tree. He used the freedom to caress and fondle, tracing a torturously slow route down the back seam of her jeans, between her cheeks and beyond. When he finally palmed her humid center, it was all she could do to hold on.

A moan slipped out of her throat as she rocked against his hand, driving for the resolution that was just beyond her reach. She buried her face in the crook of his neck as the tension built. Where was her pride, her embarrassment? She was riding him like a prize stallion, but he wasn't complaining. And she couldn't stop, not now. Not when she was so close.

Then his clever fingers shifted and pressed—just enough for her to shatter and break apart in his arms.

After a while, he kissed her on her forehead, walked over to the couch, and gently set her down. Her now-seated position gave her a front row view of his massive hard-on. She half reached for him, with thoughts of finally getting her mouth on him again filling her brain.

Suddenly his mini-comp vibrated and pulsed at his waistband. Lukas growled and gave her a ferocious kiss. "I'm late for a meeting with Gideon."

Scarlett sat back on the couch. They just couldn't seem to catch a break.

"Why are you so sad all of a sudden?"

She grabbed the afghan off the back of the couch, wrapping it around her protectively. "Stop trying to read me! Because I can't read you." She stared at the cold fireplace, at the wooden floor. At anything but the rock-hard bounty in front of her. "I always feel like I'm at a disadvantage when I talk with you."

Lukas crouched down. "You're so wrong," he said quietly. "I can tell you're sad, but not why. I can tell you feel guilty, but not why. Even after you fly apart in my arms, you feel sad and guilty." His chest expanded and contracted with the heaviness of his sigh. "That's no advantage."

She matched his sigh with one of her own. "We're going to be living here together for awhile. For starters, why don't we do what parents tell toddlers to do—use our words?"

Lukas rested his forehead against hers. "Okay, I'll start. If I didn't have to meet Gideon right now, I'd carry you over to that bed and bury myself in you. Repeatedly." He stroked a rough finger along the line of her jaw. "I want to make you feel good."

Taking nothing for yourself? Typical.

He reluctantly stood. "Gideon wants to talk about what he found in the parking ramp across from Crackhouse. It shouldn't take too long. Why don't you unpack and get settled in while I check on a few things downstairs?"

She nodded. She needed some time to think, to get her equilibrium back. To consider what Sasha had revealed about her brother, and what she was going to do about it.

"I'll bring some dinner back," he called from the door. "That pizza smelled really good."

"Sold. Later," Lukas said as he left.

Later. Scarlett looked at Lukas's orgy-sized bed. She couldn't let herself think about all the things she and her new roommate could do... later.

Chapter 16

"WHY DID YOU STOP?" STEPHEN ASKED.

Antonia stood in front of single snare drum, her sticks in the air. "You know, when I asked you for drum lessons, this wasn't what I had in mind."

I know exactly what you had in mind. Her slim body positively quivered with frustration and desire. Trying to ignore her luscious scent, Stephen said, "You have to learn the fundamentals before you can do anything behind the kit." He indicated the set of drums he'd detached the snare from, a decent backup he kept here at Scarlett's recording studio at Underbelly.

The crime scene techs were done with the room, and the cleaners had been in, so he and Antonia had decided to meet here for the drum lesson he'd promised to give her back when he was in the hospital.

Her sense of rhythm was crap. Was there a metronome around here? "Just a sec." He searched the room, avoiding the area where the soundboard used to be. In his mind's eye, Annika was still spread across it like an all-you-can-eat buffet.

No metronome, no soundboard, no computers. The crime scene techs had removed so much equipment that the room hardly looked like the same place. What could he use...? "Ah." A synthesizer stood near the window—one of the few items he hadn't touched or damaged. He plugged it in, flicked a button, fired it up.

Finding a simple click track, he manipulated the pace and tone.

Approaching Antonia again, he explained, "You can't just sit down and start flailing away. Each piece is an instrument in its own right, with its own technique," he said. "Snares. Hi-hats, bass drum, cymbals. The only tools you have at your disposal are two arms and two legs, moving simultaneously but each playing a different rhythm—everything in time to the beat—" he indicated the click track "—playing in your head. Which had better be damn accurate, because you're the only thing keeping everyone in the band playing at the same speed." He pointed to the lonely snare. "And it all starts there, with stroke work. I still do stroke work, every day. Gotta stay limber."

"Stroke work? Every day?"

The innuendo in Antonia's voice hit him like a Jäger shot. His eyes flicked to the closed door. He had all the privacy he would need to— "Let's get back to work, brat."

He could tell that the "brat" reference annoyed her, but damn it, he had to do *something* to keep her at a distance. Surely he could handle a teenage succubus with a crush.

"Can you show me how you like to… grip the sticks?"

And touch you again? I don't think so. "What you're doing is correct. Start again. I'm listening." Good thing this was just a lark for her, because her hands, wrists, and arms were really too delicate to hold up to the pounding for long. As she started playing a slow, single stroke roll, he gazed around the room. He hadn't been back since the night Annika died.

"Stephen?"

She thought the spike of lust was for her. Shove it down. "Hear that?" he said, ignoring the question in her voice. "One, two, three, four," he called aloud, clapping his hands for emphasis. "Hear it?"

She banged on the snare with more enthusiasm than skill.

"Kick those boots off. They're fucking with your balance." *And with my concentration.* She plopped on the floor and unzipped the boot down the length of her calf. It sounded too much like she was undressing. Thankfully, when she stood back up in her stocking feet, it seemed like she'd shed several crucial years along with the boots. Now she looked a lot more like a tween cruising the mall than a succubus with every right to flex and test her burgeoning sexual skills. "All right, now we're talking," he said aloud. "Let's try it again."

She started again, a hopeful look on her face.

Nope. Didn't help at all. But he nodded and smiled encouragingly. "Better. Keep going." Roaming the room while she played, his thoughts wandered. When he'd agreed to teach Antonia to play drums, he thought it would be a distraction, a good way to kill some time—and to pay the Fontaines and Sebastianis back for the care and hospitality they'd lavished upon him while he was recovering from his injuries. Did he need groceries? Groceries appeared. Did he need to talk to a faerie therapist? Referrals were proffered.

He'd declined the therapist—probably a good indication that he needed one—but visiting with Madame Bouchet was just as good. It distracted him, gave him something to do.

So, yeah, he needed a distraction, but he hadn't factored in that Antonia Sebastiani might have plans of her own. She was luscious, leggy, and barely legal—the stuff of intergalactic fantasies.

He had to stay away from her. There were some lines even he wouldn't cross.

So, it's okay to kill someone, but not to have sex with a succubus over the age of consent? Who wants you? How ironic. He shook off the thought. "Stand up straighter, Antonia."

She complied, her raised eyebrow letting him know she'd noticed the bite in his voice. Looking at her was a mistake. Her nipples poked at the softness of her vintage INXS T-shirt, and his dick came to life with a languid stretch. Even wearing *South Park* socks, she was absolutely fucking lethal. What delusional thought process had ever convinced him that he could handle this? That he could handle *her*?

"It's stuffy in here, isn't it." Rubbing at his breastbone, he tore his gaze away from her chest and opened the door to the studio, looking up and down the empty hallway. Where was Elliott Sebastiani? Where was the parental supervision on a school night? Right now, Stephen wanted the president's steely gray eyes pinning him to the wall like a bug.

"Stephen, are you okay?" Antonia put down the sticks and approached, biting her bare, vulnerable lip, her hips swaying in invitation.

Who the hell did she think she was teasing? Did she think her actions wouldn't have consequences? And why was he thinking like a judgmental, puritanical human? He looked at the sensuality softening her face, the desire glittering in her eyes, inhaled her frank lust.

Antonia placed a soft hand on his forearm. "I'm so sorry. When I suggested we have our lesson here, all I was thinking about was that, with Scarlett at Lu—" She stopped herself. "With Scarlett not using the studio right now, it would be empty. And there was a set of drums here. I didn't consider that the last time you were here, you were nearly killed." She stepped closer and gave him a hug. "Why don't we pick up the snare, bring it upstairs, and work there?"

Upstairs in my bedroom. The unspoken words taunted him. Stephen winced as the thing in his chest nibbled his ribs. The arms holding him were so soft and delicate, yet threaded with firm muscle. Her concern felt like stepping under an awning in the driving rain.

Step back. Get away.

But he didn't. Instead, he returned her hug, let her concern bleed into him with her body heat. She was obviously aroused, but her desire to comfort him was genuine. He tried to speak past the lump in his throat. "I don't know if I'm... up to this today, Tonia."

"You're the only one who calls me that." Her eyes glowed. "I like it."

He rested his head on her delicate shoulder, smelled the light, cucumber-melon body scent pooling in the crook of her neck, so innocent and fresh. He wanted to roll in it, cleanse himself somehow. The sensation in his chest changed from nips to sharp scratches, but instead of backing off, he tightened his arms around her slim body, bringing their hips closer together. She shuddered, and then pressed her lips to his.

Such innocence. Was this her first kiss? Whether it was or not, her lust prowled through the room, and the beast was licking its chops. He smelled her salty-sweet arousal, tasted the bubble gum she'd been chewing.

She ate at his mouth like she was starving, but kissing Antonia brought out protective instincts that he didn't know he still possessed. "Slow down," he whispered.

She complied, giving the roof of his mouth a wicked little lick that buckled his knees. Their noses bumped as she twisted for a better angle.

And it was his startled laughter that saved him.

"Are you laughing at me?"

"No, I'm—"

She pushed him away. Hard. "You dick." The desire misting the room shifted from embarrassment, to hurt, to flat-out mortification so quickly he could barely register the changes. Her lower lip quivered—once—and then she whirled and left the studio, leaving her black boots and bubble gum behind.

"Antonia!"

Inside his chest, the beast howled its disappointment. A hard kick to the underside of his sternum drove him to his knees.

"Run, Antonia," he gasped. "Run."

Lukas's stomach rolled as he was awakened by the rancid taste of ashes creeping onto his tongue. "Shit," he muttered, shoving back the blankets comprising his makeshift bed on the couch.

He was at it again.

Lukas went to his desk to check the Hot Sheet. A slice of light glowed under the bathroom doorjamb. Scarlett was in the bathtub—again. Scarlett spent almost as much time in the bathtub as he did in the basement workout room. The gym was his sanctuary. Perhaps the tub was hers.

He didn't blame her for needing one, because the tension between them stretched as taut as a zip line.

He could hear every shift of her weight, every splash and eddy of the water. Imagining her nude body lying a mere twenty feet away was torture. And how the hell was he supposed to sleep when she was singing a raunchy, cheerful song about all the men she'd had?

Jesus.

He flicked on the desk light and woke up his monitor with a stab of a finger, trying to block out Scarlett's voice. There was nothing on the Hot Sheet, but hundreds of unread emails sat in his inbox, the bolded number glaring at him accusingly. His Council workspace was flooded with items requiring his review, his feedback, his sign-off, his vote. The latest racist screed from the Genetic Purity League still sat open on his desktop, and Krispin Woolf had fast-tracked a proposal that they RFID tag all their citizens "to ensure their protection, safety, and security."

He reached into the top desk drawer for the liquid antacid and swigged a big mouthful straight from the bottle, perversely enjoying its chalky, cherry flavor.

Hell, he was as frustrated as Krispin was with how little progress they'd made finding Andi's assailant, but there was a line—and apparently Krispin couldn't see the irony of his request. Lukas remembered many Council meetings after the attacks of September 11, 2001, at which Krispin had held forth, with a great sense of theatre, about the absurdity, the epic stupidity, of people blithely giving away their civil liberties in the name of a security which wasn't achievable in the first place.

Krispin was letting his personal issues cloud his judgment. Lukas clicked no to both proposals, sending his votes into the digital ether.

Scarlett's voice wisped from the bathroom. Lukas took another slug off the bottle of chalky antacid.

Mentally consigning Scarlett's iPod to the seventh circle of hell, he called the hospital to check on Andi's condition. No change, still in a medically induced coma. There was nothing from Gideon in his email or text message pile. Still nothing on the Hot Sheet, damn it.

ping

[ESebastiani:] Saw your votes coming through. Couldn't sleep either?

Lukas cast a look back to the bathroom. What the hell was she listening to now? He wished she would switch to some mindless, bubbly pop, or hell, even go back to singing about dicks, because the pain in her voice jabbed like a knife to the gut.

[LSebastiani:] Thought I'd get some work done.

[ESebastiani:] Me too. Ready to have some of the work taken off your plate?

Lukas stilled. Was his father finally ready to name Antonia as the Incubus Second?

[LSebastiani:] Do NOT kid me about this.

[ESebastiani:] Antonia signed the Succession paperwork. Once we get your sig, we send it to Valerian for his, and then it's a done deal. I didn't want something this important to show up in your queue without giving you a heads up first.

Lukas leaned back in his chair. It was finally happening. Once Lukas signed the paperwork, the smallest slice of his official workload would shift from his broad shoulders to his sister's delicate ones. *Delicate, my ass.* He couldn't wait to see Antonia going toe to toe with Krispin Woolf.

[LSebastiani:] Sure, send it.

Several seconds passed. When the Sebastiani Succession Plan showed up, he opened it and carefully reviewed its contents, parsing the language for loopholes, logic lapses, any possibility of a less-than-precise interpretation, because this update to the succession plan introduced a unique twist, which Lukas hoped to Jupiter would never have to be enacted: If Elliott Sebastiani died within the next ten years, Lukas would hopscotch up the Incubus succession line so that he, not Antonia, would ascend to the Council Presidency, finishing out his father's term until the next regularly scheduled election.

The provision, unfortunately, was a political necessity. Krispin Woolf would never accept a teenager as Council President, no matter how precocious she might be, so Lukas and his father had cooked up this transitional plan, both to protect Antonia and to reduce Council chaos.

Lukas paged down to the document's Appendix to verify that Wyland's legal brief vetting the unorthodox plan was attached and signed. His sister's looping signature, scrawled at the bottom, indicated her agreement with the document's contents. Rafe had signed off his approval of being removed from the direct line of succession with bold, slashing strokes.

Lukas blinked when he saw the effective date. When he woke up tomorrow morning, he would no longer be the Acting Incubus Second.

[LSebastiani:] You work fast.

[ESebastiani:] No reason to wait. Is there?

No reason except his sister was… so young. Did she know what she was getting into? Lukas's eyes drifted over the other items in his confidential workspace. Sentencing decisions, budgets, paperwork, and endless political machinations.

The learning curve was massive. Hell, he still learned new things from his father every week. He particularly admired his father's conflict resolution style. While Lukas tended toward vocal brute force, Elliott cut through the Council's choppy political waters like a good-natured shark, striking and moving on to the next subject before the person even knew his blood stained the water.

His mouse hovered over the sig button. This was harder than he thought it would be.

[ESebastiani:] Did you find a problem? Second thoughts?

Second, third, and fourth. What the hell were they getting Antonia into? Lukas took a deep breath.

[LSebastiani:] If you die on me, I'll kill you myself.

[ESebastiani:] Consider me warned.

Imagining his father's wry expression, Lukas clicked to apply his electronic signature with a quick stab of his forefinger. Several seconds passed.

[ESebastiani:] Got it. How is Scarlett?

Lukas leaned back in his desk chair, jamming his hands in his hair. How the hell was he supposed to be able to answer that question? He couldn't answer it for himself. Despite their agreement to "use their words," Scarlett wasn't giving him much to work with other than the lyrics she sang—

He sat up abruptly. When had Scarlett stopped singing? All he heard from the bathroom now were intimate swishes and rustles of fabric as she stroked the water off her long, slim body with one of the soft green towels Sasha had insisted he buy. His dick twitched at the thought.

ping

[ESebastiani:] I didn't think I was asking such a difficult question.

Lukas scowled as he considered how to respond to his father. How *was* Scarlett? She no longer leached grief and exhaustion 24/7, but what she emitted now was a vexing cocktail of anger, sadness, hurt, and… desire. She slept a lot, was eating well enough, sang too often, and if his evil sister had packed Scarlett any bras, he saw absolutely no evidence of it. The tension between them felt like an over-inflated balloon just before it popped. He tried to alleviate this by spending almost all his waking hours downstairs at the office, or in the basement gym. When he came upstairs, dead tired, Scarlett was usually in the bathtub, or in bed, where she tossed and turned, seemingly having as much trouble sleeping as he was.

She was sleeping in his bed, right across the room— and nothing but his faltering willpower kept him from joining her.

[LSebastiani:] She's… hanging in. Her ear is healing, and the scratches are nearly gone.

[ESebastiani:] I'll tell Claudette. She'll be relieved. Well, I'm for bed. Suggest you do the same. Give Scarlett our love.

[LSebastiani:] Will do. Good night.

Scarlett's sudden sadness poked at him like an accusing finger.

He half-got up out of the chair, then sat right back down. *You're three-fourths naked, sporting the mother of all hard-ons, and you don't have a clue what would make her feel better.*

The bathroom door opened, and Scarlett flipped off the bathroom light—but not before Lukas caught a glimpse of her snug boy-cut panties, a strappy camisole T-shirt, and those ridiculous cat slippers on her narrow feet. As she walked to the bedroom, she wished him a soft "Good night," and then disappeared behind the wall section. Before long, the sheets rustled as she settled in.

He bit back a groan. The woman was trying to kill him. The sooner she went home, the better.

"She's homesick." He remembered Tomas's words the night of the show. His eyes narrowed as an idea occurred to him. *I can't let her go home, but…maybe I can bring a piece of home here.* Not giving himself a chance to change his mind—he already knew he was going to regret this—Lukas quickly opened a new email, typed his request, and sent it to Sasha.

"You are so fucking whipped," he muttered to himself.

Ashes wisped across his taste buds again. Lukas glared at the Hot Sheet, still indicating Code Green. "Bullshit."

But all he could do was wait.

Chapter 17

"GARRETT, WHAT DO YOU EXPECT ME TO DO ABOUT IT?" Scarlett paced and tried to placate her manager, who'd spent the last five minutes complaining about how the band's message board was exploding with rumors about her whereabouts, each one more outrageous than the last.

"I just cleared it with Lukas," Garrett said. "Having you post a short message thanking your fans won't be a huge security risk."

Bailey Brown was under Lukas's desk not three feet away, puttering with the computer network. She bit her lip. Maybe Bailey could hack her password. Scarlett couldn't post a personal message without it, and right now she couldn't remember what it was to save her life.

"I'll take care of it," she told Garrett. She could call Sasha and have her read the password off the sticky note she stupidly kept taped to the underside of her laptop. Bailey would no doubt be horrified.

"Today," he responded.

Damn it. "Okay."

After paraphrasing the high points of what he thought Scarlett's message should say, Garrett shifted into ruthless prioritization mode. "I talked with Tia Quinn's editor yesterday. The interview's postponed indefinitely."

Scarlett murmured her thanks. She just wasn't ready to speak to the press yet, even if that member of the press was a friend. A blog posting, yes—but an interview would be more than she could handle right now.

When would media coverage die down? She glanced at Lukas's monitor, and just as quickly glanced away again. Regardless of which website she hit, every story seemed to use that intrusive picture taken of her and Lukas as they stood on the cliffs at Annika's funeral. The wind whipped the hem of Lukas's dark coat behind him like a superhero's cape. His face seemed frozen tight, but the photographer had captured something blazing in his eyes that drew her attention time and time again.

A shuffling noise caught her attention as Bailey backed out of the knee well of Lukas's desk. "I have to go now," Scarlett told Garrett. "Yes. Yes. Yes, I'll post a message today." She finally hung up, snatching her hand back from the phone. "Geez." Scarlett collapsed into Lukas's oversized chair and stared at the ceiling. "What is it about men?"

"That's a rhetorical question, right?" Bailey asked around the screwdriver she held between her lips. She grabbed some green cabling before diving back under the desk.

Yawning hugely, Scarlett scooted the chair further away from the desk to give Bailey more room in the knee well. She was exhausted, yet oddly exhilarated at the same time—because for the first time in a long time, her insomnia hadn't been caused by burnout or nightmares.

It was him. She felt... ready to explode.

When she'd finished her bath last night, and had seen Lukas sitting, barely clothed, at his desk, it had been all she could do to keep walking to the bedroom. The desk light had cast such fascinating shadows and hollows. He was bigger now than he was when they'd slept together so many years ago, but rather than looking tight and muscle-bound, he looked sleek, ready to rocket out of the chair.

And all he'd been wearing was a pair of thin cotton gym shorts that had done nothing to hide his reaction to her.

She hadn't slept at all, and it was entirely his fault.

A knock on the door startled Scarlett. "Expecting anyone?" she asked Bailey.

"Nope. Remember to—"

"—look at the monitor first," Scarlett finished with a roll of her eyes. "We're inside one of the most secure buildings in the Twin Cities metro. It's either Lukas or Jack."

"Probably," Bailey agreed, "but the first thing either of them will do is verify that you checked to see who was at the door before you opened it."

Another knock rattled the door, followed by a feline howl. "Scarlett, hurry up," Sasha called.

"Sasha?" Scarlett hopped out of the chair, sending it skidding. Taking an admittedly cursory look at the monitor, she saw Sasha and Antonia's dark, familiar heads—and Sasha losing her wrestling match with a huge cat carrier.

Scarlett tore open the door. "Calamity!"

Sasha stepped in, gently setting the heavy cat carrier on the floor. Calamity promptly banged his body into the side wall of the carrier, tipping it on its side.

Antonia put down the empty litter box that was being used to carry a bag of litter, a small pair of speakers, a snarl of other wires and peripherals Scarlett hoped

included her iPod dock, and her battered laptop.
"How—why—oh, I don't care." She hugged Sasha, then
Antonia. "I'm so glad to see you!"

"What did I tell you, Toni? I knew she'd be bouncing
off the walls with no one other than Lukas for company."

"Hi there." Bailey's greeting was muffled from her
location under Lukas's desk. She backed out of the knee
well again, jean-clad butt first. "Is Jack downstairs?"

"Yeah," Sasha said.

"Why don't you like Jack?" Antonia asked. "You two
fight all the time, but the car smelled like—"

Sasha quickly clapped her hand over Antonia's
mouth. "Jack drove us over. Rather than escort us upstairs, I told him to just leave us alone for awhile."

Tugging her sister's hand from her mouth, Antonia
added, "He said he'd bring up the rest of Scarlett's stuff
from the car."

"He has some use as a pack animal," Sasha admitted.

"The rest of my stuff?" Scarlett asked. "There's more?"

Sasha nodded. "Lukas emailed me last night, asking
if I could think of anything you might need or want, and
to bring it over today. We have some clothes and stuff
in the car. We also brought your four-track."

Yes. With her laptop and simple mixing board, she
was all set. "Bless you. I need something to do here,
because I'm going nuts. Might as well channel all this
angst into some songs."

Calamity growled. The box jostled and skittered
across the floor several inches.

Antonia indicated the litter box. "Where should we
set him up?"

"He hates riding in the car." Scarlett kneeled down

and peered into the carrier. Seeing her, Calamity let loose a pathetic meow. "I know, sweetie," she murmured. "Can you shut the front door?" she asked Antonia. "The last thing we need is for him to make a break for it. God knows what kind of havoc he'd wreak if he got downstairs."

Bailey spoke up from the desk, indicating the wiring she'd just finished working on. "How does he do with wires and cables?"

"I'm more concerned about the leather couch."

After getting the litter box set up near the pantry, Scarlett brewed a fresh pot of coffee for the women sitting at Lukas's big kitchen table, and settled in to catch up.

"I hate to admit it, but you've gained a few pounds, and your energy seems better," Sasha said.

"I've been nothing but pissed off since I arrived." Okay, that wasn't quite true. She'd been horny as hell, too.

"But you actually *have* some energy now," Sasha said, nostrils twitching. "You were so wiped out when you came home from tour, you were practically sleepwalking. Then, before you had a chance to recover your stamina, Annika died, and then you were shot..." She reached for Scarlett's hand with one of hers, and traced the healing scab on the tip of her ear with the index finger of the other. "You just... disappeared somewhere, and now you're back. Crabby, but back. Being here with Lukas seems to agree with you in some perverse way."

Scarlett's mouth opened and closed like a fish gasping for water.

"Now we don't have to lie to Claudette," Antonia chimed in as she peered into the pantry, extracting a box of individually wrapped Little Debbie snack cakes Scarlett hadn't known were there.

"Why would you lie to my mother?"

Bailey joined them in the kitchen, gesturing to the box Antonia held. "Bring those over here, kid, and no one gets hurt."

Antonia complied. Cellophane crackled as they each opened a cake. "She's worried about you," Antonia said, her mouth full.

Ah, damn. She hadn't talked to her mother since Lukas had kidnapped her nearly a week ago. Her mother hadn't called her, either. In fact, her phone hadn't rung for—

She sat up straight in her chair. She hadn't received a single phone call the entire time she'd been here? *As if.* "That son of a bitch."

Sasha and Antonia exchanged a guilty glance with Bailey.

"Damn it." Her anger went into the red zone. She looked at Bailey accusingly. "You helped him?"

"Didn't have to. He did it all by himself. It's pretty easy, actually, you just have to—"

"You all knew?"

Sasha sighed. "Lukas insisted that you needed some time."

Damn it. It was just like Lukas to be an uptight control freak and considerate at the same time. "I need to pick up my messages, damn it."

"Take it up with Lukas," Sasha recommended, glancing at her oversized watch. "He and Jack should be up with the rest of your stuff soon." A mischievous look crossed her face.

Uh oh.

"I really need to get back downstairs." Bailey stood. "Let's get that laptop plugged in."

"I'm officially pissed at you about my phone, but thanks for helping with this," Scarlett said as she joined her. "I know you have other work you should be doing."

Bailey waved off her thanks. "It's a nice change of pace. God knows the other work will be there when I get back."

In short order the laptop was plugged in and working. Scarlett watched over Bailey's shoulder as the other woman sat at Lukas's desk, her fingers flying over the keyboard, testing this and that.

"Want to hand me those speakers?" Bailey asked without turning around.

Scarlett passed them over. Bailey connected them, found Scarlett's music library, and randomly clicked. Justin Timberlake's "SexyBack" pulsed into the room. Before long, all four women were bopping along with the infectious beat. Bailey opened a dialog box Scarlett hadn't known existed, and with a couple of clicks, sharpened the sound.

"Wow," Scarlett said, narrowing her eyes. "How did you do that?"

"Skillz," Bailey said with faux humility. "I haz them."

Antonia swayed her hips. "Justin Timberlake is so hot."

"As hot as Stephen?" Scarlett teased.

Antonia's upper lip curled. "As if."

"Over your crush already?" Sasha asked, her own body moving in time to the music.

"What crush?"

The sisters grasped each other's hands and started dancing.

Bailey bobbed her head to the beat. "Your OS is two service packs back, and your security updates are from the Mesozoic Age," she said to Scarlett. "Want me to update them as long as I'm here?"

"If you have time. Thanks. My password is—"

"Don't insult me." Bailey waved her hand. "Go dance, have fun. I'll be a few minutes here."

She joined Sasha and Antonia, who giggled madly as they tried to samba to the thumping beat. They segued through to the tango, the foxtrot, and the cha-cha.

"Minuet!" Sasha called in challenge.

Antonia crossed her fingers in a warding motion. "Nope. That's just... wrong." Jamming by herself, she wandered off to snoop through Lukas's stuff.

Sasha bowed deeply over her extended leg, and then held her hand out to Scarlett with a flourish. "Shall we?"

When was the last time she'd simply danced without thousands of people watching? Sasha's excitement was infectious. "Yes. We shall," Scarlett responded, joining her hands with Sasha's, assuming the opening position of the centuries-old dance, letting her voice soar.

—∿∿—

Lukas felt music throbbing through the floor from two floors above as he and Jack climbed the stairs to the loft carrying the rest of Scarlett's belongings. A squeal of feminine laughter echoed in the stairwell. "It feels like we're at the club. What the hell are they doing up there?"

"Relaxing?" Jack suggested with a shrug.

Lukas scowled. Sasha and Antonia had been upstairs for well over an hour, and whatever was going on, at least the music they were listening to wasn't drenched with grief. He'd been right to allow Scarlett to have some visitors. Though he was certain he'd regret the cat, her happiness sparkled into him like fairy dust.

Gritty rock and roll pounded from the loft. A gravelly male voice slurred about a hottie with a million-dollar body.

"Nickelback," Jack murmured as they reached Lukas's door. "Hey, I don't live in a cave like some people I know."

Lukas juggled two duffle bags and a portable soundboard, trying to free a hand to ring his own doorbell. Jack's arms were empty. "Make yourself useful and hit that, will you?"

Jack pressed the knob. "You're the one who grabbed it all." They waited for a good half-minute, yet no one came to the door. "Music's too loud."

"Open it."

Jack did as he asked, entering the apartment first. Not watching where he was going, Lukas bumped right into him, because Jack had stopped dead not three feet from the door. "What the…"

Lukas had grown up watching Sasha dance, up to and including an unfortunate vogueing phase, but Sasha's current hyperextended side-straddled leg position was better suited to the strip club across the street than a dance floor.

Scarlett laughed as she sang along, her hips swinging in a way they never did when she performed, thank god, or he'd never let her out of her dressing room. She brought her hands to her head, tossed her hair, and arched her back, dancing in her own little world.

Lukas hadn't realized Scarlett was that... flexible.

As his traitorous lizard brain exploded with positions, with possibilities, Antonia whirled her long hair like a Whitesnake video vixen. "Hey, Thursday is Amateur Night at Sex World," she called. "Whadda ya think?"

The Incubus Second, slithering on a stripper pole? Lukas dropped the duffle bags to the floor. *Over my dead body*.

Sasha's leg froze in position. Scarlett stopped singing. Bailey's butt stopped twitching from side to side as she typed on a laptop at his desk.

"Hey, guys," Antonia greeted them, skipping over to kiss them both on their cheeks. "Did you know that Sex World is right across the street?"

Instead of answering, Lukas carefully set Scarlett's electronics beside the duffle bags. A loud yowl from the kitchen distracted Antonia, and she trotted away to check on that big, black cat.

"My soundboard." Scarlett's eyes glowed like she'd found buried treasure. She gave Sasha a hug. "Thank you!"

"You're welcome." Sasha blithely accepted thanks that rightfully belonged to him, and gestured to the duffel bags. "I packed a few other things I thought you might need."

Scarlett shot a dirty look at Sasha, dropped to her knees, and quickly pawed through the duffels. "You *didn't*."

Sasha snorted with laughter. "I most certainly did. Lukas said to pack things you needed."

"How about some bras?" Lukas muttered under his breath.

"What were you thinking?" Scarlett hissed at Sasha.

Scarlett's cheeks were on fire. Lukas could taste her embarrassment, and a spike of helpless mandarin arousal, across the room. Why was Sasha looking at both of them with such an evil expression on her face? "What are you two talking about? What did you bring?" he asked Sasha.

"None of your business."

"It's entirely my business. Is it dangerous?"

She considered. "In the right hands, yes. It could be dangerous."

A phone. Damn it. "Give it to me."

Scarlett's jaw dropped.

"Scarlett, either you show me what's in that bag voluntarily, or I search it myself. Your choice."

Their gazes clashed. Finally, Scarlett stepped back. Sasha burst into merry laughter.

Lukas knelt down, extracting items from the duffel bag as he searched. Several soft sweaters. A pair of butter-soft leather pants. Books. Silky bikini underwear, delicate lace thongs, and wispy bras that his rough fingertips longed to stroke.

His hand bumped against a colorful, oblong box made of hard cardboard. Lukas lifted it out of the duffel, examined all sides. Stationery, writing paper? Note cards?

Sasha was bent over double, holding her belly as she laughed.

What was the big frigging deal? He carefully pulled off the top of the box. Looked in.

And saw a bright yellow vibrator.

Chapter 18

THREE DAYS LATER, LUKAS SLOGGED UP THE STAIRS like an old man, pushing lank, sweaty hair out of his face. The workday was over, but the workout he'd just pushed himself through tipped his body from comfortably tired to uncomfortably sore. Between his Council work, transitioning Antonia into her new role as the Incubus Second, keeping Sebastiani Security running, and working with Gideon to find Annika's killer, he wasn't simply burning the candle at both ends—he'd aimed a flamethrower at the thing, and wax was melting all over the place. Guarding Scarlett on top of it?

Scorched earth.

If he hadn't already hit the wall, the conversation he'd had with Claudette a couple of hours ago would have sealed the deal. A "relaxed" family dinner? When he and Scarlett were bickering one minute and drooling the next? *Riiiight*. Like he was looking forward to putting *that* on display for his nosy siblings.

In retrospect, working off his frustration sparring two-on-two with Jack and Chico probably hadn't been the smartest idea he'd ever had. He'd rolled his ankle, his scuffed knuckles stung, and Chico had clipped his kidney with his sneaky left foot. Nope, he'd been distracted, slow, his timing a critical split second off—and once Jack and Chico had recognized it, they'd gone medieval on his ass. He still tasted blood from Jack's massive roundhouse kick.

He had no one to blame for his current condition but himself. *You're the one who insisted Scarlett live with you until Annika's killer was caught*. It wasn't Scarlett's fault that he'd criminally underestimated the impact her proximity would have on him.

He trudged to the fourth floor landing and shouldered open the fire door at the top of the stairs. The fact they hadn't caught the guy yet stung a lot more than his cut tongue did.

On the other hand, having Scarlett live with him was jacking his short-term productivity through the roof. To escape her luscious taste, and to give her a little bit of the privacy she so clearly craved, after dinner he spent long hours at his downstairs office desk, chipping away at his backlog long into the night, until exhaustion drove him to his too-short couch. But there was no escape in sleep, either, because despite the availability of a very large, very comfortable bed, Scarlett had gotten into the habit of crawling onto the couch with him in the middle of the night, ruining what little sleep he got.

Was she sleepwalking? Conscious of her actions? Lukas didn't know, and for a reason he hadn't probed into too deeply, neither of them had talked about it. He'd come to both dread and treasure that moment in the middle of the night, when the bed sheets rustled behind the partial wall, and she padded across the wood floor in bare feet. Once she lay down, she seemed to settle and drop off to sleep quickly, spooning back against the warmth of his body with a sigh.

She might have found the position relaxing, but it left

him wide awake and rock hard, wanting nothing more than to slip into her hot, tight body from behind.

How had he managed to simply wrap his arm around her for three nights running? His control was fraying fast, his frustration ratchetting into the stratosphere. He had to find this guy and get Scarlett out of his house before he did something he couldn't take back.

The guy was still out there, still up to something, because low-grade nausea plagued him like he had the flu. Still, no crime with their guy's signature had hit the Hot Sheet. If he was doing anything serious enough to result in a body, they hadn't found the corpse yet.

Lukas tasted Scarlett before he approached his door—mandarin, mixing with the slightest bit of ozone. Electricity? Was she using that foolish, yellow, bunny-eared vibrator?

He would not think about that inanimate rubber... *thing* touching her where he couldn't.

Ah, damn. Of course he thought about it, and the clingy, sweaty workout shorts he wore were too thin to provide even a whiff of camouflage. He'd never taken so many cold showers in his life, hadn't jacked off this much since he was a teenager.

It was hard enough to shove his feelings down when it was just the two of them—but now, thanks to Claudette, they had a damn family dinner to contend with. He had a couple of days to get himself under control, or else his family would be able to smell his salacious feelings for Scarlett like week-old garbage.

He heard Scarlett's voice as soon as he opened the door. It didn't take him long to find her, humming in the late afternoon sun, an open notebook and that damn black cat on her lap, her eyes closed, a headset clapped to her head. Her voice twined around his spine, tunneled into his brain stem, tugged at his dick from across the room.

She was sitting right in front of the goddamned window with the curtains open.

He strode across the room to whip the curtains closed. Calamity launched from Scarlett's lap with a hiss and a spit, and the notebook and headset went flying as she quickly stood to face him, arms defensively raised.

She let her arms drop and glared at him. "You scared the crap out of me."

She'd been ready to fight. Good. "Good," he repeated aloud. "You need to move away from that window. Now."

She gestured to the pink flashing lights across the street. "To avoid sniper fire from Sex World? Come on, don't you think you're overreacting just a smidge?"

"How does your ear feel today?" he snapped. "The one with a damn bullet crease in it because you were *shot at through a fucking window*?"

She stared at him. "Okay. Okay. Just calm down."

"I have to look at that damn gash in your ear every time I look at you. Every time I talk to you." And every time he did, failure sliced like razor wire. "What's the use of hiding you here if anyone with a camera—or a gun—can simply look up and take an easy shot?" He knew his anger was irrational, but, damn, if she couldn't follow even simple instructions, he couldn't protect her.

"Okay, okay. Point taken. I was just trying to enjoy the sun," she groused. "You don't have to be so bitchy about it."

"Bitchy?" he repeated mildly.

Scarlett whirled away from him and walked to her desk. "Jeez, someone woke up on the wrong side of the—"

"You really wanna go there?"

She didn't answer, which was an answer in itself. Instead, she busily shuffled and sorted papers on her makeshift desk, cozied up next to his. After just a few days here, the table he'd muscled up from the storage room for Scarlett to use for a desk was a mix of neat and messy, covered with electronics, torn-off scraps of paper, CDs in jewel cases, what looked to be a stack of legal documents, various writing implements, and a mug of cold tea.

Lukas picked her notebook up from the floor, staring at the scratches, scribbles, and sketches on the page. Damn good thing Scarlett was a singer, because if she was a painter, she'd surely starve.

She muttered something about prisoners and dungeons. Lukas looked down at his sweat-dampened workout clothes. Yeah, he smelled like a dungeon, all right. Her voice whipped, stung, and damn it, flicked over him like a tongue. She was really pissed.

And really aroused.

It was probably better if he left her alone, because if he touched her, he'd explode.

Suddenly she whirled toward him with her hands on her hips. "Do you get off on being my jailer, Lukas?"

A picture of Scarlett writhing in chains popped into his mind, and under his thin shorts he could feel his groin pound in time with his pulse. "It would be nice to get off on something," he muttered under his breath.

"Your sex life, or lack thereof, is not my problem." Her words were so stiff he heard them creak. "This is not a joke. This is my life."

"I'm not any happier with this situation than you are." He paced to the window and stood with his back to her so she wouldn't see his raging hard-on. Lowering his voice, he said, "Scarlett, we haven't found this guy yet, but it's just a matter of time." He scowled, remembering her comment about dungeons. "You're not a prisoner here."

"Are you kidding me? I can't even follow you to that window and throttle you until your teeth rattle. What did you say when I first got here?" She pitched her voice to Lukas's low rumble. "'You don't go beyond the door. Ever.'"

Given the control she had over her vocal cords, he probably *had* sounded like that much of an asshole. For his part, he barely remembered walking her through his door. What he most remembered was being scared out of his mind. If the bullet had been one inch to the right... "Cut me a little slack here, okay?" he said, jamming a hand into the hair at his temple. "You were still dripping blood when I brought you here."

"Like you care."

Frustration surged through him. "Keep going," he said in a too-mild voice.

"What?" She put her hands on her hips again. "What'll you do?"

"Turn you over my knee, you little brat."

Her pupils dilated, and tart mandarin spurted in to his mouth. Her nipples were erect. "This is..." He swallowed heavily. "This is hardly a prison."

"Yeah, your place is gorgeous, and your bathroom is beyond decadent, but I'm going nuts here, Lukas. Other than the people who work here, I've had exactly two visitors—Sasha and Antonia."

Guilt poked him in the gut. Was he really such a selfish bastard? "You can have people over." He quickly rattled off the names of people who posed no threat. "Your mother, my family. Your band. Garrett and Jesse."

"Thanks. That helps. But the fact remains, I can't leave. Do you know how frustrating that is?" She sighed. "I know this guy's on the loose. I get that." Her voice edged higher. "But I don't know how much longer I can—"

"Can what?" He stepped closer.

"Just forget it. Could you put on some clothes, please? And give me my notebook back."

He held it up over his head. "No."

"What are you, twelve? Give it to me." She leaped up, trying to grab it.

He choked back a groan as her breasts brushed against his torso. Tastes and smells clouded his thoughts, drove a stake into his common sense. No twelve-year-old, no matter how hormone-addled, could possibly imagine everything he wanted to do to her long, lean body.

On her next leap, he gave up and simply caught her— caught her and held her against him with one arm, the childish game of Keep Away the furthest thing from his mind. Her lethal legs scrambled for purchase against his. Was she trying to move closer to him, or to get away? He didn't know because he was too busy staring at her soft, pink lips. Moving his head closer to hers.

She stilled, and with a whispered "damn," wrapped her arms and legs around him, her body aligning against his, like a series of dead bolt locks slipping into place. Her chilly hands clamped against his upper back. Her cashmere-covered breasts nestled against his hard chest. Her hot, humid heat cradled his rock-hard dick.

Her lips crushed against his.

Lukas dove at her mouth. Her tongue slid against his, tangling and tumbling, and her gasp of delight nearly did him in. Could she taste herself on his tongue? The fabric of her yoga pants was as substantial as mist, and as he stroked his violently aroused flesh against her, he swore he could feel each soft petal of flesh underneath.

Scarlett squirmed against him. "You don't feel twelve," she breathed before licking her way back into his mouth with a devastating flick of her tongue.

Where was the music coming from? Scarlett wasn't singing—her mouth was too busy mapping the inside of his—but she must have heard the music too, because her breasts brushed against his chest in rhythm to it. Swish, swish. Swish, swish. He exhaled harshly as the cashmere dragged against his nipples. He moved his arm under her ass so she could keep right on doing it.

Lukas didn't like to dance, but as Scarlett's lithe body undulated against his in time with the music, he knew this was a rhythm he could keep.

The music must be coming from her headset. He couldn't hear individual notes, but whatever she'd been listening to made him think about plunging into salty ocean waves in the dark.

Damn her. He took her mouth again, the one part of her body he could get inside right now. The notebook fell, unheeded, to their feet. When her hands grasped and clutched at his bare shoulders for balance, he abruptly re-membered what he'd been doing before coming upstairs.

Shit, he reeked. He reluctantly pulled his mouth away from hers. "I really need to take a shower."

She laughed lightly, biting his lower lip. "You don't know smell until you live with three men on a tour bus for a year. No, you smell…" She buried her nose in the notch between his collarbones, where pheromones pooled and bloomed. Licked him. "Fabulous."

Saliva spurted under his tongue as her response flooded into him. With a moan, he rolled his hips against her, once, twice. Her response glittered back, coursing down his spinal cord and tightening his balls with a snarl of pleasure he couldn't possibly survive.

He couldn't do this. He couldn't have—

"Lukas." Staring into his eyes, she stroked herself on his cock.

Okay, maybe he could.

But she had to decide. Lukas couldn't allow her to mindlessly hitch a ride on his pheromones. She had to be perfectly clear, with simple words, simply said. "Are you sure this is what you want?"

Scarlett nearly laughed. "Want" was far too mild a word to describe the exquisite rush of blood, nerves, and hormones pulsing through her body. Lukas was bare to the waist and standing with his legs slightly spread, easily supporting her weight with a big, muscled body straight out of her most shameless warrior fantasies. His soft cotton compression shorts clung damply, lovingly, and did absolutely nothing to hide his bulging muscles or the long, erect ridge of flesh underneath. Pheromones pumped off him; she could almost see them steaming off his heated, aroused body. She couldn't help but breathe them in. Didn't want to stop, even as they clouded her common sense.

Mine.

Scarlett hardly recognized the voracious hunger battering her body. Why was he holding back? Why wasn't he touching her? Remembering what Sasha had told her just before the bullet had crashed through Crackhouse's window, she drew a fingertip along his clenched jaw. "Yes. This is what I want. This is what I need."

His entire body jerked at her words. She longed for his plundering, ransacking mouth to crash down on hers, to take her down, take her over, but instead, Lukas's eyelids drifted closed, and he breathed deeply, in and out, in and out, like he was meditating, or worshiping the aurora.

Damn the man. She tightened her arms around his linebacker shoulders, squirming to get his attention. He dragged her more tightly against his body, clamping his hand on her ass. His body radiated heat like a blacksmith's forge, and when he opened his eyes again, his irises had softened to molten gold. Scarlett half thought that they'd drip on her as he bent his head and slowly—too slowly—brought his lips back to hers. She gasped at the first touch, gasped again as his rough suede tongue caught her breath. He tasted of coffee and desperation and a dark flavor entirely his own, and damn him, he knew exactly when to coax, and when to plunge and take. Her body moistened, softened. Jealousy nudged as she wondered exactly how many women had tasted that wicked, wicked tongue.

What had started off as a languid, gentle kiss quickly turned urgent and feral. Lukas was barely holding on. Teeth clicked as they dove at each other, and when he felt Scarlett's tongue chase his back into his mouth, the groans he'd been throttling back escaped like a living thing. Dragging her against his body, he angled his head for better access. He could feel her heat, her wetness, the give of her intimate lips spreading for him. Smell her arousal as she readied for him. It wouldn't take much at all to just bully through the clothes, to—

She pulled back, audibly sucking in breath.

Shit, he'd scared her. "I'm sorry. I didn't mean to—"

"Nothing's wrong. I just need some air." When she unwrapped her long legs from around his waist, he felt the loss like an ache, but he set her down, and watched her step away. He wasn't surprised she wanted to call a halt to things. He'd crowded her, moved in too fast, and she was—

She was taking off her sweater.

He blinked and shook his head to clear it. No, this wasn't his fevered imagination; she was drawing the soft sweater up her torso and over her head, uncovering pert breasts covered by a sheer black knit camisole that he barely had time to appreciate before she whipped that off too, leaving her wearing only clingy pants, fiery red hair, and soft white skin.

He swallowed heavily. Were they really going to do this? Was he?

All the old arguments flagellated him as she turned away and walked to the bathroom, her tight ass shifting under the snug pants. She was too young? Not anymore. She didn't know what she was doing? As if. The night Annika had died, Scarlett had tested his hardness and length like a connoisseur, and just now, she'd rubbed against him like a woman who knew exactly what satisfied her.

As for hurting her? It was probably inevitable—but he'd hurt himself far worse in the process, because if he did this selfish thing, he'd have to get over her all over again.

As if you got over her the first time.

Steam rose from the shower, billowing out of the open bathroom door. The rhythm of the falling water changed as Scarlett stepped under the shower head. When she started humming, her voice bouncing off the rough tiles, he moved toward the bathroom like a marionette on strings. Despite his certainty that making love with Scarlett would be the most selfish thing he'd do in his lifetime, a sense of inevitability settled in. Ignoring the sexual tension between them wasn't working. Maybe it was time for them to work it out of their systems with a vengeance.

Like you'd ever get enough.

When he entered the bathroom, Scarlett was stroking his pine-scented body wash over her long, lean body, rivulets of water turning his functional soap to exotic suds. Bubbles clung to her stiff pink nipple like a dollop of whipped cream. She crooked a saucy brow. "I thought you said you needed a shower."

Lukas worked the stretchy compression shorts down his clenched thighs and dropped them to the floor. He vaguely registered her indrawn breath as he reached into the medicine cabinet for condoms and stepped into the tiled enclosure.

He survived losing her the first time. He'd probably survive again.

—ᴧᴧᴧ—

Nearly a half hour later, the water still ran hot, but Scarlett was standing in the shower alone while Lukas did… whatever had driven him from the shower like a fire had been lit under his very luscious ass. Her body was humming, and the slight soreness between her thighs left her in no doubt that she hadn't imagined his presence. But… had her memory been that faulty? Her dreams that outrageous?

Where was the flash, the fury?

He'd been so gentle with her. Her eyes narrowed. Too gentle. Damn it, he'd held himself back. His brain had been in the driver's seat the entire time.

She felt inexplicably cheated. She yearned to open her mouth and ream him out, to scream at him, but… what would she say? "Fuck me like you mean it?" "You can't break me, damn it?"

Unless she didn't make him as mindless with lust as he made her.

They'd spoken no words, made no promises. It didn't seem fair to be pissed at him for giving her three glorious orgasms.

But she was. Scarlett reached for the bottle of body soap that stood on the ledge. Her eyelids drifted closed as she sniffed. Here it was, the origin of the dark mossy scent that so intoxicated her when Lukas let her get close enough. And yeah, he'd gotten close all right, lifting her and pressing her back against the rough green and beige tiles, the breadth of his body spreading her knees wide. The first kiss of the broad head of his cock against her wet core had rocketed through her like an earthquake. She'd tried to hurry him up, to just get inside her already, but he would have none of that. Instead, he'd buried his head in the crook of her neck and slowly, gently, tunneled himself into her, pressing the very breath from her lungs and leaving her gasping for air. She'd waited for his big body to pound into hers, but instead she'd gotten gentleness and ruthless control. Yes, he'd found his own release, but he'd barely stopped quaking inside her before he'd withdrawn from her body, quickly showering off, stepping out dripping wet, muttering something about needing to get back to work.

Had he thrown her a pity fuck? Poor Scarlett, with nothing but a tacky yellow vibrator for company? "I'm a sex demon with outrageous skills and time to kill, so I might as well help Scarlett out with her little problem." No. Lukas wouldn't do that.

Would he?

Scarlett mentally played back the scene from the shower. Lukas's eyes had been on her face, on her body, the whole time, wholly attuned to her pleasure—but taking the bare minimum for himself.

Sasha was right. Stupid, stupid man.

"I'll... be downstairs," the stupid, stupid man called from the front door, not waiting for her to answer before it softly closed behind him. He'd set a speed record for dressing, unless he'd walked out the door wearing nothing but a towel.

So frantic to get away.

It was just as well, because right now she had no earthly idea how to deal with him. How would she ever convince him that she not only could take what he could dish out with that big, bad body, but that she yearned for it? Demanded it?

Stepping out of the shower, she grabbed a bath

sheet, dried off, quickly yanked on her yoga pants and a Ramones T-shirt, and pulled a wide-toothed comb through her damp hair. Before Lukas had come upstairs and distracted her, she'd had the wisp of a song in her head. As long as she had the place to herself, she might as well get a little bit of work done.

Loose-limbed and energized, she walked to her work area, smirking at Lukas's big, wet footprints marching from the bathroom to the bedroom to the front door. On her desk, her iPod still shuffled away. Picking it up and clapping it on her head, she rolled her eyes when Sigmund treated her to Adam Lambert's "Whataya Want From Me."

She couldn't let Lukas back off, back away. A frisson of excitement bumped low in her abdomen. She refused to live the way she had during the last year—hell, the last decade. By the end of this, either she and Lukas would be together, or they wouldn't. No more living in this gray netherworld.

She glanced at the door. *Enjoy this respite, big man, because it's the last one you'll get.* Until he came back, she could channel her current lazy satiation into a—

Her mixing software's Record button glowed bright red. Her jaw dropped. Snatching off her headset, she stopped the recording, dragged the slider back, and clicked Play.

Heavy breathing, his and hers. Her thready moan, his muttered curse. Even with the laptop's middling sound quality, she distinctly heard each collision of their lips, slippery, wet, and erotic. "Oh, my."

Inspiration hit.

"C'mon, c'mon, don't lose it," she muttered as she

quickly started another recording and snatched up her acoustic guitar, mindlessly playing the melody that exploded in her brain, fully formed. She visualized the layers they'd record: Stephen's syncopated taps down at the bottom. Tansy's steady bass line, pulling the song along. A slow, steady tension from Joe's rhythm guitar, a screaming lead from Michael—and her vocals surfing on top of all of it, as waves fought to the beach, crashed, and finally came to rest.

"Undertow," she whispered. She snatched up her notebook, opened it to a blank page, and scribbled down the words pounding in her head.

Get them down. Edit later.

Finally, the words flowed.

Chapter 19

"CAN I HELP YOU, SIR?" AN UNSMILING MAN WEARING nondescript scrubs asked from behind the desk the moment Stephen stepped off the elevator on the top floor of the hospital.

Stephen smiled through the jitters. He needed a jolt, and a few steps beyond the big man's shoulder, Andi Woolf's hospital room beckoned like the Promised Land. His skin felt ready to explode off of his frame.

What would he do if he couldn't talk his way past this guy?

Bits and pieces of last night's debauched tour of the city's underground sex clubs flitted through his mind. He'd blacked out again, but had somehow woken up in his own bed, clammy and nauseated, with a pack of paparazzi on the street and the beast sharpening its teeth on his ribs.

Stephen had tried to stay away from the hospital, he really had. It wasn't like he had fond memories of the place, but after losing the paparazzi who'd followed him from home, he'd aimlessly cruised the hospital most of the morning, first spending some time with his little buddies down in Pediatrics, even sitting down and making a couple of friendship bracelets with them, posing for pictures with their families, signing some autographs. Surprisingly, he enjoyed the little buggers' inane, cheerful chatter, and their endless questions had distracted him from how shitty he felt. After the kids had all gone back to their rooms, leaving him alone, he'd simply tailgated, making himself part of the anonymous stream of people pouring through the corridors of the Level One Trauma Center.

Unfortunately, the energy he absorbed passing Maternity, Physical Therapy, and the Chapel had been feeble, negligible. He couldn't get into the Morgue due to a new security door, but the ER had hit the spot for awhile. Helicopters whapped and chopped overhead, and pain drifted from the curtained-off treatment rooms into the hallways. But it still wasn't enough. Soon, an insidious mantra chanted in his head: *She's right upstairs. Right upstairs*.

Hot chills shook his frame. "Sir, are you okay?" the nurse—bodyguard?—asked as he stepped out of the elevator.

Do I look like I'm okay, asshole? Stephen nearly snarled in response, but he throttled it back. The guy was already studying him far too closely. The place was crawling with cameras they didn't bother to hide.

He could smell her from here.

"Sir?"

"I'm okay," he snapped.

But he wasn't. Nothing had satisfied him since the day he'd shot out Crackhouse Coffee's picture window—the day he'd made Lukas Sebastiani feel fear.

"Sir." The man moved from behind the curved desk and stood next to him, no longer bothering to hide the menace behind a professional façade. Their heads both turned as Andi's door opened and a middle-aged man emerged. Though impeccably suited and barbered, Krispin Woolf still looked rumpled. It was his face,

Stephen decided. The man looked like he'd aged a decade in two weeks.

Woolf's parental guilt, helpless anger, and curiosity wafted across the room as he looked Stephen up and down with imperious eyes. "Do I know you?"

Showtime. "Likely not," Stephen said, introducing himself and shaking the WerePack Alpha's hand. "I'm a friend of Andi's. I've been hospitalized recently myself, and haven't been able to visit until now. I thought I'd stop by and see how she's doing."

The other man took in the line of stitches marching across Stephen's forehead, and the yellow/green discoloration still mottling his eye. "You're the musician who was with Annika Fontaine the night she was killed."

Stephen didn't quite know how to respond. Woolf hadn't given the word "with" the judgmental sexual twist that some did, but that didn't mean anything. "Yes," he said.

Woolf tightened his thin lips. "If the police don't catch this man soon, they're going to get some help, whether they want it or not."

Stephen barely managed to keep his face still. If the rumors were true, this man operated on the shadowy fringes of fair, right, and legal, even though no one had ever been able to prove anything. "How is Andi doing?"

"She's still in a coma," Woolf said stoically. "She won't be able to talk to you."

"But maybe she'll know I'm there." Excitement coursed through him. "Sir, why don't you take a break? Go to the cafeteria, get a fresh cup of coffee. I'd love to keep Andi company for a while."

Woolf stared at him for what seemed like ages,

then finally gestured the guard back behind his desk and indicated that Stephen should follow him into Andi's room.

As he walked into the room, the first thing Stephen noticed was the sunlight. It poured in through the wide-open curtains, and the bland, white walls were covered with cards and colorful banners. A profusion of potted plants and flowers stood on the windowsill, and spilled over to stand along the floorboards. And finally, there was Andi, his Candy Girl, lying motionless on the bed, looking for all the world like she was simply napping.

Stephen's gut clutched as he stepped closer to the bed. Her eyes were closed, and her coloring was so pale that he could see capillaries threading under the skin of her lids. But her face was slack and relaxed, despite the tracheotomy tube protruding from her throat. A ventilator hissed rhythmically, and an IV needle was embedded in her left wrist. Her brown hair was slightly mussed on the snowy white pillow, reminding him of when he'd plowed his hands through it in the hallway the night they met.

"Look what that son of a bitch did." As Woolf stroked Andi's hand, there was a quick blip on the heart monitor, and then it steadied out again. "You know I'm here, don't you," Woolf said softly. "Yes, sweetheart, Daddy's here." To Stephen, he said, "She's recovering, but she's still in a medically induced coma. She keeps trying to tear the tubes out, don't you, my little fighter?" he crooned. Woolf leaned over his daughter, kissing her silky cheek before stepping back. "It's nice Andi's friends are visiting. She has so many friends. Commander Lupinsky stops by every day." Woolf's expression hardened. "There's no news, but he provides me with status reports nonetheless."

No news. It was the first information Stephen had heard from a reliable source. Rumors were running rampant, and of course the tabloids were having a field day printing whatever the hell they wanted to, but Lukas Sebastiani's news blackout had held firm despite the determined digging of both human and Underworld press.

"Thank you for visiting my daughter."

Stephen smiled gently and laid his hand over Andi's. "You couldn't keep me away." The heart monitor blipped, and then steadied out again.

Woolf's brow rose. "She must recognize you."

"I hope so," Stephen replied. *Not that we talked very much the night we met.*

"Enjoy your visit," Woolf said, walking to the door. As it closed behind him, Stephen overheard him telling the bodyguard, "She seems to be responding to him. Maybe she's ready to come out of it."

I hope not. The minute she does, I'm toast.

He didn't know how long he simply stood there watching her, lying so still in the middle of the hissing and blipping around her, but he finally found the courage to touch her again. When he put his hand on her shoulder, the monitor bleated in warning. Excitement and apprehension battled, but he didn't remove his hand. Instead, he leaned in toward her body, brought his head close to hers, and drew his tongue along the delicate shell of her ear.

A kiss. Surely, even with the cameras picking up his every move, he could get away with a kiss. He brought his mouth to hers and nibbled his way in. Her nipples hardened under the flimsy hospital gown despite the revulsion he inhaled from her. Her mind might protest, but her body remembered him, responded to him.

Stephen inhaled greedily as the monitor kicked into overdrive. Leaning over, he licked her ear again. "I'm going to make you feel so good." His head dropped to her neck, where her pulse raced under his tongue. He cupped her breast in his shaky hand.

Stephen. Child.

Huh? What—who—was that? Release coiled at the base of his spine. He was going to come. On the monitor, Andi's heartbeat jerked along with his body.

It took forever for the shuddering to stop, but when it did, Stephen lurched away from her bed. Groping wildly for the doorknob, he stumbled to the elevator with his hand over his eyes.

The guard stared at him as the elevator doors closed. Let him think Stephen was overcome with emotion. He was—just not the emotion the man might think.

After a quick stop in the first floor washroom to clean up, Stephen passed Madame Bouchet's room. Thankfully, she was asleep. What the hell would he say to her?

Had hers been the voice in his head? Or had it been his conscience? That sorry, atrophied thing?

Reaching into his pocket, he grabbed one of the garish red and purple plastic bracelets he'd made with the kids, and placed it near her hand, where she'd be sure to find it when she woke up.

Just as well she was asleep. He didn't want her to see him like this—stinking of semen and shame.

—⁓—

"I said I'm not touring anymore."

"What?" Sasha yelped.

Scarlett lowered the phone. What was that clicking sound? Lukas had been downstairs at Sebastiani Security all day long. Again. "Can you hang on a sec?" Without waiting for Sasha to answer, she lay the phone down on the quilt beside Sigmund and clambered out of Lukas's bed, where she'd spent hours refining the lyrics for "Undertow."

The song still cratered into her brain.

Calamity, draped at the foot of the bed like a sultan, yowled as she jostled the bed. "Yeah, yeah," she muttered. "Deal with it."

Clickity-click.

She peeked out from behind the heavy velvet panel and saw Lukas sitting at his desk in front of the open window. He wore battered jeans and a T-shirt despite the autumn chill, and scowled at something on his computer monitor.

When had Lukas come home?

Over a day had passed since they'd had sex; her body still hummed like a well-oiled machine. He'd been up and out of the apartment by the time she'd woken up. Despite his physical absence, his presence had been everywhere: in the scent of the full pot of coffee he'd left her, in the toast crumbs he hadn't wiped off the counter, in the damp towel hanging alongside hers in the bathroom.

Stepping into the shower that morning, finding it already wet from his use, had felt unbelievably intimate. She'd spent too many minutes imagining him running his hand over his body as he washed. How long would it be until she could use the shower without remembering being pressed between the cool sage tiles and his big warm body, with nothing to hang on to but him?

A frisson of excitement snapped down low. At his desk, Lukas swore, closed his eyes, and slowly inhaled before returning focus to his work. When he idly pushed a hank of hair behind his ear, she saw the buds nestled in his ears. At least she didn't have to worry about him overhearing her conversation with his sister—who still waited while Scarlett mooned over her brother.

She crawled back into bed, shivering a little as she snuggled back under the warm blankets. "Still there?" she asked Sasha as she clamped the phone to her ear.

"You drop a bomb like that and then walk away? Damn right I'm still here. You've actually decided to do this." Sasha's voice sounded disbelieving.

"Yes." Scarlett heard water splashing in the background. Sasha must be doing the dishes, a task Scarlett knew she hated. "Sasha, why don't you—I mean we—" she corrected carefully "—get a cleaning service?"

"Now that Annika isn't here to keep things scrubbed up?"

The verbal gut punch drove the air from Scarlett's lungs. On the other end of the phone, she heard the water shut off.

Sasha took a shaky breath. "Damn. Damn. I'm... sorry."

She wasn't the only person who'd had Annika's death upend the ground beneath her feet. "It's okay, Sasha," she said, injecting every lick of comfort into her voice she could.

"No, it's not. It was a horrible thing to say. I'm a terrible friend."

"Sash—"

"Sometimes I forget she's gone," Sasha interrupted starkly. "I hear Jack move around in her bedroom at night, hear the water running in her bathroom... and for just a minute, I forget it's not her. Then I remember she's never coming back."

Scarlett pinched the bridge of her nose with thumb and forefinger. Silence hummed on the line, a silence that said everything. "I miss her too, Sash."

"Yeah." Sasha cleared her throat. "I really want you to come home."

"I want to come home too," Scarlett responded, though she didn't know if it was entirely true anymore.

"About the cleaning service. I don't want strangers pawing through our stuff. And let's get back to the matter at hand." Sasha's sigh transmitted clearly over the line. "Are you sure about the touring thing?"

"Yes." This one thing, she was sure about. She settled back against Lùkas's big, king-sized pillows as Sasha immediately launched into all the reasons she shouldn't do this. Couldn't do this. Consider the fans. The roar of the crowd.

Hell, consider the money.

Scarlett just listened quietly as Sasha talked herself through the shock. "Sasha," she finally said, "I didn't say I wasn't going to perform again, or record again. I just said I wasn't going to tour."

A pause. "Oh."

"And guess where home base is going to be? Underbelly's going to make a mint."

Scarlett could almost hear Sasha mentally counting money over the line. "I can see where that might be beneficial, but I still don't get—"

"Sasha, even without assuming Annika's role as the Siren Second, I... have to stop. Running away to the road isn't healthy for me. It's way too easy to just blank out, to channel other people's emotions instead of feeling my own."

On the other end of the phone, Scarlett heard Sasha sigh. "It just seems like such a damn shame."

"But it's the right thing for me to do, Sash."

They both sat in companionable silence, until Sasha said, "Did Garrett shit a brick?"

"Yes, but you know Garrett. Before the end of our conversation, he had eleventy-thousand different ideas to capitalize on the situation."

"Thought so." Through the phone line, Scarlett could hear Sasha pour a cup of coffee. Sip it. "So, are you and Lukas are shagging each other blind yet?"

Whoa. "Not exactly," she finally managed—a vague non-denial which might fool some people, but probably not Sasha. For once Sasha didn't call her on it, and the reason for her distraction quickly became apparent.

"Don't you dare dirty up any more dishes. Drink it from the can. I'm not your maid."

Speaking of shagging each other blind... "The tension sounds pretty thick over there," Scarlett teased. "Why don't you two just do it already?"

"What?" Sasha squawked. "In his dreams."

Scarlett lay back against Lukas's sinfully soft pillows as Sasha rattled off a litany of complaints about her current nighttime roommate. "Sasha, it sounds like you're busy over there. I'll talk to you tomorrow."

"You'll see me tomorrow," Sasha corrected.

"What?"

Sasha's voice muffled momentarily as she covered the phone mouthpiece and said something to Jack before she responded. "Family dinner tomorrow night. Dad's place. Didn't Lukas tell you?"

Momentary pleasure streaked through her, but it was quickly overtaken by annoyance, and then anger. Of course Lukas hadn't told her. "No, he didn't mention it."

"Hmm." Scarlett heard four or five different opinions flit through Sasha's single-syllable response. "Your mother talked to him yesterday, and he said you'd both be there. You're getting sprung, girl— for one night, anyway." A pot clanged in the sink. "You need to spend time with someone other than my crabby brother."

Not that I'm spending a lot of time with him, either. Lukas could have said something, damn him, instead of ignoring her all day long. "I feel the need to give your brother a piece of my mind. Right now."

"Give him hell."

"Will do. See you tomorrow." Scarlett hung up and took a fortifying breath before padding out of Lukas's bedroom. Unfortunately giving Lukas a piece of her mind meant talking to him. Looking at him. How would she do it without staring at his lips? Without remembering what they felt like as they cruised over her wet body, waking up nerve cells she'd forgotten she had? Her steps faltered when she saw him sitting at his desk, listening intently to something on his computer. The expressions chasing over his face were impossible for her to interpret. What was he listening to that took him from concern to bliss in a mere ten seconds?

His nostrils suddenly flared. With a couple of

lightning-fast moves, Lukas hid his desktop and tugged the buds out of his ears.

Was that a blush staining his cheekbones? "Did I bust you watching porn or something? Can't it wait until after I go to sleep?"

"I am not watching porn," he responded through clenched teeth. "There are all sorts of things on this computer that no one else should see."

She gestured to herself with her thumb. "Siren Second, remember? We're colleagues now." One more thing tying them together, not that she'd learned anything about her new responsibilities yet. But yes, that was definitely a blush creeping up his cheekbones, and curiosity was killing her. "What is it? There's no way you can embarrass me, you know," she said with a laugh. "You can't imagine some of the things I've seen on the road. If it's not porn, what is it? Show me."

His body stilled like a deer in the woods during hunting season. For some reason, her heart galloped faster in her chest. Slowly reaching for his keyboard, he made his desktop visible again.

Not really knowing what she'd find, she dragged her gaze away from his face and studied the wide, sleek monitor dominating the space on his desk. *His music library. So what?* Almost everyone had a few songs in their library that embarrassed the hell out of them. What music did Lukas listen to when no one could overhear?

Placing her hand on his tense shoulder, she leaned over and squinted. Stilled when she saw herself in an open window, a video clip paused in motion, a microphone clasped in her hand. Froze when she saw the name of his playlist, highlighted in tiny letters.

It was called, simply, "Scarlett."

Her stomach took a loop-de-loop. Yes, it was her—and the band, of course. She snatched his mouse and scrolled, barely feeling her fingers. Song after song after song. The albums, the videos. The singles. Interviews. Her one official concert DVD, and a collection of audio and video bootlegs that would make her manager and webmistress weep. Amsterdam, Atlanta, Copenhagen, Detroit. Gstaad. Los Angeles. Mexico City, New York, Paris. Red Rocks, Rio. Sao Paulo. Zurich. The collection spanned her career and followed her around the world.

But the performance he'd been watching was a rough cut of her last show.

On the screen, she was frozen in position as she sang, pointing into the crowd, her eyes blazing and chock full of attitude. Unplugging the ear buds from the computer so she and Lukas could both listen, she clicked the Play button to resume the performance, wrapping her arms around his torso from behind and resting her chin on his shoulder. He relaxed slightly, but a quick look down into his lap revealed that at least one part of his anatomy was as hard as a rock.

She and the band were halfway through Queens of the Stone Age's "I Never Came," a slinky kiss-off song. Despite the sea of upraised arms from the crowd, the cameraman had a great angle, and hadn't lost sight of her and the band. Her black T-shirt dress was damp with perspiration, and the camera faithfully documented how it clung to her unfettered breasts. The hand on her hip and the sneer in her voice shouted pissed-off sexuality.

"You sounded so angry, but I couldn't look away, no matter how much I wanted to." Lukas's voice resonated in his chest, raising gooseflesh on her arms. As the song ended, she held her breath. If there was any justice in the world, the camera hadn't caught her helpless, hungry reaction to the moment she'd seen Lukas standing stoically backstage, his jaw clenched and the front of his pants bulging.

Nope, no such luck. There she was, staring backstage, wetting her lips before blindly segueing into Pink's "Fingers," a wicked ode to solo pleasure.

"Jesus, you're killing me," he muttered under his breath, and before she knew what was happening, he picked her up and plunked her down on his lap, on top of his outrageous hard-on. She shuddered in delight, but instead of kissing her or gobbling her up like she wanted him to, he just settled her more firmly in his arms so they could watch the rest of the show.

The longer they watched, the more certain Scarlett became that her decision to stop touring was the right one, because damn—she was one hot mess. Her sweat-dampened hair whipped up a storm, and her eyes positively burned as she worked the crowd with frantic energy. Every now and again, she caught sight of Jack's bright blond hair as he stood in the crowd at her feet, spreading his arms or jabbing an occasional elbow to hold back an overenthusiastic fan, his concern clearly etched on his face. She winced as she watched herself reach for her guitar and sling it over her body, as the homesickness, weariness, and loneliness all crashed in on her. The crowd quieted as the spotlight narrowed in, ruthlessly lighting her upper body as she strummed the opening chords of Stereophonics' "Maybe Tomorrow."

From this angle, she looked exceedingly frail and vulnerable.

She'd sung the entire song solo, accompanying herself with jangling, plaintive chords, her strumming propelling the sad, wistful song along to its oddly hopeful conclusion. As the last notes faded out, leaving her blinking in the spotlight, there was a hushed moment of silence—the ultimate performers' compliment—and then applause filled the void. The enterprising cameraman had chosen that moment to zoom in on the VIP box, catching her mother with tears in her eyes, raising a shaky hand to her mouth.

As the show galloped to an end, Scarlett thought that maybe, someday, she might be glad to have this emotional train wreck recorded for posterity, but right now she felt positively stripped bare. A lifetime of events had happened in the handful of days since then: they'd lost Annika. They'd almost lost Stephen. The assailant was still at large. She'd been shot. She'd become the Siren Second.

And she'd realized she'd never be able to extricate herself from this man who sat, hard and aching, beneath her.

Lukas's arms tightened. "Are you going to miss touring?"

He'd overheard her after all. "My touring days are over, but that doesn't mean I'll never perform again." She rested her head back against his big shoulder. "I came home completely burned out. Absolutely wiped." She gestured to the monitor, where she, Dave, and Tomas waved to the crowd. "The evidence is right there, in glorious Technicolor. I need to make some changes."

Lukas wrapped his arms more tightly against her. "Ramping up as the Siren Second isn't going to be a pleasure cruise."

Were his lips brushing against her hair? "No," she replied, "but I'll have a home base, and more control over my day-to-day activities." Her eyelids drifted closed. "No more wake-up calls. No more shuttling from event to event, from activity to activity, from car to bus to car, never breathing fresh air." She paused. "No more putting my life on hold."

Under her, Lukas's big body tensed, but he didn't respond. Lying quietly in his arms, she felt precious, protected. Like nothing could ever go wrong.

When Lukas's playlist moved on to an acoustic performance of "Pisces" that she hadn't played at the Underbelly show, her stomach dropped to her feet. Written mere days before she and Lukas had made love for the first time, her younger voice absolutely throbbed with longing and a desire she didn't yet know how to satisfy. Scarlett closed her eyes as her younger self poured out hopes, dreams, and fantasies about a nameless man who was bigger than life.

The man who held her right now.

"What's wrong?"

She cleared her throat. It took serious effort to not squirm against the hardness in his lap. "You've... got some video footage here that even Garrett doesn't have."

"It was the only part of you I could let myself have."

Scarlett opened her mouth to shriek like a harpy that he'd been the one to walk away without a word. The words were on the tip of her tongue, but she choked them back. It wouldn't help. He thought things through very carefully, and he had a sacrificial streak a mile wide. But in the case of their relationship, he'd based his decisions on faulty data, and damn it, his actions had cost them both dearly.

She twisted in his arms so she faced him, draping her legs over his thighs and her arms over his shoulders. "You're so wrong, Lukas."

His hands clutched convulsively at her hips. His jaw looked ready to shatter. "Wrong about...?"

Bringing her hands to his broad cheekbones, she leaned in until their lips almost touched. "About not being able to have me," she breathed. "You can, you know. Have me. Any time, any way." Her voice cracked. "You always could."

His pupils dilated at her incendiary words, but he jerked his head back as far as the desk chair could allow. "I—"

"You what? Feel absolutely wonderful?" she interrupted with a ruthless shift of her hips, stroking herself along the ridge jutting in his pants. "Know exactly how to touch me? Yeah." Scarlett threaded her fingers through his hair, tugging his head so he had to look her in the eye. "Please don't talk to me like I don't know my own mind, my own body. Listen to the lyrics of this song, Lukas, listen very carefully. I knew exactly what I wanted from you, long before we slept together, and I certainly know now."

In his expression, desire and duty battled for supremacy. She could tell he was trying to find the strength to deny himself—to deny her—and damn it, for what? She'd had enough of this martyr crap. "Just... love me, Lukas," she whispered against his lips. "And let me love you."

The seconds that ticked by felt like an eternity. Then Lukas closed his eyes, drew a ragged breath, and touched his lips to hers.

She surged against him, opened her mouth against his, bit at him in her frantic haste to taste him again. Dark and smoky, like the forest at night, and she'd never get enough of it. As their tongues stroked and twined, lyrics streaked through her head. His arms vised in, dragging her more tightly against his body. Had he read her mind, or had she gasped her demands aloud? It didn't matter, because she finally felt that wild spark that had been missing when they'd made love yesterday.

For endless minutes, their mouths clashed and fought, nipped and gorged. Scarlett tasted blood. Hers? His? It didn't really matter. Their hips rocked and surged against each other, but it wasn't enough. Scarlett's wet core clenched against a maddening emptiness that only he could fill. Delight shimmered through her when Lukas burrowed his hand under the waistband of her yoga pants and panties, hopelessly stretching them to get to her scalding heat. She raised herself up on her knees and shoved them down to give him more room, and was rewarded with a swirl of his big, calloused fingers before he plunged them into her body.

It was too much, and not enough. And Lukas must have either felt the same or read her mind, because he abruptly pulled his fingers from her clinging sheath, lifted her in one arm, and swiped the other across his desk, sending paper and files flying and the computer mouse and Pepto-Bismol bottle clattering to the hard wood floor. Plopping her on top of the chilly desk, he took his hands off her just long enough to tug off the yoga pants and panties, baring her from the waist down, and tear his jeans open at the fly.

Thank the universe he wasn't wearing underwear, because it meant nothing impeded her access to the treasure mounded underneath. Finally freed from confinement, his penis positively sprang into her hands. Twining her legs around his bare hips, caging him, she wrapped both trembling hands around his outrageous length and gently pulled him toward her aching heat.

Or tried to, anyway. At her touch, Lukas's massive body stilled. Scarlett tightened her grasp in warning, challenging him with her eyes. If he was going to pull away from her for good, she was bitch enough to make him stroke himself through her hands to do it.

A sigh shuddered through his frame, and then his expression smoothed out in resolve. Sweat popped at his hairline and above his upper lip before he finally dropped his forehead to hers. Finally flexed his hips toward her, pushing his hardness into her grasp.

"You're going to regret this," he breathed against her lips.

"Never." Letting go for a moment, Scarlett threaded her fingers through his hair again and kissed him, blinking back tears of relief. She didn't know where this would ultimately go, but at least now they had a chance to find out. "I need you inside me, Lukas."

His eyes were molten as he pulled her butt to the edge of the desk and spread her knees with his hands. Stepping closer, he fit his blunt tip against her wet opening.

Scarlett moaned as she looked down to where their

bodies were about to join. Seeing his big hand clasped around his own cock with such authority was about the hottest thing she'd ever seen.

Lukas pushed, breaching her with the broad head. Then, with a sharply indrawn breath, he suddenly withdrew. Backed away.

Her jaw dropped. "No way. I'm—"

"Condom," he gritted, his expression looking like a man walking to the gallows. "No condom."

Relief sheeted through her. "Go get one." He did, returning from the bathroom before she could miss his body heat, with the condom already in place. She strummed the triangular band of muscle bracketing his groin with her thumbs before bringing him back to her lush portal. "Now let me have you. I don't want to feel anything but you."

His eyes flared with heat at her words, and he pressed himself into her ever so slowly. Scarlett tossed her head as he fed her the first stinging inches.

She wanted fast and frantic. He couldn't fill her fast enough to suit her. Stroking him where her body stretched desperately to take him, she reached underneath his penis to cup his heavy sack.

He surged into her, knocking the breath out of her lungs. He loomed over her body, his eyes screwed tightly closed, breath heaving as he fought to keep himself still, even as she dug her heels into his ass, a rider spurring a stallion.

"Love me, Lukas. Love me. Let me love you."

So many emotions flitted across his face: wonder, guilt, desperation, stark pain chased by voluptuous pleasure. And finally the pleasure won. With a groan that sounded like he was being dragged to the depths of hell, she felt him finally slip the leash.

Chapter 20

"LUKAS, I'M GOING TO BREAK AN ANKLE," SCARLETT said, tottering on high-heeled boots. "Slow down. It's just our family."

He complied. They were really late, and despite their shower not a half hour ago, they probably still reeked of sex. "Why do women wear shoes they can't walk in?" he asked the cement ceiling of the Sebastiani Building parking ramp.

She shot him an exasperated look. "Whose fault is it that my knees are knocking? Help me out here."

Wrapping an arm around her waist, they walked to the private elevator at a more leisurely pace. Lukas swiped his keycard and glanced about the parking ramp as they waited for it to descend from the penthouse level. "We're over an hour late," he said testily. "I thought your friends would never leave."

"Hey, don't blame Tansy and Stephen. I could have showered a lot faster if you hadn't 'helped' me." She couldn't control the heat that flashed in her eyes even as she rolled them. "I'm starving," she muttered. "Rafe's probably eaten all the cheesy bread."

"I'm sure your mother saved you a piece or two." And if she hadn't, he'd make another batch himself, because Scarlett having an appetite was not an occasion to waste. While she'd filled out slightly since she'd been staying with him, she was still too thin.

Not that that stopped him from pounding into her body like a jackhammer at every opportunity in the past day.

The elevator announced its arrival with a soft chime and a swoosh of doors, and they stepped in. "I think Stephen really needed some company today," Scarlett said. "Thanks again for letting me invite them over."

Waking that morning with Scarlett still draped over his body, he'd told her she could have some visitors over if she wanted to. Her smile had rivaled the sun, and she'd peppered his face with thankful kisses. One kiss led to another, and… Lukas inhaled as he remembered the sight of Scarlett's fiery hair spread over the quilt the faeries had pulled kicking and screaming from his subconscious. Pushing into her body as she lay atop it felt like a long-lost puzzle piece finally clicking into place. He wanted to wallow in her, to never leave his bed, but Scarlett's stomach had growled. After eating, she'd showered and then immediately picked up the phone.

He'd attempted to work at his upstairs desk, but once Tansy, her bondmates, Stephen, and Michael arrived, the noise level scraped like claws, and someone smelled like an ashtray. He'd abdicated host duties to Scarlett and went downstairs. Leaving for a while had probably been for the best, because who was he kidding? It would be a long, long time before he could work at that desk without remembering how Scarlett looked spread upon it, a quivering, fragrant feast, demanding that he love her.

He had.

He… did.

As the elevator rose, so did the heat and tension between them. Clearing her throat, Scarlett reached into her purse, withdrew a tube of lipstick, and turned to the elevator's mirrored wall to reapply the color he'd kissed off at every stoplight between Sebastiani Security and his father's place.

Lukas stared as she stroked the moist color over her lips. After so many years of ignoring each other, of most emphatically not touching each other, now they could barely keep their hands—or their eyes—to themselves. He was absurdly proud that he'd put that blissed-out expression on her face, but he didn't want anyone to see it yet but him. His siblings didn't have an ounce of discretion, couth, or sense of personal boundaries between them.

The night to come had train wreck written all over it.

"Stephen thinks you're hot," Scarlett teased. "He couldn't stop looking at you." She mumbled something under her breath as she capped the lipstick and threw it back in the purse.

"What?"

"I said, I can't fault his taste." A smile lit her face. "Are you blushing?"

"No." His hot face contradicted his words.

"Yes, you are. Why?"

He shifted his weight on feet that suddenly felt like they'd grown five sizes. While he knew he was a competent lover, and prided himself on never leaving a partner unsatisfied, he was under no illusions about his looks. His brother Rafe had the face and body that women swooned over. Him? He was a throwback. He had size, muscles, and a preternatural ability to fight and protect. He lived in his body, and in most places—particularly between her fragile thighs—he felt too big, too rough.

She waited for him to answer, her head tilted up to his on a twig of a neck he could snap between his fingers. She was so small, but she'd taken him like a custom fit. He cleared his throat. "I didn't have anything to do with what I look like."

Scarlett rolled her eyes. "Yeah, right. Your parents may have provided the basic genetic material, but for as much time as you spend riding a desk, I notice you're not succumbing to middle-aged spread." She stroked his flat midsection, her hand coming to rest at his belt buckle. "You work out more than any person I know."

Because otherwise I'd fucking explode. Lukas eyed her steadily. Neither of them moved, but her eyes had softened, darkened. Mandarin sparked into the elevator like someone had peeled an orange. She might just as well have grabbed his dick and stroked. He stepped closer, whispering, "Just so you know, Stephen's not my type."

Scarlett tipped her head back. Shifted her weight toward him.

Ting.

The elevator bumped to a stop on the tenth floor. And they just stood looking at each other. Breathing each other. The doors started to close, and Lukas cleared his throat, pushing his hand into the gap to stop them. "After you."

As Scarlett stepped out, she glanced at her apartment door on the other side of the foyer. "As long as we're here, I'll pick up a few things. Why don't you go on over? I'll catch up with you in a couple of minutes."

Lukas's imagination ignited as he remembered the last batch of supplies that had come from Scarlett's apartment. "If you have any other toys like that yellow vi—"

"Shut. Up."

Face flaming, she stalked across the foyer, digging in her purse for her key. As she unlocked the door, Lukas eyed her spectacular ass as it shifted and flexed under her snug jeans. He didn't want to let her out of his sight, but she was as safe here as she was at his place, and they both knew it.

And maybe he'd have better luck jerking his unruly body back under control if he was alone for a couple of minutes. Remembering the ecstatic moans he'd coaxed from Scarlett with that diabolical yellow toy had made him as hard as a rock.

"Don't take too long," he said as she ducked inside.

She rolled her eyes and disappeared, the snick of the closing door echoing in the empty foyer.

After a couple of minutes, he entered his father's apartment. Noises and smells assaulted him while he hung his leather jacket up in the closet. Antonia's violin squawked from behind her closed bedroom door, fighting with the jazz playing softly in the living room. Sasha and Rafe sat on the couch, arguing about something. He walked past them with a wave, got two waves back, and followed his nose to the kitchen.

The scent of garlic and onions permeated the place as spaghetti sauce simmered on the stove top. Pillows of homemade ravioli were lined up on the cluttered granite cooking island, and a big pot of water boiled, untended, next to the sauce.

A quick glance around the room told him why. His father had Claudette pressed up against the door of the stainless steel refrigerator as he delivered a blistering kiss. Her hands twined into his father's hair while they devoured each other.

At least I'm not alone in this madness. What was it about the Fontaine women that turned Sebastiani men into slobbering beasts? "You're corrupting me," Lukas said with a grin, despite the bittersweet feelings that unexpectedly hijacked him.

His father loved again.

Elliott abruptly lifted his mouth from Claudette's, and Lukas crossed the room to greet them. As he leaned down to hug Claudette, she swiped her manicured thumb across the corner of his lip, blandly displaying smudges of Scarlett's lipstick. Plucking a tissue from the box on a nearby counter, she handed it to him and asked, "Just where *is* my daughter, anyway?"

Damn it. "Next door. She'll be back in a minute." Lukas scrubbed at his mouth. Sure enough, the tissue came away stained with Scarlett's red lipstick. Thankfully he could wipe away the evidence before talking with his siblings, all of whom would bust his balls over this with loud, smacking relish. Tucking the tissue in his pocket, he gestured to the boiling water. "Need some help?" Without waiting for an answer, he transferred pasta to the pot.

"The bread should be nearly done," Claudette said, opening the oven. "Better snag a piece now before Rafe smells it."

Elliott poured them each a glass of pinot noir. While the three of them worked companionably, Claudette grilled him about the investigation into Annika's death and asked pointed questions about Scarlett's well-being.

"Let's eat in here tonight." Claudette reached into the cabinet for a stack of casual plates.

Elliott gently took the plates from her grasp. "I'll set the table. Why don't you tell everyone we're ready to eat?"

Lukas shook his head. Did he look at Scarlett as hungrily, as possessively, as his father looked at Claudette? Were his feelings as nakedly displayed? Christ, he hoped not.

He heard the apartment door open and close. The squawking violin blessedly stopped. Greetings and laughter filtered in from the foyer, along with the mildest taste of mandarin. Scarlett was back.

"This get-together was a good idea," Elliott said softly. "Claudette is so worried about Scarlett."

Lukas's inner antennae twitched as his father's voice trailed off. Worry? His father stank of it. "What's wrong?"

The swinging door burst open, and the kitchen filled with squabbling Sebastianis. They were followed by Scarlett and Claudette, who walked with their arms wrapped around each other's waists, heads close together.

"Oof!" Lukas caught Antonia as she launched herself at him, her knobby knee narrowly missing his balls. Rafe winced in commiseration.

Antonia sniffed. "You and Scarlett are having sex, aren't you?"

Jesus. Lukas felt like he'd just taken a shot to the testicles after all. Scarlett's jaw dropped. "Remember what we talked about, Antonia?"

"But you're not a stranger. Are you boyfriend and girlfriend, or are you just sleeping together?"

"Excellent question, Antonia," Sasha said with a shit-eating grin. "Lukas, is Scarlett your girlfriend?"

Lukas shot Sasha a look that said "bitch" every bit as clearly as if he'd spoken it aloud, and then looked at Scarlett, who suddenly seemed very interested in the kitchen's hickory hardwood floor. How the hell was he supposed to answer such a question? "Girlfriend" was much too tepid a word to describe his snarled-up feelings.

"It's really none of your business," he said to his sisters.

"That means 'yes,'" Antonia told Sasha.

"Girls, quit teasing your brother," Elliott said. "Everyone, please sit down. We're ready to eat."

Everyone grabbed a dish or an item needed for dinner, setting the table as they went, as was their routine. Without thinking about it, they'd set the table for eight. Annika's chair sat empty, like a socket missing its tooth. And until he felt his siblings' eyes on him, Lukas didn't realize that he'd taken the seat next to Scarlett rather than his usual position across the table, next to Antonia.

Elliott approached the table with a bottle of chilled Moët, and Claudette followed, carrying champagne flutes. Lukas turned to Scarlett, a question in his eyes.

"Don't ask me," she murmured, placing her hand on his upper thigh under the table. "I've been your prisoner for over a week."

Everyone waited until Elliott poured the champagne. "Claudette and I have an announcement to make."

"You're sleeping together too?" Antonia said. "Duh."

Elliott looked to the ceiling, took a deep breath, and then said, "Claudette has agreed to become my bondmate."

While Scarlett, Sasha, and Antonia congratulated

his father and Claudette, Lukas looked on with mounting concern. It was one thing to know their parents were companions, in a relationship. But… bondmates? This news would rock the very foundation of the Underworld Council.

Rafe sidled close, jabbing him in the ribs with his elbow. "Sleeping with your stepsister? Pretty kinky, dude."

Lukas shot his brother a withering look and joined in the congratulations.

It was well past 2:00 a.m. when the last toast was offered, the last dish was washed, and last hugs good-bye were bestowed. As Lukas pulled out of the now-empty Sebastiani Building parking ramp, Scarlett tipped her head back against the soft leather headrest. "Oh, man." She looked at Lukas, sitting in command in the driver's seat, and thought about the comment she'd overheard Rafe make to Lukas upon hearing the news. "This is officially weird."

Lukas smiled slightly, tapping his big fingers against the steering wheel as he navigated the short route back to Sebastiani Security. "After everything that's happened lately, it's great to finally have something to celebrate."

Scarlett looked over to the man who'd shared so much of her life. Their parents were going to be bondmates. If their relationship didn't work, she'd never be able to escape him.

Lukas braked the car to a stop as they approached a snarl of traffic. Scarlett dragged her eyes away from his flexing thigh muscles. "Sure is a lot of traffic for a weeknight," she said, covering a yawn with her hand.

"I'm glad we're almost home. I really shouldn't have had that third glass of—"

"Get down," he ordered, jerking the steering wheel. The car swerved violently.

But she wasn't fast enough. Flashbulbs blinded them as Lukas wove the big car through the gauntlet of people and haphazardly parked vehicles blocking the entrance to Sebastiani Security.

"Shit."

Crouched down in the front seat, Scarlett shivered at Lukas's feral tone. As they drove past Sebastiani Security, she poked her head up and saw what Lukas had: Chico, relieving a trespasser of a handgun, ejecting a clip into his hand.

Finally clear of the crowd, Lukas hit the gas and sailed down Washington Avenue, not stopping for lights, and not speaking until they hit the exit for northbound 35W.

"Where are we going?" Scarlett said with resignation. Tears stung. She was so tired of feeling like an animal in a cage. Just so tired.

Lukas's hand covered hers. "Fancy a trip to the lake?"

She appreciated the effort, but all she could do was lean back against the seat and try not to cry. "Sure. Anywhere. Anywhere but here."

———

"Hey," Lukas said softly. "We're here."

Scarlett cursed as she blinked into the bright morning sun. NPR's "Morning Edition" droned sonorously from the radio as Lukas muscled the big car around the last hairpin turn on the rutted logging road leading to the

Sebastiani lake property, one hundred and fifty acres of pine-and-birch-treed privacy on one of the dozens of lakes strung along the border between Minnesota and Canada. When he reached their private road, Lukas stopped the car and slid out with a fluid shift of muscle that didn't show any indication that he'd driven nearly three hundred miles in the dark with no sleep.

He left the door ajar while he unfastened the rustic fence blocking the entrance. As chilly air filled the car, Scarlett clutched the soft fleece blanket more closely around her shoulders.

She'd been to the Sebastiani cabin many, many times before. When they were teenagers, she, Annika, and Sasha had practically lived here for weeks on end, their most important goal being obtaining the ultimate summer tan. She'd certainly never been here alone with Lukas before, and suddenly the rustic surroundings were full of sensual possibilities.

Annika, I could really use some advice right about now.

Lukas slid back into the car with a swoosh of T-shirt over the seat. His nostrils flared. "You okay?"'

"Yeah," she said. "It's just that the last time I was here, Annika was with me." She suddenly giggled. "Remember the time Annika fell asleep in the sun with her hand on her stomach? It took her days to even out her tan."

"Too many memories?" he asked. "Do you want to go back?" Lukas's hand flexed on the shifter, just as willing to turn around and drive five hours south as he was to continue on to their destination less than a minute up the rise.

"Keep going."

Dragging his gaze back to the road, Lukas put the car into gear.

The thick canopy of leaves and branches scraped the roof as the big car bumped and lurched over the rugged dirt road. As the narrow road opened onto a cut grass clearing and the backside of a sprawling log cabin, a squirrel scampered by with its cheeks packed with food for the coming winter.

"Logs need to be restained," Lukas muttered as he braked the car to a stop.

Scarlett shrugged, saying nothing. She liked the look of the faded logs. The cabin and outbuildings came by their weathered appearance honestly, standing stalwart against northern Minnesota's long, brutal winters and hot, humid summers. Elliott Sebastiani had bought the land and built the cabin shortly after Dasha Sebastiani's death, to help his children heal and to get away from life and death decisions, if only for a few days at a time.

Lukas got out of the car, popped the trunk, and extracted three grocery bags bulging with food. *He'd let her sleep while he grocery shopped?* Grabbing her purse, she dragged herself out of the car and scrambled after him as he unlocked the door.

"Rafe was here last weekend, so at least the place is aired out," Lukas said as he walked into the kitchen and set the bags down on the scratched butcher block counter top.

"I'll put away the groceries," she offered. Time to start pulling her weight.

"Thanks," he said. "I'll go unlock the outbuildings." He picked up a yellow kayak leaning drunkenly against the dining room wall, swung it up to his left shoulder, and carried it outside with him.

Scarlett dropped her purse on the dining room table and swiped open every cheerful orange cotton curtain to let the light in. The first floor of the cabin was basically two huge rooms—on one side, a multipurpose kitchen/living room/dining room, and on the other, a communal sleeping area furnished with a hodgepodge of beds bearing mismatched quilts. Above the sleeping area was a loft with two bedrooms, one used by Elliott Sebastiani, and the other by guests, or more typically, by her mother. Scarlett giggled softly. How long had her mother been sneaking across the hall to Elliott's room while their clueless children slumbered below?

Her *mother, not theirs*. Her smile dimmed. Her subconscious was processing Annika's death whether she wanted it to or not.

On a shelf near the door, battery operated lanterns, flashlights, bug spray, and sunscreen stood at the ready, and a menagerie of sweatshirts and coats in various sizes and colors hung on sturdy hooks. Good thing, too, Scarlett thought, because other than the underwear she'd presciently grabbed while she was at her apartment last night, she had nothing to wear but the clothes on her back.

What would Lukas do about underwear?

Don't go there. Scarlett snagged a sweatshirt at random, pulled it over her head, and went back to the family room, which was a mix of rough and luxe that suited the Sebastianis perfectly. A rust-colored cashmere throw lay over the back of the battered leather couch, and pieces of Rafe's sculpture were prominently displayed on the fireplace mantel, covered in enough dust to make a museum curator gasp. A clear quart canning jar containing an

arrangement of dried grass, cattails, and pussy willows
sat on the coffee table next to a well thumbed Ellery
Queen mystery novel. Bookshelves along the north
wall groaned under the weight of haphazardly stacked
books, CDs, DVDs, and board games. Framed snapshots
elbowed for their share of the space.

Scarlett turned away from the bookshelf and went to
the dining room. She couldn't face the pictures just yet.

The previous weekend, Rafe had pushed all of the
mismatched dining room chairs against the outer walls
to give himself room to work, and pieces of wire and
chunks of metal littered the newspaper-covered table.
She wasn't going to touch any of Rafe's things—especially that scary-looking soldering iron—but she turned
on the small boom box.

Her own voice. Her first CD, she realized with a
sinking heart. The songs she couldn't let herself sing.
It was past time she put on her big girl panties and
confronted them.

Leaving the player on, she checked the open kitchen
shelving unit for supplies, glad to see dried pasta, jars
of sauce, microwave popcorn, and cans of soup. On top
of the refrigerator were two unopened bags of potato
chips, and the ingredients for S'mores. No matter what
Lukas bought or didn't buy at the grocery store, they
wouldn't starve.

Someone, probably Rafe, had left half a package of
Oreos in a Ziploc bag sitting out on the kitchen counter.
"Bless you," she breathed as she tore the bag open and
ate breakfast over the sink looking out at the water.

She'd forgotten how relaxing it was here at the cabin.
And she'd forgotten that the family snapshots were

scattered everywhere, without rhyme or reason. Here in the kitchen, a decorative grouping of items hung near the double oven: several antique kitchen utensils, a vine-laden tile that asked, "Want some whine with that?" and a snapshot of her, Annika, Sasha, and Rafe tanning down on the dock as teenagers, their chaise lounges slanted to maximize the angle of the sun.

The memory stung like lemon juice on a paper cut.

She tore her eyes away from the picture and put away the groceries Lukas had bought. No junk food, of course—just plenty of lean meat, fruit, and vegetables. He'd even bought dried fruit. What the hell for, survival? Scarlett snorted. While the cabin's location might seem wolf-howl desolate—and yeah, in the middle of winter you definitely had to think about what you'd do if you got snowed in, or lost heat—there was a thriving tourist town less than ten minutes away. If push came to shove, all they had to do was hop in the car, and they could quickly have food, alcohol, tossed-to-order pizza, Internet access, shopping, cappuccino, and fresh bait.

After she folded and put away the grocery bags, she stood in the middle of the kitchen, at a loss about what to do next. If she was here with Sasha, or Annika, or as part of a larger group, she'd already have chosen her bed.

Scarlett bit her lip as she walked to the bedroom. The sexual tension between her and Lukas was thick enough to cut with a knife—and god knew that within the last twenty-four hours they'd had each other left, right, upside down, and backwards—but it seemed presumptuous to assume that they'd share the largest bed in the communal bedroom, a queen-sized mattress which had been Lukas's since he'd outgrown the others.

Would Lukas even want to share a bed with her?

Quit mindfucking it to death. Where do you want to sleep? She dropped her purse on Lukas's bed. She was sleeping here; he could make his own decision.

The morning sun struggled weakly against the room's west-facing curtains, and Scarlett crawled across Lukas's bed to open them. Outside, the lake was glass smooth, and while a few stubborn red leaves still clung to the maples, most of them had fallen to the ground. She didn't see or hear ducks and geese. They'd probably already packed their bags and flown south for the winter.

She heard Lukas down on the ancient railroad tie dock, winching the fishing boat into the water. He must have left some clothes in the sauna, because he'd changed from the khakis and pressed oxford he'd worn to dinner the previous night to a pair of jeans that were clearly his, worn nearly white at the stress points. The ratty U of M sweatshirt was stretched beyond structure at the neck, waist, and armbands, and his hair was lashed into a ponytail.

She wanted to lift the waistband of that sweatshirt with her teeth, and wash his cobblestone abs with her tongue.

Lukas's head whipped toward the cabin.

Busted. Rather than duck, she stayed right where she was, kneeling on Lukas's bed. The air stilled as they stared at each other.

Finally, he moved.

~~~

Indecision and lust battled within him in an epic tug-of-war. Scarlett was exhausted, and the dark shadows under her eyes had haunted him for most of the drive up north. The last thing she needed was for him to fall on her like a lust-crazed beast. But her voice called to him, tugged at him, even though her mouth was closed. Had she finally found a way to burrow directly into his brain?

It must be the boom box, he thought with one of his few remaining brain cells. But then jealousy gashed its teeth. What the hell had Rafe been working on that he needed to channel such sexually charged inspiration? From Scarlett?

Hell.

If you're going to get jealous of every man who fantasizes when Scarlett sings, you're in for a lifetime of hurt.

Up at the window, Scarlett smiled a Mona Lisa smile, and then backed out of sight. She might as well have grabbed onto his dick and pulled. She had to be on his bed, where he'd spent far too many nights trying to ignore the flame-haired girl sleeping across the room.

His legs quickly ate up the ground between the dock and the cabin. The screen door snapped closed behind him like a trap.

Scarlett came out of the bedroom to meet him wearing a faded Sorbonne sweatshirt that was four sizes too large.

She was so beautiful.

She'd opened the curtains, and sunlight blazed into the room, setting each strand of her hair crackling with fire and bleaching away the shadows under her eyes.

He drew his index finger along the sweatshirt's frayed neckline. "Is this Rafe's?"

She shrugged, unconcerned. "Probably."

First things first—getting his brother's clothing off

her body. Lukas tugged the sweatshirt up and over her head, taking her sweater with it, leaving Scarlett wearing only yesterday's jeans and a delicate lace camisole. It was a confection of lime green, hot pink, and bright purple, and it clung to her cupcake breasts like butter cream frosting. As he licked along the lacy border, he felt her hands fumbling with his ponytail until his hair loosened and spilled. She tugged his head to her erect nipple, and made a demanding sound deep in her throat that shivered up his spine.

He could only obey. As he suckled her through the silk, it was all he could do not to just bite down to see if her mandarin taste would spark into his mouth. But when he let her feel the edge of his teeth, her nipples pebbled even harder.

I need to have her. "I need to have you," he said aloud, wincing as soon as the Neanderthal words left his lips.

Scarlett cruised her eyes over his face, his body, and arched a brow. "Same goes."

His breath hitched at the thought of being... had. But he had to throttle back, keep his head. This was going to be all about her, he thought, even as she brought their torsos together and lifted her mouth up to his, dragging the dampened silk and lace against his sweatshirt.

There were too many layers of fabric between them. He wanted to feel that silk against his skin. Separating his lips from hers with a groan, Lukas set her back and whipped off his own sweatshirt and T-shirt. She shuddered. With desire, or with the cold?

Lukas quickly crossed to the fireplace, mentally thanking Rafe for restocking the kindling and logs before leaving last weekend. He built a fire, impatiently feeding it until it sparked and blazed. Behind him, Scarlett's mandarin essence ripened to mango.

Christ, he could get drunk on her taste alone.

Rising from his crouch, his shoulder blades brushed up against bare legs—yards of silky, bare legs. *She'd undressed for him*. He smiled when he saw her thick white ankle socks. How far had she gotten? If he tipped his head back toward her body, would his hair tangle in her luscious bush?

With a hitch in his breath, he did it—and brushed against even more silk.

Standing behind him, Scarlett stroked her chilly, clever hands over his shoulders and chest, and traced the downy trail of hair leading to the waistband of his jeans. Her silk and lace camisole slipped against his skin. "You're wearing too many clothes," she said, her voice shivering into his ear as she tugged at his fly.

The buttons slithered open, and Scarlett's guitar-calloused fingertips burrowed under the elastic waistband of his snug boxer briefs. Strumming his length, she dipped her head to the crook of his neck and nibbled.

He thrust heavily into her hands, once. Twice. *Jesus*. If he didn't slow this down, it would be over before it began. "Let me get these off," he said.

She stepped back so he could wrestle out of his boots, jeans, and briefs.

"Stop right there," she said suddenly. "Let me look at you."

Taking several crucial steps back from the crackling fire, he obeyed. Waited. He shifted his weight impatiently, almost feeling her gaze stroking his butt.

Finally he shot her a look over his shoulder, and she twirled her forefinger in the air, giving him permission to turn around. Before she could treat his twitching dick to the same ogling she'd given his ass, he closed the distance between them. The scraps of candy colored silk she wore were in his way. Lukas edged his big hands under the hem of her camisole and drew it up her narrow torso, felt her breath snag as he avoided her breasts and lifted it over her head.

Shadows from the fire flickered over her pearly skin. He lowered his mouth and traced the shifting patterns with his lips and tongue, skimming over her shoulders and collarbone before taking a meandering route between her breasts.

When he finally licked her pebbled nipple, she clutched his head and held him against her breast. "Don't move."

Moving was the very last thing on his mind. When he leaned in, latched on, and suckled, she rose on tiptoe, clutching at him for balance. Before she could entirely right herself, he nudged his foot behind hers and tipped them onto the worn, leather couch in front of the fireplace. He lifted his head for a moment and stared at the picture she made, with her torso arched over the arm of the couch, breasts kicked up into the chilly air, her neck bared, and her hair waterfalling over the edge.

"Lukas," she moaned, removing her hands from his head to clutch at her own breasts. She mindlessly arched off the leather, bumping her crotch against his mouth.

Jesus. Covering her hands with his own, he buried his face in the fuchsia silk and wallowed.

Lukas half-expected to be dragged from the dream any minute now, waking lonely in his bed with his dick in his hand. But no, that was the couch leather rasping against his bare skin as he shifted over her. Those were the narrow elastic bands of her panties snapping in his hands. That was Scarlett, spreading her legs for him as he whisked the scrap of silk out of his way.

The firelight turned her pubic hair to flame. He covered her mound with his hand, threaded his fingers possessively through the soft decoration. Her taste already effervesced on his tongue, and he hadn't touched her with it yet. Lukas closed his eyes momentarily, and then parted her with his big fingers. Her soft, pink center glistened with dew, and when his fingers slicked over her slippery center, Scarlett moaned, cupping his cheek with her hand.

His mate was ready to take him. Lukas thanked the universe for the snarled genetics that allowed him to experience her as no other man could.

Her hands latched onto his hair. "Lukas?"

"Hmm?"

She shuddered as his response vibrated against her most sensitive skin. "Don't stop. Don't... leave."

You've got to be kidding. "I'm not going anywhere." Against his will, his hips flexed against the leather, trying to get some relief for his aching dick. He had to please her—now—because once she got her hands on him, he'd be a goner.

He held her in place as he licked and teased, taking endless minutes to respond to her every twitch and moan. When he finally gave her the firmer touch she craved, she crossed her cotton-clad ankles behind his head to hold him in place, her nails scratching against his skull. Her body clenched, gathering itself under his mouth and tongue.

She exploded with a sharp cry that rattled the windows in their frames. His vision went gray around the edges as he frantically inhaled, lashing himself to the mast to ride out the storm.

───∿∿∿───

When Scarlett opened her eyes, Lukas sprawled over her, leisurely suckling on her hipbone like he had all the time in the world. Even though he outweighed her by more than two to one, his weight felt oddly comfortable, like a favorite blanket.

She swiped at the damp hair at his temples. "Hey."

He lifted his head and smiled. "Welcome back."

She tugged at his hair. "You don't have to look so proud of yourself. So I passed out for a couple of seconds."

When Lukas levered himself up and got off the couch to put another log on the fire, she missed the weight immediately. He looked really satisfied—far too satisfied for someone who hadn't come himself.

After poking at the fire and closing the grate, Lukas turned back to her. Backlit by the fire, he looked absolutely huge, hewn from stone and larger than life until you looked for the softness. His small copper nipples nestled in a bed of fine hair, and a tawny trail bisected his lower abs, the hair broadening and coarsening as it reached his cock, which was rampantly and unapologetically erect. A well-healed scar marred the surface of his left thigh, but his legs looked as sturdy as tree trunks. Even his gunboat feet were sexy. His body looked hard as the mountains, and she felt like a boneless jellyfish washed up on the shore.

No wonder no one else had ever measured up.

He moved closer to her, leaning down for a kiss—the softest, most reverent kiss. Her salty musk mixed with the dark sin of his mouth.

She had to touch. His jaw would be clenched one hell of a lot harder by the time she was done with him.

She tugged him down onto the couch with her, painting his tongue with hers. While he was occupied, she cupped his balls in her hand, swallowing down his grunt like caviar. When he tried to pull back, she tightened her grasp. "You said you weren't going anywhere," she reminded him. "You can dish it out but you can't take it?"

Yes, his jaw was definitely clenched.

"Scarlett…" he gritted out, "there's nothing I want more than your mouth on me. To be inside you." His eyes wandered her body, and his hands followed. "But… look."

Scarlett looked at the whisker burns he'd scraped onto her breasts and stomach. Reddened fingertips tattooed her hips, and she had a hell of a hickey on her hipbone. "Yes," she breathed as desire rocked her anew. "Look."

He brought his forehead to hers.

Damn that sacrificial streak of his. What could she do that would—a brilliant idea popped into her head.

Oh, this was gonna be good. "So you think that you hurt me just by touching me."

He nodded.

"So… don't. Don't touch me." She treated the head

of his penis to a wicked twist of her wrist. "You *can't* touch me."

She scooted off the couch and knelt between his knees. "You can look, but you can't touch. Does that make you feel better?" She indicated his hands, clenched into fists at the side of his legs on the leather couch. "Keep them right there. You don't want to hurt me now, do you?" The mocking smile in her voice didn't match her schoolmarm expression.

Sacrifice and need warred on his face—but his body was ready for action.

Scarlett sat back on her heels, raising her hands like she was poised in front of a piano. "Where should I start?" She stroked her fingers along the tendons of his feet and ankles, surprising a grunt from him. Wrapping her hand around his lumpy calf muscle, she lifted his foot to her mouth and quickly, sneakily, suckled on his baby toe.

His hands clenched the seat of the couch.

She was going to drive him mad. "Close your eyes, Lukas," she invited. "Where will I touch you next?"

He obeyed, shuddering as her hot breath puffed against his sensitive anklebone. She nibbled her way up his shinbone to his knee. "Spread your legs," she whispered. "Give me some room to work."

He complied, and she rewarded him by skimming her lips and tongue over the gooseflesh pebbling his inner thigh. When she shouldered her way between his legs, pushed them open even wider, his cock jerked against his belly button.

"Do you want to touch yourself, Lukas?" she asked silkily. "You can, you know. You can touch yourself—you just can't touch me." She met his eyes with a mischievous dare. "I really wish you would."

His hands stayed stubbornly clenched at his sides. She laughed against his inner thigh. "Okay, if that's the way you want it."

"You can't imagine all the ways I want it," he gritted.

"Even now, you're denying yourself." She licked his hip bone, and settled in to give him a hickey to match hers, nestling his cock between her breasts. "I don't like it when you deny yourself, Lukas."

It took longer than she thought it would for Lukas to finally stroke his hard flesh against her soft skin. When she abruptly replaced her breasts with her hands, and then took him into her mouth, he clawed welts into the leather with his fingernails.

He tasted like the midnight sea.

His hands lifted toward her head, hesitated, and then fell back onto the couch. Scarlett could feel his eyes on her, watching her explore his most intimate terrain with her mouth.

She licked him from root to tip and back again, taking the scenic route, breathing into the humid crevice where his balls rubbed against the leather couch. His breath stuttered from his throat when she bathed them with her tongue, and finally—*finally*—he lifted his hands from their death grip on the couch, tangling his fingers in her hair.

Scarlett didn't know how much time had passed when she became aware of Lukas's body tensing under her mouth and hands, of him pushing back gently against her shoulders. When she eased back, he reached down to the floor for his discarded jeans and got a condom from his wallet.

After donning it, he opened his mouth as if to speak, then closed it again. She crawled up onto his lap, pouring her soul into a blazing kiss. He wound his arms around her—too tightly, but she didn't care. Raising herself up on her knees, she held his eyes and lowered herself onto him, the broad head of his cock spreading her wide. He put his hands under her ass, stopped her dead, then lifted her slightly, allowing both gravity and her wetness to help him work his way into her tight, clinging sheath.

Up, down. Up, down. Millimeters at a time, until she was writhing in his hands, wiggling and straining against him. "Let go of me, damn you." She was desperate to take more of him. To take all of him. It was imperative.

He obeyed, sending her sliding down the rest of his cock down to the root. She caught her breath as her clit settled against his pubic bone.

It felt like he'd flipped a switch deep inside her.

Inside them both.

Grabbing her hips in his hands, he pistoned in and out, dragging endless inches against her delicate tissues. "I can't... stop," he groaned.

"Don't you dare."

So he surged and pounded, wild as the sea, until the anchor finally snapped, freeing them both.

Chapter 21

SHE AND LUKAS HAD SHARED THE QUEEN-SIZED BED after all—not that they'd slept a whole lot.

Lukas was gone. His pillow was cold, but the smell of bacon wafted from the kitchen, so she just might forgive him. What time was it? She'd been so dead to the world she hadn't even felt him get out of bed.

She stretched and snuggled deeper into the nest of blankets, feeling the tug of every deliciously sore muscle. Did sex qualify as a workout? It must, because she hadn't done anything else the previous day to earn her exhaustion. After she and Lukas had made love in front of the fire yesterday morning, she'd been diligently lazy for the remainder of the day, either reading in the hammock, or sitting on a chaise lounge writing, soaking up the sun like a solar panel.

Lukas, on the other hand, had done enough work for three people, putting away most of the summer recreational equipment and knocking off most of the winterizing tasks that prepared the cabin for the brutal weather to come. Most of the work required a lot more muscle than she possessed, so Lukas had waved off her feeble offers of help.

Scarlett felt oddly proud that he'd slept through the night—hogging the bed, yes, but given his size, she couldn't really blame him for that. No cell phone buzzing at all hours. No 3:00 a.m. forays to his desk to catch

up on email, or to take a quick call from one of his workers. No conference calls with Gideon Lupinsky and his
investigative team, reporting yet another dead end that
sent him to his stash of antacids.

Outside, birds chirped, and a dog barked down the
shore. A small buzzing motor meant that a fisherman
trolled for breakfast—or was it brunch? Then she heard
a rhythmic thunk she couldn't place.

Throwing back the covers, Scarlett got out of bed,
hop-scotching from rug to rug to avoid putting her bare
feet on the chilly wood floor. Quickly dressing in yesterday's jeans, cami, and sweatshirt and jamming her
feet into a pair of too-large flip-flops, she went to the
kitchen. She was absolutely starving.

THUNK.

What was Lukas doing? Scarlett poured coffee into
the thermal mug he'd set out for her, snagged a handful
of the bacon, and then padded out onto the lake view
deck, a big wooden platform without sides that supplied
a level surface for the huge grill, an outdoor dining set,
and cozy twin Adirondack chairs. To the left side of the
deck, a pair of faded board shorts hung on the clothesline strung tautly between two sturdy birch trees. The
hummingbird feeder was empty.

THUNK.

Lukas wasn't down on the dock, or over by the
sauna. She walked to the edge of the deck so she could
see the broad expanse of shaggy lawn on the north side
of the cabin.

And there he was. Out of habit, she stepped back so
he wouldn't see her, but immediately reversed herself.
To hell with skulking around corners, because Holy

Mother—if a man was going to chop wood looking like that, he deserved to be ogled.

Gauging from the pile of split logs, and the sweatshirt and T-shirt lying in the grass, he'd been at it for a while. The strengthening sun gleamed off his shoulders, and the waistband of his sagging cargo shorts was damp with sweat. His hair was loose but lashed to his head with a faded blue bandana.

She swallowed audibly. There was definitely a cause-and-effect relationship between the line of tortoiseshell hair disappearing into Lukas's waistband, and the tugging sensation between her thighs.

Of Sasha's two brothers, why did she have to fall in love with Lukas? Why not Rafe, the easygoing, unabashed sensualist? He'd be far easier to have a relationship with, but some critical alchemy was missing between them.

And it was definitely premature to define this... thing as a relationship. Sure, she'd slept with Lukas a handful of times, each one more memorable than the last. Though she'd mapped every inch of his body with her hands, mouth, and tongue, she hadn't spent nearly enough time touching him to take his body for granted. Despite these physical intimacies, and the front-row seat she had into his work life, she didn't have a lot more insight into his thoughts about them now than she did when they first slept together. But she was done hiding from him.

And he'd seen her. He stared, pupils dark and dilated, his nostrils flaring. Her nipples pebbled under her sweatshirt in reaction.

Lukas shot her a look so feral, so frantic, that she moaned aloud. He looked wild enough to do anything. Everything.

With a twist of his wrist, he buried the head of the axe in the stump.

Scarlett ran.

—∿∿—

The need to chase Scarlett down and pin her to the ground thrummed through him, but, ever the hunter, Lukas stilled, watching her instead. She couldn't get away from him wearing his brother's sloppy flip-flops.

She didn't run far. After scurrying down toward the lake, she veered off to the sauna, disappeared for a couple of minutes, and emerged carrying a bottle of shampoo and an armful of beach towels. Shooting him a look over her shoulder, she sauntered onto the dock, and set the items down.

She was definitely up to something. His mind exploded with sensual possibilities.

He joined her, his steel-toed boots thunking against the wooden railroad ties with each step he took. He brushed against her body before sitting down on the wooden bench at the end of the dock, unlacing his boots and peeling off his socks like he had all the time in the world. Standing, he watched her as he unzipped his cargo shorts over a mother of a hard-on, and dragged them down his body.

She stared. Licked her lips.

Shit. She was better at this game than he was. Picking up the bottle of shampoo, Lukas threw it out into the water and quickly dove in after it, his gonads shriveling as he swam underwater a good sixty feet before breaking the surface. He needed a little cooling off, or he'd be on her like a shark on chum. The woman turned him into a snarling, unthinking beast. Hell, he might as well wash as long as he was out here. Grabbing the bobbing bottle, he poured some shampoo in his hand. "Come on in, the water's fine," he called to Scarlett, standing back on the dock.

What had he been thinking, bringing her here? He'd never be able to sleep in that queen-sized bed again without first thinking about how she'd shared it with him.

What would he do when she decided she'd had enough?

"Hey, be careful. I like that hair too much to see you scrub yourself bald."

Despite the water temperature, her voice brought him surging again, as strong as when he'd first seen her standing at the corner of the cabin, watching him. He could taste her from here.

Ducking under the water to rinse the soap out of his hair, he surfaced and turned toward her, only to find her stripping off at the end of the dock, like he'd so blithely done a few minutes ago. The bright sunlight caught each wavy filament of hair and lit it like fire, and her skin was so pale it was nearly translucent. He would have to remind her about sunscreen when the sun rose higher.

He'd apply it himself—very, very carefully.

"Keep going," he murmured, his voice carrying on the water as he swam toward her.

She'd removed her sweatshirt—Rafe's again, damn it—and stood in jeans and that gorgeous camisole he'd had his hands all over yesterday. She peered up and down the lakeshore.

Reaching the dock, Lukas lifted a hand out of the water and stroked her ankle. "The nearest cabin is over a mile down the shore. No paparazzi here." His voice softened. Dropped. "It's just you, me, and… the wildlife."

Scarlett glanced at his hand, latched around her ankle like a manacle. He could taste her excitement sparkling on his tongue. She dragged the camisole up over her body and shook out her hair as she dropped the scrap of silk to the rough wooden dock. A loon called, and the scent of creosote filled the air as the railroad ties used to build the dock heated in the sun. He was certain that every bit of the hunger, lust, and awe he felt was etched on his face for her to read, but he didn't care.

"Keep going," he repeated, tightening his grasp on her ankle.

Goose bumps sheeted her body. Holding his avaricious gaze, she removed her jeans and stood in the sun's spotlight wearing only purple lace panties that displayed a hell of a lot more than they covered. Sliding her thumbs into the lacy waistband, she slowly dragged the useless scrap of silk down her thighs.

Jesus, was there anything more gorgeous on this earth? Lukas gobbled her long, slim form with his eyes. Where to look first? Her teacup breasts, their raspberry tips perking up before his eyes? The slender waist? The curving hips? Her luxuriously full bush, a humid wilderness he yearned to explore?

Throttle it back. "C'mon." He extended his hand. "Bath time."

Her eyes narrowed suspiciously. "How cold is the water?"

"Feels great," he said cheerfully before tugging at her ankle and pulling her in.

Her shriek bounced and echoed, hurting his ears and

driving birds from the trees, but even as she hit the chilly
water, he felt her joy and delight sparkle into him. She
quickly surfaced and climbed up his chest, latching onto
his body like an octopus.

"Damn you," she gasped, slinging ropes of long, wet
hair out of her face. "It's freezing!"

Lukas grinned and wrapped his arms around her,
pulling her closer to the heat pumping off his body. She
twined her arms and legs more tightly around him, so
tightly that no water molecule could find its way between them. Her nipples scraped his chest. Helpless, he
lowered his head.

Scarlett suddenly yelped. "Seaweed!"

"You're such a girly girl," he sighed as she shim-
mied even higher to get away from the slippery plants.
Nope, nothing was going to happen here and now, not
with algae twining its way around Scarlett's ankle, or
with her teeth chattering from cold rather than pleasure.
When he slipped inside of her, he wanted every bit of
her attention.

"Come on. As long as you're wet, let me wash your
hair," he said. "And then I'll start the fire in the sauna
for later."

Her eyes heated and locked onto his.

Yes, later.

Scarlett slipped the headphones off and looked up from
her notebook. Clouds were rolling in, and the sun had
dropped just enough in the western sky that despite the
day's unseasonable heat, her borrowed bikini top and
shorts weren't quite warm enough anymore.

The notebook pages fluttered in the breeze. She'd written twelve pages of puke-it-up lyrics since sitting down after lunch. Yeah, they needed serious editing, but at least she now had something to fix.

And she was uncomfortably horny. Lukas had no idea she'd been listening to a recording of him moaning for most of the afternoon.

After washing her hair—the most sexually loaded shampoo she'd ever received—Lukas had simply lifted her out of the water onto the dock, bundled her in a beach towel, then suggested she relax. He'd started the sauna, the scent of the wood stove becoming more pungent and evocative as the day went on. After raking leaves together, Lukas had mowed the lawn, put away the kayak, taken down the badminton net, removed the motors from the boats, and drained everything of gasoline for winter storage, while she napped like a cat in the sun. Mid-afternoon, the sound of him firing up one of the snowmobiles had awakened her, and then she started to write.

And they'd watched each other.

Now, from her position up on the deck near the cabin, she had a great view of Lukas finally taking a break, fishing down on the dock. He still wore nothing but those ratty cargo shorts that seemed to drop lower and lower on his hips with each hour that passed—not that she was complaining, because she now had a primo view of those lickable dimples where his lower back met the curve of his butt.

It was a miracle she could hum a thing when her tongue kept falling out of her mouth.

Lukas swore without heat as the fish he'd been

slowly reeling in spit up the hook. "Took the bait too, you son of a bitch," he muttered, reaching into the white Styrofoam container at his feet and extracting another leech. Muscles shifted as he put the squirming leech on the hook and lifted the fishing rod over his head. With a flick of his wrist, line sang out of the reel, and the hook and leech hit the surface of the water with a soft plop about thirty yards out.

The tension lines around Lukas's eyes had smoothed out a little, and regardless of what happened with their relationship, Scarlett was glad that he'd gotten this time away. He'd needed this as much as she had. Before she moved in with him, she had no idea he worked with the police as often as he did. It was after those calls from Gideon Lupinsky that Lukas most often reached for the Pepto-Bismol bottle.

Before last night, she hadn't seen him get more than three hours of sleep at a time. But last night, she'd worn him out.

When she looked down to the dock again, she found him watching her with a glint in his eye. "Wanna help bait the hook?"

"Yeah, right." They both laughed. Scarlett's loathing for leeches was well-established. The screeching teenage hissy fit she'd pitched the one time a bloodsucker had innocently attached itself to her ankle had cracked most of the cabin's windows. "Let's not risk it. But I might be able to help." After theatrically clearing her throat, she sang a series of high, clear notes that shivered over the water.

The fishing rod yanked in his hands, and he quickly set the hook.

While she mentally planned their menu, lightning

flashed off to the west. The clouds were black and blue
against the darkening sky, and thunder grumbled softly.
Earlier in the day, the weathercaster on the scratchy
local AM radio station had predicted a chance of thun-
derstorms, but… this was more than a chance. The front
was coming in fast. "Lukas!" she called, pointing to
the sky.

"Damn. Be up in a minute."

She quickly rose from her chair and started buttoning
things down. Folding the chaise, she put it inside the
sliding glass door along with Sigmund, her recorder, and
her notebook. Traveling the perimeter of the cabin, she
closed and latched all the windows, closed the fireplace
flue, and then went back outside to yank the flapping
beach towels off the clothesline.

The lightning was getting close, and Lukas was landing a fish.

One eye on the sky, she trotted down to the dock to
gather up the fishing gear so it wouldn't blow into the
lake. "Forget the damn fish!" she hollered into the wind
as it pushed the scent of rain and ozone out ahead of it.
Lukas unhooked the fish, placed it in the live box in the
shallows adjacent to the dock, and then just… stopped.
The muscles of his torso tensed and leaped. His nostrils
flared. He tipped his head back to the elements, shuddering as he inhaled energy from the storm.

The wind gusted and swirled, but she was riveted to
the spot. He looked glorious, with chest muscles ripped,
and his loose hair streaming away from his face. Rain
started to fall on the far side of the lake, a soft hush
growing louder as it approached. Suddenly the hair on
Scarlett's arms stood up, and a lightning bolt cracked

into a tree across the lake. Lukas latched onto her hand, pulling her to the nearest shelter—the sauna.

The spring loaded screen door snapped closed behind them, and they were enveloped in cedar scented heat.

"Wow, that was…" Scarlett dropped Lukas's hand and rubbed at the gooseflesh on her arms. "That came up really fast."

Lukas plucked a towel off one of the dressing area hooks and wrapped it around her. "Are you okay?"

"Yeah, just wet."

What a massive understatement. She couldn't stop staring at him. He was as hard as a statue, and veins stood out atop his muscles in bas-relief. Raindrops glittered on his hair and skin, and barely leashed power seemed to spark off of him, just looking for an outlet.

For release.

She rested her hands on his rocky shoulders, felt him jolt at her touch.

Lukas erupted like a match set to gasoline, diving at her mouth like it was a lifeline. Rain blew in, soaking his calves. She was surprised the water didn't turn to steam.

Rain pounded against the tin roof. Lukas picked Scarlett up and lay her on the worn cedar planking table. In the dim light, neither of them could see very well, but her nimble fingers worked the button and zipper of his shorts, spilling his hardness into her chilly hands. He peeled off her shorts and sodden bikini top, dropping them with a splat onto the cement floor.

Thunder rocked the small structure as lightning-hot pleasure streaked up her spine. Moaning, he plunged into her, as if doing so would save his life.

Chapter 22

STEPHEN CAUGHT HIS BREATH AS HE STOOD IN MADAME Bouchet's hospital room doorway, taking in the military-straight white bedding, the bare shelves, and the freshly mopped floor. Her riotously colored quilt was gone, and the bedside table held a shrink wrapped plastic pitcher and glass for the next patient. It was anonymous. Sterile. Spotlessly clean.

Madame was dead.

Stephen rubbed at his sternum with his knuckles. Madame was dead, and Andi was fighting her medication—hard—and would soon regain consciousness. His only two sources of comfort were gone. What was he going to—

"Stephen," a familiar voice said from behind him.

Dashing the wetness from around his eyes, he turned to see Peggy, the nurse who'd cared for him when he was in the hospital, wearing her habitually rumpled purple scrubs. Her face was soft with sympathy—sympathy for him. It was all he could do not to fall into her arms.

When she placed her hand on his shoulder, the beast nipped in warning.

"Ouch!" Peggy jerked her hand away.

"Sorry, I must have picked up some static from the carpet," he said. *Static, my ass. You left Andi before you were topped off.* "When?" he choked out, indicating the empty room.

"About an hour ago," she responded quietly, cradling her hand. "She died in her sleep."

And her room was cleaned out already? Where were her family pictures, her memories? He sniffed deeply, but smelled nothing but industrial cleanser.

They'd completely wiped her out.

"What's that?" Peggy said, pointing to a shot of color just under the bed.

The friendship bracelet he'd given her. As he stooped to pick up the cheap memento, his face crumpled like Kleenex. Madame was gone, and once Andi regained consciousness, he'd be captured, arrested, and thrown into whatever qualified as a prison on this backwater planet.

How long did he have before he was caught? Days? Hours?

As he turned to leave the room, he wondered if it really mattered.

The gut punch of ash jerked Lukas from a sound sleep. "Shit." Stomach clutching with warning and his forehead blooming with sweat, he unwrapped his arms from Scarlett, slid out of bed, and broke all known land speed records to reach the toilet before he heaved.

While his body purged itself, a greasy ecstasy stained his psyche like a broken sewer line.

After long minutes, Lukas finally backed away from the toilet and leaned against the chilly wall tiles. *Who died to get you off this time, you sick fuck?*

If his reaction was an accurate barometer, the death had just occurred. Hours could pass before anyone found the victim—but that didn't mean that he and Scarlett couldn't leave now, so when the call came from Gideon, they'd be that much closer to home.

After a quick look in the bedroom to ensure Scarlett was still sleeping, he brushed the foul taste out of his mouth and then hopped into the tiny shower to wash the clammy sweat from his hair and body. Dressing in the dark, he grabbed the keys and a flashlight from the shelf by the door, then walked down to the dock to liberate last night's catch from the live box. After a guilty glance up at the cabin, the leeches followed.

Picking up the fishing pole, tackle box, and net he'd dropped to the lawn when last night's storm had broken, he carried them to the garage, put them away on their hanging hooks, and locked the door. He saved the sauna for last, ensuring that the wood stove fire was completely out. The essence he and Scarlett had left behind when they'd swallowed each other up the previous evening soothed him like a balm, taking the edge off the perp's violent crap.

After one final gulp, Lukas walked back to the cabin. Quietly closing the screen door behind him, he turned on a single kitchen light to pack up perishables they'd have to take home. After setting the last grocery bag down next to the door, he went to the bedroom to wake Scarlett.

Her head was half-buried in the blankets, with just a hank of hair exposed, and she snored ever so lightly. It was a shame to wake her; they'd worn each other out last night. When they'd gotten back to the cabin after the worst of the storm had passed, she'd… taken control, gifting him with the hottest sexual experience of his life.

Sure, he could have broken the ties lashing his wrists to the old iron headboard at any time, but he... hadn't.

And what a reward he'd received for relinquishing at least the illusion of control to Scarlett. She'd been ravenous, ferocious, determined to drive him wild. He couldn't remember every mindless demand that had spilled from his lips, but she'd not only taken everything he had to give—she'd returned it tenfold.

After she'd untied him, kissed his wrists and lips, and then fallen into an exhausted slumber on his chest, he'd whispered aloud the words that had seethed inside him for so long—that he loved her. Loved her until he was sick with it.

"Scarlett. Wake up," he whispered, kneeling next to the bed and stroking her hair back from her cheek.

She swatted vaguely at his hand, and then rolled over. When he nibbled on the vulnerable bump connecting her neck to her spine, she finally lifted her head from the nest of pillows. "What?"

Unfortunately there was no time to tip her annoyance to arousal. "There's been another attack. We need to go home."

She pushed up onto her elbow. "Who is it?"

"Jack hasn't called yet." Scarlett's gaze darted to the bathroom, then back again. Yeah, she'd lived with him long enough to know how his low-tech early warning system worked. "I'm packing the car now. How long will it take you to get ready to leave?"

"Let me hop in the shower. I'll be ready to go in twenty," she said, sitting up and swiping her hair out of her face.

Lukas swallowed as the bedclothes fell to her waist.

He tried not to look at her hard-tipped breasts, but it was a losing battle—especially when she lifted her arms over her head and stretched. He barely managed to hold back a possessive growl. With a sleepy, knowing smile, she dropped a soft kiss on his lips, hopped out of bed, and walked to the bathroom, her lean body gloriously and spectacularly nude.

He wanted her—as always—but rousing Scarlett from a sound sleep had felt cozily domestic. Intimate. There'd been no complaints about being woken up at the butt crack of dawn, no recriminations for cutting their time at the lake short. Just a trusting kiss, then up and at 'em, no questions asked.

What a woman.

It was actually closer to forty-five minutes later before they hit the road. The first part of the journey was slow going, with both of them keeping their eyes peeled for the twitchy deer that had an alarming tendency to dart across the road without regard for the gas-powered predators rumbling through their habitat. The gravel road finally dumped out onto pavement as the sun was rising. They shared coffee and a companionable silence as the big car chewed up the miles.

They finally reached the interstate. "Do you mind if I work for awhile?" Scarlett asked.

"Go ahead."

She smiled her thanks and reached into that suitcase of a purse, whipping out her notebook and a portable recorder with a headset. And she hummed. Scribbled. Chewed on the end of her plastic pen. Hummed again, then opened her mouth and sang. About wetness, sinking, cresting waves, drowning.

"I'll take you down with me..." she sang softly into the recorder, her lethal voice tugging at his dick with the same thoroughness as her lips and tongue had the night before. Her eyes glowed as she worked, and her mandarin essence quickly filled the enclosed space.

Lukas inhaled the erotic energy, shifting uncomfortably in his seat. *Great. Blow jobs on the brain, driving 75 mph on the interstate.* Thank the aurora for small favors; at least she couldn't hear him grinding his teeth to dust while she wore that headset.

On the center console, his mini-comp suddenly woke up, vibrating to a raucous "Me So Horny" ring tone. "What the hell." He didn't download ringtones. A flash of Antonia jumping into his arms for a hug the night of the family dinner flashed into his mind.

The little shit had picked his pocket, and he hadn't felt a thing.

He looked at the tiny display window. *This was it.* He put the mini-comp on speaker. "Jack."

"Lukas, where are you?"

"Southbound 35, just south of the Cloquet split. Who—"

"So you *did* taste it. Good." Jack paused. "Well, not good, but you know what I mean. Two humans, one male and one female, discovered at a sex club operating out of a private home in Minneapolis. Place is zapped and trashed. Your corroboration indicates that it's our guy."

Humans. "Anyone we know?" Bailey must be fine, or Jack would be a mess.

"No."

Lukas closed his eyes as relief washed through him.

"I'm about to leave the office and join Gideon at the

scene," Jack said. "The guy left this couple trussed up like Thanksgiving turkeys. Together, if you get my drift."

"Christ," Lukas muttered. "COD?"

"Looks like strangulation, with some electrical burns. Gideon thinks it's possible that at least some of the bondage was consensual." He sighed. "The scene is a mess."

He glanced at Scarlett out of the corner of his eye. Last night he'd let her tie him up, surrendering more control than he ever thought he was capable of, but he knew her. Loved her. He couldn't imagine what drove someone to take such risks with perfect strangers. "Consensual or not, I think it's a pretty safe bet that this couple didn't walk into that club last night thinking they'd never walk out again," he said. "I place TOD at about 4:30 a.m."

"That helps. Gideon did an initial run on their ID— no Council ties, no apparent Underworld ties, though a deeper dive is going to take awhile. Bailey's on it."

Lukas's thoughts raced. What were they missing? What was *he* missing? Whoever this guy was, he was quickly racking up charges. Sexual assault. Attempted murder. First degree murder. But victimizing humans tipped the first degree murder charges into special circumstances territory. Automatic life sentence, with no opportunity for release. Though the human courts would never know about the trial, justice would be swift and sure.

If he ever caught the guy.

"Any witnesses? Surveillance equipment?"

Jack's frustration was palpable over the phone line. "The owner claims not, says that her clients pay dearly for confidentiality, and that she provides it. People find out about the club through word of mouth. Very exclusive. Pay the cover, clear the metal detector, and you're in."

"Who takes the money?"

"A machine. A freaking machine, like at the car wash, can you believe it? Cash only."

Damn. Even if they managed to lift some usable prints off the bills, they'd be absolutely useless if the guy wasn't already in the system.

"But we might catch a break with Andi," Jack said. "She's fighting the medicine with all her might, and her doctors plan on bringing her out of her coma today."

Lukas sat up straight. Scarlett glanced over at him and slipped off her headset.

"The case could be closed today."

Lukas glanced at Scarlett as she closed her notebook and gazed out the window. Her intoxicating scent was clouding over. "Keep me updated, Jack," he said.

He disconnected the call and waited. Guilt and sadness swirled through the enclosed space, and Scarlett eyed the notebook like it was a snake. "I forgot why we came up here in the first place." The self-condemnation in her voice sliced right through him. "How could I forget about Andi? About Annika? I—"

Her voice cracked, but she didn't cry—thank god. Lukas didn't think he could handle Scarlett's tears in an enclosed space. "Don't feel guilty for living your life," he said. "Annika wouldn't want that for you." Lukas reached for her hand, laced his fingers between hers. Saw the faint bruises forming on her slim wrists.

When he tried to pull away from her, Scarlett simply tightened her grasp on his hand. "Don't start that again."

"Don't feel guilty about bruising you?" Lukas dragged his attention back to the road momentarily, but made himself look at their linked hands again. "Damn, Scarlett—"

Her gaze bored into him as she morphed from sad to angry like quicksilver. "Do you remember me saying stop, or ouch, or making any protest of any kind? No, you don't," she answered before he could open his mouth. "You were right there with me, for every gasp and moan, every step of the way. As I begged you for more." She paused. "Don't you dare feel guilty for giving me exactly what I need. For *being* exactly what I need."

The shock of what she said pushed the breath out of his lungs as effectively as one of Sasha's sucker punches.

"Would you feel better if we had a safe word?"

Lukas gulped. Scarlett couldn't fathom the things he'd done to her—the things she'd done to him—in the depraved safety net of his imagination. He was a sick bastard who needed to change the subject, fast, because his dick was as hard as steel, his thoughts were on fire, and he was navigating a two ton missile down the interstate.

"I think that was a yes," Scarlett teased.

Lukas jerked his head to her notebook. "Why haven't you been writing?"

A self-deprecating expression slid over her face. "Where should I start? Exhaustion? Fear?"

Scarlett, scared? He sat up straighter, felt his chest expand. Of what? Of... whom?

"Will you throttle back?" she said with exasperation. "I can see you revving up from here. If there's any ass to be kicked here, it's mine. I was a mess when I left to go on tour. Running scared. I couldn't sing my own songs, because to do that, I had to actually let myself feel the lyrics first. And I… couldn't. It was easier to channel someone else's emotions rather than my own."

Lukas shot her a look. "You didn't have any problems with emotion the night of the show at Underbelly."

Scarlett winced. "I wasn't ready to deal with you yet, and there you were, everywhere I looked." She looked out of the passenger window. "I wanted to make you suffer, to imagine me with someone else. To feel even a fraction of the pain I felt the morning you made love to me and walked away."

Lukas's hands tightened on the steering wheel. There was nothing he could say to—

"And you're still uncomfortable about the same thing, even after last night." Scarlett pursed her lips. "I was joking before, but maybe we need a safe word after all."

Oh, man. Lukas sighed, and reached over to take her hand again. "This is going to sound like a massive cliché, but it's not you. It's me. And I'm… working on it."

"It would help if you worked on the right problem in the first place. What do you call it, root cause analysis?" She stroked the bruises smudging her wrist like they were bracelets of precious jewels. "Some of those problems you're so worried about aren't problems at all; they're entirely in your imagination."

The air turned electric as their eyes met. He helplessly inhaled her desire, the taste he would always crave like the very air he breathed.

"You know the song I was writing earlier? Any idea what it was about?"

He snorted a laugh. "I know what my dick thought it was about, but tell me anyway."

"It's about how I feel when we make love—then, and now." She was silent for a moment. "I haven't written a new song in a really long time."

"Why?"

"When you walked away that morning, you took my voice with you. I couldn't sing, I couldn't write, I couldn't—" She stopped. "No, strike that. I'm responsible for how I reacted after our... night together. I shut down, and I can't let you take responsibility for that."

It didn't matter what she said. The responsibility was his. He was older, and he should have known better. He should have controlled himself—

"Don't! Damn it, I can see you flagellating yourself from here. You're so wrong." She looked to the ceiling of the car as if to request guidance from above. "You didn't physically hurt me, then or now. What hurt me was that you just... walked away, Lukas." She turned her head back toward the window, like she couldn't stand looking at him anymore. "You walked away from me—from us—without saying a word."

Her hurt ricocheted into him like a bullet to the heart. How could he make her understand the regret he'd felt that morning? Make her understand that he'd walked away for her own good? "I looked down at you that morning, saw what I done to you," he started.

"What you'd done? You melted me into an orgasmic puddle of goo! You horrible, horrible man."

Lukas dragged the memories out to the vicious light of day and tried again. "Your wrists. Your thighs, your breasts. I could see my fingerprints all over you."

"Yes." Her voice deepened with desire. "And after you left, I ran my fingers over and over them until they finally faded, and only memories remained. Do you remember how much I begged? Screamed? Just like last night."

No. No way. His subconscious fought to keep hold of the lifeline he'd grabbed onto all those years ago—that leaving her was for the best. But she yanked it out of his grasp, leaving him to sink or swim.

"Lukas. Don't you understand? I love what you do to me, love what we do together. I love—" She swallowed, then forged ahead. "I love you, you stupid, stupid man."

He blinked dumbly.

"And I'm tired, Lukas. I'm tired of running from this—" she gestured vaguely with her hand "—whatever this is. Push me away if you have to. Walk away, again. But if you do, you're going to damn well look me in the eye when you do it, not slink away in the middle of the night, leaving me wondering what I did wrong."

Guilt, joy, and testosterone battled inside of him. The need to take, to claim, pounded with each beat of his heart. The words welled up from his throat like lava. "I love you too."

"I know—and I'm glad." She leaned over from the passenger seat, bringing her hand to his jaw. "Listen. I need you to be exactly who you are, and I need to know I can be myself with you." Stretching the seat belt mightily, she licked his chin with her clever tongue. "I love how you make me feel. I love knowing I can make you lose control. That's only fair," she breathed, "because you make me forget my name."

The car swerved when he captured her mouth with his. "Damn," he muttered, jerking his eyes back to the road. Black Bear Casino loomed off the highway to the right, thank the universe, because he needed to be inside her—now—and at this moment, pulling off onto a gravel hunting road and bending Scarlett over the hood of the car would have been sufficient.

Andi Woolf could wait. Killers could wait. He jerked the steering wheel and squealed down the exit ramp.

From the passenger seat, Scarlett hummed with approval, the sound bubbling like champagne on his tongue. "I like how you think."

Chapter 23

SCARLETT GLARED AT THE PORTABLE MIXING BOARD. "You worthless piece of crap."

She saw the song in her head. She saw how to build it, layer by layer. The final version of "Undertow" glowed in her imagination like the proverbial pot of gold at the end of the rainbow, and she was stuck here with this... this... Paleolithic piece of shit that didn't have a chance in hell of producing the percussion transition she absolutely required for the song's bridge.

She was dead in the water.

Oh, in the reasonable portion of her brain, Scarlett knew she could work on other areas of the song, but the bridge was lodged in her psyche like a sliver. Adding insult to injury, her own state-of-the-art recording studio sat empty less than a mile away. But the last thing Lukas had said to her before leaving for the hospital? "This isn't over yet. Stay put."

"Stay put," she mimicked, shoving the chair back away from the desk with a satisfying clatter of wheels against the hard wood floor. "Damn it." The taste of his blistering goodbye kiss still lingered in her mouth, but it didn't make his decree any less annoying.

So, now what? She whirled the chair in slow pirouettes as she considered her options. For all she knew, Andi had named her attacker and the combined force of Sebastiani Security and the MPD had already come down on the guy like the proverbial ton of bricks. He might be in custody right now, no longer a threat to anyone.

Whether they'd caught the guy yet or not, Lukas wouldn't be home for hours. She could go to her own studio, get in some solid work, and be back before he even knew she'd been gone.

No. Scarlett discarded the idea almost as quickly as she'd formulated it. No matter how annoyed she might be about his autocratic tone and her worthless equipment, leaving would not only be monumentally stupid—it would be a violation of trust that she wasn't sure their fledgling relationship could recover from. She was stuck here.

But she didn't have to like it.

She hugged her legs to her chest and plopped her chin on her knees. Why was it okay for him to take risks, to put himself in harm's way, while she sat home, cocooned in bubble wrap? She'd seen enough scars, scabs, and scuffs on Lukas's body to know that he wasn't content to stand back and let the police do their job without his help. No, at this very minute, Lukas could be pounding his fist into someone's face, dodging a knife, or diving to the pavement. Fighting for his life. Scarlett's fists clenched. Didn't Lukas know that people worried about him, worried about his safety? He was hardly immortal.

Once this guy was behind bars, they needed to have a serious talk. The conversation they'd had in the car was a good start, but they needed more than a long weekend at the cabin and a few stolen hours at a roadside hotel.

The hotel. Three precious hours of lust and love and laughter, of muttered demands, of whispered promises. Of having all of his attention focused solely on her pleasure. After a shower that was supposed to be fast but most emphatically was not, they'd stumbled back out to the car, leaving behind a wrecked bed, a room reeking of pheromones, and an outrageous tip for the housekeeping staff.

But the minute they'd hit the highway again, Lukas shifted back into work mode, returning the messages that had piled up during their little time-out at the hotel. Andi Woolf was coming out of her coma, and Lukas made plans to meet Jack at the hospital just as soon as Lukas dropped Scarlett off back home. He'd told Gideon Lupinsky that he'd stop by the latest crime scene. He set up a con-call with Bailey, Valerian, and Wyland for the next day.

His previously relaxed expression tensed and hardened a little more with each phone call, with each southbound mile.

Scarlett's eyes shifted to the bottle of Pepto-Bismol sitting on his desk. How did he juggle all his responsibilities, and still hold on to his sanity? His sanity might yet be intact, but his stomach lining was another matter entirely. Trying to be everything to everybody—and damn it, succeeding at it—was definitely taking its toll. At this very moment, Lukas was probably putting himself in danger to catch her sister's killer, and while she wanted justice for Annika, and certainly for Andi and Stephen, she didn't want Lukas to hurt himself to achieve it. The price would be too high.

Scarlett dropped her legs to the floor. "Um, duh." *Stephen*. Drummer. Percussion. Percussion effects, and damn good ones, too. She shot out of the chair with new energy. Lukas had told her to stay put, but he hadn't said

she couldn't invite anyone over—and after all, Stephen
was on her approved visitors list.

Yes, she thought, creative juices already flowing as
she near skipped to Lukas's desk. She picked up the
phone and dialed Stephen's cell.

She and Stephen could do this the old-fashioned way.
She'd drag Stephen away from whatever—or whom-
ever—he was doing, ask him to bring over a few drums,
some sticks, brushes—hell, as much equipment as he
could donkey over on his motorcycle.

Win-win. Problem solved.

Lukas could hear Andi half-screaming, half-howling the
minute the elevator doors opened onto the empty reception area of the VIP floor. Something shattered against
the inside of her closed hospital room door, followed by
unmistakable slams and bumps.

Fighting, hand-to-hand in an enclosed space.

Gideon pulled his police-issue.

"Where the fuck's the guard?" Lukas, Jack, and
Gideon approached the door, using instinctive choreography: Gideon on point, Jack to Gideon's right, his gun
pointed to the ceiling, and Lukas coming in low and left
with no weapon at all.

"Police," Gideon called loudly. "Open the—"

The door abruptly swung open. "Come in, gentle-
men," Krispin Woolf said, gesturing them into his
daughter's room with a courtly sweep of a hand bleeding from several small cuts. He stood in shattered glass,
and several peony stems lay on the floor in a puddle of
water. Andi sagged against the bed in her hospital gown,

breathing heavily behind a hand covering her mouth. The bodyguard stood between father and daughter, cradling a broken wrist.

"As you can see—"

"Quiet. Everyone stay put." Gideon skirted the perimeter of the room, ducked his head into the bathroom, and then entered, sweeping back the shower curtain. Lukas wondered who the hell they should be covering.

"Clear," Gideon called out to Lukas and Jack before exiting the bathroom, closing the door behind him. He approached the guard and asked for his weapons, then approached Krispin Woolf. "Are you carrying?"

Lukas took Krispin's deadpan expression as a yes. Gideon did too, because he politely but methodically frisked the WerePack Alpha, coming away with a semi-automatic handgun, a clutch piece, two knives, and a garrote.

"A man can't be too careful these days," Krispin said blandly.

"Dad, you're not helping matters any," Andi said hoarsely. The trach tube she'd been sporting the last time Lukas had visited had been removed, replaced by white gauze bandages. "It was me."

"What was you?" Gideon asked before Lukas could.

Andi's arm gesture was very much like her father's, somehow managing to encompass the entire room with a flick. "The guard approached as I was waking up, and I... overreacted." She cleared her throat, raising a hand to the bandages. "Sorry. Hang on a sec."

Andi picked up the small plastic pitcher on the bedside table and drank, not bothering to pour the water into a glass. While she quenched what had to be a vicious thirst, Lukas and Jack entered the hospital room, cheerfully cluttered with colorful cards, banners, and enough flowers to stock a florist shop. A bouquet of Mylar balloons hovered near the ceiling.

It wasn't until Andi tipped her head back to get the last drops of water from the pitcher that Lukas noticed the mark on the underside of her chin. The matching love-bite Scarlett had suckled onto his left hipbone a few hours ago throbbed. "Andi, where did that mark on your neck come from?" he asked, careful to keep his voice neutral.

"What mark?"

"There's a red patch under your chin that wasn't there when you were admitted."

A quick flash of something—fear?—flickered into her expression, quickly followed by copper-flavored anger. "That fucker." She walked to the bathroom door and wrenched it open, completely ignoring Gideon, who followed her.

"What fucker?" Jack asked.

Krispin had a rueful expression on his face. "Her young man was certainly enthusiastic."

The hair on the back of Lukas's neck rose. He'd done dozens of interviews with Andi's friends, family, and acquaintances in the days following her assault. No one had mentioned a boyfriend. "What young man?"

Jack shot a look at Lukas as he hurried from the room. "I'll check the guest roster."

When Andi came back from the bathroom, her gown was unfastened and her face pulsed with temper. She opened her mouth to speak, but nothing came out but a lupine growl.

"Breathe, Andi. Breathe. We'll wait." Gideon tied the back fastening of her hospital gown. "She's covered in them," he said to Lukas and Jack. His expression flattened as Krispin lapped the blood from his hand. "Okay, one thing at a time. What happened here? Report," he ordered the guard.

Despite his injured wrist, the man Krispin Woolf hired to guard his daughter spoke steadily and cogently. "Approximately ten minutes after the doctors left, Ms. Woolf became agitated. I entered her room to check her status. Mr. Woolf followed. When I approached the bed, she reached out and…" A tinge of embarrassment crept into the guard's voice as he indicated his broken wrist. "She then threw the vase at Mr. Woolf, who used his hand to deflect it."

"I just—reacted," Andi said. "I didn't know it was you, Dad."

"Understandable, my dear," Krispin responded. "Just coming out of a coma, in bed for days, and she's still strong enough to protect herself," he said proudly to the men. "What a girl."

"He's not my boyfriend. We hooked up at Subterranean. He nearly killed me that night, and he's been… visiting me here at the hospital." A shudder wracked her frame as she looked down at her gown-covered torso. "Visiting me, over and over again."

Krispin and his handpicked guard exchanged a shocked glance that said it all. Andi's assailant had waltzed right into her hospital room, victimizing her anew? Krispin's face froze up, as solid as a lake in January, but underneath the surface, his rage and guilt roiled so violently that Lukas had to shake his head to clear it.

"Dad…" Disregarding the glass, Andi walked to her father and stepped into his embrace. To comfort him or to receive comfort? Lukas wondered. Probably a little of both.

Krispin picked up his daughter and set her on the bed. When he finally spoke, it was with all of the authority of the WerePack Alpha. "Who is this man? His name."

Jack answered his question from the door, where he stood holding Andi's visitor's log. "It's Stephen. Scarlett's drummer, Stephen."

Lukas's extremities went numb.

"What?" Gideon snapped incredulously, though they'd all heard the name perfectly well.

Stephen had taken himself off the suspect list the very night of Annika's murder, by turning himself into a victim.

They hadn't even questioned it.

Jack shook his head in amazement. "He almost died making it look like he'd been—"

"We didn't even look at him twice. Fuck." Lukas snatched his mini-comp out of his jacket pocket. "Where are you, you sick bastard?" he whispered, his fingers flying over the tiny keyboard to issue a comm blast telling all Council members and their families to ping back, STAT. At least he knew that Scarlett was safely at home.

Gideon called in an APB, then pulled up a chair, turned on a recorder, and began to interview Andi. She described the hookup at Subterranean as being completely consensual, until she'd been hit with a blast of something that had scrambled every synapse in her head. The longer she talked, the more pissed off she sounded, though she wasn't letting emotion get in the way of the facts.

Good. Stay pissed. Fight back. Lukas was massively pissed off too. He hadn't seriously considered Stephen, even after tasting those damn ashes at his own fucking house. The fact that Stephen had given Antonia drum lessons, alone and with the family's blessing, chilled his blood.

From the bed, Andi's voice was getting louder. "When I get my hands on him, I'm going to—"

"—do nothing, except recover and regain your strength," Krispin said firmly as he bundled her back under the covers. "Let the Commander do his job." *Or there will be bloody hell to pay,* his flinty expression finished.

Lukas's mini-comp vibrated as people checked in, and a gaggle of white-coated doctors hovered near Andi's door, waiting to examine their now conscious patient. Gideon was taking Andi through it again, the repetition fleshing out the details of what had happened to her at Subterranean. Andi seemed lucid and calm, but her father looked ready to crack as he listened to the details of what Stephen had done to his daughter. For once, Lukas couldn't blame him.

There was nothing more he and Jack could do here. "We're going to hit the street," Lukas said to Gideon. "We'll get him, Andi. You're safe here."

"Better late than never," Krispin said, his voice dripping with accusation and a fair dose of self-recrimination.

Lukas nodded in acknowledgement. There was more than enough blame to pass around.

On the way to the elevator, he and Jack passed Andi's

guard and a couple of Gideon's investigators fine-tuning the security procedures. Lukas stopped them cold. "It's simple. No one else comes up that elevator. Krispin Woolf doesn't leave." Weapons or not, Lukas didn't trust the WerePack Alpha not to take matters into his own hands. To the guard he said, "Get one of these doctors to take care of your wrist."

"Don't beat yourself up," Jack said as they stepped onto the elevator. "He fooled us all. We'll take him down."

"Better late than fucking never. And we have to find the bastard first." The next ping reported that his father, Claudette, and his siblings were all at Elliott's penthouse.

Jack looked up from his mini-comp. "Scarlett hasn't checked in. Did she contact you privately?"

"No." Lukas shoved down a spurt of panic. "Probably has those damned headphones on." He dialed his home phone number.

"Why didn't Stephen attack Antonia? Drum lesson, just the two of them—talk about an opportunity. Why didn't he take it?"

Phone to his ear, Lukas paced the elevator like a lion in a cage. "Let the prison shrinks figure it out. C'mon, Scarlett, pick up."

"Well, it shouldn't take too long to run him down." At Lukas's raised eyebrow, Jack said, "The guy trails paparazzi. He can't hide for very long. We just have to keep everyone out of his way until we catch up with him."

Lukas grimly hung up the phone. "Scarlett's not picking up."

"Maybe she's in the tub," Jack said, even as his index finger stabbed at the already-lit first floor elevator button.

It was an entirely rational explanation. Feasible—even probable—but it didn't explain why the hair on his neck stood on end, or why adrenaline seethed through his body. When the elevator finally reached the first floor, Lukas wedged his hands in the door and pulled.

He hit the lobby floor at a dead run.

Chapter 24

"OH, JEEZ, LET ME TAKE THAT," SCARLETT CALLED from the door as Stephen approached Sebastiani Security. She reached for the unwieldy mike stand as she propped open the door with a hip. "How did you ever carry all this stuff on a bike?"

"It wasn't easy. Thanks." Stephen rebalanced the load of percussion equipment he carried, barely saving the maraca case from falling to his feet. After Scarlett's phone call, he'd stopped by the Underbelly studio and picked up a little bit of everything because he had no idea what she had in mind. "Sorry it took me so long."

On the nearby Mississippi, a barge horn bellowed. Stephen looked back at the empty parking lot. "Where is everybody?"

"I have no idea. Ten minutes ago, the place just cleared out."

How ironic. He'd half-hoped that Lukas Sebastiani would take him down the second he turned into the parking lot and put him out of his misery. Stephen's stomach twisted as he followed her into the building and onto the elevator, unable to rub at the now-constant gnawing behind his breastbone. Last night's debauchery had left him feeling so shaky that he'd almost dumped the bike on the way over.

Truth be told, he hadn't tried very hard to right it.

Even death energy wasn't satisfying the beast

anymore. Stephen was out of options. He just… wanted this to be over.

"Stephen? Coming?" Scarlett asked with a quizzical look on her face.

The elevator had stopped on the top floor, and she was holding the doors open for him.

"Are you okay?" she asked, wrapping an arm around his shoulders. "Are you up to this?"

Lukas's scent was all over her. With both arms full, he couldn't touch her, so he simply rubbed his head against her shoulder. "I need some coffee. Rough night last night."

Scarlett rolled her eyes and gave him a good-natured pat. "I don't even want to know."

You're right. You really don't.

At Scarlett's invitation, he stepped into Lukas Sebastiani's home again, wading through musk, dark forest and the deep, salty sea. The place was drenched with the residue of their combined sexual energy. He couldn't blame Scarlett for shagging Lukas Sebastiani blind, deaf, and dumb.

He put down the drum case, inhaling deeply. *It wasn't just sex.* Underneath the lusty top notes was a complex bouquet of laughter, annoyance, concern, and a delicious male dominance that set fire to Stephen's body and imagination.

And love. They loved each other. How long had it been since he'd felt—he grunted as the beast nipped him in warning.

"Stephen?"

"Sorry," he said, rubbing at the sting. "Just a little heartburn."

She trailed Lukas's scent as she moved, and it tugged him in her wake. The speakers crackled as he approached. "That's annoying." Scarlett adjusted several levers on the soundboard. "I wish we could work at Underbelly, but…" She shrugged.

"Why don't you put on what you've got, let me listen while we set up?"

"Okay."

Listening to her voice would give him a plausible explanation for his erection.

Scarlett bent over the desk and pressed a button, starting the music. "The song is called 'Undertow.' I want the music to convey the feeling of being caught in a riptide. Pounding. Timeless. But… soft and throbbing, if you get what I mean."

Scarlett stared at the desk. Stephen would bet his last pair of sticks that Lukas and Scarlett had had each other on its very surface.

He sat down in Lukas's desk chair, crossed his hands over his lumpy lap, and tried not to be too obvious about his interest in the other man's possessions. The requisite computer equipment, all dark, dominated the surface. A near-empty bottle of Pepto-Bismol stood next to his mouse. There was a notebook, and an aluminum pencil, the type used by architects or draftsmen. Hung on the wall at eye level was a picture of a man, a woman, and four children. Stephen recognized a younger Elliott Sebastiani, but not the black-haired beauty holding the baby. The gap-toothed little girl—Sasha—grinned as she held rabbit ears up behind her oldest brother's head. "What gorgeous hair," he murmured.

"What?"

"I said, it sounds gorgeous already." He meant the response as a cover-up, but, as her recorded voice shivered through him, it didn't make his statement any less true. The glissando, slipping and sliding to a minor lift... it was pure siren, and every man who listened would willingly wreck himself on the rocks. He issued an admiring whistle, and grinned at Scarlett. "Hot stuff. When you sing this, there won't be a soft dick in the house."

A blush suddenly reddened Scarlett's cheeks. Stephen narrowed his eyes and listened more closely. Was that... yeah, way down in the mix. Feminine gasps and moans—and a soft baritone groan.

Scarlett had recorded them having sex. The beast shoved to its feet, and it was all Stephen could do not to groan along. "You naughty little minx," he said in what he hoped was a teasing voice, because he could barely talk.

He'd imagined Lukas would be a near-silent lover, all throttled control, and the recording proved him right. He never would have thought that Scarlett would be so vocal and demanding—very much like her sister Annika.

How much time and skill would it take to make Lukas Sebastiani shout his pleasure out loud? The speakers snapped as the challenge shrilled through his nervous system. "Okay, I think I know what you're going for," he said. "Put it on loop and let me try a few things."

Scarlett flipped a switch to record the session, put her headset back on, sat in Lukas's chair, and let him experiment awhile. He grabbed a set of brushes from the pile of sticks and stood at the snare, losing himself in the music, in her voice, in their bodies as they crashed together. He cocked his head. There was a mild syncopation in the movement of their bodies; Lukas's stroke wasn't quite steady. He tried to put himself in Lukas Sebastiani's head as his hips rolled in and out of Scarlett, the rhythm steadying out as his speed increased. Swishing the brushes over the skin of the drumhead, he tried to replicate the sound of shifting beach sand. A tap against the rim as they crashed on rocks, slow and steady as a metronome.

"Yeah. That. Keep it going." Scarlett flipped more switches, increasing the reverb and layering in a throbbing digital bass line, humming along, harmonizing with her recorded voice.

Aaah. His groin ached and burned. They'd found the seed of it.

The beast scraped teeth against his sternum. Scarlett's big black cat poked his head from the kitchen and hissed.

"Calamity, stop it." After scribbling a quick notation, she sat back, closed her eyes, and simply listened as he continued to play. A slight syncopation, a double stroke, a tap on the snare to catch the crash of the wave—or the groan of a man bottoming out in his lover's body.

Stephen took a deep breath. Scarlett might be dissatisfied with the mix she'd produced before he arrived, but he was absolutely enthralled. Did Scarlett realize what a talented producer she was? With nothing more than her voice, Lukas's voice, and this ancient board, she'd layered the sounds in such a captivating way that anyone who'd ever been in lust—in love—would feel the emotions as they listened.

She'd captured the essence perfectly.

Scarlett's recorded moans grew thready, picking up

speed and volume, rising in pitch. Her voice now dominated the mix, making the occasional moan or bitten-off
groan from Lukas all the more precious. In the chair, her
body tensed. He inhaled deeply. Yeah, he'd found the
groove all right. Would she come from simply listening
to him play along? And if she did, would Lukas's scent
be stronger? Because he wanted—

Ah, damn. Electricity surged in his lower torso, traveling a circular route from tailbone to balls to cock and
back again. His mouth opened, but he didn't make a
sound, the speakers crackling and popping. Under the
headset, Scarlett's eyes were still screwed shut, her body
poised on the knife-edge of release, so lost in the music
that she hadn't noticed the hitch in the beat, that he'd
stopped playing.

Putting down the brushes, he walked toward her. The
skin over her cheekbones was drawn tight. Her neck
craned in submission. Lukas's scent bloomed from her
body. She was almost ready to—

Ah, there. Scarlett's body quietly quaked. Suddenly
he was standing over her, mouth open, huffing her release with deep, lung-filling breaths. His hands were
clenched around her throat.

Her eyes flew open. His soft mental "no..." was
completely drowned out by the beast's howling demand. Electricity arced off the board as he breathed in
her musk, her fear, and her frantic need for air. Her body
still shuddering in aftershocks, Scarlett clawed at his
hands and wrists, tearing open the scabs Andi Woolf had
carved there with her wicked nails. The metallic scent of
blood stung his nose.

Bad move, Scarlett. The beast loves blood.

As glorious music vibrated in his bones, Stephen covered her mouth with his and pressed with his thumbs, swallowing as she gasped into his mouth.

He could almost hear the beast smacking its lips as it suckled and gorged on every strangled moan, kick, and desperate toss of Scarlett's head. He burrowed his tongue into the dark corners of her mouth to catch what remained of Lukas's flavor. Power sparked and surged into him, bathing away the ache on the underside of his skin

Rage. Adrenaline. Testosterone. *Lukas was nearby.* *Of course.* His penis kicked in response as he moaned into Scarlett's mouth.

I'm going to taste him if it's the last thing I do.

It very well might be, his common sense replied.

But what a way to go.

The faintest wisp of ashes hit Lukas's tongue as the car cornered into Sebastiani Security's parking lot. The lot was completely empty—except for Stephen's motorcycle, parked next to the door.

Fuck. He'd left her wide open.

Knee-knocking fear shot through Lukas's already-overloaded system. He squealed to a stop next to the door, knocking down Stephen's bike in the process. Slamming the car into park, shattering the stick with his forceful action, he vaulted out of the seat. Let the fucker roll right into the Mississippi, he thought as he eyed the fourth floor windows on the run. He had to get upstairs. Scarlett was fighting for her life.

His opening yank nearly tore the heavy outer door off the hinges. He ran past the empty reception desk to the stairwell and pounded up the stairs, shoulders careening off the walls as he wound his way up. The closer he got to the top floor, the stronger Scarlett's terror tasted.

Fuck stealth. He went in hard, splintering the thick wooden door, not bothering to hit the threshold in a crouch. The sun shone. Music throbbed, saturating the room with Scarlett's lush sexual energy. He smelled ashes, semen, ozone—and iron-tinged blood.

A garbled scream came from the desks. Stephen had Scarlett pinned to Lukas's desk chair, his hips churning between her kicking legs, Calamity's teeth latched firmly to his calf. Stephen's hands were wrapped around her throat, his thumbs pressing into her windpipe. Scarlett was fighting for air—and losing.

With a roar, Lukas barreled across the room, grabbed Stephen, and simply threw him. He landed in a heap under the windows, his elbow jammed in the drywall. A foot higher, and he'd have flown through the glass to land with a splat on the asphalt four stories below.

Lukas spared a glance to make sure he was down, then brought his attention back to Scarlett, who lay still on the desk chair, arms limp at her sides, eyes rolled back in her head.

Not breathing.

"Don't you dare," he said, bowel-loosening fear turning his voice surly. CPR. He knew CPR. He dropped to his knees and poked his index finger into her ribs, where he knew she was most ticklish. "Breathe for me, sweetheart."

Her chest heaved in response, setting off a paroxysm of coughing. *Good.* Coughing meant air was moving in and out. The hand she raised to cover her mouth was stained with blood. He quickly examined it. She had tissue under her fingernails—she'd nailed the bastard good, but… Jesus. The scent of semen sliced at him. He hovered his hands over her body, afraid to touch her.

Don't panic. Analyze the scene. He took a shaky breath and did his best. Pants. Scarlett's black stretch pants were still on her body, the waistband snug against her hips, right where it belonged. Unlike Andi Woolf or Annika Fontaine, Scarlett's belly-baring T-shirt still covered the essentials.

What the hell had happened here?

Scarlett finally stopped coughing. "Lukas?" she rasped, looking at him with eye whites speckled with pinpoint hemorrhages.

Petechiae, his left brain noted. His right brain simply roared. "I'm right here," he said, holding her bleary gaze as he quickly probed her skull and jaw line for injuries. She recoiled when he examined her throat, jabbing an icy spear through his heart. "It's me, Scarlett," he said. His own throat was clenched so tight he could hardly force out the words. "It's just me. I need to make sure you're okay." He ran his hands over the slim tendons in her neck, over her shoulders, down her arms, her torso, abdomen, hips, and legs. He tried to keep his touch professional and businesslike, but he couldn't help stroking her cheekbone with his fingertip. "I don't think anything is broken," he said. "Sweetheart, can you sit up? Here, let me help—"

A shockwave hammered into his upper back. He clutched at his chest as he instinctively rolled away from Scarlett. *Jesus.* His heart was flip-flopping against his ribs like a fish on a hook.

"Lukas."

The horror in Scarlett's voice penetrated. Stephen stood, his left elbow cocked at an odd angle. He held the other arm out in front of him, staring at the electricity arcing between his outstretched fingers.

"Well. That's new," Stephen said.

Heat flashed against his upper back, quickly licking its way up his neck. He smelled singed hair. Lukas rolled, but the hardwood floor didn't do a damn thing to—

"Here!" Scarlett's T-shirt was in his hand. He quickly snuffed out the fire, reducing the pain from nuclear to merely excruciating, and lurched to his feet.

"Get back." He shoved Scarlett behind him.

"We really don't want to hurt Scarlett." Stephen inhaled deeply, momentarily holding his breath like he was taking a hit from a bong. When he released the breath, pleasure hazed his eyes. "But you? That's another matter entirely."

We? Shit, he hadn't cleared the room. Lukas opened his senses, his gaze darting to every corner and entrance. Behind him, Scarlett scraped breath into her lungs. He didn't hear anyone else.

"So nice of you to join the party. We were sure you'd arrive sooner or later."

Lukas stared at the electricity arcing and snapping off the smaller man's body. The gun closet hidden behind a slab of wood at the far end of the maple shelving unit might just as well be on Mars. *This'll teach you not to carry, you arrogant asshole.*

Behind him, Scarlett rasped, "There's no one else here."

As she spoke, Stephen jumped. Lukas grunted as another surge of electricity slammed into him. His knees buckled like someone jacked him from behind with a crowbar. "Jesus," he gasped, trying to tug Stephen's legs from around his body. The little bastard was burning him alive.

Lukas staggered toward the wall, ramming Stephen's back against the windowsill. As wood splintered, the smaller man hollered in pain, but he didn't let go. Lukas twisted and launched them toward the heavy maple shelving unit, ruthlessly banging Stephen's ruined elbow into the hard wood.

Stephen shrieked and dropped to the floor, but not before delivering a massive jolt that turned his muscles to mush.

His legs collapsed underneath him. He raised a hand to his jittering heart. Scarlett's hoarse scream was the last thing he heard before it all went dark.

<center>~~~</center>

Scarlett watched in horror as Lukas fell like timber. As Stephen scuttled over to Lukas's stunned body and climbed on top of him, she searched frantically for a weapon.

Electricity arced between them. Scarlett smelled charred skin, and the soles of Lukas's boots were starting to smoke.

As Stephen slowly lowered his mouth to Lukas, Scarlett grabbed the mike stand, holding it like a baseball bat.

Lukas, don't move. Please don't move.

She planted her feet and swung, her banshee wail shattering the windows and raining glass onto the sidewalk below.

There was a horrible, hollow thunk. Blood sprayed as Stephen slumped on top of Lukas, and the full body contact sent him into spasms. "Oh gawd." Scarlett dropped the mike stand and tugged woozily at Stephen's leather belt. Smoke wisped off Lukas's eyebrows, and the skin on his lips was crisping before her eyes. "Damn it." Breaths sobbed from her throat as she pushed at her drummer's shoulders. "Damn it."

Footsteps pounded up the stairs. Jack burst through the door with his gun drawn, quickly followed by Gideon Lupinsky. They were both bleeding from the ears, though neither man seemed to notice. Together, the men rolled Stephen off Lukas, whose veins popped and jittered like they were about to burst out of his skin.

"Jenny!" Gideon snapped into his headset. "We need the defibrillator. Now."

Scarlett collapsed against the wall as people exploded into motion around her. Jack's voice was tight as he called an ambulance. Gideon's partner trotted in, breathing hard, carrying a small yellow box that she handed to Gideon before cutting Lukas's shirt off with a pair of scissors.

I should be helping. A white haze pushed at the edges of her vision. More police filled the room, but the loudest thing she heard was the rasp of Calamity's tongue as he lapped at her face.

Jack crouched beside her. "Scarlett? Let me check you out."

She touched his bloody ear with a hand she couldn't feel. "Sorry." Her teeth started chattering, and her head, suddenly too heavy for her neck, sagged back against the wall. Black speckles flew into the white clouds, blocking her view. Were they birds? Bats? "So many of them," she whispered through her stinging throat.

"Medic!" she heard Jack yell as the blackness engulfed her.

Chapter 25

"I'M LEAVING NOW," SCARLETT SAID WITH EVERY LICK of command and influence she could wring from her sore throat. "Thank you for the excellent care, but I feel fine and I have to leave now." She shoved back the blanket and stood, picking at the adhesive tape holding the IV in place at her wrist. Once she had the tape completely torn off, she held out her arm to the nurse. "Either you yank this, or I will."

The nurse goggled at the unsecured needle, now leaking blood. "Ms. Fontaine—"

Scarlett pulled the IV herself. *Wow, that needle's... really, really long.* "Do you have any gauze? A Band-Aid? No?" She wadded the pristine white sheet in her hand and pressed it against the welling blood.

"Ms. Fontaine, please. The doctor will be here to speak with you very soon. You're upset—"

"Ya think?"

The nurse recoiled and scurried out of the room, whether to get a Band-Aid, the doctor, or hospital security, Scarlett didn't know, and she didn't care. She peeked under the red-flecked sheet. The bleeding had almost stopped.

Where was Lukas? And where were her clothes?

Stepping out of the flimsy hospital gown they'd insisted on bundling her into when she arrived, she walked, shivering, to the closet. There, on the floor, was a yellow plastic bag containing the meager belongings she'd arrived with. She dumped the contents on the bed, swallowing hard as she picked up her black yoga pants. How could she ever wear them again without remembering?

Stephen, what happened to you? When did we lose you?

And where was Lukas now?

As she dressed with shaky hands—having no shirt, she had to put the hospital gown back on—she tried to sort the memory fragments into some logical order, but her brain wasn't cooperating. She didn't remember being transferred to the ambulance, just waking up in one—with Lukas jerking and shuddering next to her, the defibrillator and leads still attached to his bare chest. His arms and legs spilled over the sides of the gurney, and the compartment reeked of singed hair and skin. After the ambulance screeched to a stop at the entrance to the ER, they'd hustled Lukas out and away, separating them. She hadn't seen him since.

The essentials covered, Scarlett walked out of the examining room. She was going to get some information, from someone, somewhere.

Now.

Dozens of people milled in the hallway and in the waiting room, most of them with cameras. "There she is!"

The pack swarmed toward her like rabid hyenas. Quickly surrounded, she raised her hand to protect her eyes from the bright flashes of light.

"Scarlett! How are you?"

"Scarlett! Did Stephen rape you?"

The excitement in their voices made her sick. Before she could speak, Gideon Lupinsky waded into the mass, wrapped his arms around her midsection, and bodily extracted her, roughly pushing through the crowd. "Get this garbage out of here," he snapped at the uniformed officers trailing in his wake.

He carried her until they rounded a corner leading to a hallway blocked by four posted officers. Beyond them, the hallway was blissfully empty. "You okay?" he asked as he set her on her feet, holding on to her shoulders until she steadied.

"Yeah. Thanks for the rescue."

Gideon escorted her to a family room where her mother, Elliott, Sasha, Rafe, and Antonia waited. Her mother and Elliott were dressed for the boardroom, but the younger Sebastianis had all apparently dropped other activities to come quickly to the hospital. Sasha was wearing a leotard, tights, and toe shoes. Rafe's clothes, face, and hair were flecked with clay. Antonia cuddled next to her father on the couch, completely wrapped in a thin, hospital issued blanket.

Rafe approached quickly and took her hand. No doubt fear was pumping off her like water from a fire hose. "He's okay," he said. "He's going to be okay." Before she realized he'd done it, Rafe led her to a chair and she was sitting down.

Her mother kneeled next to the chair, carefully touching the red marks on her throat, stroking her temples. A film of tears glazed the steely anger in her eyes.

"I'm fine, Mom. A little hoarse, but I'll recover. Where's Lukas?"

Claudette and Elliott exchanged a look. "We just left him," Elliott finally answered. "He's a little singed, banged up, but his heart rhythm is normal again." He smiled ruefully. "He's already complaining because the doctors won't release him."

"And... Stephen?"

Gideon unconsciously rubbed at a red mark on his hand. "He's being treated at Quarantine."

"Being treated" meant he was alive. She wondered why she cared.

"He's drifting in and out of consciousness," Gideon said. "It'll be awhile before we can interrogate him."

There was a knock at the door. Before Gideon could open it, a raven-haired, white-coated valkyrie entered, her gaze immediately zeroing in on Scarlett. "Ms. Fontaine. You left your room before we could discuss your test results." She smiled and indicated the door. "Would you please come with me?"

"No."

"Scarlett, please go with the doctor," her mother urged.

"Tell me here. Cut to the chase." Scarlett met the older woman's eyes. "Then I'd like to see—"

"—see Mr. Sebastiani. I know." The doctor, whom the embroidery on her pocket identified as "Dr. Melvin," sighed as she sat in the chair adjacent to Scarlett's. "It feels good to get off these tired, old feet."

Scarlett eyed the doctor's stylish, low-heeled boots, the gorgeous tangle of necklaces at the neckline of her red, silk blouse, the incisive intelligence in her eyes. *Tired old feet my ass.*

"Your heart checked out normal. You have some bruising at your throat, but your trachea, esophagus, and vocal cords aren't damaged. Your singing voice won't be impacted." She hesitated. "He didn't latch on to you long enough to do much harm."

But he had latched on to Lukas.

Dr. Melvin glanced at Elliott. "Mr. Sebastiani took quite a jolt, but thanks to Commander Lupinsky and his partner, his heart rhythm's back to normal and it seems to be staying that way. Brain function is currently normal. He has some rather painful burns which are being treated as we speak, and we still have to test his muscle function."

Scarlett relaxed, just a bit. "When can I see him?"

Dr. Melvin and Elliott exchanged a glance.

"What?" Scarlett snapped.

The doctor finally spoke. "Mr. Sebastiani doesn't want visitors at this time."

Scarlett's stomach tightened. The doctor's bland, diplomatic response didn't quite ring true. "You've all seen him?"

Silence. Then Sasha answered, "Yes."

Scarlett glanced around the room, mentally cataloguing the occupants. "Where's Jack?" Holding up her hand, she said, "Don't even bother. He's with Lukas right now, isn't he?"

Other than the birds chirping in the small aviary in the corner, the silence was deafening. *Damn you, Lukas.* "So it's just me he doesn't want to see."

"I'm sorry, Ms. Fontaine," Dr. Melvin said.

He was walking away from her, without moving a muscle. Without saying a single goddamn word.

Again.

Not this time. Scarlett stood and stalked to the door. "Excuse me a moment, please. I need to visit the restroom."

As she left, she caught Sasha's approving nod from the corner of her eye.

—ww—

Lukas barely held back a groan as he dropped his head back to the pillow. Why had he refused pain medication?

Bad call. He was full of bad calls today.

Now that the adrenaline had worn off, the aftereffects of every injury Stephen had inflicted, and every procedure he'd undergone, screamed and hollered for his attention. The back of his neck hurt like a bitch, and every now and again random muscles twitched like grasshoppers were jumping under his skin. His jaw and teeth sockets hurt, and he'd kill for some ChapStick. He smelled ozone and singed hair, could taste his own crisp skin.

His balls were burned.

An EKG machine softly blipped his heart's rhythm, and leads trailed from his noggin to a silent machine next to it. IVs snaked into both wrists. But he could see. His arms and legs moved. And most importantly, he couldn't taste Stephen any longer.

Thankfully, Scarlett wouldn't see him like this.

Jack stepped into the hospital room, his eyes widening momentarily before returning to their typical implacability. Lukas sighed. The nurses had done their best to clean him up, but he probably looked like he was at death's door.

"You definitely need some grooming help," Jack said as he approached the bed.

"Look who's talking." Jack's suit was a rumpled mess, and trails of dried blood snaked from his ears to his jaw line. "How's Scarlett?"

"Arguing with the doctor. She'll be fine."

Relief flooded into him. The sight of the little shit's hands wrapped around Scarlett's throat would be burned into his retinas for a very long time to come.

"How—" Lukas coughed against the sting in his throat. Jack grabbed the glass of water from the bedside table and held the straw so Lukas could drink. "Thanks," he said when he finished. "How did that little shit get the drop on me?"

Because, Christ, that stung. How had a man half his size taken him down?

"Wyland's floated a theory that, instead of absorbing emotional energy passively, like most incubi, he might be tapping into it as an energy source, and can transfer that energy to others when he's agitated or excited. Basically, he tased you, bro." Jack paused. "Gideon took a pretty good shot when he cuffed Stephen. He's okay," he quickly added. "Superficial burn."

Lukas pursed his cracked lips and swore at the sting. His mind raced. How could Stephen possibly do that? "Genetic anomaly?"

Jack shrugged. "Who knows? But for someone his size, he certainly packed a punch. Speaking of which," he smiled grimly, "Scarlett bashed in the bastard's skull but good."

Lukas didn't know whether to be proud or appalled. Reality was an uncomfortable mixture of both. "She shouldn't have had to. He was at my house. I tasted the fucking ashes. He was right there, and I didn't pick up a damn thing."

So much for his so-called talent.

"We had no reason to suspect him, and you know it. He was Scarlett's friend, a co-worker she'd safely traveled with for over a year—a victim found seriously injured at the same crime scene where Annika lost her life. We never thought to cross-check his DNA with the sample we collected from under Andi's fingernails. If you're going to beat yourself up, you'd better save a punch for me, and for Gideon too. Stephen fooled us all."

Intellectually, Lukas knew that Jack was right, but... damn, Stephen had hurt so many people. People he loved. He hadn't saved Scarlett, Scarlett had saved *him*. Unacceptable. "Are you sure we got him?"

Jack nodded. "Gideon said Stephen momentarily regained consciousness in the ambulance, rambling about hurting Andi, hurting Annika, hurting Scarlett, hurting you." Jack cleared his throat. "Apparently, a beast living inside him forces him to do things. He also claimed he was from another planet. Gideon entered his recording into evidence, but, to use a highly technical term, the guy's whacked. He may not ever be able to stand trial."

Lukas stared at his right quad twitching under the blankets until the surge of anger drifted away. "We have to let the process play out." As a witness—hell, as a *victim*—he'd be recused from rendering judgment.

A light mandarin scent soothed his charred nostrils. She was here. And she was really, really pissed.

Scarlett stood in the doorway with her fists clenched, looking more like an avenging valkyrie than a siren. Her face was ghost-pale, and she wore those damn black stretch pants and a hospital gown. There was a trail of blood on her hand, and he could see the bastard's hand-prints on her neck from here. Clenching his sore jaw, he steeled himself for what he had to do—remove himself from her life, once and for all. It was the best solution for everyone concerned.

"Don't you even think about it." Scarlett stalked into the room, blood-flecked eyes flashing. "I've had enough of your martyr crap."

Jack held up both hands and headed for the door. "You're on your own." He kissed Scarlett on both cheeks as he passed, squeezing her hand. "Give him hell," he murmured.

Lukas heard. "You're supposed to be on my side."

Jack looked at him with pity. "I am."

—∿∿—

Scarlett's heart took a slow swan dive, right off the cliff. He was going to do it again. He might be flat on his back in a hospital bed, with hanks of his glorious hair singed off, but she could read the resolve in his eyes.

"You chickenshit."

"What?" His expression didn't shift one iota, but beside him, the EKG blipped.

"You heard me." She paced the room in her bare feet. "Tell the doctor to keep me from your room? You coward. You're getting ready to walk away again. What's your excuse this time?" She didn't give him a chance to respond. "'I should have known.' 'I should have protected Andi, protected Annika.' 'I should have protected Scarlett.'" She stared at him with hands on her hips. "Am I close?"

"Yes. I should have protected you."

"Damn you!" Her voice rolled through the room, rattling the windows in their frames. "You're one of the strongest beings on this earth, but you're not invincible."

"Scarlett, you could have died. The bastard should never have—"

"Who pulled Stephen off of me in the first place, Calamity? No, it was you, Lukas. You." Scarlett plopped on the edge of the bed and tried to take his hand. He pulled it away, but not before she saw the burns.

"Thank you for saving my life," he said.

His voice was so polite, and oh-so-remote. "We saved each other!" she said, anger bubbling over. Across the room, the mirror cracked. "We saved each other," she repeated more quietly. "There's no one I trust more. I trust you with my life."

"Bad bet, babe. You nearly lost it today."

"I know you'll always be there for me, Lukas."

"Of course. You're my stepsister—and the Siren Second."

Her heart smacked the water and sank to the depths of the deep, but she rose from the bed, stood beside it and stared down at him.

"I… can't do this," Lukas finally said.

He couldn't meet her eyes. "Yes, you can, but you're choosing not to—because then you'd feel as vulnerable as the rest of us." The ambulance sirens wailed outside. She wanted to wail along with them, but damn it, she wouldn't do it here.

She refused to do it here.

"I love you, Lukas, and I know that you love me." She walked to the door, the tile floor so, so cold against her bare feet. When she reached it, she turned back to her injured warrior, watching her with such pain in his eyes. "Let me know when you're brave enough to admit it."

Chapter 26

ONE. MORE. REP.

His torso was sweating so much he practically slipped off the weight bench. What remained of his hair was dripping wet, and his arms wouldn't stop shaking, but he was going to finish one last rep if it killed him. And it very well might, he thought as he eyed the heavy black slabs bending the metal bar he held suspended over his head on locked out elbows. He could see the embarrassing obituary now: "Underworld Council Member, Risk Assessor Lukas Sebastiani, Killed in Entirely Avoidable Weightlifting Accident." It would serve him right for lifting so much weight without a spotter.

Would Scarlett even mourn him if he died?

The weight swayed overhead. *Okay, focus. One more, and you're done.* His abs and biceps burned as he lowered the bar to his chest, whooshed out a breath, and grunted out the last punishing bench press. "Now get the bar into the stand before it kills you, you dumb shit." He did so with a hard clank, dropped his dead arms to his sides, and lay there with his eyes closed, waiting for his breathing to even out.

Scarlett was right. He was a chickenshit.

He hoped Scarlett was wired like her mother was, because Lukas's father had told him not two hours ago that when he pissed off Claudette, a heartfelt apology usually sufficed. The twinkle in his father's eye led

Lukas to conclude that his father's apology technique also employed judicious amounts of make-up sex.

Funny how you never stopped learning from your parents.

His lips quirked. Yeah, he could get behind the make-up sex, one hundred percent. But unfortunately the apology had to come first.

His house was filled with emotional booby-traps. No matter how much weight he lifted, no matter how many punishing sit-ups he crunched, he couldn't erase the memories: Scarlett laughing and splashing water at him while they washed the dishes together. The cute little scowl of concentration between her eyebrows when she wrote. That goddamn headset, permanently clamped to her ears. The way hot showers turned her skin a rosy, carnation pink. That haunting, infernal humming that turned his cock to rock in the span of a heartbeat. The way she throatily demanded more of him, more and more, when they made love. The way he willingly gave it to her, every way she asked, and then some.

"Damn it," he whispered. He owed her an apology whether she gave him another shot or not.

"I told you he'd be here." As Jack entered, he set a shopping bag on the floor, his expression darkening as he took in Lukas's shaking body, the sweat-darkened workout clothes, and the slabs racked up on the bar.

Rafe walked in behind him and immediately eye-balled the weights. "Are you trying to kill yourself?"

Lukas didn't dignify his comment with an answer. He sat up, grabbed a towel, and dragged it across his sweaty face. "What are you two doing here?" Jack and Rafe didn't run in the same circles. Seeing them together, without him to bridge the gap, was a little unusual.

Jack picked up the head of the sparring dummy that Lukas kicked off earlier, setting it on the table where Scarlett used to work. "This is an intervention. You haven't left this building in almost two weeks. You need a change of scenery."

"Blow off some steam," Rafe said with a grin. "Maybe get laid."

Jack raised placating hands at the killing look Lukas speared them with. "Or not. But you're coming out with us."

"You might want to shower first," Rafe suggested.

Lukas stared at them. He wasn't in the mood for a Saturday night bar crawl, and the way Jack and Rafe were dressed, it didn't look like they had a biker bar in mind.

"Brother or not, Sasha won't let you in the door if you show up looking like this."

Underbelly, then. A bite of cinnamon hit his tongue. Despite Rafe's casual slouch, his brother was worried about him. *Damn*. But he couldn't go clubbing, not tonight. He had to apologize to Scarlett, try to—

Scarlett's place is right upstairs from the club, you dumb shit.

He stood. "Okay. But you're buying." At Rafe's surprised look, he said, "Hey, I can drink a beer or two if that's what it takes to get you off my back."

He stripped off and stepped into the shower, feeling more energetic than he'd felt any day since Stephen's attack. He turned the knob and stood out of the way until the water warmed up, staring at the girly purple puff, a pumice stone, a can of watermelon-scented shaving cream, and a bright blue razor that still sat on the shelf in the shower. Sasha hadn't looked in the shower when she'd come over to retrieve Scarlett's things, and Lukas couldn't make himself move them under the sink.

Steam rose from the shower, and he stepped under the spray with a moan, letting the water pound his tight muscles. *What the hell*. He snatched the purple puff off the shelf and used it.

With her scent filling in his nostrils, Lukas strategized, then reviewed his plan for flaws. He'd spend an hour or so at Underbelly with the guys, long enough to assuage their concern, but no longer. He'd let Rafe buy him a couple of beers, steering clear of Sasha, who'd taken it upon herself to give him regular, torturous updates about how busy Scarlett was, how she was gaining weight, getting her curves back. Finally sleeping well, and working like a demon. She'd finished one song, and was collaborating on another with Dave Grohl, "now that they'd reconnected."

Lukas turned off the water with a twist that threatened to break the heavy knob, and stepped out of the shower. Sasha had known the mere thought would lodge under his skin like a fucking sliver.

"Hey, I have a puff like that at home," Rafe said from the open door. "Feels great, doesn't it."

Shit. The steam wasn't thick enough to hide the damage Stephen had inflicted upon his body—damage he hadn't shared with his family.

Rafe silently examined the healing burns on Lukas's collarbones, sternum, hipbones, and spine, taking in the singed body hair on his chest, abs, and underbelly. "What the hell…?"

"Your guess is as good as mine." Lukas snatched a towel off the hook, ran it over his upper body, and slung it around his hips as he stepped out of the shower. He didn't have any answers himself. The last report he'd received from the secure medical facility where Stephen was being held had been maddeningly inconclusive. "I just know it itches like a bitch."

He surveyed his collarbones in the mirror hanging over the sink. The blackened skin had finally sloughed off, leaving shiny red welts. He could hide those wounds under his clothing, and had for two weeks, but there was no hiding his singed eyelashes and eyebrows, or his tattered hair. He met Rafe's eyes in the mirror. "Sure you want me to come along? I might scare all the women away."

"With that scowl, you hardly even notice you don't have eyebrows."

Lukas sighed.

"Jack? Can you bring that shopping bag in here?" Rafe called. He opened drawers, the medicine cabinet, the doors under the sink. "Where the hell's your hair product?" he muttered.

"Huh?"

"No wonder your hair always looks like crap. Keep drying."

"Okay, Kyan."

Rafe smiled at the reference to the *Queer Eye for the Straight Guy* hair stylist, and knelt to better root through the items stored under the sink. "Ah."

Lukas recoiled at the scissors in his hand.

"Lukas, we have to cut your hair." Rafe indicated his

brother's uneven hanks. "You can't get your woman back looking like that. You shouldn't throw out your garbage looking like that."

Jack walked into the bathroom carrying a stool and the shopping bag. He reached into the bag and handed Rafe a clipper.

"Sit," Rafe said, indicating the stool. "Let's get this done."

Lukas sat and watched long strands of hair drop to the rough bathroom tiles. Once most of the length was gone, his brother carefully plied the clipper over his skull.

"Okay, shower off. Jack, check the closet and see if there's anything worth wearing. I'll—"

"Out, both of you. I can take it from here." The bathroom was the one room in the place that had a door on it, and it was about to get slammed. Hard.

As he washed his prison-inmate brush cut under the shower's massaging spray, he decided he'd wear whatever clothing Jack chose for him.

Tonight, he needed all the help he could get.

Music rumbled through the concrete walls as the three men pulled into the Sebastiani Building's underground parking garage twenty minutes later, Jack at the wheel of his Volvo sedan, Lukas riding shotgun, and Rafe sprawled across most of the backseat. As Jack cruised the lot for an empty parking space, Lukas's gaze, as always, momentarily flicked over a very specific parking slot—innocuous enough, smack in the middle of the row, and currently occupied by a gray SUV dripping with sleet.

But in his mind's eye, it was forever a crime scene,

partitioned off with yellow tape—the place where his mother had fought off a mugger like a tiger, turning a purse-snatching into a stabbing that wouldn't have happened at all if her oldest son hadn't stomped away from the car in a testosterone-fuelled teenage huff, about some perceived slight that Lukas couldn't even remember anymore. He'd left her alone and defenseless. Sometimes, in the deepest recesses of his psyche, that teenager still raged, "Why didn't you just give him the fucking purse?"

But with no surveillance cameras in place to find the criminal, Lukas had discovered his wild talent, and helped bring his mother's killer to justice.

Was Scarlett safer with him, or without him? And did it really matter? He couldn't stay away from her either way. Earlier today, his father had punched a hole in his ego by musing that self-blame was self-indulgent, allowing a person to retain the illusion that they had control over the outcome of a bad situation in the first place.

Lukas knew that his control issues stood in the way of any future he and Scarlett could have together. Intellectually, he knew he had to step back, let her take risks, to live her life—beautiful, wild, and free. He just hoped it wasn't too late to convince her to do it with him rather than without him. Tonight he was flying without a net. He'd better get used to it, because if tonight went as he hoped it would, he'd be getting a hell of a lot of practice.

He joined Rafe and Jack near the trunk. "Remember, you're buying," he reminded his brother.

They took the stairway from the garage up to the first floor, and the music blasted them as soon as the doors opened. It didn't take long to find Flynn holding court at the back bar, spilling his Irish charm over a trio of tipsy women.

"Hey, guys," Flynn greeted them with a wave, reaching for two Heinekens. He popped off the caps with a twist of his wrist, and then skidded them down the bar to Lukas and Jack. Turning to the taps, he started building Rafe's Guinness. "Place is hopping, and look at all the pretty ladies here tonight." He grinned at the women he was serving. "Ladies, meet Jack, Rafe, and Lukas."

"You weren't kidding about the eye candy here, were you?" the buxom redhead murmured to her friend. Her gaze stopped on Lukas. "I'll take door number three."

Jack smiled and saluted them with his bottle of beer. "Ladies."

Lukas tried not to scowl as he acknowledged the women's greetings with a nod. Though the redhead was perfectly attractive, she wasn't the redhead he was looking for. He wasn't interested in picking anyone up, watching his brother work his infallible hookup mojo, or even standing here at the bar talking. He wanted to find Scarlett, apologize to her, and see if there was anything left to salvage of the relationship he'd stupidly shot down.

The pheromones drifting from the dance floor didn't help. Someone had set Buffalo Bill's disturbing "it puts the lotion on its skin" dialogue from *Silence of the Lambs* to a slow, grinding beat. The juxtaposition made him twitchy. "What is this shit?"

"Forgive my brother. He's antsy tonight," Rafe apologized. "Where's Sasha?" he asked Flynn.

"It's Guilty Pleasures night, so she's either on the floor or in the DJ booth."

Lukas snorted. Suddenly the music made a lot more sense. On Guilty Pleasures night, Sasha picked the tunes.

Flynn scanned the dance floor and gestured. "Over there."

Lukas looked over to where Sasha and Bailey danced together, cheerfully hanging on each other in that platonic way girlfriends often did, but which caused the assholes dancing around them to spin hopeful ménage à trois fantasies. The two women were being circled like baby seals, drawing all the wrong kinds of attention. *Great. Just fucking great.* He picked up his beer and took a healthy swig. He'd come here to relax, but he was going to end up knocking some heads together before the night was over. And apparently Jack felt the same way, because he stood up straight, at full alert beside him.

Rafe shook his head at both of them. "They're fine. Relax, enjoy yourselves."

Suddenly Scarlett sauntered down from the DJ booth, joining Sasha and Bailey. What was she doing down here instead of upstairs? Lust punched him in the gut. Rafe smirked beside him, but didn't say anything.

Jesus, she was beautiful. Sasha was right; Scarlett had gained a crucial seven or eight pounds since he'd last seen her, and in all the right fucking places. The way her well-worn jeans cupped her ass made his hands itch, and the heeled boots she wore canted her hips flirtatiously. He wasn't the only one who admired her curves, or noticed that she wasn't wearing a bra. She swayed to the music, eyes closed, with a slight smile on her face.

She lost herself in the pleasure of the sound, and drew every eye.

"Damn it."

"Jesus, Luk, give it a rest. They're just having some fun." Rafe placed his half-finished Guinness on the bar. "Watch that for me, would you?" He winked at the women. "I wouldn't want anyone to slip me a roofie."

Rafe had spotted his quarry for the night, and Lukas didn't have the heart to tell the women avidly babysitting Rafe's beer that it wasn't going to be one of them. His brother waded through the people on the dance floor, cheerfully fending off a few arms slung around his waist, and finally stopped when he reached Scarlett, Sasha, and Bailey. He tipped his head back and laughed at something Bailey said, then he—

Lukas's eyes bugged as Rafe wound his arms around Scarlett's torso from behind, cuddling every inch of his lanky body right up against hers. She smiled up at him, placed her arms over his, and leaned her head back against his shoulder as a singer throatily implored that he wanted to see her stripped down to the bone.

Lukas looked at Jack and Flynn, chatting and flirting with the women as if there was nothing out of the ordinary going on, like his brother's long, wavy hair wasn't twining with Scarlett's blazing red mane. Like Rafe wasn't grinding against Scarlett's ass not thirty feet away.

Lukas slammed his beer onto the bar and plowed through the crowd.

He didn't see Jack and Flynn high-fiving behind him.

His eyes locked onto his brother's the whole way. The son of a bitch saw him coming, and his expression was filled with challenge and an almost unholy glee. As he approached, Lukas raised a singed eyebrow and flashed his right hand with every digit extended, silently giving Rafe to the count of five to back the fuck off. He was down to one and actually had his fist clenched when Rafe finally stepped away from Scarlett with a theatrical "she's all yours" gesture, and turned his attention to Bailey.

Scarlett kept moving to the slithering tune, eyes closed, as happy to dance by herself as with someone else. He hesitated, and then stepped behind her as Rafe had, pressing his whole body against hers, wrapping his arms around her abdomen. She halted momentarily, inhaled, then relaxed back against him.

Lukas absorbed her essence, her helpless reaction to him. To him, he reassured himself, not to his brother, who was too damn good looking for his own good.

But good Christ, he hated to dance. Lukas felt the moving throng close in on him, so he closed his eyes and swayed, focusing on the feel of Scarlett's soft breasts resting on his forearm.

No wonder his brother liked clubbing so much.

Scarlett squirmed, and then turned in his arms so she faced him. "Hi," she murmured, raising her hand to stroke his shorn head. "You look much better than you did the last time I saw you."

His senses were wide open, but he couldn't find a whiff of anger or recrimination mixed in with the emotions swirling from her. Did she really find it so easy to forgive him? He wrapped his arms around her waist and opened his mouth to apologize. To grovel. To beg her to take him back into her life, to sing to him and only him. But before he could speak the words, she pulled his head down and kissed him.

Despite his good intentions, he dove in, all too willing to take advantage of her generosity, because she tasted like home. Yes, he'd apologize. They'd have a serious talk, but... later. Lukas tunneled his skinned-up fingers into her hair and feasted on her mouth like a king at a banquet.

They grasped and groped, swaying a bit for propriety's sake, but no one could mistake the pheromones blooming around them. "Shit," Lukas whispered, reluctantly dragging his lips from Scarlett's to see Rafe, Sasha, and Bailey grinning at them from nearby.

"Never mind them. Come back here," Scarlett said, pulling him back down to her mouth.

He drifted back into the kiss, heard her haunting voice, calling to him. *How can she sing when she's kissing me?* Then he noticed that people around them had stilled, and were craning their heads to the three-story speaker system.

Scarlett tensed in his arms and pulled back slightly. The glorious voice continued, though he could see that her mouth was closed. *Scarlett's new song.* Sasha had mentioned that Scarlett had been on a creative tear, but *wow*. Lukas wrapped his arms around Scarlett and rested his chin on top of her head as the extraordinary sound system pulsed.

Waves crashed. Voices emerged from deep in the mix. A man and a woman, murmuring softly to each other, barely audible, but their pleasure was unmistakable. There was Scarlett's breathy moan. And... his face flamed.

She'd recorded them making love? He hardened to granite in a rush. He looked around the dance floor, but no one, absolutely no one, was paying attention to them. Instead, people had started to pair up, to couple, to sway to the music. Scarlett listened with her eyes closed, her face rapt as she cuddled closer to him, shifted her hips against his as the waves pulsed harder and crashed louder. Her siren's voice twined around him, beckoned to every person in the room:

> *"Let me pull you down below*
> *Through the blue-green undertow"*

The day he'd interrupted her as she worked, she'd pulled him down all right, riding him until they both exploded. He didn't have to understand the mixing techniques she'd used, the writing skill she'd employed, to understand that her song was building to the same shattering conclusion.

Pheromones saturated the dance floor. Lukas noticed more than one man adjusting the front of his pants, saw dancers with their tongues buried down each other's throats.

Rafe backed away from Bailey with a dazed look on his face.

But the song continued. Scarlett had added a final, wistful verse:

> *"I know you'll pull me down below*
> *To the blue-green undertow…*
> *To the blue-green undertow"*

The yearning. The trust. The love, passion, and commitment. All of it pulsed into him, everything he wanted, and nothing he ever thought he could have. Lukas pressed his forehead to hers, wrapping his arms around her like he would absorb her into his skin if he could. Useless words wrestled for supremacy in his head, but all he could say was, "I'm so sorry."

Her soft, forgiving kiss, her unmistakable mandarin champagne response, made his head swim.

He took a deep breath and boldly crashed his ship into the cliffs. "Sing to me, Scarlett. For the rest of our lives."

"Be careful what you ask for," Scarlett whispered with a smile that rivaled the aurora. "You just might receive it."

He brought his lips to hers. The kiss was a benediction, a promise. But when her soft pink tongue touched his, he groaned and let his join in, tangle and dance.

"Can you two get a room?" Sasha complained, bumping Lukas with her shoulder as she walked by. "This is a respectable place of business."

Lukas looked at the dancers who all but copulated in the shadows. It was business as usual at Underbelly.

Scarlett tugged on his hand, leading him off the dance floor. "I have a room, right upstairs." She wrapped her arm around his waist as they walked to the penthouse elevator. "Did you notice that my bedroom has a skylight? Maybe we'll see the aurora tonight. Or a shooting star."

Lukas eyed Scarlett. "You know that shooting stars are just space debris burning up as it hits the atmosphere, right?"

"You're such a hopeless romantic."

Their eyes met and locked. "So, you want to see stars?" Lukas murmured. "I'll show you stars."

He lowered his head as the elevator doors closed, and showed her the moon, the stars. The universe.

Scarlett's Set List

"Desire (Come and Get It)" — Gene Loves Jezebel
"Maneater" — Nelly Furtado
"Line Up" — Elastica
"Sex (I'm a…)" — Berlin
"Ice Cream" — New Young Pony Club
"Ain't Talkin' 'bout Love" — Van Halen
"Erotic City" — Berlin
"Blue Monday" — Orgy
"I Never Came" — Queens of the Stone Age
"Fingers" — Pink
"I Touch Myself" — Divinyls
"Too Drunk To Fuck" — Nouvelle Vague
"Stripped" — Depcche Mode
"Perfect Strangers" — INXS
"All Day Long I Dream About Sex" — JC Chasez
"Are You Happy Now?" — Michelle Branch
"Do Ya Wanna Touch Me" — Joan Jett
"Lovestoned" — Justin Timberlake
"This Is Love" — PJ Harvey
"Future Love Paradise" — Seal
"Such Reveries" — Duncan Sheik
"One Part Be My Lover" — Bonnie Raitt
"Maybe Tomorrow" — Stereophonics
"Home" — Zero 7

Acknowledgments

While writing a novel is a solitary endeavor, producing a book is a massive undertaking which cannot be accomplished without the support and expertise of countless others.

Many thanks to my eagle-eyed critique partner Brenda Whiteside, for asking just the right questions and zapping extraneous words dead. Thanks to my agent Cherry Weiner, who helped seal the deal, and to my editor Deb Werksman and all the people at Sourcebooks, whose skill and talent turned this long-held dream into a reality. To my Midwest Fiction Writer chapter mates and my blogmates at The Ruby Slippered Sisterhood, thanks for your friendship, wise counsel, and for always having my back. Let's keep those red heels clicking.

Last but definitely not least, countless thanks to Mark—for holding down the fort, for herding the cats, and for the gift of time.

About the Author

Tamara Hogan loathes cold and snow, but nonetheless lives near Minneapolis with her partner Mark and two thoroughly spoiled cats. When she's not working as a quality and process engineer for a global networking company, she enjoys writing edgy love stories with a sci-fi twist. A voracious reader with an unapologetic television addiction, Tamara is forever on the lookout for the perfect black boots.

In 2009, *Taste Me* (previously titled *Underbelly*) won the Daphne du Maurier Award for Mystery and Suspense and was nominated for the Romance Writers of America's prestigious Golden Heart® award.

DEMONS
ARE A
GIRL'S BEST FRIEND
by Linda Wisdom

A BEWITCHING WOMAN ON A MISSION...

Feisty witch Maggie enjoys her work as a paranormal law enforcement officer—that is, until she's assigned to protect a teenager with major attitude and plenty of Mayan enemies. Maggie's never going to survive this assignment without the help of a half-fire demon who makes her smolder...

Praise for Linda Wisdom

"Hot talent Wisdom does a truly wonderful job mixing passion, danger, and outrageous antics into a tasty blend that's sure to satisfy."
—*RT Book Reviews*

"Entertaining and sexy... Ms. Wisdom's stories have something for everyone." —Night Owl Romance

"Wickedly captivating... wildly entertaining... full of magical zest and unrivaled witty prose."
—Suite 101

978-1-4022-5439-0 • $7.99 U.S./£4.99 UK

FUGITIVE

BY CHERYL BROOKS

"Really sexy. Sizzling kind of sexy...makes you want to melt in the process." —*Bitten by Books*

A mysterious stranger in danger...

Zetithian warrior Manx, a member of a race hunted to near extinction because of their sexual powers, has done all he can to avoid extermination. But when an uncommon woman enters his jungle lair, the animal inside of him demands he risk it all to have her.

The last thing Drusilla expected to find on vacation was a gorgeous man hiding in the jungle. But what is he running from? And why does she feel so mesmerized that she'll stop at nothing to be near him? Hypnotically attracted, their intense pleasure in each other could destroy them both.

PRAISE FOR THE CAT STAR CHRONICLES:

"Wow. The romantic chemistry is as close to perfect as you'll find." —*BookFetish.org*

"Fabulous off world adventures... Hold on ladies, hot Zetithians are on their way." —*Night Owl Romance*

"Insanely creative... I enjoy this author's voice immensely." —*The Ginger Kids Den of Iniquity*

"I think purring will be on my request list from now on." — *Romance Reader at Heart*

978-1-4022-2940-4 • $6.99 U.S. / $8.99 CAN / £3.99 UK

The Werewolf Upstairs

BY ASHLYN CHASE

SHE SHOULD KNOW BETTER...

Attorney Roz Wells is bored. She used to have such a knack for attracting the weird and unexpected, but ever since she took a job as a Boston Public defender the quirky quotient in her life has taken a serious hit. Until her sexy werewolf neighbor starts coming around...

Roz knows she should stay away from this sexy bad boy, but she can't help it that she's putty in his hands...

—⁓—

What readers say about Ashlyn Chase

"Entertaining and humorous—a winner!"

*"The humor and romance kept me entertained—
a definite page turner!"*

"Sexy, funny stories!"

978-1-4022-3662-4 • $6.99 U.S./$8.99 CAN/£4.99 UK

THE FIRE LORD'S LOVER

by KATHRYNE KENNEDY

IF HIS POWERS ARE DISCOVERED, HIS FATHER
WILL DESTROY HIM...

In a magical land ruled by ruthless Elven lords, the Fire
Lord's son Dominic Raikes plays a deadly game to conceal
his growing might from his malevolent father—until his
arranged bride awakens in him passions he thought he had
buried forever...

UNLESS HIS FIANCÉE KILLS HIM FIRST...

Lady Cassandra has been raised in outward purity and
innocence, while secretly being trained as an assassin. Her
mission is to bring down the Elven Lord and his champion
son. But when she gets to court she discovers that nothing is
what it seems, least of all the man she married...

---

*"As darkly imaginative as Tolkien, as richly romantic as Heyer,
Kennedy carves a new genre in romantic fiction."*
—Erin Quinn, author of *Haunting Warrior*

"Deliciously dark and enticing." —Angie Fox, *New York
Times* bestselling author of *A Tale of Two Demon Slayers*

978-1-4022-3652-5 • $7.99 U.S./$9.99 CAN/£4.99 UK

Backstage Pass

SINNERS ON TOUR

By Olivia Cunning

"Olvia Cunning's erotic romance
debut is phenomenal."
—Love Romance Passion

. . . .

FOR HIM, LIFE IS ALL MUSIC AND NO PLAY…
When Brian Sinclair, lead songwriter and guitarist of
the hottest metal band on the scene, loses his creative
spark, it will take nights of downright sinful passion
to release his pent-up genius…

SHE'S THE ONE TO CALL THE TUNE…
When sexy psychologist Myrna Evans goes on tour
with the Sinners, every boy in the band tries to woo
her into his bed. But Brian is the only one she wants
to get her hands on…

Then the two lovers' wildly shocking behavior sparks
the whole band to new heights of glory… and sin…

. . . .

"These guys are so sensual, sexual, and yummy.
[T]his series… will give readers another wild ride,
and I can't wait!"
—Night Owl Romance
5/5 Stars
Reviewer Top Pic

978-1-4022-4442-1 • $14.99 U.S./$17.99 CAN/£9.99 UK